THE FIRST TIME
SHE MET HIM

It was at a sumptuous party in Manhattan that Yvonne St. Cyr first met Seán FitzGerald—and instantly decided he was everything she despised in a man. All too attractive and supremely self-confident, he was clearly used to having any woman he wanted, and clearly wanted every woman he met.

Yvonne turned her back on him, and walked to stand by the side of the husband she adored. She had the delicious pleasure of knowing that for once Seán FitzGerald had met a woman he could not conquer.

But that night seemed so long ago now—that time when Yvonne's life had overflowed with happiness and love. It was a different Yvonne who faced Seán FitzGerald now . . . a woman suddenly alone and vulnerable . . . a woman who had to struggle against this arrogant man's strength . . . a man who would break through her defenses and leave her open once more to passion's wonder. . . .

TO LOVE FOREVER

Great Reading from SIGNET

To Noble —

Love — Dian and Anthony

24 September 1983

To
Love
Forever

by

Page Anthony

Ⓢ
A SIGNET BOOK
NEW AMERICAN LIBRARY
TIMES MIRROR

PUBLISHER'S NOTE

This novel is a work of fiction. Names, characters, places, and
incidents either are the product of the author's imagination or are
used fictitiously, and any resemblance to actual persons, living or
dead, events, or locales is entirely coincidental.

To Eric: without whom it never would be

Stanzas

Could Love for ever
Run like a river,
And Time's endeavour
   Be tried in vain—
No other pleasure
With this could measure;
And like a treasure
   We'd hug the chain.
But since our sighing
Ends not in dying,
And, formed for flying,
   Love plumes his wing;
Then for this reason
Let's love a season;
But let that season be only Spring.

—George, Lord Byron
   Venice, December 1, 1819

1

Every morning Yvonne St. Cyr Reed awoke to what her husband, Gregory, called "ballet-on-tap," a combination tape recorder and alarm which he'd found for her. This morning, the overture to *Swan Lake* had woven into her dreams, the woodwinds gently hinting at the romantic theme, the strings swelling and expanding the notes, and she dreamed that she danced. Not the true dancing of straining muscles, deep breaths, or vigilant attempts, but her dream dancing. Floating weightlessly, without effort or pain, she moved across the floor in *pas de bourrées*, on her *pointes*, taking tiny steps. Then she flew into the air, separated her legs into a complete split and in the *grand jeté* position soared across the stage, freed from gravity and the weight of her own body.

Yvonne saw the Prince approaching from the distance. He stopped only for an *entrechat*, leaping high into the air and crossing his feet, *entrechat-six*, six times crossing; *sept*, seven; *huit*, eight, and in the ballet paradise, still not descending but continuing in what could be an eternal step, except he chose to glide to the floor and continue toward her. Choosing his Princess.

When he lightly reached out and pulled her toward him, she recognized Gregory's features. Only then did she realize they were both nude, but that didn't matter, for theirs was a private dance. As they began an *adagio*, a slow dance of love, his strong muscled body skimmed her slender form. He lifted her high, her black hair swirling and playing in the breeze of the ascent. Then he nestled her in his arms while she floated *en pointe*, his hands free to gently stroke her breasts, his lips at liberty to explore hers.

A crash of cymbals and a strident call of trumpets darkened the atmosphere. They cried of sorrow, warned of disaster, and Gregory moved away, sadly leaving until the crescendos of despair surrendered once more to the triumphant love song.

Yvonne smiled. Unconsciously her muscles tensed, then relaxed, responding to the music even in sleep and beginning the warm-up that real muscles, true dancing, required. She slowly opened her eyes as the dream receded into darkness, and reality rushed in with the morning light. It was time to get up.

Still immersed in the morning's music, she reached across the bed for her husband. Just as her hand glided through the cool satin sheets, she remembered. Gregory was still in Dallas, busy with one of the business deals the Texas millionaire orchestrated. Regret mingled with relief. At least with his absence she need only worry about herself. The man of inner strength and quiet self-confidence always dissolved on the day of one of her performances. It wasn't such a change that anyone else noticed, of course. It was a subtle matter of emphasis: the tone in which he asked if she needed anything, a stiffness that marked his smile, a devastating glare at a fan who'd ambushed her.

This was an especially important performance, a gala to celebrate her tenth year with the Ballet American Company and her twenty-fifth birthday. Former dancers, critics, fans, all would be present, thousands of critical eyes watching. *Swan Lake*, her first starring role, was by coincidence the first role Gregory had seen her dance.

Lying on her back, Yvonne carefully stretched her muscles to warm them up before climbing out of bed. Her violet eyes stared into the lavish gathers of heavy flowered silk that flowed from an ornately carved circle in the ceiling in a river of hand-woven material over the bedposts, and down to the floor. Gregory so venerated her art, it was hard to believe that two years before when they first met, he'd never seen a ballet.

*   *   *

They had met in Dallas. While in town for a performance, Yvonne took a rare afternoon off to shop, and wandered through stores looking indecisively at various outfits. In Neiman-Marcus she stopped to watch a fashion show benefiting a local charity. The models, all local socialites, sauntered through the store. From a side aisle a man approached Yvonne.

"Nice! Very nice."

Yvonne glanced coldly at him, smiled slightly, then looked away. Could be a fan, she thought, but it sounded like a pass. "Thank you."

"How much?"

Her glance darted back to the errant stranger, taking in the brash set of his shoulders and handsome masculine features. "I beg your pardon!"

"I'll only go so high, of course. We Texans are willing to pay for what we get, but I won't be taken." His accent trickled to the floor and pooled around his boots.

Yvonne looked around wildly. "I don't know what you're talking about."

"You're not from here, are you?"

"I do wish you'd just go away and leave me alone."

"Now, now. That isn't going to make many sales." His cool stare raked her as if weighing the merchandise and drew a deep blush to Yvonne's cheeks.

"I have nothing to sell, and if you don't leave me alone immediately, I'll call the management."

"That's a good idea." He looked dramatically around the store. "Manager! We need a manager."

"You're crazy!"

"There's a vice-president now. Thomas? Oh, Thomas. Do you have a minute?"

A gravely authoritative figure approached. "Mr. Reed. And what can we do for you this afternoon?" Respect colored his voice as he rubbed his hands together.

"I was interested in purchasin' this little number here." The manager looked at Yvonne, shock playing across his face. "The dress, that is. You're having a little fashion show here this afternoon, aren't you? A benefit, right? I need a little present for my secretary come Christmas, and this might do a good deed at the same time."

They had all burst into laughter, realizing the error. The

manager then introduced the ballet dancer to Gregory Reed, respected millionaire, and before she knew it, Yvonne found herself invited to dinner.

She had hesitated, shy before his determination, his poise. Ballet was her world and she had rarely ventured off its careful path. Within its confines she had found not only fortune and fame but also confidence in herself, an image to project, behind which she could hide her real self, her fear.

Yvonne's diffidence about her ability in all matters other than ballet left her vulnerable. Still, a certain twinkle in his eyes, his hardy refusal to let her slip away following polite excuses, his tender and protective manner, caused Yvonne to think twice and accept.

That was the beginning. Months had passed before she realized he had not mistaken her for a model at all. Gregory just had his own way of meeting her, his own form of whimsy.

He could still play a Texas rancher, an icy aristocrat, and, she supposed, a cutthroat businessman. These roles slipped on effortlessly, a second skin separating him from the world. Only Yvonne penetrated his defenses, and even she was often unsure if she knew the real Gregory. He was a man of mystery, she admitted to Maxine before her marriage.

Yvonne knew little of his past or background; Gregory brushed off her questions with the brisk answer that a man's present and future mattered, not his past. With pride he acknowledged having made enemies by his fast rise and absolute determination to achieve, but prided himself on his ethics.

Unlike Yvonne, he never felt defensive or inferior to the wealthy, well-educated businessmen among their acquaintances. Under his protection, she had learned to garner the aura of her stage persona and extend it to her personal life. But she and Gregory were so different.

Gregory enjoyed the thrill accompanying risk, and he gambled fast and often—on cards, on high living, on business—calling Yvonne his lucky charm, joking that he needed her by his side for wagers in life.

Yvonne clung shyly to Gregory and security. She wanted neither risk nor chance in her life; she needed Gregory for sanctuary, and too desperately to joke about it.

She knew of unanswered questions in their relationship, knew and didn't care. To her, he was friend, lover, protector, all she wanted in a man. Everything else, anything else, he would take care of.

At his Texas ranch just two weeks before their wedding, they lay in his bed, temporarily satiated after a night of passion. She'd burrowed into the chinchilla-fur spread and prepared herself to offer her sacrifice, her attempt to show how much she appreciated all he'd given her.

His love, concern, and emotional shelter spun a net supporting and protecting her, compensating for years of fear and neglect. The gems that followed—expensive houses, lush jewels, luxurious life-style—only gilded the package.

Gregory radiated security, leaving Yvonne with absolute assurance that she was valued for herself, not just for her fame. She was only that certain of one other person, and she'd known Maxine all her life. Having Maxine and Gregory, she felt loved and cherished no matter how vulnerable or exposed in her professional life.

In nervous anticipation she had blurted it out. "I'll retire."

"You'll never get a pension." Gregory's gray eyes sparkled. "Not at twenty-two."

"I'm serious." She reached out, lightly touching his broad strong chest, her white skin sharply contrasting against his tan. "I'll give up dancing."

The cleft in his chin deepened as he looked quizzically at her. Indignantly she sat up in bed. Yvonne was a tiny woman but full-breasted, especially for a dancer, with a deeply curving waist and soft hips. Her black hair flowed freely around her shoulders, reaching down to her smooth, round bottom. "And why would you do that?"

"For you. For us. You live in Texas. The house is here, the ranch too. I can't dance in New York and live here too."

"We'll arrange it. Anyway, I like a woman who knows how to work. Gives two hundred percent. I didn't get where I am by actin' the playboy. Besides, would you ruin me for life?"

"What?"

"I refuse to be known as Gregory Reed, the male chauvinist who married the legendary—the scintillating—Yvonne St. Cyr and made her retire. The greatest Dying Swan since

Pavlova, and I plucked her feathers!'' He shivered in mock fear. "If the feminists didn't get me, the balletomanes would. I'd be found lynched with tiny pink ribbons strung together from your revered toe shoes, a single swan feather in my hand. The mark of death by Friends of the Dance.''

"For a financial genius and Texas millionaire, you're very frivolous.''

"A mark of my great intelligence, forceful personality, and''—he suddenly rolled over, pinning her softly under him—"Texas virility.'' He smothered her neck with kisses. "And I'll gladly demonstrate the latter,'' he said, ending the discussion.

Could she have kept that promise? Yvonne would never know. Her life had revolved around dance since she was ten, and by then she had already known for two years that she'd be a ballerina. Her friends were dancers, choreographers, or designers; her talk involved muscles, roles, or ballet gossip; her dreams concerned elevation, extension, and perfection. She'd traveled the world: to London to dance at Sadler's Wells, Sweden for the Royal Swedish Company, Stuttgart, La Scala, Tokyo, Paris. In her travels she discovered the universal appearance of a ballet studio—the same box of tacky rosin, bare wooden floor, barre-lined walls, and the pungent smell of sweat—and that backstage, all theaters were basically alike. She was a star, but one bound within the constellations of dance.

Her horizons had exploded outward since her marriage. Her home, once in New York, now embraced Dallas and Houston. Her acquaintances still included Misha and Rudolph, but also Houston oil men, Dallas ranchers, New York socialites, and Hollywood film stars. Her conversation no longer was limited to toe shoes and liniment; rather, it expanded into new art trends, the best season to visit Japan, and who was sleeping with whom in the jet stream of society. She'd seen the Eiffel Tower on a spring day, and the Taj Mahal in moonlight. Gregory helped Yvonne define her desires, backed her choices. By carefully arranging her schedule, she needn't dance every night, and could see Pavarotti when he was in town. She had power over her life. Only her dreams remained unaltered. She still wanted, wanted more than anything, *the* perfect role, *the* most exquisite execution of a step.

One of those dreams could—might, she prayed—be realized this very evening. She would dance the twin role in *Swan Lake* which required a change in character from a trembling Swan Queen in Act II to an evil Black Swan in Act III, then to the faithful lover in Act IV, when the Swan Queen is victorious in love if not life. Yvonne was acclaimed, especially for the first act, when she first danced Odette the Queen, a trembling, frightened creature transformed into a swan by an evil magician. And why not? While making her debut at fifteen, terror and uncertainty came easily to her. Later, when she danced Odile, the evil Black Swan, fans as well as critics had flocked to see her. All reveled in her interpretation of the puppetlike being of her magician father as she became a truly evil creature intent on possessing the Prince.

But Yvonne knew her dancing in the last act was emotionally weak. How could she show undying love, wild passion, and total abandon, emotions she'd never experienced? Until now. Now that her life included Gregory, now that she'd learned to give herself totally. Tonight could be her crowning achievement, which books on ballet would record for posterity and whispered remembrances would transfer into legend.

Suddenly Yvonne laughed and leaped out of bed. With the performance over, if she chose to complete the wildly dramatic scenario, she could happily sink to the ground dead. She slipped off her pale blue silk nightgown trimmed with handmade lace that Gregory had purchased in France, and stood before the antique dressing table. She picked up another of Gregory's presents, a Victorian silver brush, and with long deliberate strokes she brushed her shimmering hair into a loose chignon at the back of her neck.

Performance day dictated a rigid routine. Breakfast at nine; then, at eleven, class; one, lunch; three, theater for another lesson; five, a supper of yogurt; six, make up and dress; eight, performance time. She cooked a large breakfast of steak, salad, and one cup of coffee, a hardy meal to keep her until an after-the-performance dinner. She needed all the energy she could muster, and by the time of her light lunch, her stomach would churn with nerves.

Madame Lisa had determined her eating habits. She'd been Yvonne's first teacher. "The body is an engine," Madame had reiterated in her heavily accented English. "It must have good-quality fuel." When Yvonne saw the kids at the company munching candy bars and drinking Cokes, she wondered how their engines held out. The thought brought a smile to her lips. Kids. At twenty-five, she was hardly an old lady, after all.

Their New York apartment conveniently divided into two floors. The lower, with its immense living room suitable for parties, a vast dining room, three guest bedrooms, a kitchen, and even quarters for the help, acted as their public area. But upstairs was for them alone. Only Nellie, her personal maid and dresser, and Maxine, her best friend, had access to their private area.

"Make our living quarters look like a ballerina's life," Gregory had ordered. And Yvonne was pleased with her effect: all romantic flowers, frills, and lace, but with furniture large and comfortable enough for a six-foot-two husband. One end of their spacious bedroom housed an intimate living room dominated by an ornate fireplace that was banked with fluffy sofas covered in a cabbage-rose Liberty print. In a small kitchen-dining room off the hall, she cooked their intimate dinners whenever they needed complete privacy. Here she made her breakfast, anxious not even to speak with the cook on a performance day. Beyond their bedroom and next to her soundproof dance studio lay the only nondancer's area, a library, where she'd reconstructed an English hunting lodge for Gregory's use as an office. A suite of dressing rooms, baths, and a sauna completed their private space.

Yvonne had finished eating when Nellie appeared. "Good morning," the white-haired woman, neatly attired in a plain black dress, murmured.

"Is it a nice day?"

"Beautiful spring weather. What will you wear to the lesson?" She disappeared into the vast closet.

"Jeans and a sweater?" Yvonne asked hopefully. "I'll just be going down to the car and straight to class."

The older woman replied with a meaningful silence.

"My black sheer wool dress?" Yvonne sighed. "The one with the slit on the side and tiny buttons up the front."

"Much better."

"No one will see me," Yvonne insisted. Too often Yvonne

failed to meet Nellie's stringent standards, and the woman's age and poise intimidated her. Although Gregory had a background as unfamiliar with servants as her own, he always managed to strike the right note.

"Someone always sees you. It's the price of fame."

The phone by the bed rang. All calls were screened downstairs; only Gregory and Maxine were put through. "I'll get it." Yvonne flew to the bed. "Hello."

"Hello, darlin'. Sleep well?" Gregory's rich voice filled the line.

"Wonderfully." She paused in thought. "I dreamed about you."

"Doing something real naughty with you, I hope."

"As a matter of fact, you were." She laughed, tingling at his remembered touch.

"You ready to dance?"

"A dancer's never ready."

"It'll be real fine. Perfect."

"Will . . . will you be there?" Suddenly she wanted him present, nerves and all, to see her, to know his eyes caressed her inside the blackened theater.

"Darlin', I can't. This business deal is more balled-up than I dreamed. I'm ass-deep in contracts, papers, and whiny little lawyers. I'll try to be back before the end of the week. Forgive me?"

Yvonne thought of his curling brown hair, his softly cleft chin. "I could forgive you anything." She paused. "Unless, of course, there is a woman in your room and you're planning to leave me. I don't think I'd be inclined to forgive that." She affected a deep stage Texan accent. "We hang men for that, you know."

"I believe you would." Gregory chuckled. "You'll get to Maxine's party all right?"

"Yes. You'll miss my dress. It's special."

"Well, now, you can just show it off for me the night I get back. Then I can admire it—inside and out." His voice deepened.

"Hmm . . . that sounds rather nice." She glanced at the clock. "I have to leave now."

"The Lesson." Verbally he capitalized the L. "Tell the dragon howdy for me."

"No chance. I'm not going to remind her I'm married."
Madame firmly believed a dancer was married to her art, and
only to her art. They laughed and, sharing soft good-byes,
hung up.

2

Madame Pauline rapped on the floor with her stick. "Let's get started, class. Some of us still have things to do today."

Yvonne looked around the room. It was filled with New York's ballet stars, but from Madame's attitude one would assume they were a group of five-year-olds eager to run frivolously out to play. Yvonne straightened her shoulders and commenced her *grands pliés*, those deep knee bends that began every lesson, every day.

Now it was a relief for her, a constant in a life that had changed so much in two short years. Her three-room apartment had been exchanged for the lavish set of living areas Gregory maintained. Everything gleamed, was more luxurious, easier. But not the classes. They were unchanged.

"It was so nice of you to come." Madame's voice, heavy with sarcasm, addressed a male dancer. "Perhaps you might drag your mind along too?" She poked his back foot with her stick. "I think the fifth position is still done with the back foot tucked against the front, toes pointed in different directions. Or maybe you are now such a great dancer, you don't worry about how the rest of us do it? You make your own positions, perhaps?"

The dancer—a temperamental man who had once abruptly dropped a partner he was assisting in a lift and had stormed off the stage during a performance because a member of the audience took a flash picture—smiled sheepishly. He blushed, tucked in his foot, and muttered, "Thank you, Madame."

The dragon, Gregory called her. At their first and only meeting, she'd clearly have enjoyed beating him instead of the floor with her stick. "Marriage." She'd spat out the word. "Sex," she hissed. "Babies, I suppose." She looked with angry pity at Yvonne, her face contorted as if carved from a dried apple. "And you were such a good dancer." Madame wore a large black shapeless dress, soft black leather shoes, and coal-black dyed hair pulled back into a skull covering. It was impossible to tell her age. Had she announced she had entertained the troops during the war, Yvonne would wonder if Madame was referring to the American Civil War.

Gregory had taken one look and fled without attempting to use his confident charm. "One more minute and she would have beaten me into a saddle," he claimed later.

"To Madame, nothing is as important as dancing," Yvonne explained with a smile.

"Madame"—he laughed—"doesn't think there is anything *other* than dancing."

"She hopes not."

But the ballet greats still came to her. Because she knew. Some extraordinary vision let her peer into their sinews, dissect their muscles, identify what was being done incorrectly, and more important, what could be done to correct it. Not that she would tell you if you asked. Her advice was scattered, dropped in tiny, often obscure hints. She knew everything, and while no one saw her at performances, she knew how you'd performed, where you'd failed, and most embarrassing of all, when you were faking.

Today she stood by Yvonne's shoulders, apparently watching the dancer behind her, who was nervously sweating. "Swan tonight," Madame hissed. "Swan, swan, swan." Without losing the beat, keeping her movements clean, and maintaining a perfect posture, Yvonne wondered if that remark called for a response. "Second act. You're too old to keep up with fluttering young-girl princess. Enchanted creature caught in body of beautiful swan." She whipped around. "Kathleen, are you planning to sleep all through class?" she asked a suddenly quivering woman. "Slow, dragged out. Upbeat!" How had Madame seen that? Yvonne wondered as Madame's sharp, bright eyes slowly returned to rest on her.

"Your thirty-two *fouettés* will be perfect, of course." A *fouetté* required the dancer to stand on one toe shoe, open the other out at waist level, then by whipping her outstretched leg around, propel herself into a turn. The third act necessitated thirty-two successive *fouettés* without the ballerina moving across the stage or losing balance. A flashy trick for a ballerina. "Maybe too perfect."

Jolted by Madame's final words, Yvonne almost stopped dead in a leg circle. Too perfect? How could any movement in ballet be too perfect? It would do no good to ask, of course. Madame would look innocently at her, then stare contemptuously into space. I don't teach dummies, she would say, and refuse to speak further.

An hour later, the class ended. "Thank you, Madame. Tomorrow." They parted and Yvonne bounded down the stairs, pleased that Jimmy would be waiting with the limousine. She was spoiled, she knew, surrounded by luxury, so pampered and cushioned. But she loved it.

Before Yvonne reached the open door of the car, a flurry of movement to her side caused her to halt. "Miss St. Cyr, please, can we have your autograph? We see all your performances." Fans surrounded her with a look of adoration.

Graciously she signed the proffered sheets of paper, then quickly slipped into the car, shielded by Jimmy's broad back. Silently she thanked Nellie, whose vigilance had assured that Yvonne was wearing the soft, flattering dress, with her hair pinned up becomingly, and her makeup discreet.

At home, another group waited by the door, resisting the doorman's scowling discouragement. Nellie was right, the public always saw her. She was a public figure, private only in the safety of backstage or her houses.

Upstairs, she walked into the entrance hall, and remembered the first day she'd seen the apartment. "I bought a place," Gregory had announced. They were living in her apartment at the time, Gregory looking too large and feeling too cramped by the low ceiling and dainty furniture. She wondered about their life in New York, especially where they would live. "Would you like to see it? I think it's a nice little place."

"Very much."

Gregory often bought things without consulting her. Control was important if not essential to him: control of his life, control of his work, and now control of her. His desire was not to domineer, but to protect and cherish, Yvonne felt, so she was not annoyed, but relieved that he was willing to take over. One more decision was made, one less thing for her to think about.

Although Yvonne was aware of Gregory's wealth and his luxurious life-style, the apartment still came as a shock. When empty, the first floor looked so much like a museum that Yvonne couldn't imagine it furnished. A home for two? And with half another floor above!

"You don't like it!"

"Oh, it's splendid, Gregory. I was just thinking about decorating it."

"Don't worry about that. Just hire one of those decorator fellows."

Yvonne did. "Brown is in," the man assured her. "Brown on brown, accented with black. Something amusing in the living room." His idea of amusing was the stuffed figure of a bear. She fired him, had the walls repainted white, and hired another decorator.

This decorator suggested bright colors. "A flurry of little chairs here around the fireplace, bright cushions scattered like confetti." Yvonne, trying to imagine Gregory curling up in a confetti shower, said, "I don't think so."

So she pored over the last two years of *Architectural Digest, House and Garden, House Beautiful, Designers West,* and *Interior Design.* She considered materials and styles, rugs versus carpet, while exercising. Her mind flittered toward curtains and drapes amid routine performances.

Finally she decided. Downstairs would be used for entertaining, for their public life. She chose a monocromatic color scheme—all neutrals accented with black and white. Large backless sofas sat in the middle of the room, bright impressionistic art was scattered along the walls. The result was both efficient and expensive, just as she'd hoped. It was the home of a successful, sophisticated man and his glamorous and equally successful wife.

Upstairs she had rebuilt and rearranged the area according to their personal needs. It was then that Gregory asked her to decorate it for a ballerina, and she had chosen the lyrically romantic style that best suited her.

Still, downstairs had not completely pleased her. Too static, she decided, too safe. It lacked surprises. What good was life without surprises? Again she pored over catalogs and magazines and slowly added pieces to the room.

To the light gray entrance hall which stretched almost the width of the apartment, she added two nineteenth-century samurai warriors. Massively impressive and almost life-size, the gilded bronze statues stood on heavy wooden bases, perfectly detailed in their highly decorated armor and realistic faces. One look and Gregory had whistled. "I'd like to see a burglar's expression if he broke in on those babies."

The dining-room table, black lacquer but too subtle, was replaced with a glass panel floating on two abstract gold rams' heads, their noses resting on a floor now covered with red carpeting and their horns curving back in a huge arc supporting the tabletop. In the guest bathroom she hung a large mirror, a moonlike sphere with a white china dragon curled around its diameter. Yvonne beamed at seeing their apartment featured in the very magazines she'd consulted earlier.

Nellie came out to greet her. "Good lesson?"

"I *think* so," Yvonne said, suddenly restless.

Nellie recognized the symptom at once. Some alchemy was beginning to occur, transforming Yvonne from a mere mortal of the twentieth century to a swan, a queen, a princess, or whatever the role required. "Maxine is on the phone."

"Phone?"

Solicitously Nellie took Yvonne's hand and led her to the stairs. "Go. Up. Pick up phone. I'll be there with lunch in a few minutes."

Yvonne snapped out of her trance and laughed. "Yes, Mother."

Maxine's husky voice, aged by too many cigarettes and hoarse shouts at assistants, poured out the words before offering any greeting. "Your dress is ready."

"I wear swan feathers in this role," Yvonne teased.

"I meant for the ball afterward. You haven't forgotten?"

"Neither forgotten nor am I unappreciative. I suppose what clothes I'm wearing after the performance would be more important to a dress designer than my dancing."

"Not true, not true. Your performance will be wonderful. You always are." Although sure that Maxine spoke truthfully,

Yvonne knew the compliment was meaningless. After all, Maxine believed everything Yvonne did was perfect, ever since she was six and Maxine nine and both had been stranded on that island of loneliness called a boarding school.

"The dress is ready, just waiting for me. You know Nellie would not allow anything to happen to such a work of art." The gown couldn't be worn by a less than stunningly beautiful woman, at least not without damaging her appearance. In black velvet, deceptively plain in front, and constructed with all the style of a master designer, it hung perfectly on Yvonne. Each of the magnificent sleeves contained yards of material, tucked and controlled to reach her wrist in undulating folds. The neck demurely round, the dress skimmed the outer contours of her back, leaving creamy skin exposed to the waist. Gregory would love it. No one would take his eyes off her when she wore it. Exactly what Maxine had in mind when designing it.

"Perish the thought."

"Thanks, Maxine. I'll look like the belle of the ball."

"You are the belle of the ball, remember?" Maxine brusquely deflected the compliment. "Well, tell me. Which ballet is this?"

"*Swan Lake*."

"Let's see. You flutter around the stage and die."

"That's *The Dying Swan*. This has a prince and happy peasants."

Maxine thought. She often said she had not only a tin ear but also steel eyes, since she couldn't remember the ballets' stories, no matter how often she watched Yvonne dance. "I remember. You love the Prince, and when he marries someone else, you die and turn into a Dickey."

Yvonne snickered. "A *Wili*, dear, and that is what is loosely known as *Giselle*. No, this is the one where I love the Prince, then I get to change into the bad swan, and then die as the good Swan Queen."

"I was right about the death," Maxine crowed.

"You're ready for tonight?" Yvonne asked.

"No, but after six months of preparation, I should be. Will Gregory be there?"

"Can't. Business in Dallas. I'll miss him."

"Poor baby. I know, but I promise you'll have a wonderful time. The best ever."

"I'll trust you completely, as always," Yvonne answered. "I have to run. Lunch." Her sentences grew clipped as her mind drifted to thoughts of her role. More wild creature, Madame had recommended. She agreed with that. But whatever did Madame mean about her turns being too perfect?

"I know. Luck."

"Thanks."

Yvonne sat down to a bowl of soup, a helping of pasta, and a crystal glass of Mumm champagne brut. The dress had been Maxine's birthday present. "It's too much, Maxine. So beautiful. It should be placed in a museum."

"Do you know how much publicity I'll get just having that dress on you? Anyone who hasn't fainted with desire at a whiff of Yvonne perfume will be finished off at the sight of the gown." Maxine had devised a regally romantic perfume exclusively for her friend, a blend of roses, jasmine, and one hundred and fifty other rare essences.

"You are impossible."

"Yes, so the gossip columns tell me."

Maxine Andrus wasn't beautiful, never had been as a girl, never developed the gentle gift as a woman. But it didn't matter. One didn't criticize an orchid for having no smell. Maxine had always been so uniquely herself that mere lack of beauty offered no handicap, and in fact might have proved too jarring, only one more reason why she was noticed.

Maxine stood out like a woman dressed in red at a black-and-white artists' ball, a perfect white lily in a field of red roses. Intelligent, witty, icily independent, with thick red hair and deep green eyes, she was soon seen all over New York, her impossibly slender form wrapped in her own dramatic creations.

In no time, the clothes tagged with the soon famous Andrus label—a black background and the name Maxine Andrus in shocking-pink letters, the A formed with a stylized open pair of cutting shears—were considered required dress by the beautiful people. They flocked to Maxine's studio begging for costume gowns and to her parties, whenever they could wangle an invitation. She was part of the new élite.

Maxine had always known the value of placing a high price

on herself and her skills, always understood the cachet of a vivid gesture. The more intuitive, reserved Yvonne could only gaze in awe when, aged twelve, Maxine had refused to wear the school uniform, claiming it made them all look like turtles. Old, leathery turtles, she had yelled at the headmistress.

Although she had lost that fight, Maxine had the satisfaction of having her father summoned from Washington, D.C., where he'd been busy solving the world's problems. Ever since, Maxine had made a point of losing as seldom as possible. "It's amazing," she once told Yvonne, "what people won't do to you if you don't invite them."

Yvonne still remembered vividly the day they had dined in the Birdcage, the newest, chicest French restaurant in town. They celebrated the success of Maxine's new line of "moderately priced" dresses. Yvonne had swallowed twice at the seven-hundred-dollar price tags.

That day, as she and Maxine finished their cream-of-sorrel soup, Maxine glanced around the room, then at a large floor-to-ceiling cage of exotic birds in the center. "Why do I keep thinking of decorated hats?" Maxine raised a disdainful eyebrow.

"That's horrible," Yvonne scolded. "Those nice little creatures."

"They smell."

"Maxine, you're going to get into trouble one of these days."

"I hope so. I've been bored lately."

At the time, Maxine was juggling three different male friends, none of whom knew about the others, planning a new line of cosmetics, and keeping the company in its usual uproar. But then, Yvonne considered wryly, Maxine always did have extra energy.

"I don't believe it!" Maxine exclaimed softly.

"I won't either," Yvonne agreed. "I don't see how you do it."

"I didn't mean *that*! Do you see that woman over there?" Maxine pointed with a finger topped by an inch-long nail, bloodred. "In the pink dress."

Alarmed at Maxine's ominous tone, Yvonne peered slowly around. "Yes." She looked again, this time more carefully. "I don't know her, do I?"

"You'd better not. Recognize the dress?"

"Well, yes. It's yours, isn't it? The top seems different, though. Changed."

"It's the neckline. She's had it altered so it dips lower and she can display her chest." The word seemed obscene as she spat it out.

"Maybe it was uncomfortable," Yvonne joked.

"And the sleeves. They were longer, the correct length for the line of that dress." When Maxine stood up and marched across the room, a dismayed Yvonne hurriedly followed. The hapless woman sat innocently finishing her chicken.

"Excuse me . . ." Maxine's red hair shimmered around her head like a devil's halo. "Isn't that an Andrus?"

"Why, yes," the woman preened.

"Not now, it isn't," Maxine hissed. "Ruined. My dress ruined!"

"Your dress. What are you talking about?" the woman sputtered, finally realizing this wasn't an admirer.

"These sleeves . . ." Maxine fingered the material.

Yvonne tugged at her. "Don't you think we should—"

"This neckline!" Maxine yelled.

"How dare you!" the woman cried, trying without success to edge her chair back, but the iron legs caught in the thick grasslike carpet.

"The newspapers," Yvonne whispered. "Your career."

"How could you!" With amazing strength from hands that had cut and shaped for years, Maxine ripped both sleeves off the dress. "And don't you dare do it again!" she yelled.

Turning, Maxine carefully and calmly left the room. Yvonne could only follow, trying to keep herself from giggling. Behind her, she could hear the woman wail.

That was Maxine. Bold, brash, but with a heart of pure gold.

3

"You have everything?" Yvonne asked Nellie.

"Checked my list twice. The car's waiting; let's go down." They rode in the elevator to the ground floor and entered the car.

Yvonne sat silently on the ride to the theater, only her hands moving in unconscious mime of the Swan performance. Could she do everything she planned with the role? And what had Madame meant? A nervous lump tingled in her throat. She wanted this to be a magnificent success, but in a performance, so much could go wrong. An accident, a sudden cramp, a fatal mistake by her partner—any one of these could ruin all her hopes.

Dressed in leotard and tights, she slipped into the practice room for the short lesson meant, not to perfect steps, but to warm up the company. No one danced full out, but reserved energies and intensities for the coming performance. Anton Lynne, the Prince for the evening already stood at the barre.

The smashingly handsome blond glanced in her direction, then hurried to her side. "You're looking wonderful." Anton kissed her lightly on the cheek.

Yvonne smiled, knowing she must be chalk white with nervous anticipation. "I hope you remember that, if I step on your toes."

"Impossible, my Swan Queen. We all know your dainty feet never touch the ground." With a slight bow he resumed his place at the barre and the fighting of his own fears.

It pleased Yvonne to have Anton partner her that evening. His romantic, regal bearing made him a believable prince and a perfect *danseur noble*, partner for a ballerina. Unlike some men, he was a good sport. The first time they'd danced together, Yvonne came out of a *pirouette* and turned a fraction too far, accidentally kicking Anton. He had gritted his teeth but never complained. Another partner would have taken his revenge by standing in her way during a turn or dropping her during a lift.

Yvonne, too nervous by now to chatter any longer, exercised with slow, careful movements. Stretching and toning now would help avoid tearing a cold muscle later.

Back in her dressing room, Yvonne smiled, noticing Nellie standing guard over the Swan Queen costume. Several sets of toe shoes lay in a heap on the floor, waiting for Yvonne to choose the pair she would wear. The black tutu of her Odile costume peeked out of a closet. "Any word from Gregory?" Yvonne asked casually, changing into a loose bathrobe. Nellie was not fooled.

"Not yet. I have your yogurt—orange."

"Thank you." Yvonne laid out her makeup on the table. First she brushed her hair, wrapped it into a tight chignon at the back of her head, then put on her stage makeup, pausing occasionally to eat her creamy supper. While she worked, the transformation began. As Yvonne St. Cyr drifted into obscurity, Odette emerged, a magical creature, half-woman, half-swan.

A knock on the door broke into her thoughts. Nellie answered. "Thank you."

"What is it?" Yvonne asked, carefully applying false eyelashes.

"Flowers. From Gregory." Bouquets from management, her admirers, Maxine, other friends, and several from Gregory already lined the walls of the small room.

"Beautiful!" Reaching out, Yvonne gathered the four dozen pale pink roses into her arms. She separated one rosebud and placed it on her dressing table. Later Yvonne would pin it inside her costume for luck, a tradition since her marriage. She handed the flowers to Nellie, who promptly arranged them in a vase.

"There's something here." Nellie pointed to a small box tied to the stems of the roses.

"A present." Yvonne smiled. "That's just like Gregory." With trembling hands she untied the ribbon, careful not to prick her finger on the thorns. It was a jewelry box. When Yvonne lifted the cover, she gasped with delight at its sparkling treasure—diamond earrings. "Oh, look, Nellie!" Where the earring touched the lobe of her ear lay a circular cluster of stones; another cluster formed a tear shape at the bottom; and in between, two delicate flowers branched in opposite directions. There were dozens of diamonds in each earring. A tiny hand-printed card at the bottom of the box explained they dated from the Georgian period, circa 1790. With a girlish laugh she held them to her ears, the sparkling of her violet eyes vying with the glimmering diamonds.

"They'll look lovely with your dress," Nellie commented.

"You'll guard them for me?"

Nellie replaced them in the box and buried it deeply in her pocket. "Safe as the bank."

Yvonne continued with her makeup, a secret smile of pleasure on her lips.

High-strung, but by no means among the most difficult of prima ballerinas, Yvonne had been temperamental in the past. She was never vicious to the younger dancers; she enjoyed seeing new faces being promoted within the company, and never resorted to playing unpleasant tricks on other dancers to ruin their performances. She was *the* star in the company, and quietly but firmly insisted on the deference to which she felt entitled. But before she met Gregory, Yvonne had become a little too sharp, too imperial. Now she was calmer, more sedate.

And had a better sense of humor. She had become entirely too serious about her role as a great dancer, too accustomed to recognition and public acclaim.

Gregory was her lover, her life. With little gifts and big words, he continuously reminded her of what she meant to him, how highly he valued her, and how much he loved her.

The PA system cut into her thoughts. "Fifteen minutes." That meant twenty minutes until curtain. Yvonne didn't hurry; she wasn't in Act I.

Before long, she heard the five-minute call. Then the overture swelled over the PA. Even as she dressed, Yvonne could see the first act replayed in her mind. Prince Siegfried celebrates his twenty-first birthday, and is told that the next night during the celebration ball, he must choose his future bride.

"Five minutes." It was time. Yvonne walked to the stage area, Nellie by her side. Stage right, the wings were crowded with organized confusion—machinery to operate the curtains and give cues to the crew technicians and the stagehands. To both sides, scenery and props were strategically cluttered, waiting to be used. The other dancers arrived from their dressing rooms, walking carefully to avoid tripping or stepping on electrical cables.

Earlier, Yvonne had glued her shoes to her tights. Now she dipped her toes in the rosin box, the sticky powder that would add traction to her shoes. It was hot and very noisy backstage as crews moved scenery and prepared the stage. The heavy curtain blocked out all the noise from the seated audience, but she could feel the mass of people awaiting her entrance. Just above the din, the dancers heard the orchestra tuning.

"Clear, please."

The dancers moved to the sides of the stage. They whispered to each other, wishing luck. Already the swan, Yvonne scarcely heard a word and restlessly waited to glide onstage. The music began, embracing the foreboding theme, and when the curtains opened to reveal a forest scene, a great lake whose shining surface glimmered in the moonlight, the hunting party entered. Act II of the ballet had begun.

Soon Yvonne made her entrance, her face encircled by swan feathers which clung to her hair, her pure white costume embellished with soft, downy feathers, and the Swan Queen's crown perched on her head. She paused, then slowly posed in *arabesque*. Balancing on one leg, she bent her cheek against her shoulder in a gesture reminiscent of a swan smoothing its feathers. As the dance continued, Yvonne so merged with the character of Odette that she didn't know which she was.

At one point when she ran offstage, Nellie stood before her, handed her tissues to wipe perspiration from her face, and made a slight adjustment to her crown. "Thanks," Yvonne murmured vaguely. Someone passed and tried to chat with her. "Don't talk to me," Yvonne whispered. "I'm sorry" —she smiled apologetically—"I have to concentrate."

Yvonne returned to the stage and danced the romantic

adagio with Anton the Prince. Then as dawn approached onstage, she danced a variation of great speed which ended in a series of *pirouettes*, turns on one foot, that diagonally moved her across the stage. Finally she left with the other swans, and morning arrived.

Panting, Yvonne moved to her dressing room. In the next act she danced as Odile, the black swan—a conniving, treacherous creature. Too perfect.

She looked in the mirror, narrowing her eyes, hardening them. They must be cruel, without pity or tears. Yvonne felt the evil of Odile sprout inside her, consuming her character, changing to allow her to dance within the evil creature's body. She changed costumes and sauntered back to the stage. Too perfect.

It wasn't until she was dancing that Yvonne realized what Madame meant. Yvonne's perfection made the strenuous movements look too easy. If she made the steps seem just a trifle more difficult, and somehow implied—without altering the step—that she might not be able to complete them, then the audience would be more appreciative. From that moment until the final curtain, she remembered nothing.

She *was* the evil Odile, the conniving Odile. Seductively alluring, she danced to trick the Prince into betraying his love. Her magician father, the court, all disappeared in her raw determination to possess, to consume the man for whom she lusted.

At the moment of the thirty-two *fouettés*, a minute part of her heart whispered, "Too perfect, too perfect," and Odile-Yvonne, for she was now unable to separate the two, lingered for the smallest second. The Prince and the audience caught their breath. As the whipping turns continued with dazzling perfection, the applause began, then swelled, and finally drowned out the orchestra.

When Yvonne finished, "Bravas" cut the air, forcing the ballet to pause. Yvonne automatically acknowledged the ovation, her heart still beating in Odile's breast.

Changing into the white feathered costume in concentrated silence, she was dazed when anyone spoke to her. The final act began with Yvonne as the dying Odette, sacrificing herself to save the Prince, her only love. The Prince, Gregory, were now one and the same. Yvonne's undying love, wild passion, and total abandon for her husband shone through the emotion of the dance in the electric touches between her body and Anton's. Finally came her sacrifice, dying to regain her soul from the power of the evil magician, dying to join the Prince in the life beyond, safe in eternal love.

The audience was on its feet cheering before the last notes faded. As she took her bow, Yvonne graciously accepted a large bouquet, and loosening a rose, she presented it to Anton. More cheers. A fan scurried up the aisle and hurled a small bouquet onto the stage. Others followed, causing splashes of yellow and red in the lights. The atmosphere was electric. Eventually the curtains closed, but reopened as the "Bravas" continued. Three, four, even five more curtain calls were demanded to lull the audience into silence.

Yvonne recognized her success, saw that hers had been an interpretation that would be remembered. Yet she felt removed from her triumph, as if she were still a creature of the other world.

Slowly Yvonne walked offstage, a shaky smile her only response to Anton's praise. Temporarily drained and exhausted, she felt her breath come in sharp, painful gasps. Sweat stung her eyes and moistened her lips with salt. Her legs ached, her feet seemed swollen with pain. When Nellie led her to the dressing room in silence, Yvonne collapsed into the chair, her body dripping with sweat. "I can't see anyone for a few minutes," she begged.

"I'll wait outside and bar the entrance," Nellie replied, and softly closed the door as she left.

Yvonne's head collapsed in her arms. Scarcely a minute passed before she heard the door open. "I didn't want . . ." Yvonne began to speak, then looked up and smiled with sudden delight.

4

At an early age Maxine Andrus defined her philosophy of life. "Cheer up, things can only get worse," she whispered to herself for wry comfort. "It's amazing what people won't do to you, if you don't invite them. Aim high, and don't look back to see who's gaining on you," she muttered through fear-chattering teeth. They decorated her mind like Victorian needlework samplers would an antiquated drawing room, embroidered with cross-stiches of neglect, chain stitches of rebuff, French knots of cruelty—the unhappy threads from a wealthy, privileged, arid childhood.

Yvonne first met Maxine in the barren cell of an Atlanta Catholic girls' school, neither girl Catholic, religious, or boy-crazy—the conventional reasons for enrollment in the school.

Both had been recently orphaned: Yvonne by a flaming car crash; Maxine by a bitter divorce, drugs, and finally the death of her mother and uninterest of her father.

At six Yvonne found herself ripped from an airy, sunny New York apartment overlooking the harbor, and plopped down in the cluttered dark Atlanta house owned by her maternal grandfather, a man she was meeting for the first time.

Her mother's best friend had dressed her for the flight south, spilling false cheer and true tears. Then in Atlanta, standing in the library which was shuttered against the feeble winter, Yvonne nervously smoothed her pleated cotton dress, stared down at her black patent Mary Janes, and tried to swallow back the tears. She couldn't look at the wizened old

34

man haloed by a single pool of yellow-green light. Around her, the room clanged and ticked. The old man collected clocks.

Words, phrases, swirled through her head: orphan, that cheap bastard (that uttered by the friend's husband before being hurriedly hushed by his wife), estrangement—words she didn't grasp in detail but knew too well in essence: her world had ended.

The meeting was brief, fragmented, and cryptic in Yvonne's memory. Her mother had seen fit to live her life as she wished, the old man snorted, damn fool she married—disconnected phrases remained in Yvonne's memory. Now he, the grandfather, would pay for her inconsiderateness. (Death as a social gaffe, Yvonne later considered.)

Almost immediately she found herself repacked for boarding school by the cowed older woman Yvonne assumed to be the housekeeper.

Only two years later, she returned to the house, forced to live there when the insurance money ran out, and discovered it was her grandfather's sister, her great-aunt. The woman, kindly but ineffective after years of subservience, offered little besides pity.

When Yvonne was thrust upon the older girl, Maxine had gazed at the tall, slender stranger with an evaluating eye. At first she noted a sweet, demure girl with long black hair, high cheekbones, and a gentle smile. When about to dismiss her as a toad, Maxine looked into Yvonne's deep violet eyes and recognized frenzied determination only waiting to be channeled.

Yvonne, three years younger and desperate to find a *raison d'être* now that her beloved parents were gone, never doubted Maxine. She never dared.

Maxine had an advantage over Yvonne: she knew what she wanted from life. "To make beautiful clothes," she announced, much to the younger girl's intrigue. Yvonne's mother would, at the most charitable, have been described as trim and neat. She must have worn something, but nothing Yvonne could recall. "To be famous." Again, Yvonne didn't know what such a goal implied, but decided she wanted it too. "To be rich." Already Yvonne knew what that meant, or more to the point, what *not* being rich signified.

Rich—what her writer father had never become, as her

grandfather caustically and repeatedly griped. The insurance money dwindled, and Yvonne became first a day girl, then a "scholarship" student. The rich bad-girls were contemptuous, the religious good-girls charitable. Yvonne didn't know which she hated more. The experience was iced with the knowledge her grandfather possessed money.

Except for Maxine, life would have been unbearable. "We're going to make it," Maxine assured her new friend. Recollection of Yvonne's parents dissolved with time, her mother's large happy eyes and her father's strong capable hands and booming laugh her only surviving memories.

She had no one to share them with. Her grandfather acknowledged her only as an invasion. Her Great-Aunt Ethel, dwarfed by years with her brother, could show concern and affection only in awkward bursts.

Once, as ten-year-old Yvonne stood in the kitchen shelling peas, Ethel's eyes filled with tears. "You'll be a real beauty," she predicted, with a vicious sweep of a dishcloth over the counter.

Considering her long skinny legs, flat chest, and straight hair, Yvonne thought it unlikely.

"Like your mother," Aunt Ethel added, her back turned, her piece spoken.

"Why did Grandfather hate her?" Yvonne dared.

"Hate? Why, he loved her very much." The words dragged reluctantly. "Very much. But love can be complicated for adults."

And life for children, Yvonne thought.

From the beginning there was the Tale, the myth that Yvonne and Maxine survived on during the years when they fashioned their dreams into realities. "Once there were two orphans," one or other would begin, casting Mr. Andrus into an early symbolic death.

"They were going to be famous and rich."

But there the story stalled for a year. With her friend still unfocused in life, Maxine was too tactful, too sensitive to add the next line. "One would be a world-famous fashion designer." Her lips almost formed the words, but she always bit them back. Who would Yvonne be?

A year later, following a school trip to a second-rate ballet production of *The Nutcracker*, a new line could be added.

Less than halfway through, Yvonne turned to Maxine. "I'm going to be a ballet dancer," she whispered. "A great ballerina." Maxine noted her friend's violet eyes had turned black with emotion.

"A ballerina. That's perfect, Yvonne. You'll be famous and rich, and a ballerina."   .

It had been an uphill struggle all the way. Aunt Ethel's pathetic Social Security check, earned from years of clerking in a dime store, paid for her first lessons.

When Yvonne was thirteen, Aunt Ethel died. Yvonne could only continue ballet lessons because her teacher recognized her talent and drive and took her on without a fee.

The next year Maxine left for New York and the Fashion Institute of Technology, leaving Yvonne feeling twice orphaned, with only Maxine's command to follow to give her solace. Her grandfather barely noticed her from day to day. Her teachers found her suddenly recalcitrant; her classmates, uninterruptedly dull.

A year later, Ian Thorn, choreographer and backbone of the Ballet American Company, swept through Atlanta, teaching and talent-spotting. He recognized Yvonne's ability at once and offered her a scholarship to the company.

Immediately and with galling irony, Yvonne splashed to her school's attention. Her name and picture trumpeted in the local newspaper; she was invited to dance at a school assembly.

She unexpectedly found herself a minor celebrity. Girls invited her home for the holidays; the illicit but very active sororities fought over which would take her in; older brothers made discreet inquiries through their younger sisters.

It was too late. The years of rejection and dismissal racked too severely. If they hadn't wanted to know her before, she didn't want them to pretend friendship now.

It had taught her a lesson about the importance of ballet, what it meant to people and what it could mean to her. Dance had been a private passion, a future plan with a clear goal—wealth and fame—yet indistinct milestones. For the first time she had tangible feedback: praise, attention, recognition.

She might never think of the clever thing to say, but her legs were witty. She might hesitate about what to wear to a party, but onstage she was elegant. She might feel lost and forlorn in real life, uncertain of her abilities and skills, but as a dancer she knew her talent was real, her ability supreme. Yvonne realized ballet meant acceptance—a salve for the years of rejection since her parents died.

When she asked her grandfather about the scholarship, he scoffed. "Where would you stay? Be writing me for money. Just like your mother."

"She didn't." Yvonne refused to believe her mother would have groveled to the vengeful man.

"She would have," he countered. The insult to her mother goaded Yvonne into rare rebellion. Carefully she forged a letter from Maxine's father offering to allow Yvonne to stay with his daughter, and prompted by his interest in the arts, he suggested an allowance. With a shrug her grandfather conceded and returned to his clocks. He might not have been fooled, Yvonne decided, but appearances had been met.

She hoarded the bus fare penny by penny from the small housekeeping allowance. Once packed, she fled before the old man could change his mind.

At seven on a bright Sunday morning she was outside Maxine's door in New York, and down to her last twenty dollars. Fear clutched her stomach. What if Maxine weren't home? What if she'd forgotten their friendship? Maxine, not much of a letter writer, had sent only three messages in the last year. Sick with fear, Yvonne rang the bell.

Nothing happened.

Yvonne rang again.

Still nothing, until the door tore open and Maxine stood with wild red hair, a very white face, and flaming green eyes. Then she recognized Yvonne. "Well! What took you so long?" she asked.

They were going to be famous and rich.

And happy? The thought flickered through Maxine Andrus' mind as she looked over the apartment, awaiting her first guests. A trace of boredom, a soupçon of ennui, had crept into her life lately. Maxine didn't tolerate monotony. She smashed, exploded, tore at the world until it delivered excitement. She would have to consider that—not now, but tomorrow, with the party behind her.

She liked giving parties, and gave good ones heaped—like Tiffany's with diamonds—with delicious food, beautiful settings, and fascinating people. From the beginning, every-one wanted to come, everyone feared being left out. They came to her parties to avoid being talked about or to assure being talked about or to talk about others. Some came just to have fun. Maxine always did. Parties of contrast, she called them. Food, setting, themes, people—all were mixed in the caldron of her imagination and swirled with a drop of malice. Contrast sparkled, especially obvious in the guests Maxine combined: Pavarotti with the latest punk-rock star, Dolly Parton and Renata Scotto, Jonathan Miller and Suzanne Somers.

Maxine dreamed of luring Jerry Falwell and Roman Polanski to the same room, adding a drop of provocation, shaking well, and watching the fireworks. They might accept, other improbables had. The desire to meet an opposite was a strong lure, seeing one's reflection in a fun-house mirror.

For Yvonne's party, that particular tingle would be absent. Interesting parties, truly memorable parties, often ended in glowing invective, broken champagne goblets, and thin blonds crying their mascara off. That hardly seemed an appropriate scenario for a ballerina's anniversary.

Not that the party would be lacking in fascinating people. Guests included dancers, choreographers, balletomanes, and wealthy patrons, all of whom felt they deserved to be there. All excitedly accepted the invitations, but to Maxine the guest list was incomplete. As a close friend and star, Yvonne deserved an even more important party. So notables and luminaries from other arts, writers, theater people, other fash-ion designers, were necessary. And all the rest of the jet set.

The guest list eventually balanced out, but not without leaving a casualty. Maxine. She felt exhausted.

The apartment was satisfactory, Maxine thought, examin-ing the large, spacious set of rooms, painted and decorated in white with mild touches of silver. Hardly the vivid display expected for a person with Maxine's personality. But, having worked with clothes, material, and design all day, Maxine suffered from color fatigue, and a mild sensory deprivation was, to her mind, a relief.

Tonight the room had been transformed into a park with masses of flowers, groves of potted trees with tiny white lights, and a miniature mirrored dance floor to one side. Two walls of the vast living room normally covered in mirror heightened the image of the magic park. Maxine had considered live swans wandering freely among the guests as a scenic touch, but vague memories of a cygnet attack prompted her choice of the only feathered creatures present having shiny, pointed satin feet, not little webbed ones.

A small orchestra would soon begin to play. A long buffet table and bar lined one wall, with a fleet of roving waiters of both sexes in trim tuxedoes to spread champagne and keep the table in order.

The buffet bristled with goodies. Canapés of smoked salmon decorated with butter piped through a pastry tube into a swan outline nestled next to diamond-shaped canapés filled with Bayonne ham. Thick slices of truffle-decorated pâté competed with scrambled eggs placed in their shells and topped with caviar. Plates flowed with crêpes of assorted meat, crab, cheese, and dessert fillings. Caviar was regally represented with light gray beluga, golden-yellow Ossetra, and small-grained sevruga. Maxine knew all of Yvonne's little weaknesses.

Maxine's chef would provide the *pièce de résistance*, his own invention, Cherries Yvonne. A combination of cake, cherries (Yvonne's favorite fruit), whipped cream, and liqueurs would be flamed and served in a graceful ice sculpture of a swan, wings spread as if near flight.

Yvonne nestled in Gregory's arms as the limo sped through the streets toward their apartment. "I never thought I'd herd you away from your adoring public," he murmured, nibbling on her ear.

"I'll only complain when they aren't there." Yvonne giggled. At the stage door, fans had immediately surrounded her, clamoring for autographs and delaying her departure. "I can't believe you are really here. Why didn't you tell me?" She pretended to pout.

"Because." His finger traced the line of the V-necked top, dipping down over the swell of her breasts.

"Not a sufficient answer." Yvonne removed his hand, capturing it in hers.

"Because I wasn't sure I could come, and I knew you'd be disappointed. Besides, I just make you more nervous." With a sudden movement he pulled her close for a kiss. "Like the earrings?"

"Beautiful! You always pick out the most beautiful things for me." She looked out the window. "How did you find the performance?"

"I think your turns in the second act were a little sloppy and I don't know about the—" Gregory broke off in laughter, responding to her surprised gasp. "Darlin', you were wonderful, perfect, never better. Let's face it, I'd always think that, no matter what. But at intermission the *Times* critic assured me of your perfection."

Gregory could be an astute critic. Once attracted to Yvonne, he delved into ballet with the same intensified concentration applied to anything that interested him. But he knew there was a time for criticism. Now wasn't the time.

"Really?" Yvonne purred. It was a game. Yvonne doted on Gregory's praise, thrived on good reviews, but still had to satisfy herself. That rarely occurred; tonight was the exception. She had been marvelous, she thought with satisfaction.

"Really!"

"Maybe I should have died tonight. I'm not sure I'll ever top this performance. It will be downhill from now on." Gregory's shoulders began to shake. "Are you laughing at me?"

Quickly he cleared his throat. "Never. I was just choking. You are hardly over the hill, my dear. Top of the hill, maybe."

"I don't know."

Gregory recognized the symptoms. With so much invested in a performance—energy, hopes, reputation—the letdown afterward could be crushing. "How does the dress look? Some little rag that Maxine threw together?"

"You'll have to wait and see."

"Give me a hint," Gregory pleaded, happy to feel Yvonne relaxing against him. "Is it red?" he queried, indicating one of his favorite colors. "Or the violet of your eyes?"

"Neither. Very subdued."

While riding the elevator to their apartment, he lightly kissed her. "Cut low in front?" His hands moved to cover her breasts.

Yvonne twirled lightly away from his grasp. "Cut very high and respectable in front."

"I don't know if I'll like this dress."

"Just wait and see," Yvonne said.

Once inside their apartment, each walked to his own dressing room. Gregory didn't hurry, drank a leisurely Irish whiskey with water, chose a wing-collared shirt, and picked out the jade-and-gold cufflinks Yvonne had given him. Half an hour later he left his room and checked his watch. "We'd better be leaving."

"You go downstairs," Yvonne suggested. "I'll be down in a few minutes."

While Gregory waited in the vestibule at the foot of the stairs, his eyes drifted to one of the gilded bronze samurai. "I just hate waiting. How about you? Of course, I guess you've gotten used to it by now."

"Do you think this will do?" Suddenly Yvonne's voice floated down the stairs, a welcome greeting to his ears. Slowly she came toward him, the sleeves dramatically flaring, the velvet skimming her perfect figure, hinting at all her charms.

Gregory's eyes lit up; he leaned back against the wall for support. "Very nice." He spoke in a low and gravelly voice.

"Not too dull, too calm?"

"You look like the greatest ballerina ever." His gray eyes turned velvet black and narrowed with passion as Yvonne lightly pirouetted before him, displaying her naked back. "My God! You'll be arrested."

"Do you think so?" Yvonne batted her long black eyelashes. "Maxine would be *so* pleased!"

5

Yvonne and Gregory entered the room to coos of reverence as guests admired her dress and beauty. Then came the pattering of applause, a quiet tribute to her dancing. With regal composure Yvonne smiled in gratitude before gliding across the room to Maxine.

Maxine glittered. With characteristic verve, she had not chosen one of her own dresses but wore a 1960 Norman Norell sequin sheath of emerald green which sparked the color of her eyes. Her red hair flamed out around her shoulders. The combined effect was like a configuration of exploding fireworks.

Yvonne smiled at the dress. Maxine was proud of her open-minded attitude. "Some designers won't have any other designers' clothes near them," an interview in *Harper's Bazaar* had quoted her. "I have any number of other people's beautiful creations." With characteristic aplomb, Maxine casually mentioned a few: the 1933 Schiaparelli suit, severely tailored but ultrafeminine in trimming, a 1950 Balenciaga ball gown, her beaded evening suit made by Mainbocher about 1938, two classic Chanels, and four Adrians. Yvonne never pointed out that all the designers were safely dead.

The party sparkled with Andruses—this year's, last year's, carefully preserved classics denoting the owners' devotion to Maxine and their recognition of her talent from the beginning.

"It's beautiful." Yvonne gestured to the trees and flowers. "Like the setting for a romantic ballet."

"I should hope so." Maxine motioned toward one of the waiters and plucked a crystal tulip of champagne from a tray.

"You were even more wonderful than usual." As Gregory came up, she handed him another glass. "Aren't you proud of your wife?"

"You bet."

Across the room, Yvonne spied herself and Gregory in the mirrored wall. Always graceful, Yvonne seemed to float after a performance, her lithe figure more willowy, her neck longer, her walk more elegant. Beside her, Gregory appeared even taller and stronger. He epitomized that rare kind of man who looked equally well and felt equally comfortable in a tux at an elegant soiree or in dirty jeans around the ranch. His deep tan made Yvonne's skin glow a pearl white in contrast; his chiseled, handsome face with high cheekbones made her all the more delicate when beside him.

Yvonne nodded hello to a clique of balletomanes, then saw Ian Thorn gently disentangle himself from a coterie of admirers and sweep toward them.

Maxine was studying her with a professional eye. "The dress works," she finally declared.

"That's like saying Yvonne dances," Gregory teased. "I am just a little starving, so I think I'll see what erotic, I mean exotic treats Maxine has for us. Want to come, Yvonne?"

"Not yet, I think Ian wants to see me."

"I'll come," Maxine offered. "Must make sure we haven't run out of boiled eggs."

"Boiled eggs?" Suspicion colored Gregory's voice.

"Darling." Ian closed in, bowed to kiss her hand, then gingerly held her at arm's length. "It was perfect. You should donate your shoes, those shoes, those little bits of satin, to a museum in honor of your performance." The choreographer gazed past her shoulder in thought. "I've never liked that ballet."

"I know." Yvonne laughed. How like Ian to continue with the truth no matter what the occasion.

But they had known each other too long, too intimately for lies. After only two months in the *corps de ballet*, the chorus of dancers relegated to group dancing, Ian had selected her for an important if small role in one of his ballets. This allowed him to judge her, to test her determination, ability, style, and most of all her passion. Yvonne was not found wanting, so a starring role in *Swan Lake* followed.

Ian Thorn was tall and slender. Semi-balding, he wore a neatly trimmed beard the same black-kissed-with-silver color of his hair. Although close to seventy, he looked twenty years younger. "I wish to talk with you alone."

"Anything in particular?" Yvonne waved to a famous women's magazine editor entering the room in a five-year-old Andrus original. Perfectly appropriate, Yvonne thought, a tribute without fawning.

"Ireland. I don't mean the country, although it is a charming isle. Green. Mystic. My second wife was Irish, but I never held that against the country."

"I know," Yvonne murmured.

Ian, in what he called his baroque years, had had four marriages. Recognized if not always legal, all were to dancers. "They were all flamboyant, my dear, and richly ornamented. Plus," he once said, "at least two were pearls of irregular shape." Yvonne admired his tactful impartiality in having chosen two women and two men.

"I'm helping the ballet company there put on a performance of *Honoré*."

Ian was noted for his witty and sensual ballets. Epigrams of dance, they were concise and cleverly planned statements, slyly making pointed observations and usually concluding with a satirical twist.

Honoré et Eve was Ian's presentation of Honoré de Balzac's improbable love affair and eventual marriage to Countess Evelina Hanski. Eve sent Balzac a fan letter. They met, and eighteen years after Eve had sent the letter, they were married. Ian staged the ballet with lush sets and costumes presenting a wildly romantic story. Until the last act. Only six months after the wedding, Honoré died, and Ian displayed his sardonic humor and cynical temperament, showing Eve dancing on his grave, taking lover after lover.

"You want me for Eve?" Yvonne said as she watched the party pass like its own elaborate ballet.

"If not you, perhaps you could teach the role to one of the younger girls. Not that you're not young," he quickly added.

Yvonne smiled. "The legs still work, dear." But twenty-five wasn't young, she knew that only too well. Not that she needed the role of Eve. She still had the cream of the company's ballets to dance. No ballerina could have them all.

Gregory appeared at her side. "Come have something to eat. Maxine slaughtered a school of Russian sturgeon for this party."

"You two go without me," Ian murmured. "I have to go tell Leon how the tutus for his performance of *Giselle* were too, too." Ian laughed gleefully.

The party kaleidoscoped around them, precious jewels of dresses mixing with diamonds, gold, and all the glittering trappings of the wealthy. The sound of murmured gossip, whispered confidences, and exchanged endearments drifted toward their ears. People parted as they passed, pretending not to stare, but eyes were instinctively drawn to the couple of gold.

Cliques still hung together, ballet people not mixing with designers, the stars greeting each other. What Gregory called "the aggressive nipple set"—the groupies, would-be models and hopeful actresses with their sheer tops and thick ambitions— eyed one another with malice and care. As the evening and champagne wore on, the cliques merged and mingled.

A quiet stir near the door drew Yvonne's attention. Which star had arrived? Through the throng she gazed with doubtful, disbelieving eyes. It was Madame. With her usual black dress and soft leather flat shoes, she wore an ornate jeweled necklace, sumptuous burnished golden bracelets, and careful but vivid makeup. A gilded Buddha, Yvonne decided.

Only then did she notice Madame's escort—Tor N. Curtain, the new young choreographer of nude ballets with sexual themes. Maxine flittered to Yvonne's side. "I never thought she'd accept the invitation," she whispered. They approached the old woman, neither sure of what to say. Madame took care of that, as usual.

"Interesting." Madame scrutinized the room and crowd. "Fascinating. I've read about this, you know. I decided to see for myself."

"I'm so pleased you did," Maxine squeaked.

"You said I could bring an escort." Madame motioned toward the choreographer.

"Of course." Maxine nodded, repressing a smile.

"Sometimes I like to try new things." Yvonne wondered if Madame meant the party or Tor. "Come on." Madame motioned to Tor's rotund figure and moved into the party as if wading through a shallow pool.

Later Yvonne found Madame sitting by Gregory, a slim hand resting on his knee. "Your husband is an intriguing man, my dear." If Yvonne hadn't known better, she would have said Madame was flirting. Truly a most memorable evening.

"You were fabulous this evening. Perfect." A slim blond young woman smiled tentatively at Yvonne.

"Thank you . . ." Yvonne recognized the younger dancer, a recent recruit from the San Francisco company.

"Aisling Nolan."

Yvonne remembered the name on a memo. "You pronounce that like 'Ashling'?"

"Yeah. It's Gaelic for 'dream.' Not that I'm into Ireland. My grandparents came over . . . you know how it is."

Eighteen, Yvonne decided. No older. One of the many faces she didn't know well. Wealth, age, and position separated them.

"Mr. Thorn said it might not be long before I can dance Eve in *Honoré*."

"Next season, maybe." Yvonne studied the girl. "I'll be glad to introduce you to some of the tricks."

"Swell! It's not an easy role. But when *you* dance it, you looked as if you were floating." Aisling tugged nervously at her flowing blond hair.

"Yes. I sailed home every single night, soaked my feet for an hour, and scheduled an extra hour of massage. Ian can devise fiendish movements."

"Oh-oh!" Aisling gazed over Yvonne's shoulder with wide-eyed alarm.

Yvonne turned to see Justine Stelle bearing down. In their dance world, Justine reigned as artistic director of the company.

"Yvonne!" Justine theatrically embraced her, kissing the air by her ear. "There are no words." Sharp eyes moved to Aisling and glittered. "Missed a turn this evening, didn't you?"

Aisling giggled nervously. "A little one. It was real nice to see you, Yvonne. Wonderful party." She nodded at Justine, then tossed her head shyly and excused herself.

Yvonne watched her slender form receding. Eve called for passion, wanton emotion. Aisling appeared timid and controlled, but this could be a reaction to being with Yvonne. What emerged during her dancing could be entirely different. Dancers often displayed unexpected, flaming personalities when dancing, personalities alien to their nondancing lives.

Young dancers were so sheltered, so protected from life outside ballet that their personalities often did not develop until late, leaving them uncomfortable outside a dancing environment. Watching Aisling, Yvonne thought of a young girl, waiting and uncertain.

"She's not bad." Justine's voice brought Yvonne abruptly back to the present. "Needs seasoning."

Yvonne wondered if Justine planned to devour the dancer. The director's fulminations made even the most secure dancer nervous. Yvonne had once overheard Justine say to a recalcitrant dancer, "Some ballerinas don't have rich husbands to turn to, or their negotiating skills." Now, no trace of venom penetrated Justine's smile. "You were perfect. The company is very proud. But, I must mingle."

As Justine moved away, Ian appeared at Yvonne's side. "There's Her Latest."

"Whose latest what?"

Ian nodded toward a woman of about forty. "Jessica Graham."

"The novelist? I've never met her." So that's Jessica Graham, writer of romances of an especially innocent variety, Yvonne thought, half-ashamed to find herself looking with interest. The writer combined snow-white skin, which blushed pink at the slightest impropriety, and innocent blue eyes with a predilection for very young boys.

When the crowd swirled, Yvonne and Ian found themselves at the woman's side. "So nice to meet you, darling," Jessica twittered when Ian made the introduction. "An unbelievable performance."

"Thank you. It's a lovely party, isn't it?"

"Just gorgeous." Coyly the woman peeked over Yvonne's shoulder, and a look of calculated licentiousness entered her eyes. "I think I see someone I know." Jessica excused herself and moved toward a handsome young man clad in a tight leather suit and a sullen smile.

Yvonne turned to Ian. "Isn't she afraid of being arrested for contributing to the delinquency of a minor?"

Ian shrugged. "Which is the innocent, I can't help wondering?"

"Yvonne, I want you to meet someone," Maxine interrupted. "He's come all the way over from Ireland."

"Someone special?" Yvonne, noticing Maxine's faint glow, hoped for love. Love with someone as wonderful as Gregory would make her friend's life perfect.

"If you mean special 'romantic,' don't be silly. I have enough to keep me busy here," Maxine laughed. "Seán," she called softly, "come meet the guest of honor." She held him lightly by the hand. "Yvonne, this is Seán FitzGerald. He's from Dublin. We're going into business together."

"Charmed." Seán FitzGerald was about thirty-three. He was yummy—black hair and deep blue eyes—and he knew it, Yvonne thought, irritated. Every inch of him screamed charm and self-assurance, from the casual expensiveness of his clothes to the slightly condescending twinkle in his eye.

"Come to New York often?" Yvonne made a special effort for Maxine's sake.

"Not often enough," Seán said smoothly. "More of Paris or Tokyo."

"How cosmopolitan! You must work hard."

"I try not to."

Yvonne's smile faded, her suspicions confirmed. Seán FitzGerald was part of the inherited rich, the European landed gentry who slipped and slithered into a position of power, not climbing inch by inch the mountain of success as she and Gregory had. "Have you known Maxine long?"

"Just a couple of weeks in person, although we've written before." Sweet charm and a lazy grace were a part of him, and he was attracting appreciative glances from the women present.

Gregory too was charming and self-assured, but his boyish manner and Texas cowboy mien made it impossible to take offense at him. Seán, on the other hand, was entirely too sleek, and he wouldn't do Maxine any good, Yvonne thought.

But the designer was old enough to choose her own poison, as Gregory would say.

Maxine openly admired him. "And to think I pictured a dignified old man."

"I am dignified," Seán protested.

"But not old." Maxine winked at Yvonne and slipped back into the crowd.

"I do wish I could say how much I enjoyed the performance tonight." His blue eyes hypnotically held her attention. "But alas . . ."

Yvonne stepped back a few inches to regain her poise. "Alas?" The nerve of the man!

"Alas . . . I wasn't able to attend. But I'm sure you were fantastic as always."

"You've seen me before?" Yvonne was unwillingly, disturbingly aware of Seán's hand holding the champagne glass. Hands had always attracted her, and his were both masculinely large and strong, yet sensitively shaped.

"No." His eyebrow lifted in amusement. "I haven't, but I'm certain you are as exquisite on the stage as off." Seán moved closer and took her glass, brushing her hand as he did so. "It's empty," he explained, answering her startled glance.

Yvonne ignored both the compliment and the shiver of excitement from his touch. How dare he openly flirt with her at Maxine's own party? Whatever Maxine's faults, she never threw herself at unwilling men. If Seán openly intrigued her, it could only be with his encouragement. "I don't want any more wine." Yvonne gestured away the glass Seán had plucked from a passing waiter. "I have to circulate." She turned away.

"Tell me, Terpsichore, what do you do when you're not dancing?" Seán called after her.

Yvonne hesitated at his use of the name of the Greek muse of dance, wondering if Seán knew more about ballet than he pretended. "I *always* dance," she called back, determined to escape.

Yvonne felt suddenly isolated at her own party. Snakes of gossip slithered by her, names and details lost. Across the room she saw Gregory's broad shoulders, but couldn't see to whom he spoke.

Maxine suddenly returned, a small balding man in her wake. "Melvin." Over his head she mouthed silently: "The money."

"So nice to meet you. This is so exciting." He flushed and enthusiastically shook her hand.

Maxine pushed him away, whispering over her shoulder, "Might finance the new expansion!"

A surge of the crowd, and people around her changed position. Behind her an enticing male voice said, "Whenever choosing between two evils, I always like to try the one I've never sampled before."

The voice was deep and Irish, and as Yvonne turned, she found herself once again facing Seán FitzGerald, his companion gone. "Are you often given a choice?" Yvonne asked.

Seán laughed at her response. "Too seldom."

"How unfortunate." She tried to escape, but people surrounded them, pushing her even closer to Seán.

Seán's eyes boldly inspected her dress. "A creation of Maxine's?"

"Yes." He's bold, Yvonne thought, looking at me like that and even mentioning Maxine's name.

"Tell me something." Seán moved her around so her back was against the wall, as if protecting her from the crowd.

Yvonne didn't feel any safer in this position—too close to Seán, too isolated amid the throng. "Yes?"

"Don't you have any spare time? Are you alone?" He leaned closer as if murmuring over the other voices.

"No. Gregory is over there."

"Gregory?" Seán raised a fine eyebrow.

"Gregory Reed." Yvonne attempted to inch away.

"Oh, yes. The Texas millionaire."

"Yes." Yvonne preened.

"I didn't realize he was your . . . what is the latest American saying?" Seán smiled urbanely.

"Husband," Yvonne snapped. "Gregory is my husband."

Seán was stricken. "I'm so sorry. You are St. Cyr, and . . ."

Yvonne didn't wait to hear, but murmured a quick goodbye and left to find Gregory and safety.

What an obnoxious man that Seán FitzGerald was! How

could Maxine fall for someone like that? Yvonne shrugged. Maxine's taste in men wasn't always discriminating, but to be fair, it was difficult to find a good man.

Yvonne smiled as she rejoined Gregory, floating happily to his side. How lucky she was to have her husband. Unbelievably lucky.

6

"It was a wonderful party." Yvonne smiled happily and relaxed into Gregory's arms. They watched the sleeping city pass, their car zooming trough the empty streets.

"Wonderful," Gregory murmured, rubbing her neck.

"Maxine looked perfect. That dress was spectacular on her. How typical of Maxine not to wear one of her own designs."

"She didn't look nearly as good as you." Gregory moved to her lips, first kissing the corners, then pressing tightly against her.

She had been utterly beautiful. The black dress highlighted her cameo white skin, and the sparkling diamond earrings drew attention to her face. With her long, slender neck, her hair elaborately knotted at the nape, and violet eyes that sparkled with pleasure, she had undoubtedly been the most beautiful woman at the party.

"The food was absolutely delicious!" Caviar and pâté. Quichettes soubise, tiny onion quiches; croustades savoyardes, cheese tartlets; petits chaussons au Roquefort, pastry turnovers with Roquefort cheese. Yvonne loved to eat miniature food. It didn't seem to count as calories. "And the swan was spectacular!" When the lights had dimmed, a flaming diamondlike swan was wheeled out on a cart, appearing to glide through the air.

"That reminds me . . ." Gregory sat upright in the car. "I'm hungry."

"There was tons of food!"

"Little bits of food. Nothing to feed a full-grown husband who traveled all the way from Dallas."

Yvonne turned, sliding her arms around his neck. "Thank you for coming. I wanted you there so much, although I'd have been nervous if I'd known." Gregory had flown in by private jet. "And the earrings are beautiful. You shouldn't have."

"Yes, I should." They drove up to their apartment buildling. "But I will take a present in return."

"That wouldn't be a pot of chili, would it? It will take too long to cook! My fastest recipe takes over an hour, and it's so late."

"Never too late for some things." Gregory's eyes wrinkled with laughter. "You wouldn't deny a drowning man, would you? I have to leave before too long."

"Oh, darling."

"I know." They held hands in the elevator. "It came just at the wrong time. I know your season's just startin' and all, and you can't get away, and I hate bein' away from you." He drew her close, kissing her again. "But this is important. It's a big deal."

"What's it about?" Yvonne stared trustfully into his deep gray eyes.

"Computer chips."

"Not related to chocolate chips, I guess."

"Much less interesting, I promise; and nothin' you need worry about. I take care of those things, and don't you forget it." His finger stilled the question that sprang to her lips.

Yvonne was satisfied with his answer. She wanted to be pampered and sheltered, and in a way didn't really wish to know about Gregory's business dealings.

Once inside, she slipped off her floor-length dark mink cape. One last time she pirouetted before him, displaying her dress. "I can't cook chili in this."

"The way you look in that, I wouldn't leave it on you anyway," Gregory growled. His arms closed around her, pressing her body tightly into his. As their lips met, he stroked her bare back, teasing her skin.

"Are you certain you're hungry?"

"Am I ever," Gregory groaned, "but I'll wait for this

until after you start the chili. Besides, I have to make a phone call.''

''In the middle of the night?''

''It's mornin' in Europe.''

''What a wonderful thought.'' Yvonne smiled. ''It's always morning somewhere.'' She changed in the bedroom, carefully placing the dress on a hanger and the earrings in her jewel box. She had a sudden happy thought, quickly stripped off her underthings, and without replacing a stitch, slipped on a red-and-black mohair sweater which, she noticed with pleasure, reached just below the curve of her bottom.

In the kitchen, she started the chili. Gregory loved Mexican cooking and she'd become an expert on such dishes as *frijoles refritos*, fried beans with onion, which he ate for breakfast; *frijol con puerco*, black beans with pork, chopped radishes, tomato sauce, and coriander leaves; and *carne con chile verde*, beef with green chili. To her surprise, she'd learned to love them too, but her weight was not allowed to climb above one hundred pounds, so Yvonne never ate too much at one sitting.

''Mmm . . . good.'' Gregory's voice was low.

''Yes, it should be delicious.''

''I wasn't referring to the meal,'' Gregory said, on his way to the stove. ''Have I seen that sweater before?''

''I don't think so. You've been out of town so often, you've missed a lot of things.''

''You're tellin' me!'' Gently he reached down and raised the bottom of the sweater. ''That's what I thought.'' He whistled. ''Don't look now, but you forgot something.''

''I don't think so.''

His arms circled her, pulling her body into his. ''I've missed you.''

''I've missed *you*. When will this deal be finished? I'm tired of not having a husband.''

''I know. I tell you what. When the deal is done, and you can get away from the ballet, we'll take a trip to Europe. Wherever you want. Sound good?''

''Oh, yes!''

His hands moved up to cover her beasts. ''So how is the chili coming?'' Gently he moved his fingers, arousing her.

''It won't be ready for a while.''

"Really? Maybe we could find something to fill the time." His hands moved lower, exploring, exciting her. Slowly he removed her sweater. "That's better."

"Better for what?"

His hands cupped her bottom, pulling her closer. "I'll show you." He picked her up and carried her into the living room, settling her on the thick rug before the fire. With smooth gestures he took off his own clothes and lowered himself to her side.

"You're so handsome," Yvonne whispered, and ran her hands over his body, feeling his strong muscles. Then she moved her grasp lower. When they were both yearning for each other, he moved over her, gently leading their movements until they clung in a passionate embrace, crying out their love and need for each other.

As they rested in each other's arms, Yvonne smiled with pleasure. She was planning more than a trip in Europe. It was time for a change in her life, in both their lives.

An arid smell sent her bobbing to her feet. "The chili! It's burning!"

"Just the way I like my chili—as well as my women!"

Slowly Yvonne awoke, surrounded by cool linen sheets, the scent of Yvonne perfume, and a satisfied longing for her husband. Gregory is home! With a tentative hand she explored his side of the bed. Cold and empty.

A soft murmur wafted in from the library; Gregory must already be at work. She punched the pillow. She wanted to snuggle up to her husband, not a cold bed. Their life necessitated separation; she had known that when they married. Gregory had business in Texas, among other places. Yvonne danced in New York, and on occasion, Europe. Until recently they had seen each other often, but this business deal had ended that. More and more Gregory traveled and in his time with her he was preoccupied. She wrinkled her nose. The deal would be finalized soon, allowing Gregory back into her life.

Yvonne slithered out of bed and shivered as the cool air caressed her skin. She'd slept, wrapped only in her hair, perfume, and Gregory's embrace. She slipped into a sheer magenta cashmere bathrobe, tying it snugly around her slim waist, and hid her feet in furry slippers. Like most dancers' feet, hers were marked by her craft: misshapen and callused. At the end of the room a small fire crackled in the hearth. How thoughtful of Gregory!

Down the hall she strolled, stopping at the door of the library when she heard Gregory's deep voice. "Right, Jerry."

Jerry was Jerry Brandner, Gregory's chief lawyer. She should have known that Jerry would be intimately involved in this special deal.

"How soon?" Gregory's voice held a hint of emotion. Could it be worry? Instantly she banished the thought. Gregory wasn't the worrying type.

"You push him, you hear? We need it by the ninth. I'm not going to have anything mess this up. . . . I know, I know. I swear, Jerry, you're turning into an old woman. You don't get anywhere without gambling."

Yvonne smiled. That was pure Gregory. You might as well play to win, not just to survive, was his philosophy, and he'd been playing and winning since he ran away from home at fifteen.

When Gregory replaced the receiver, Yvonne entered the room and settled happily into his lap. "Did you sleep well?"

"Very." He kissed her tenderly. "And you?"

"Very well. Ready for breakfast?"

"You look good enough to eat." He cradled both of her hands in one of his.

"How is Jerry?"

"Cautious."

Yvonne led him toward the kitchen. "No one could ever accuse you of that."

"Thanks." Gregory swatted her on the bottom. "Would I have taken you on if I were?"

Together they prepared breakfast: Gregory started coffee; Yvonne scrambled eggs and toasted muffins. Just one of their many traditions, Yvonne thought with a happy sigh; cooking together. Both worked extremely hard, but still shared so much.

Yvonne chose their breakfast china, almost translucent and decorated with pale yellow roses. She placed cups, saucers, and plates on a rolling cart of Victorian design next to antique silver place settings and cream-colored linen napkins. The whipping cream fit into a deep rose dish, the muffins and toast under a covered silver tray. Yvonne loved a romantic breakfast with perfect linen, silver, china, and food. For a crystal bud vase she culled a yellow rose from one of her bouquets of the night before.

Gregory wheeled the cart into the living area, and they sat on the fat overstuffed sofa before the fire.

As Yvonne sipped the thick coffee and stared into the orange-yellow flames, she suddenly realized Gregory's gaze was fixed on her. "What are you thinking?"

"Did you know your skin is the color of peaches? Just a kiss of yellow, a touch of pink." He ran his hand up her leg.

Yvonne folded her leg underneath herself. "I was thinking, too."

"What about?"

She carefully considered her answer. She wanted to tell Gregory her plan, but something made her reluctant to discuss it now. As Gregory reached over to capture a strand of her hair, she quickly began speaking. "Maxine." It was a safer, easier topic.

"What's wrong with Maxine? She looked fine last night."

"That's because she doesn't know." Yvonne placed the cup on the table, absentmindedly picking up the plate of eggs.

"Doesn't know what?"

"That there's anything wrong," she continued darkly.

"Then it can't be all that bad," Gregory suggested hopefully. Sometimes conversations with Yvonne had a way of wandering into thick forests of confusion.

"She needs a husband."

"I seem to remember another discussion like this. Maxine was sitting right where I am now. You were there, telling her about the joys of married life. And if I still remember correctly, she turned to you and said, 'Marriage is a great institution, but I'm not ready for an institution yet.' " He laughed heartily, until he noticed her stern expression.

"I didn't think it was funny." Yvonne turned on the couch to face him, her arms folded. "Aren't you glad we married?"

Gregory couldn't tell if she was teasing, but her lips were straight and unnaturally thin. "Of course I am."

"Why don't you think Maxine would enjoy marriage?" Yvonne asked with what he feared was deceptive calm.

"I don't know. She doesn't seem to be missing anything in her life."

"Sometimes you don't realize you are missing anything until you find it." She'd thought of that a lot lately.

Gregory felt the forest of confusion catch fire. "Maxine has lots of men around."

"Not the right ones. That tennis player, for instance. Really! They're all toys. Playthings. She needs a real man."

"Like me?"

Yvonne reached out and caressed him. "I'm tired of not seeing you."

"I know, Yvonne, and it won't be that much longer."

"Jerry couldn't take care of things for you?"

"Not on this. The psychology is important. It will only work out because I'm part of the deal . . . but I don't want to talk business." He never did, except in the vaguest terms— oil, heavy machinery, land speculation. Yvonne really had no firm idea how Gregory made his money.

"But we will go to Europe? You promised."

"I did and we will. Soon." Gregory kissed her neck. "Where will we go?"

"I thought Paris to begin with." They had visited Paris on their honeymoon.

"By all means Paris. We can stay in that romantic little hotel." Gregory loosened her robe, his kisses reaching lower, eventually skimming the top of her breasts.

"The Ritz, you mean?" Yvonne giggled.

"That's right. Where next?"

"Venice. I want to see it before it sinks. A night ride on the canals in a gondola doesn't sound bad."

"Sounds wonderful." One hand cupped her breast, slowly brushing it against his bare skin. Yvonne looked into Gregory's eyes. He looked tired, Yvonne suddenly worried. Their vacation would do them both good. And maybe it would be a beginning, as well.

For more than a year Yvonne had been considering having a child. At first it seemed an impossible dream. How much time would she have to take off? How would she care for the child and continue her career?

When she had first met Gregory, Yvonne had had a cat—a large black Persian. But with their life of travel the animal was too often left alone in the apartment, so with tears she'd given it to a friend. If she couldn't keep a cat, how could she possibly raise a baby?

Time passed, and somehow Yvonne changed her mind. Her visualizations expanded and deepened during those long nights spent alone. She pictured a little girl, dainty and beautiful; a small boy in Gregory's image; a nursery with a white wicker crib, eyelet lace curtains—and an efficient governess.

Why hadn't she told Gregory about her plans? She didn't know. He was so preoccupied, she told herself. Later. When there was time. . . . But right now, she had to go. It was almost nine-thirty.

"Class!" Gregory frowned as Yvonne got up. "I don't suppose I could talk you into skippin' it. Just once."

"I can't. You know what they say. If you miss one day's class, you know it; if you miss two, your teacher knows it; and if you miss three, the audience knows."

"What they don't know won't hurt them, I always say."

She leaned over to kiss away his frown. "I'll be home this afternoon."

"Yes." He looked embarrassed; one finger rubbed his nose. "But I won't. I have to be back in Dallas."

"Oh, Gregory!" Yvonne stood back, her arms akimbo, looking annoyed.

"I know. I have to go. I didn't want to tell you earlier. Didn't want to spoil last night."

"When will you be back?"

"As soon as I can. I'll call tonight. Why don't you arrange to do something devilish with Maxine?"

Yvonne shook her dark curtain of hair. "I would rather be doing something devilish to you."

7

From her massive glass desk Maxine stared past the open door of her office out to the workroom beyond. Sparkling lamés, thick tweeds, scintillating silks flowed off tables. Tiny, awkward sketches lined one wall—Maxine's shorthand for her design ideas.

"Here are your letters." Kili Weatherspoon, Maxine's first assistant designer, interrupted.

After glancing at them, Maxine signed and returned the papers. "Any important calls?"

"I have a list." The small oriental woman was organized, efficient, and immune to Maxine's temper—all qualities helpful in her job. "The accountant needs some papers from last year. The Seventh Avenue office wants to know about material and if you're coming over today. Ian Thorn, and"—she paused to glance at Maxine—"Silvia Rosen."

"Silvia Rosen?" Maxine's voice bristled with warning flags.

"The gossip columnist. She wants an appointment."

"Silvia Rosen!"

"She begs, pleads. Her daughter's wedding is coming up. She needs . . . has to have . . . will die without a whole new wardrobe."

Maxine pulled her hair and screamed. "That woman—that creature—will never touch a dress of mine again. Never! Not if she climbed up the stairs to this office. Not if she clawed up all twenty flights on her knees."

"She annoyed you in some way?" Kili's eyes were wide with innocence, her voice calm and light.

"Snake!" Maxine hissed. "White stockings! She wor
white stockings with one of my dresses. What does she thin
she is, a nurse?"

"I'll tell her you haven't time now."

"Never, never, never!" Maxine's fists beat on the desk
rattling the papers. With a dramatic sigh she slid back in he
chair, closing her eyes. "Fools!" A silence for sixty space
seconds followed while Kili waited patiently. One heavy
lashed eye opened. "When is the wretched creature plannin
the wedding?"

"Six months."

"Take a note. We'll call in two. But"—Maxine swun
upright, a wild gleam in her eye—"she'll pay."

"Yes, Miss Andrus."

Maxine reached for her phone, dialed Ian Thorn's number
spoke briefly with the choreographer, then hung up. Ki
waited patiently. Patience also helped when working wit
Maxine. Kili didn't care how much patience, organization
efficiency, or thick skin she needed to keep her job. She'
wanted to work with Maxine since she'd seen the first Andru
collection featured in *Vogue*.

She had known of Maxine's reputation when she applie
for the job. To Maxine, life meant combat. Some claimed th
chips on her shoulder could be assembled into a log cabin
An upturned nose, dismissive gesture, or social snub un
leashed rage within her. High or low society, colleague o
customer, media or academia, all at one time or anothe
incurred her wrath. Few were immune.

But Kili also saw Maxine's soft side—her friendship an
loyalty to Yvonne, the help given to an ill employee, an
frequent, quiet charity. Maxine was a bronze-covered marsh
mallow, Kili concluded. It didn't stop the dramatics, however

"Ian is interested in us designing costumes for a new balle
for him. I've designed for him before."

"Will I get to work on it?" Kili asked hopefully, suddenl
interested. She remembered Ian's burning dark eyes: intimat
yet mysterious. And to design costumes for a ballet!

"Whither I goest . . ." Maxine gestured to the bookcase
lining one wall. "Bring me the green album and the boo
underneath it."

Kili opened the books on Maxine's desk and scanned a series of photographs. "Your designs?"

"Yes. Thorn likes costumes evocative of the period he's chosen, but somewhat bizarre, theatrical. And of course dancers must be able to move in them." Maxine gestured at the books. "Take those with you and study them. It won't hurt you to work on the ballet. Fashion is a tough life, and having a sideline is a good idea. By the way, I was trying part of the new line on Yvonne St. Cyr the other day. She looked fabulous." Maxine suddenly looked preoccupied. "That is an idea. Yvonne in Andrus. Yvonne *as* Andrus." Maxine sighed. "It wouldn't hurt Yvonne's career, either. There is no such creature as too much publicity."

"Yvonne does not need publicity. She's at the top."

"Of a very steep, pointed mountain. Surrounded by a quagmire of competition and jealousy." Maxine tapped her fingernails on the desk. "Greased with the sweat of hungry young dancers. Pulled at by foreign ballerinas with flaming publicity. Nipped at the heels by Justine Stelle."

"I get the picture." Kili moved to straighten Maxine's desk.

Maxine smiled. "Call Yvonne at the company and ask her to have dinner with me at the apartment. Where are the models, anyway?" She glanced impatiently at her watch. "It's getting late."

"The party lasted late," Kili pointed out.

"*I'm* here."

"Everyone doesn't have *your* energy!"

That night Maxine and Yvonne ate dinner together. "You're not eating." Maxine looked critically at Yvonne's dish of linguini with white clam sauce, shrimp, and scallops.

"It's delicious."

"Of course it's delicious. Do you know what I pay my chef? You want something else? He can whip up a handsome omelet."

"I'm not very hungry." Yvonne sighed. "I miss Gregory."

Maxine twirled a strand of linguini and neatly drew it toward her mouth. "I'm glad marriage makes you so happy."

"But it does," Yvonne protested. "We're so happily married—"

"That it makes you sad," Maxine interrupted. "I under stand perfectly."

"You're impossible," Yvonne scolded. "When are yo going to settle down?"

"I've always thought that sounded like something a chea house might do."

They sat in Maxine's apartment, restored now to its white purity, the trees and blossoms stripped away. Yvonne coul see their reflection in the mirrored wall across the room Maxine wore a simple black dress, her hair pinned back in a untidy bun. Yvonne had arrived straight from an interview with *People* magazine wearing a softly shaped pimento-colore raw silk jacket with gold-striped pants blossoming out like full skirt. Her thick hair was fastened in a coil on each side o her head with beaten gold decorations.

"You need a man."

Maxine smiled. "I have three."

"That isn't the same. It's too much of a good thing."

"Too much of a good thing can be fantastic." Maxin looked pleased with herself.

"All right." Yvonne threw up her hands. "I give up. Fo now," she added *sotto voce*.

"I'm thinking of expanding my business." Maxine sud denly pushed herself away from the table. "Let's have brand and coffee in the living room and I'll tell you about it."

Maxine thoughtfully took out her hair pins, shaking he hair around her shoulders, and relaxed on the sofa.

"Is that why Seán FitzGerald was here?" Yvonne asked.

"Partly. Didn't you love him?" Fortunately she didn't wai for Yvonne's reply. "His company makes a beautiful rang of tweeds and mohair fabric that I'm thinking about using fo my upper two lines."

Already Maxine produced two kinds of collections. From her Madison Avenue custom salon she worked on clothe specially ordered by individual customers who attended he couture collections. On Seventh Avenue she made ready-to wear—very expensive ready-to-wear. The custom line carrie a label with only the stylized A, made for those who didn' need to be told, or to tell, who made their clothes. Th ready-to-wear collection carried the more obvious Maxin Andrus label.

"What would you expand into?" Yvonne asked.

"Better sportswear, modestly priced, that would sell in department stores across the country. I was thinking of calling them Andies."

"That's cute."

"I've also been thinking about other things. Most designers license their names to an entire range of products: furs, cosmetics, perfume, towels, shoes, uniforms."

"From head to toe with Maxine Andrus." Yvonne smiled.

"Maybe. Anyway, I'm thinking about a line of fragrances, cosmetics, and sportswear. *Real* sportswear. Tennis, swimming, exercise. What do you think?"

"Anything you do will be successful. What about money?"

"I'm getting some financial backing. Remember Melvin?"

"It will be a lot of work," Yvonne cautioned.

"Yes. Lots of coordinated publicity."

"Will I see your smiling, innocent face peeking out at me from all the newspapers?"

Maxine laughed. "Not mine, dear. I'm hardly of the temperament or beauty to sell my own products. No, I'll need someone to become identified with my products. Someone beautiful and glamorous."

"That shouldn't be hard." Preoccupied, Yvonne didn't notice Maxine looking at her with a speculative eye.

"How long will Gregory be gone?" Maxine decided to change the subject.

"I don't know. He'll be back and forth for a while. More time for me to tag along with you."

"Yvonne, do you ever feel too dependent on Gregory?"

"Yes, and I love it." Her tone didn't invite further discussion.

They poured more brandy, talked ballet and design. Later, neither really knew how much later, they were in Maxine's bedroom, clothes from the new collection surrounding them on chairs and on the floor. "Lots of pants," Yvonne said.

"It seemed like time."

"It's a beautiful collection." Yvonne smiled. "You're so talented."

"You're depressed, aren't you? It's more than Gregory."

"It's nothing, really. The performance was so good. But

this morning in class, I felt tired, stiff. I'm not as young as I used to be.''

"Poor old thing." Maxine shook her red curls in mock dismay.

"Twenty-five *is* getting old for a dancer. Most retire by their early thirties.''

"Look at Fonteyn."

"Right. Maybe I'll be so lucky." Yvonne sat on the edge of the bed. Maxine's bedroom was luxurious with fur and satin—the soft center of the harsh designer.

Maxine sat on the other side of the bed and lay back. Head to head, hair mingling red and black together, they relaxed. "Aren't things going well?" Maxine asked.

"Too well, maybe. It makes me nervous to have everything so perfect.''

Maxine chuckled. "Let me tell you a story. Once there were two little orphans . . .''

Yvonne didn't answer at first. How often they had encouraged themselves with the Tale. First they wove it around themselves at school, determined to ignore the snubs and disapproval, determined to be neither nuns nor mothers. Later, it helped them in New York. When Yvonne's first attempt to join the company failed, when Maxine lost an important sale, it carried them forward.

"They were going to be rich and famous," Yvonne slowly added.

"One would be a famous fashion designer."

"One would be a famous ballerina."

"Maxine would win two Coty awards." The redhead's voice grew low.

"Yvonne would become a prima ballerina."

"Maxine would open a luxurious office."

"Yvonne would become renowned throughout the world."

What more could they want?

8

Tired and sore, Yvonne sprinkled a generous handful of bath salts into the deep tiled tub and turned the hot water on full. The season continued, class after class, rehearsal after rehearsal, performance after performance. She was exhausted; details of the last weeks blurred in her mind.

Which afternoon had Rosie fallen to the floor with a cry, a torn muscle in her leg? Two of her three grueling roles had been allotted to Yvonne. Which morning had Jeffery, in a sweaty fury, turned on his partner screeching that she'd gained so much weight he couldn't lift her?

Stripping off the blue satin bra and pants, Yvonne sighed and dug her toes into the bedroom rug. She was tired and discouraged and lonely. She hadn't seen Gregory for a week.

Built next to her home studio, her bathroom was a *pas de deux* of pink and peach. The carpet was pale green, entwined with pink and peach flowers. The walls were tiled pink, the deep tub-for-two peach. Pinning her hair loosely atop her head, Yvonne eased herself into the swirling, foaming green water, catching her breath as heat slipped between her thighs and caressed her breasts.

She had a man to share her life with, and now she rarely saw him. It wasn't fair. But as Maxine once remarked, who said life was fair? Shouldn't she be grateful to have Gregory at all? Especially when she had once given up any hope of marriage and a family life. Yvonne leaned back, resting her head on a bath pillow. Ballerinas met few nondancers, so she had considered marrying another dancer.

But that thought had died early. Two dancing careers

doubled the tension, meant twice as many demands and little time to be together.

The heat from the water massaged her body, relaxing strained muscles, soothing her tense bones. A gradual drowsiness overcame her, and closing her eyes, she floated in the sea-scented water.

From the outer hall came a faint noise. Probably Nellie straightening, Yvonne thought lazily.

At the sound of the bathroom door opening, Yvonne didn't bother to open her eyes. "Would you turn on the towel rack, Nellie?" The racks were wired for heating, but Yvonne had forgotten to switch them on. A toasty towel would feel good against her body. Must take my sensual pleasures wherever I find them, Yvonne thought regretfully.

"Wouldn't you prefer I turn something else on?" Gregory's deep voice, as welcome as it was unexpected, filled the room.

Yvonne sat suddenly upright, unable to hide her joy even in fun. "I didn't expect you."

"Had an impulse and decided to fly up for the night. But I will have to leave early tomorrow."

"Then we'll have to hurry and do something about your impulses."

Gregory sat on the edge of the tub and gazed at her with narrowed eyes. "Finished with your bath?"

"I hadn't washed yet. The water felt so good."

"You're working too hard."

Yvonne smiled, excited by his wide shoulders and rugged good looks. "Yes, and I need someone to take care of me."

Gregory's hand reached for the soap, a heart-shaped bar. "Don't know about that. You dancers are tough." He lathered her back.

"Tough? We ballerinas are fragile, mere floating fluff from a dandelion ball."

"Lean back," Gregory ordered. Slowly and sensually he smothered her chest with soap, massaging her breasts until her nipples were hard with desire. "You might fool your public, trippin' along on the tips of your toes, but I know better. You're all made of steel and nylon cord, not roses and moonbeams and all that romantic nonsense you'd like people to believe."

Grasping his hand, she forced it into the water and captured it between her thighs. "I'm glad to hear that. I would hate to be at your mercy."

Gregory laughed hoarsely. "Huh! That will be the day." With his free hand he stroked the back of her neck; then, tilting her head back, he exposed her face to his kiss. For an instant they clung together, his hand moving over the inside of her thighs, caressing and teasing.

"Gregory . . ." Her voice held both pleading and promise.

Wordlessly he scooped her out of the water and clenched her wet body against his.

Yvonne unbuttoned his shirt, then deliberately kissed his chest, her tongue making tiny circles as her lips parted, then reached down and unzipped his pants. Impatiently she tugged at his underpants. Kissing inch by inch, she moved down his chest to his lap, where she buried her head and deftly used her lips and hands until his breath quickened and with firm movements he took her. She gasped, holding pleasure back until it broke free, overwhelming her.

Yvonne leaned back and gazed adoringly at her Gregory. "I'm starving."

Only hours earlier Yvonne had been exhausted; now she bubbled with life. Quickly she dressed, choosing a long, very loose pair of white pants pleated at the waist and a daring blue-and-white cotton sweater-jacket which fell open almost to her waist. A carved jade necklace-and-earring set completed her ensemble. "Hurry," she urged Gregory. "I can't wait to eat."

Gregory helped as Yvonne slipped on a long, full mink, her reward from a Blackglama advertisement. "Do you feel like a legend in this, dear?"

"I always feel like a legend by your side."

They chose one of their favorite places, a quiet Italian family-owned restaurant where privacy would be assured. The proprietor greeted them at the door with cries of recognition and welcome. "Too long since we've seen you," he gushed as he ushered them along.

Soon they were seated in the rich plum-decorated room at a table adorned with white flowers, flickering candles, fine crystal, and heavy silver. Gregory turned to the owner. "What would you suggest tonight, Tony?"

"You're hungry?"

"Starving." Yvonne smiled happily.

Gregory was by her side again.

Yvonne woke the next morning determined not to lose a moment with Gregory. She would slip into her studio for a quick warm-up, taking her life into her hands by missing her lesson with Madame. Gregory's side of the bed was empty but still warm. He was not in the den either, but an almost full cup of hot coffee sat by the phone. Downstairs, she decided, probably already caught up in business.

After a brief but thorough practice, she showered and dressed in a lavender cotton jumpsuit. If she were fortunate, Gregory could stay for lunch, perhaps have time to talk about their coming year and their future family.

Downstairs, as she entered the living room, she heard Gregory's voice. "What do you think?" Two deep chairs faced the cold ash-littered fireplace, two pairs of male legs thrust forward.

Gregory's jeans and boots contrasted with his guest's London-tailored suit and handmade shoes—Jerry Brandner, Yvonne decided, Gregory's lawyer.

"I didn't know I was paid to think." Jerry's voice was coolly amused.

Yvonne hovered, uncertain if she should retreat upstairs. She didn't want to interfere with business, but if left alone, Gregory might never tear himself away.

"I didn't know I paid you for anything else," Gregory countered.

"You haven't been known to take my advice." Yvonne saw Jerry's hands remove his horn-rimmed glasses and polish them with a monogrammed silk handkerchief. Each man sounded as if he were stalling for time. Curiosity rooted her in place.

"I listen."

"You pay me a lot to merely listen and then ignore what I say," Jerry sparred.

"Don't listen to many," Gregory parried.

"It could be a disaster."

"Harsh word."

"You're overextended."

Gregory laughed. "Oh, my! How am I gonna survive?"

"You will, I suppose. Tricky field, all this new technology. Computer chips. Genetics. New companies." Jerry clearly disapproved. "But this will be one more Reed miracle. Your name, reputation for guts, will keep the money in until the deal goes through."

"We'll tie it up like a calf at a rodeo—you'll see."

"Maybe. Have you discussed this with Yvonne?"

"Yvonne doesn't worry about business; I don't dance for her."

Jerry clicked the side pieces of his glasses together. "How nice for your feet and her fans, but maybe not for her future. This is a risk, and she should know."

"I take care of her future."

"What about the borrowing? The life insurance?" Jerry's glasses clicked faster. "Dammit, man! I am her attorney also."

"A month, Jerry, two. Hell, I'm not about to drop dead. I'm too mean." His laugh cut. "J.R. never dies."

"This is not a television show, Gregory. This is real life. Don't you ever worry?"

Yvonne tensed, waiting for Gregory's response. "A little," he finally admitted, sounding as if he'd swallowed desert dust. "But I fight it every inch of the way. Worry is nothin' more than steps backward in life, and I just charge forward. When the gains are great, the losses can be total. What's the worst that can happen? I lose everythin'?"

"That does not sound highly desirable to me," Jerry primly commented.

"So we would start over. Damn, Jerry, you've known me forever. Fifty dollars and luck—that's all I started with. Fifty dollars I invested in a slightly crooked poker game, and then I won that old truck. More of a gamble than genetics and chips. Besides, haven't I already lost two fortunes? Always come up smellin' like a rose. What's one more?"

"Always like a rose. But that was before Yvonne. She would find that hard, maybe too hard. She depends on you for everything, Gregory."

"Well, then. I just won't lose this gamble, will I? It's that simple."

Yvonne relaxed at his tone as she went back into the hall. It was just that simple.

9

A ballet dancer's life has its own seasons, its own weeks, its own days. Over the next few weeks Yvonne's life swept on, a whirlwind of celebrity interviews, chic parties, gourmet lunches, and haute-couture fittings, but always with dance superimposed: class, rehearsal, performance. Gregory's visits, an oasis in Yvonne's desert of loneliness, grew increasingly rare as he flew from New York to Dallas to Houston to Los Angeles and back, plotting, planning, and promoting his deal.

When together, there was time only for hurried affection. Yvonne could not discuss the baby with him in those interludes, and certainly not on the telephone in his daily calls. When they were together, really together, she promised herself, she would talk to him.

This had been a particularly hard season, with new ballets, fewer rehearsal hours, general tension. Some of the younger dancers seemed to be under such strain. Years of dedication, practice, and hope led to joining the company, but that was only the beginning. From corps dancer to soloist to star, the future stretched a pink satin ribbon. But for some, the ribbon wound around their slim, elegant throats. Yvonne had never tarried in the corps, but was plucked like a rare flower by Ian, then tended and cared for while she bloomed and advanced almost without effort. Physical effort, yes, but not the political striving that hindered so many dancers. Ian had protected her from company infighting, intrigue, and maneuvering.

But Ian wouldn't always be there. Now at least she was an

important dancer. And she had Gregory to smooth her way through the thorns of negotiations.

In the mirrored rehearsal room, dancers milled around trying to block out *Giselle*. As usual, the soloists and corps members practiced separately.

Dory, the assistant to the ballet masters, stood staring at the corps, frustration marring her face. "Let's try that again. By count." Dory wore a black leotard and tights, thick glasses, a thin smile. "One, two, three, four . . ." For many reasons, ballet dancers don't move to the music as do ballroom dancers: too many changes of direction, too many pauses, too many shifts of accent, too many sets of phrases. Instead they count. The corps had temporarily gone astray.

Ian slid into the room beside Yvonne. "What is this supposed to be?"

"*Giselle*."

"Am I to assume those mundane creatures are *Wilis?*"

Wilis, those bewitched spirits condemned to dance for eternity, currently wore tattered leotards, sloppy leg warmers, bulging rubber pants, miscellaneous T-shirts, strained grimaces, and sweat. But during a performance the audience would see floating gauze and refined expressions.

"They'll be fine," Yvonne said.

"Impossible. I don't know how we'll get through the season."

"The way we always have, Ian, with a turn and a prayer."

"You can joke, big star." Ian's eyes twinkled. "Come into the hall. I want to talk with you." Ian loved mysteries, surprises, secrets. Now what line of gossip has he scented? Yvonne wondered as she followed his slim figure. He looked left and right, then leaned close. "A new ballet."

"Really," Yvonne purred.

"Wonderful."

"Aren't yours always?"

"A perfect role for you."

"I would be stricken if there weren't."

"Big production."

Yvonne feigned casual consideration. "Big?"

Ian's hands expanded in a wide circle. "Big! Expensive. It will put the *La Bayadère* production in the shade."

Yvonne was impressed. *La Bayadère* had cost half a million dollars. "Nice."

"I would like to get together with you. Gregory, too." Within minutes of meeting Yvonne's husband, Ian had noted the importance and influence the Texan exerted in her life.

"Why don't you come to dinner at my apartment next week. I can't promise Gregory will be there, but I'll see."

"Maxine, too?"

"Of course. You want her to do the costumes?"

Ian nodded. "It will be beautiful." He patted her face. "I will make it on you, and you'll be the most beautiful ever." Whatever his current sexual interest, Ian always appreciated a beautiful woman.

As they drifted back to the stage area, Yvonne's mind flitted to her plans for a child. Could she have the baby and the role? A new role wasn't to be turned down. She had considered not signing with the company next year, but dancing part of the year as a guest star with other companies. Not that she'd dared voice such a thought at the company. "Don't some of those girls look too thin?" Yvonne asked.

"There's no such thing as too thin." The sharp voice of Justine Stelle caused them to start. Justine liked to see bones sticking out on her dancers. She was opinionated, flamboyant, and petite, or, as Maxine once said, "nasty, brutish, and short." Maxine's opinion was influenced perhaps by the slim older woman dressing entirely in Adolfo. Ian had more gently described her to Yvonne as "a monster."

A wave of fear crept through the rehearsal hall as the dancers noticed Justine poised in the doorway, her sharp, cutting eyes darting in all directions. "Ian told you about the ballet."

"Yes, it sounds interesting."

"You'll be lovely." Justine's lips didn't move; her eyes never left the practicing dancers. "Of course, there is your contract. We've all been so busy. We'll have to get together soon and talk about it."

So Ian's new ballet was the bait, and she herself the fish. No doubt Justine had guessed that Yvonne was considering not signing, and this new ballet was a bribe. If there was a baby, there would be no ballet for her.

Once again the posturing and maneuvering of signing time

would begin. The reward of a new, taller partner for Yvonne might be offered with the threat of a favorite role assigned to another dancer. Gregory would handle her contracts, applying new rules, treating ballet as a business, and enraging Justine in the process.

Now Justine drifted through the room spreading confidence and joy. "May! A *tour jeté* is a turn, not a tour of the stage. Last night you weren't looking good. Pauline, have you gained some weight?"

Ian looked down his handsome nose. "When the tough get going, the going gets tough. By the way, have you heard that Eleanor Alexander might join us next season?"

"I hadn't heard that," Yvonne replied, proud that her voice had concealed her shock.

Back in her dressing room, Yvonne tried to calmly prepare her toe slippers. Using at least ten pairs a week, it was a constant chore. She selected a tiny satin pair in delicate pink. Eleanor Alexander was a well-known dancer in the English company. With a sharp pair of scissors, Yvonne savagely poked a hole in the smooth, slippery fabric. Alexander danced the same roles as Yvonne. With trembling hands she ripped off a circle of satin. Justine had started that rumor to pressure Yvonne into signing the contract. With a darning needle Yvonne darned cruel, hard stitches on the toe for traction. Alexander was married to Roland Martin, seducer of young girls. Holding the shoe high, Yvonne bashed it into the brick wall, softening the last. Alexander was only twenty.

Yvonne felt like a waif cast off into a hurricane of company politics, blown by winds of ill will, lashed by waves of envy and intrigue. She wanted Gregory there to take care of her.

That night, Yvonne sat in the theater dressing room wearing a dusty pink leotard and tights and stared into the mirror. Soon she would appear in *Morning Lights*, a modern abstract ballet by the famous choreographer Penn Stafford. *"Morning Lights,"* she murmured to herself. Behind her, Nellie mended a fluffy tutu and ignored Yvonne, accustomed to the dancer's preperformance jitters.

"What does 'morning light' mean? Dawn? Or is it nothing to do with day, but means the dawn of a new life?" Yvonne made a face at herself in the mirror, sticking out her tongue. Such questions had no answers.

This was not one of her normal roles. Yvonne preferred dramatic roles, with high emotion and subtleties of characterization. Stafford, a thin, bearded man, did not connect. He would almost touch, nearly kiss, appear to hug—but not quite. When speaking with people, he had a curious gesture of slowly raising one hand and leaving it suspended in air, palm flattened out, as if resting against a large pane of glass, an invisible separation between himself and the rest of the world. To Yvonne, Stafford's ballets clearly expressed this emotional detachment.

"Just dance," he told her. "Don't think. It is all a matter of movement, nothing more. Every night, do it the same way."

Yvonne had smiled coolly but said nothing. She would never dance a role in exactly the same way night after night. Once when asked about her interpretation of Odette, she had truthfully replied, "Which Odette? There are hundreds of Odettes." It was true. The role changed not only from year to year as her understanding of the character deepened, but also from evening to evening.

Each night she tried to start afresh, to think as would the character. Sometimes she was a young lover, sometimes a tortured spirit. Yvonne would attempt to live their emotions and experiences as if they were really happening to her. Often she transformed herself so thoroughly, so completely, that she was herself surprised at changes she made in her presentation. Alterations occurred onstage, interpretations she hadn't planned.

The muffled tingle of the phone jolted her. Only Maxine or Gregory had access to her number at the company. Nellie answered, and handed her the receiver: "Your husband."

"Darling . . ." Yvonne's voice filled with happiness. "I didn't expect to hear from you."

"Just wanted to check and see how you were doing." He sounded tired, tired and dispirited.

"Fine. How are you? I don't suppose you're calling to tell me you're coming home." There had been no time to discuss her thoughts with him.

" 'Fraid not. But soon, I hope."

"Ian wants to get together and discuss a new ballet. I suggested dinner at our house. Maxine will be there also. We also have to talk contracts—and plans."

"Good. When you know the date, I'll try to be there. Can't let your career escape my attention." He was silent for a second. "I miss you, you know. I love you."

"I love you. Everything is all right, isn't it, Gregory?" Something in his voice, something like fear, had alerted Yvonne. Panic rose in her.

"Everything is fine. You know I take care of everything, lucky charm. Just don't you worry about a thing." Hardy confidence again flooded his voice. "Now, get out there and dance."

When Yvonne returned home, she didn't notice Nellie at first. The older woman sat on the couch next to the fireplace. Beside her lay a coat, and on the floor at her feet, a suitcase. "Nellie? Is something wrong?" Yvonne stopped just inside the door, then moved quickly to her side.

"My sister."

"Martha?"

"Yes." Martha, Nellie's only relative, lived in Arizona.

"What happened to her?"

"I got a call this afternoon."

"Go on." Yvonne put a comforting arm around her friend. Normally calm and efficient, Nellie seemed stunned and at a loss.

"She's had a heart attack."

"That's horrible. How is she?"

"They don't know yet. I thought I would go out to be with her, but the season isn't over yet. How would you get along without me?"

"Nellie!" Yvonne's eyes filled with tears as she hugged Nellie. "Don't be ridiculous. I'll manage. Have you called the airport?" Yvonne briskly took charge: booking a flight to Flagstaff, charging a ticket, making sure that Nellie had all that she needed. The next morning, Nellie would leave for the airport.

Yvonne changed into a nightgown and curled up on the sofa. Even the glowing fire added little cheer to the room.

She stretched out her legs and stared into the flames. With Nellie gone she would be more alone than ever.

Ballet, knowing she could throw herself ever deeper into dance, consoled her. And the knowledge that soon Gregory would be free. Gregory and dance—with them she had it all.

10

Kili looked around the vast living room. This was how a famous ballerina should live, she thought with satisfaction, the bronzed samurai appropriate guards for the fragile star, the impressionist paintings—including a subtle Degas—beautifully lighted, perfectly placed. Nothing shouted, nothing clamored for attention. But when you were Yvonne St. Cyr, married to Gregory Reed, nothing needed to.

Kili's own apartment remained a carefully guarded secret. Only too well could she imagine Maxine's ironic hilarity at her careful wooden antiques, her Laura Ashley fabric, her Early American accessories. Oriental had never fascinated Kili.

"Kili, how nice to see you." Yvonne, wearing a simple black dress, her hair severely back, and diamonds glimmering at her neck and ears, swept out from the dining area. She looked very beautiful and very rich.

The apéritif was *kir au champagne*, champagne with blackcurrant liqueur. Kili grasped a slim goblet and listened to Ian, Yvonne, and Maxine gossiping, as Gregory—who had flown up for this meeting—looked at his wife adoringly. "I tell you it was a horrible performance. Just horrible." Ian looked pleased. "I think Roland is getting a little old. And Eleanor Alexander just can't seem to stay *en pointe*."

"What a shame!" Yvonne exclaimed. Kili didn't think she looked all that sorry.

"It was more of a *faux pas* than a *pas de deux*," Ian quipped.

Ian hadn't yet mentioned his new ballet, but he impressed Kili anew with his charm and grace and wit.

Dinner was served on gold-painted English bone china. Between mouthfuls of *coulibiac*, fillets of salmon and mushrooms baked in brioche, they gossiped about new dancers and styles.

"I hear Penn Stafford was hysterical last week," Yvonne commented.

"Some of us choreographers are very touchy," Ian confessed smugly.

"Something about Stafford's *Pink Glow?*" Yvonne turned to the others. "I think large passages of it are undanceable."

"That was the problem." Ian helped himself to another portion of sautéed zucchini and fresh spinach. "*Pink Glow* had changed from the way Stafford devised it. Me, I never mind small changes, not if it adds something. The dancers had worked on *Pink Glow* and made it move better, but when Stafford came into a rehearsal, he blew up."

"What will happen now?" Yvonne asked with concern. She covered for that ballet, and had no intention of reverting to those impossible combinations if she should have to dance the role.

"Easy. Justine canceled all rehearsals for *Pink Glow*. There, there, she told Stafford. All right, all right, she soothed him. Then she officially added an extra set of *Swan Lake* rehearsals for B group. B group really is rehearsing *Pink Glow*, but Stafford doesn't know that. By performance time he'll be back in England, out of our way."

"Justine is clever." Yvonne also was clever, managing to stay out of the artistic director's way. She didn't want to sign a contract, she didn't want to not sign a contract. She'd had no time to discuss the tightrope with Gregory. Once he had arrived home, they only had time and energy for love.

Open-faced apple tart with whipped cream completed the dinner.

And Ian still hadn't mentioned his new ballet.

Coffee was served in the living room. Kili curled up in a large, cushy chair close to Ian's; the others scattered on the sofas forming a circle around the modern fireplace.

"How is Nellie's sister?" Maxine asked.

"Still in the hospital, but expected to live."

"When will Nellie be back?"

Yvonne sipped her coffee. "I don't know that she will. Martha will need her, and Nellie is getting older. It isn't fair to keep her with me when she wants to be with her family."

Silence. They were all waiting.

Maxine waited with her usual enthusiasm, Kili with hope. With Maxine very busy, much of the responsibility would be hers, hers and Ian's. Yvonne waited with interest and fear. Would her role be too good to miss? Gregory waited with concern. Yvonne needed a new interest to occupy her time and ease the pain of his absence.

Ian laughed. "Well." He rubbed his hands together. "I guess I wanted this meeting, didn't I?"

"You promised me a wonderful role." Yvonne smiled.

Ian stood before the fireplace, a snifter of brandy in his hand. His slim figure elegantly displayed his Italian-cut suit. "Choreography comes from two Greek words: *choreos*, meaning 'dance,' and *grapho*, 'to record.' A choreographer is the composer of dance. Originally"—he winked at Kili—"it wasn't so grand. Dancing masters composed the dances, and often had to play the violin while teaching."

"You might not have made it back then," Yvonne teased.

"As it happens, I play the violin superbly."

"A man of hidden talents," Maxine added.

"In practice"—Ian moved with tiger grace to a large chair and slithered into place—"the choreographer is totally in charge of the ballet: he chooses or invents the story, selects the music, picks a designer and commissions the costumes and decor. As if that isn't enough for one set of frail shoulders, he directs the work, guiding the dancers in their acting, their placement onstage, and their understanding of the style and mood of the dance."

"If he could only dance all the roles," Yvonne said, laughing, "he wouldn't need to fool around with those nasty little dancers."

"Excellent idea." Ian straightened up. "Anyway, I like to start with a story, often a biographical one. People and the past fascinate me. That's only the beginning, of course. Ballets are like sculptures in music, exploring the space around the dancer, showing the emotional content of the characters . . ." He broke off with feigned exhaustion. "I don't know how I do it."

Laughter awarded him. "When I was looking through Maxine's books,"—Kili spoke for the first time—"I saw the phrase *ballet d'action*. What does that mean?"

"It means a ballet with a story. All the old ballets like *Swan Lake* and *Nutcracker* are *ballets d'action*. Traditionally they're divided into four types of movements. First the *scènes d'action*, in which the dancers tell part of the story by gesture, without dancing. Second, the *pas d'action*, when part of the story is told using dance. A large part of the ballet is either this or the *variations*, dances in which the heroes and main characters describe something about themselves—their emotions, their hopes, their plans. Then the last type is *divertissements*, dances which may have nothing to do with the story, but add more dancing to the ballet." Ian paused dramatically. "The new ballet will have all these elements. The name: *Ballet of Desire*. The main character: Colette, the French writer. You, Yvonne, will become identified with her forever."

Everyone was silent as Ian explained. "Colette was born on January 28, 1873. By the time she died, she had married three times—a lot of desire there. First we visit a young girl in the French countryside, innocent, a thick braid of hair down her back, loving animals and plants. At twenty she's in Paris, the city of lights and of Toulouse-Lautrec, married to a writer, Willy, who locked her in a room while she wrote for *his* credit, *his* glory."

There was more, much more. Plenty of material for Ian to craft a work of art, a role of genius for her. From sensuous detail, exciting plot, and shocking variations, steps would come, fascinating, awe-inspiring steps.

To dance the role of the lover of men and women, the famous writer—creator of such characters as Gigi—would be all Ian had promised.

Although not fully awake, Yvonne knew she was happy, but fearing the false joy of dreams, she struggled against the morning light. Gradually, as memory returned, the scent of the fresh linen sheets and lavender potpourri confirmed it. She and Gregory were finally together, alone at the Houston ranch, playing hooky, as Gregory said, for a four-day weekend. This was their last day, when their idyllic weekend ended.

Thursday they never went outside. Gregory made chili for breakfast. Yvonne teased him about the red-hot seasonings. She cooked lunch. He teased her about the lack of spice. They spent the afternoon in bed, and found the spice and seasonings just right. For dinner they ate chocolate cake. For dessert they sipped champagne. On the video-cassette recorder they watched Fred Astaire and Ginger Rogers dance. Well, almost the entire dance.

Friday they never came inside. They inspected the ranch, swam in the pool. She cut her finger. He kissed it and made it better. He backed into a barbed-wire fence. She kissed it, made it better, and enjoyed herself. They swam in the pool again. He suggested making love underwater. She pointed out she wasn't a fish. She learned to hold her breath a little longer.

Saturday she woke up laughing. He brought her breakfast in bed. She smeared marmalade on all his indecent places and licked it off. He covered her with baby oil and rubbed it in. She got a rug burn on her bottom. They watched Astaire and Rogers dance again, this time to the strains of "Night and Day." They danced along. Fred and Ginger had a misunderstanding. Yvonne said it was Fred's fault. Gregory said it was Ginger's. They made up in the bedroom just as the lovers made up on the screen.

A perfect retreat. No time to worry. No time to think. No time to talk. Just love talk, passion talk, romance talk. No ballet, no business deals, no contracts, no plans.

Gregory was making breakfast. Yvonne lay in bed, considering. What would it be like not to dance? To wake up every morning with nothing to do but enjoy herself? To shop as much, eat as extravagantly, play as often as she wished? Never having to consider what ballet loomed that night; never worrying about pulled muscles; never agonizing over her role?

To be no one but Mrs. Gregory Reed?

That would mean not dancing Ian's ballet, not having the role of Colette made on her. She would pass up the most demanding, dramatic, and fascinating role she'd ever danced. Her own place in the history of dance.

She could not give up the role. She could not give up her baby. So she would have both.

Several weeks earlier she had stopped taking her birth-control pills and had missed her last period. This holiday, she had planned to tell Gregory the wonderful news of her pregnancy but decided against it.

With this current business affair, Gregory had too much on his mind, too many concerns and fears as he juggled the balls of money, power, and success. Just three weeks or a month more, he had promised, and she would have his full attention.

This weekend, their last time together as a couple, should be carefree. Soon they would be a family-to-be. She did not want to think about ballet, about decisions, about the future. Soon, very soon, Gregory could turn his attention to where his heart lay, with her, Ian's ballet, and their offspring. Their future would be perfect, perfect in every way.

"Up, sleepyhead. Time to get this show on the road." Gregory appeared in the doorway of the bedroom.

"I refuse."

"I made your favorite breakfast," he tempted.

"What's that?"

"Chili eggs, of course." He grinned as he raised his arm to block the pillow she threw at him.

Later, as she walked regretfully by his side to the Ferrari, Yvonne turned for a final look at the ranch. "I wish we didn't have to leave."

Gregory reached for her, kissing her tightly. "I know. We were lucky to have these days, though. Soon I'll have all the time in the world."

11

Maxine sat cross-legged on her bed; drawings, notes, articles, pictures littered the large silk quilt. Her future lay before her eyes. She shuffled the papers, laid them out, altered the configuration, read her fortune. Now had come the time to make her move, almost. Now the money had been amassed, almost. Now her plans had jelled, almost.

Almost.

Still thinking of business, she wriggled off the bed, snatched up her brush, and began the two hundred strokes that would leave her hair gleaming. "Ninety-nine, one hundred." The phone rang. "Damn."

Casting her hairbrush on the bed, she grabbed the receiver. "Hello?"

"Is this the lady with the cat?" The voice was deep, strong and gravelly.

Maxine lay back on the bed, a silent "oh" of surprise formed on her lips. It was Fleming James, an attorney who specialized in international law, whom Maxine had met at a party last week. She tarried until she could trust her voice. "No, have you lost one?" They had met because of a misunderstanding regarding how many cats their mutual friend owned.

"How are you doing?"

Maxine paused, evaluating his tone. Real interest? Or an opening ploy? "Busy as usual." She delayed an extra beat. "I thought you had business tonight?"

"Did. Finished earlier than I expected. Want to go dancing?"

Maxine pretended to consider. "I was going over some

figures. Did you know that the total dollar volume on scent for men is up fifteen percent per annum to seven hundred and fifty million dollars a year?''

"Fascinating.''

"How many do you own?'' Maxine struggled to combine her seductive voice with her efficient business tone. Attraction without commitment.

"Cats?''

"Scents.''

"Four, but I try not to wear them all at once. Dancing.''

"You're dancing?''

"No, but I want to be. The Rainbow Room. I'm not really planning to take no for an answer.''

"Half an hour?''

"Twenty minutes.'' He hung up, not allowing her a reply.

Maxine stared at the phone, then replaced the receiver slowly. What was she getting into? Grabbing the hairbrush, she ran to her dressing table. She quickly reapplied her makeup, accenting her eyes with jade green, thickening her lashes with mascara. She didn't hurry for a man. She slipped on a flowing black jersey dress which floated around her figure, crossing one shoulder, baring the other. Finally she pulled her hair back, twisted it into a bun, and fastened in a jade clip. She glanced at the clock.

Three minutes to go. A liberal splash of perfume, a graceful settling of a shocking-pink cape around her shoulders, and she was ready. The bell rang. Fleming James was always on time to the minute. Maxine stared at herself in the mirrored wall while the maid answered the door. So what if he was a luscious blond, what was she doing?

Two hours later, she was still unsure, but Maxine didn't know if she cared. Champagne and music had left her head whirling, her heart fluttering. Fleming drew her closer. "Let's go back to my apartment for a final drink.''

"I don't think I need anything else to drink.''

"All right. Let's go back to your apartment and have something to eat.'' Fleming swirled her to the music, brushing her lips with his.

"I don't know.'' By now Maxine half-hoped she would keep her head, half-hoped she would lose it.

"I do.''

Almost surprised, Maxine soon found herself in her apartment seated before a small fire. As Fleming enthusiastically finished off the last of a large piece of chocolate cake, she sipped her coffee and fought an urge to stare adoringly at him. If she wasn't careful, she'd become one of those silly women who giggled and blushed whenever they saw their special men. Disgusting.

"Have any enthralling cases today?" Maxine ventured.

"Nothing captivating—until I saw you." He sighed. "Now you know my secret. Sophisticated man-about-town, successful lawyer, and chocolate fiend." He licked the fork. "Could you love a man who would sell his mother for ten pounds of Lady Godiva chocolate?" Maxine pretended not to notice his arm resting on her shoulders.

The phone rang. "It must be love." Fleming captured her in his arms. "I hear bells." He pressed his lips over hers.

"I have to answer." Regretfully she forced him away.

"Why?"

"It's my private line. Almost no one has this number." Maxine ran lightly across the room. "Hello?"

"Hello, is that Maxine?"

The voice was familiar, but not familiar enough to have had that number. "Who is this?" Maxine's voice was husky— the late hour and Fleming's kisses had taken their toll.

"This is Silvia Rosen. I hate to call you at a time—"

"How did you get this number?" Damn that gossip hag anyway.

"I called the operator and told her it was a family emergency."

"How dare you!"

"It's not a lie. My column is going in to the paper now and I knew you would want to comment."

Was there no limit to her nerve? That woman *would* sell her mother for a pound of chocolates. She would never, never wear another Andrus. "Comment on what?"

"You mean I am the first to tell you?" Silvia hesitated. "Comment on Yvonne St. Cyr."

"What about Yvonne?"

"She died this evening. A car crash in Texas. She and her husband both gone. Terrible."

"No!" Maxine slammed down the receiver. "No." She

wouldn't accept it. "No." Yvonne couldn't be dead. Not aware that she had screamed aloud, she started at the sound of Fleming's voice.

"Maxine, is something wrong?" One look at her chalk-white face sent him bounding across the room to her side. "What is it, darling?"

She couldn't answer, the pain too great, too all-encompassing to allow her to speak. It shouldn't be like this, she thought; shock supposedly left you numb, not filled with blinding pain. Maxine bent over, doubling with agony, balling her fists till her nails forced her palms to bleed. Slowly she regained control; her words were a dazed whisper. "Yvonne. Something has happened to Yvonne." She couldn't repeat Silvia's message.

Fleming jumped into action. Efficiently he escorted Maxine to the black lacquered bar, found the brandy, and poured her a stiff measure. "Where is Yvonne?"

"Houston. She and Gregory have a ranch there."

"What happened?" He was taking mental notes.

"She said . . . said . . ." The words would not come.

"Drink!" He watched as the liquor slid down, choking her. "Who said? Yvonne? A hospital?"

Maxine shook her head in reply. "Gossip columnist." The words came out through clenched teeth. "Car accident," she moaned.

"Sit down." Guiding her to a position by the phone, he called a friend at *The New York Times,* the information operators, the highway patrol, and finally, an hour later, he reached the hospital where Yvonne and Gregory had been taken.

Waiting. Maxine sat quietly. Worrying. Sometimes she cried. Sometimes she just hurt. Waiting. All the while waiting. What would Fleming find out? What might he discover? Yvonne couldn't be dead; Yvonne could only too easily be dead. Things always got worse.

When Fleming hung up the phone, Maxine opened her mouth to speak, but only a squeak emerged from her throat. Now that the time had come, did she really want to know the truth? Once she knew, she would never be able to heal her heart. The wound would be mortal.

Abruptly she rose from the chair and walked across the

room, like a tiger pacing its cage. As she turned, Fleming looked uncertain and uneasy for the first time that evening

"Are you ready?" he asked in a low voice.

Maxine steeled herself, preparing for what might prove an unbearable pain. "Yes."

"The news isn't good. Gregory . . ." Fleming hesitated "Gregory is dead."

Maxine paled and gripped the back of the chair. "Dead."

"I'm sorry, Maxine."

"And Yvonne?" She didn't want to hear. "How is Yvonne?"

"Yvonne is unconscious. Hurt. The car was totaled. Shall I make plane reservations? Is there anyone who should be called? Family?"

"I'm her family. How badly hurt?" Maxine hardly dared to hope.

"They don't know yet. Something about her leg."

"Damn! Damn! Damn!" Maxine leaped from the chair and ran to her bedroom. "Please call the airlines. I have to get there immediately." She pulled down a suitcase, threw things in. Later that week as she unpacked the case, Maxine discovered five pairs of silk underwear, no bras, and a pair of orange panty hose.

12

Yvonne had not been told of Gregory's death. She was conscious, drugged but lucid, having fractured her leg in two places and suffered a possible concussion. She had been so lucky, the nurses cooed. After all, the car had been ripped open like a sardine can.

Gregory had died instantly when the car rounded the curve and plowed into the semitruck blocking the road. The trucker had had no time to place his flares; speeding as usual, Gregory had had no time to brake.

"I want to see Yvonne." Maxine stared at the floor, grateful for Fleming's presence, thankful for not having to show her gratitude.

"That might not be best," the head nurse stated. She was tiny and blond and her flashing blue eyes sparkled at Fleming.

"I'm going to see Yvonne. Now." Maxine's voice was firm.

"Now, now. We're going to be reasonable, aren't we?"

"We?" Maxine's voice softened. "We? You are maybe." Her teeth clenched, she slowly raised her flaming green eyes to stare at the nurse. "The last time I was reasonable was an error I don't intend to repeat."

Although soft light illuminated the left side of the room, the bed was shrouded in darkness. Maxine's eyes took a moment to adjust; then she saw Yvonne lying on her back, her hair loose and flowing over the pillows.

Maxine moved to the bedside and lightly touched her friend's hand. Yvonne lay still, her right leg in a cast, slightly elevated.

"Maxine?" Yvonne's eyelashes fluttered.

"I'm here." Maxine moved closer. "Don't try to talk."

"I thought I was dreaming when I smelled your perfume."

"It's all right," Maxine lied.

Yvonne's eyes opened, allowing Maxine to see them, to see that she already knew about Gregory. "Nothing will be all right ever again." She was calm, frighteningly calm.

The drugs must be clouding her pain, Maxine thought. Soon after, Yvonne's eyes shut and she slept, Maxine still at her side clutching her hand.

Days passed. Yvonne, no longer drugged, still remained calm. She cried a little while telling Maxine what she remembered. "I fell asleep as we drove. I awoke just as we rounded the corner. I think Gregory cried out." She closed her eyes as large tears gathered and streaked her cheeks. "I saw the truck. There was no time to be frightened. I didn't wake until the hospital; I can't remember the crash. But as soon as I awoke, I knew Gregory was gone. I just knew."

She hasn't cried enough, Maxine thought, but is holding everything inside: panic, pain, passion. Those explosive emotions all needed expression, but Maxine recoiled at the thought of such an explosion. Yvonne was her best friend, her family. These last years, Yvonne had had love, romance, happiness— Gregory. Could she adjust to life without him?

Yvonne poked with her fork at the mushroom-and-sour-cream omelet Maxine had just cooked. The bread, toasted golden brown, with orange marmalade on the side, sat on its own fragile plate. To Yvonne it might well have been molded sawdust. Food had lost all appeal. With slow, deliberate movements she cut a piece of egg, raised it to her lips, placed it in her mouth, and chewed. She would eat.

Four times a day, with the same deliberate movements, she ate whatever Maxine prepared. She was determined to eat. For the baby.

Yvonne knew she was pregnant, and could sense life growing inside. It was her secret so far, hers and Gregory's. Somewhere he knew. Somewhere he saw their life completed.

She would be calm for the baby; she would eat for the baby; she would sleep for the baby. Somehow she swallowed the fear that filled the night when she realized Gregory would never be there again to help her. Somehow she choked back the tears that welled up when she realized her love would never again be by her side. Somehow she would be calm for the baby.

Today would be the worst yet, the day of the funeral. "Let me put your hair up," Maxine suggested. They were staying at a hotel, Yvonne unable to face the ranch with its all-too-fresh memories. "Your dress is on the bed." Maxine had flown to New York, gathered what they needed for the funeral, dropped Fleming off, and returned to Texas—all in the space of a day.

"Call if you need me," Fleming told her. Maxine was grateful he had come, appreciated his not asking why she hadn't introduced him to Yvonne, and thankful he had left without complaint. Maxine felt sure that this wasn't the time for Yvonne and Fleming to meet. Not when Yvonne had just lost Gregory, not when she needed Maxine so desperately.

For the funeral Yvonne arranged a short service by the graveside, a site she chose on the ranch. Was that what Gregory would have wanted? She didn't know; they had never discussed such a possibility. But the ranch was the first property he had owned, an area where he was most relaxed and happy—the place he should rest.

The service would be difficult, Yvonne thought, wondering if she could survive watching the coffin descend, knowing they would never be together again. On the hot, clammy day, an inappropriate sun shone merrily in the sky.

Maxine never left her side. Friends from the ballet corps, Gregory's business, and personal ones all offered their condolences. Gestures, faces, words, drifted by her; she barely recognized people. "Thank you. I know. Thank you." The words came automatically, like a bow at the end of a mediocre performance. Maxine had brought her a hat with a small veil, but Yvonne's eyes were tear-free. She knew this ceremony had nothing to do with Gregory, nothing to do with life.

Life was within her, waiting to be born.

Soon it was over; Maxine and Yvonne sat on a flight to New York. Yvonne maneuvered gracefully on her crutches, a skill acquired over the years after various ballet accidents. "I'm going to retire." She gazed blindly out the window.

Silence. Maxine looked at her hands.

"Don't you think I should?"

"I don't know if you can."

"I don't know if I could stand to dance again. I'm tired, so very tired. I think it's time to retire and let younger dancers move up. Besides . . ." She thought of Gregory's child, but stilled her lips. She would tell Maxine later.

"Besides?"

"Nothing."

Silence followed through the remainder of the flight, through the dark streets, through the elevator ride to Yvonne's apartment. As they stood in the alcove, Maxine recalled an earlier conversation. "Are you sure you want to stay at your apartment? You could come home with me," Maxine had asked, although knowing Yvonne wouldn't accept. "Or why don't you let Nellie come stay with you?" The older woman had attended the funeral, offering to return to New York and help Yvonne.

"Nellie has her own responsibilities. I'm fine, I'm staying here in my own home, and I'm not alone." Their live-in couple remained.

But as the door closed behind Maxine, Yvonne realized she was alone, terribly alone. In certain ways she'd be alone for the rest of her life.

Slowly she moved into the living room, looking around as if examining a house she had never seen before. Only ten days, she thought with wonder. Only ten days had passed since they left together, flying to Houston and their happiness at the ranch.

Her hand reached out and stroked the velvet covering of a chair as if she were considering purchasing it. The housekeeper came out of the kitchen. "I made tea." Without waiting for Yvonne's refusal, she turned and wheeled in a cart, settling it by the fireplace. "I thought you might sit by the fire."

"I see Maxine has already issued orders." Yvonne attempted a smile.

"Shall I freshen the upstairs area?"

"I'll be moving down to one of the guest rooms. The light pink one."

"I'll move some of your clothes. The cards and letters of condolence are here when you want to see them."

"Thank you."

Just as the housekeeper began to leave, she turned to face Yvonne. "A package arrived here the day you were due back from Texas." She took a small rectangular box from a table and set it on the serving tray. "Nothing else I can get you?"

"Nothing."

Nothing. Nothing she had to do. Nothing she wanted to do. Nothing she could do. "Nothing" summed up her life from now on.

Next month would have been their anniversary, two years married. Two years ago they had celebrated at the Plaza, an elaborate party arranged by Maxine, all white flowers and balloons. All happiness, but the kind of happiness Yvonne would never know again. Then she had everything, a wonderful husband, a brilliant career. Now that she'd lost the former, the latter had no meaning.

Idly she noticed the small box. What could it be? The day she was due back from Texas, the housekeeper had said, so it wasn't a message of condolence. She picked up the box, unwrapped it, lifted the lid. Inside, there was a choker of pearls and small diamonds from which hung a heart-shaped amethyst surrounded by larger diamonds. Despite tears of certainty which sprang to her eyes, she searched for a note. She found it all too quickly.

From a small card, written in Gregory's distinctive hand, she read aloud: "To Yvonne with all my love. Sorry the vacation was so short." He must have ordered it the day they left New York, arranging delivery for a time when he thought she would be alone.

And she had been alone, she thought ruefully, although he couldn't have known how alone.

The amethyst was the purple stone Gregory said reminded him of her eyes. Her eyes fascinated him, their deep violet color accented by thick black lashes. "Sometimes they are exactly the color of violets. Fresh spring violets." He had bought her a fine porcelain bouquet of violets. "Sometimes they pale," he added, "pale to the color of lavender." He bought her lavender-scented hangers, a light purple bathrobe, sugarplum candies, tiny purple-stoned earrings, orchids, dark wild strawberries.

Yvonne stared at her present from beyond life, her last gift from Gregory. Despite her intentions, her eyes filled with tears, which magnified their color, turning the violet to deep purple, black purple, the color of mourning. Slowly the tears fell down her cheeks, streaking paths of pain. The last present she would ever have from Gregory.

13

The nights were the worst.

Dreams crowded in. Nightmares in which she saw Gregory, torn and broken, hurt and bleeding, but beyond her reach. Dreams in which he was alive and well, walking, talking, and making love, after which came the reality of awakening, the pain which renewed itself each morning. She didn't know which was worse, the horrifying nightmares or the cruelly happy dreams.

She tried to see only Maxine, wanting to hide from everyone else. Ian came once, and refused to discuss her pain, a tactfulness for which she was grateful. He spoke of *Ballet of Desire*, of Colette. But she wouldn't, couldn't let herself be touched by the story.

Once she went for a drive, and looking out the window, saw Gregory. Irrationally certain it was he, she called out his name. Maxine didn't argue, but directed the driver to pass the man, holding Yvonne's hand as they saw that it wasn't Gregory—of course—didn't even look like him.

Mechanically she took a taxi to the doctor. Nothing mattered, but she would do her required duty.

Dr. Epstein seemed young to her, his mustache a disguise to confer maturity. He glanced through papers in a thin file marked "Yvonne Reed," then pulled out a series of X rays. "Mmmmm."

Yvonne began to fidget. "Well?"

"Good pictures. Those men in Houston did a good job."

"How is my leg doing?"

"Not badly. I'll want my own pictures taken, to see how

you are doing, if that's all right. Just smile nicely for the man."

New X rays took almost an hour. Yvonne felt ill and tense. When ushered back into Dr. Epstein's presence, she noticed him studying the new set of negatives. "You are making progress."

"That sounds cautious."

"It was a bad break. A double fracture, but it is healing."

"How soon before I'll be able to dance?"

The doctor looked into her eyes without expression. "What did Dr. Stans tell you? The doctor in Houston."

"Tell me?" She had been preoccupied with thoughts of Gregory, and the hospital's doctor had seemed pleased enough to drop the subject of her leg, emphasizing only that she must consult Dr. Epstein when in New York. "Nothing, really. Just that it was fractured."

"I see."

"See what?" Yvonne's lips were dry with fear.

"Your leg has been badly hurt."

"But it will get better?" Yvonne moved her hands restlessly.

"Yes, it will get better." The doctor scribbled a series of notes on the pages. "In time, you should be able to walk normally, or at worst with a slight limp." His eyes stayed with determination on his notes.

"Walk?"

"You were very lucky not to have been hurt more seriously."

"Will I dance?"

"I don't know that you will ever dance again." His eyes flickered over her, now not seeing her.

The same skill that enabled her to assume the role of the Swan Queen, the same talent which allowed her to dance before thousands of discriminating eyes, showing grace, ability, but never terror, aided her now, helped her rise from the chair. "I see," she replied, her head held high, her lips firm and without quiver, her wide-open eyes concealing her fear. "I'll be back." Slowly she left the room, scarcely leaning on her crutch. I am the Swan Queen, triumphing over the evil magician, I am a *Wili*, dancing to save my true love. I will not fall, I will not falter. I am a great ballerina.

*　　　*　　　*

At home, in a sudden change of mood, she brushed away her tears and shrugged off his sentence. So what if she couldn't dance; it didn't matter. In fact, now it surprised her that she had felt anything at all when she heard the doctor's news. She would retire, devoting herself to the baby. She would have to be a mother and a father, after all, roles not suited to moments between performances. Together they would lead a quiet life, partly in Texas, partly in New York.

Later, when the child was older, he could be told about his mother's career, that she was once an eminent dancer. He would know about Gregory from the beginning. She would tell him of his daring brilliance, his impressive achievements. Their child would know what a father Gregory would have been. Her child would not have Gregory, but she would make up for the loss. *That* would be her life, her art.

14

Three weeks later, Yvonne received a call from Jerry Brandner. "I need to discuss some business with you." As executor of Gregory's will, the lawyer had full power to handle all business affairs.

"Of course." Yvonne cringed. With Gregory she had avoided making decisions; without him she relished decisions even less. She even refused to discuss with Ian or Justine when she would be ready to dance . . . if she would be ready to dance.

The housekeeper served tea and coffee. Her leg still in the cast, Yvonne walked around the room as best she could, offering sandwiches, urging another cup of coffee. Jerry ate, drank. A mutual conspiracy of avoidance, Yvonne thought.

"Your leg?"

"I don't know how much longer I'll have to wear the cast."

"Better not be too long. Your audience is waiting!"

Yvonne smiled noncommittally. "You want to talk about business? Something to sign?"

"Not precisely." Jerry rose and paced back and forth in front of her. "I hate to bother you about anything now. I know how difficult all this is for you."

"I appreciate that." Yvonne played nervously with the hem of her dress.

Taking a deep breath, Jerry sat facing her, took out his pipe, poked at it, replaced it in his pocket. With his handkerchief he polished his glasses, then regretfully replaced them on his nose and looked at her. "You must understand"—he spoke slowly, each word measured and distinct—"Gregory did nothing illegal."

Maxine arrived later that afternoon to find Yvonne perched on the sofa as if frozen in place. "What happened?"

Yvonne avoided her friend's eyes.

"Yvonne, what's wrong?"

"Jerry was here."

"The lawyer?"

Yvonne nodded. "There are difficulties."

"Difficulties? What else could go wrong?"

Yvonne drew circles with her finger on the arm of the chair. "Insurance."

"What is the problem with the insurance?"

"There isn't any."

Maxine stared. "Now, Yvonne, of course there is. You are upset. You misunderstood something Jerry said, darling, you've never had a head for business at all. Give me his number and I'll call and straighten this out."

"No. There isn't any. It's . . . it's all gone."

"Gone?" Maxine looked around as if she expected to find it. "Gone where?"

"Someone borrowed on it."

"Someone? Yvonne, what do you mean? Who borrowed? That's illegal."

"Hardly. Gregory borrowed on his insurance."

"Oh." Maxine moaned. "Why?"

"There was a business deal . . . computers and genetics and bacteria used to manufacture drugs. A brilliant combination of ideas, put together by Gregory. He conceived it. Gregory's plans always worked." Yvonne's eyes filled with tears. "But it needed money, backers; and Gregory, to show his confidence, mortgaged everything."

"Everything?" Maxine whispered.

"Everything." A single tear slid from her right eye and glided down her cheek. "The ranch, the houses, this apartment."

"Everything! How could he! How could he have done this to you? It's careless, foolish, horrible!" Maxine's voice roared.

"Maxine! You must not talk about Gregory like that." Two spots of bright red appeared on her cheeks.

"To leave you like this, and with no money?"

"I won't hear it." Yvonne covered her ears. "I won't. Gregory was wonderful. He did it all for me. For our future. He wasn't like other men—boring and careful men. Gregory was special." She paused.

"Jerry told me to ignore the gossip," she said finally.

"Gossip?"

"Because of Gregory's name and reputation, people invested. Now . . . now that he's gone, the deal will probably fall through. A lot of people will lose their money."

"Oh, Yvonne. And you alone."

"I'm not alone."

"Of course not. Ian and I will be with you all the way. Kili, too."

"No, Gregory is still with me. I'm pregnant."

"Yvonne. How . . . wonderful." Maxine quickly moved to hug her. "How long and when is it due and what room shall we change into a nursery?"

As the next two months passed, never once did Maxine even imply that being widowed, injured, broke, and pregnant was less than wonderful.

And Yvonne also found new strength in the increasing adversity.

Gregory was gone, she told herself. She did not want to live without him, but she must. She did not feel adequate to manage her life, but there was no choice. After all, she had a life other than her own to consider.

Leaving dance was an option she no longer enjoyed. She needed the income, needed her career. Retirement was now a luxury. She was bankrupt.

But she never blamed Gregory. One last time, he had gambled, gambled and lost not only his life but also her future. Yet she could not, would not, blame him. Gregory could only be himself, a man of action, not reflection. Who could have believed he would die so young?

An immediate visit to an obstetrician confirmed she was more than three months pregnant. Maxine stayed by her side and in a flurry of excitement they examined miniature clothes, white wicker furniture, silver rattles.

Yvonne had to continue, had to heal, had to dance: all for the baby.

Without delay she made an appointment with the company's orthopedist. He recommended a specialist who dealt with dancers, understood the irony of their hypochondria regarding the most minor pain and their tendency toward total denial when suspicious that something was actually wrong.

Yvonne quickly convinced herself that Dr. Epstein hadn't understood. He was not, after all, a dance doctor.

Dr. Griffen poked and probed, sent her for X rays, inspected them, took more X rays, all the time chatting about dance, gossiping innocuously about personalities, and making bad dance jokes.

"Well, well . . ." At last he sat at his desk across from her. "How is it feeling?"

"When doesn't a dancer's body hurt?" Yvonne offhandedly remarked. "How soon can I get back to dancing?"

"Not so fast. There are a lot of things to consider."

My future, Yvonne thought. My lack of money. My child. "Such as?"

"Most of the damage is in your right leg, to the tibia. It's right here." He held up an X-ray photograph. "Two hairline fractures. That was what they found in the hospital. A nuisance, but of course they will heal. The cast sees to that."

"It won't affect my dancing."

"Not in the least."

Yvonne relaxed slightly. "Then it's just a matter of time and taking it easy until the cast comes off."

"Not exactly." He found another X ray and held it out. "This is your foot. You dance on a complex set of bones— twenty-six per foot. The sturdy tarsal bones near the ankle, then the longer metatarsals, and the phalanges which make the toes. Sometimes dancers get what we call a march fracture, a hairline break in the shaft of the second or third metatarsal. The consequence of accumulated impact and shock rather than an accident. Look here." He pointed to the X ray. "I suspect your injury is the same, although I'm sure yours is due to the accident, or at least aggravated by it."

"Is this . . . is it very bad?" Yvonne's heart pounded.

"No. No jumping for a month, but that's pretty hard to do

with a cast on anyway." He laughed. "No, that isn't really the problem."

"Then what is it?" Impatient and nervous, Yvonne wanted to scream.

"Your Achilles tendon."

"Oh." Yvonne knew that an injury in the calf-muscle tendon was always serious, and often permanent.

"It isn't ruptured, but there is damage. Some tearing, I think. We'll have to keep a close eye on it. Complicating all of this is the cartilage of your knees. Your leg was injured in such a way that the medial collateral ligament was severely sprained, and cartilage became loose in the joint. Sooner or later it will have to be surgically removed, but not yet. Let's see how everything else heals."

"But . . . but will I dance again?"

The doctor looked grave and shrugged. "I think so." He briskly continued: whirlpool therapy, non-weight-bearing exercises, massage.

Fortunately it was all written down, because when she came home from his office, Yvonne couldn't remember what he had said. She only recalled his noncommittal "I think so."

Worry about money and her career temporarily replaced her pain about Gregory. She could not give up her career, yet she might well have no choice.

Jerry promised that nothing would change immediately. She still had her salary from the company; she was on sick leave. But she needed money. The unpleasant thought reminded her of the years after her parents' death, the years when the entire school knew she couldn't afford the fees. But she refused to reveal the extent of her need or expose herself to their pity or scorn.

Something had to be done to assure her own future and the baby's. She had to dance.

Slowly, slowly, slowly her bones healed.

Impatiently Yvonne searched for another doctor, another cure. Eagerly she listened to class gossip about new cures, the latest diet combinations, the advantage of dry heat over wet, cold over warmth.

As soon as possible, she began exercising, as gently as she could and still feel progress. All dancers knew that muscles atrophied when not used, and for every week of rest, they needed a similar period of exercise to recondition the damaged areas. So she stretched and pulled, trying to minimize the deterioration from non-use. During the exercises, she wrapped layers of Saran Wrap around her legs, her natural body temperature creating a steam bath.

Every day she pushed herself to a class, attempting more each day, forcing every minute, exploring her limits and capabilities. Ian suggested a rest, but she wouldn't listen.

After one especially strenuous session, Yvonne felt ill. "Just what I need," she remarked to another dancer, "the flu."

Hot lemon juice and honey, she decided. Clear soup for dinner, and by tomorrow she would be fine. She had an appointment next morning with the obstetrician and planned to skip class.

As night gave way to morning, she felt worse and considered missing her appointment. Just when it seemed unworthy of the effort, she remembered her responsibility. The doctor had a sonar scan of the baby planned.

Only at the doctor's did she discover the bleeding. Quickly he made calculations, and muttered to the nurse, "Five months, at the most. Let's call the hospital. You'll have to go in immediately," he told Yvonne.

She couldn't ask what was wrong. She didn't want to know the answer. A frozen calm numbed her, left her dry-eyed as gentle hands settled her in the ambulance that took her to the hospital, as hurried hands pushed her into a labor room, and as a large hand placed an inhaler over her face. When she woke, her own hand was tightly clutched in Maxine's.

For the first time in the weeks of horror, Maxine cried. "I'm sorry, dear. So sorry. They don't know what went wrong."

"Was it a girl or a boy?" Yvonne asked. She was not holding back her tears, didn't have to fight to be brave. She didn't feel anything.

"A girl." Maxine fought to control herself. "I insisted on seeing her, Yvonne, so you could know and won't have to see. She looked like a baby, a tiny, perfect baby." Maxine hid her face in her hands and sobbed.

"There, there . . ." Yvonne patted her. "There, there, Maxine."

"I'm sorry. I should be comforting you." With effort, Maxine regained control. "What do you want done? I'll take care of everything."

Yvonne felt so tired and so very old. "I want her to be buried," she decided. "In Texas, next to Gregory. Just us at the funeral, Maxine."

"Right. I'll take care of it."

Less than four months after Gregory's burial, Maxine and Yvonne again stood under the hot Texas sun. This time the coffin was tiny and white. This time there were few flowers: a spray of white and pink from Kili, a larger group of white mums Maxine had arranged, an elegant set of orchids from Ian. No one else had been told.

Yvonne stood as the miniature coffin was lowered into the ground, felt the sun searing their skin. How little and unimportant they were. Just two small people in a large state, in a larger country, and on a spinning ball of earth in a vast universe. Just two insignificant people out of hundreds of millions.

Maxine touched her arm, disarranging her thoughts. "It's time to leave, isn't it?"

"Yes," Yvonne agreed, as all the while her mind and heart drifted back to the tiny form resting in the earth.

15

Yvonne touched the marshmallow with a tentative finger. "Almost done." Extending the long gold fondue fork into the fire, she watched the candy turn a light golden brown.

"I must say this is a first for my fireplace." Maxine watched, bemused.

"Hand me the graham cracker, will you?" With Yvonne's recovery came a craving for childhood foods: brown bread smeared thickly with peanut butter and sprinkled with coconut; olives mashed into cream cheese spread on Ritz crackers; bacon and banana chopped over cottage cheese; and of late, toasted marshmallows and chocolate on graham crackers.

"I don't see how you can eat that." Maxine shuddered delicately.

"Delicious. Pass the Godiva bars, will you?"

"You could at least gain weight. I've always had trouble with my weight."

"No wonder, with all this chocolate sitting around." The crystal display bowls filled with chocolate bars had set off Yvonne's latest debauch. "Are you developing a sweet tooth in your old age?"

"Guess so." With a determined smile, Maxine chose a chocolate bar, then unwrapped and nibbled on it, hiding her distaste. The chocolate was for Fleming, as yet a secret from Yvonne.

Three weeks had passed since Yvonne had lost the baby. At first Yvonne was swept by storms of emotion: floods of tears, fires of rage, hurricanes of despair. Storms, she thought, that would rip her body asunder as they tore through her.

Her bitterest regret became the child—the baby that would never be. Why hadn't she become pregnant earlier? Her arms aching to hold an extension of Gregory's life, she paced her apartment wildly, trying to outdistance her thoughts.

All day, self-accusations raged in her ears. Selfish, she screamed inwardly, self-centered. Why didn't you take a year off from dance? Why did you place ballet before everything? By night she felt physically lashed.

But slowly the swift pain of sorrow faded and died to an ache of regret.

Madame came to visit. "You must rest," she ordered "Rest and forget." This Madame was a woman she'd neither seen nor met before. She had canceled her ballet classes to be with her. Her other students—turned away without a word. She was still gruff, even caustic, but that helped Yvonne control herself, cope with her unhappiness. And Yvonne had told Madame all: the financial, personal, and ballet questions.

"You are in pain. That's natural. To be expected. But pain isn't always bad. Pain can be growth, and understanding, and new beginnings. The trick is to live through the pain, to dance through the pain."

Yvonne wasn't certain she would learn to do either. She and Gregory had had a unique relationship. Their love had been sweet and savage, burning and refreshing, the beginning and the end. Such feelings she would never rediscover, but that didn't mean she wouldn't continue.

"You're a survivor," Maxine told her. "You didn't choose to be, you can't decide not to be. You're stuck."

"I'm better now," Yvonne protested. "I can cross the street by myself and everything."

"I know."

"You don't need to use a soothing voice with me," Yvonne grumbled. "The experience might do you in."

"Don't you like my new sweet nature?"

"I think you've been eating too much chocolate."

Maxine displayed enough ruthlessness to be recognized as her old self. "The upstairs has to be cleaned out. We'll pack everything away, and later you can look through and decide what to do. There are too many memories for now."

"I can't."

Maxine hesitated. "You can. You have to."

And she could; she did. But packing Gregory's clothes, his personal items, wasn't easy. Fingering the jacket she had bought for him the previous Christmas, boxing the cufflinks she'd purchased during their trip to Mexico, took all her bravery.

Madame's words flashed through her mind: You have to live through the pain. When finished packing, Yvonne, hobbled by grief, limped to her bedroom and collapsed in tears.

While waiting to dance, she would teach at the company. Yvonne was determined to find a new area for her talent.

Dutifully she arrived at the auditions held for scholarship positions with the school. To be a dancer required years of sacrifice of time and energy and money. Especially money. Taking classes cost substantial amounts of money, and without scholarships, even most middle-class students found financial survival difficult. Competition for scholarships was, like most aspects of ballet, both brutal and heartbreaking. The emphasis was not on who deserved a scholarship, but who deserved it more.

Yvonne arrived without enthusiasm. The building overflowed with hopeful students, frantic mothers, an occasional father, many friends. The reception area seemed a sea of heads when Yvonne arrived, the dressing rooms packed tightly with bodies.

Students everywhere. Students in leotards and tights. Students in street clothes. Students in elaborate tutus. Students with cold hands and frightened eyes; students with frightened hands and cold eyes. Each wanted a scholarship. Yvonne continued on her way to Ian's office, a buzz of interest combined with envy and compounded by terror in her wake. She was there to judge.

It was a call open to thirteen- to seventeen-year-olds. Some had already survived preliminary auditions held when the company toured Miami, Houston, Los Angeles, and New Orleans. Some already attended paid classes in the Ballet American School. Some took classes elsewhere. Some knew little about ballet, attending auditions as they would a free show. What did they have to lose?

Ian stood in the middle of his office, breathing deeply. "How does it look?"

"Terrifying."

"That's supposed to be *their* perspective, Yvonne. You're in the company."

"I don't feel in the company." She glared at her leg. She now wore a soft cast, and still used one crutch.

"Patience. We must all have patience." He smoothed his shirt and inhaled once again, as if he might hold his breath until the audition concluded. "I hate this, you know, just hate it. I can't stand turning people away."

"Me either." Yvonne followed him. "I've never done this before. What do we look for?"

Ian thought. "Essence."

Hundreds of eyes from the thronged hall watched them walk to Studio Three.

Justine was already seated, Edith Conrad, the school's director, on her right. Floor-to-ceiling mirrors covered one wall of the long room, barres lined the others. A piano lurked in the corner, nestling close to folding chairs for the judges. Noel, the school's registrar, appeared at the door, a harried look in his eyes, sweat on his forehead. "About ready here?"

"Whenever you are." Justine motioned grandiosely. "How many?"

"One hundred and thirty." As he looked wide-eyed over his shoulder, the crowd murmured with increasing excitement. "Not counting the mothers."

"Get them in," Justine decided.

From the hall Noel's voice echoed. "Everyone take a numbered tag. When you have the tag, go to Studio Two. Wait there. Mothers, stay out of the studios. Mother, get out of that studio!"

Justine sighed. "The mothers are the most impossible, you know. Like animals. If the girls had half the ambition . . ." She shrugged. "We shall see."

Noel stuck his head back in. "Let's start with big groups of fifty and eliminate the hopeless."

Justine nodded assent.

"Hopeless?" Yvonne asked.

"You'll see," Ian warned.

The first fifty straggled in, no one anxious to be first or last. Noel looked them over. "You in the pink. You! This is

one through fifty. You are clearly marked eighty-nine. Leave!"
He left to assume his place with the other judges.

Ian stood. "This is an audition for dancers between the ages of thirteen and seventeen. You should all have had enough training so you can go into intermediate or advanced classes. If anyone here doesn't meet these requirements, please leave now." No one moved.

"Very well. Please place your bags, purses, towels, sweaters, toe shoes, and whatever else you're carrying along the sides of the room, under the barres." A few girls did as asked.

"Try to listen and follow directions." Ian looked stern. "Place your things under the barres." Two requests later he gave up, ignoring one girl who clutched toe shoes in her hand, another who dangled a large purse from her shoulder.

Justine motioned Ian over. "Let's eliminate the obvious."

"Is there anyone here over seventeen?" Ian scanned the room. Several mature young women watched the piano, the floor, the ceiling, anywhere but Ian. "Please raise your hands. This audition is only for those under eighteen." Finally five timid, reluctant hands rose. "I'm sorry. You'll have to leave."

"Next the figure faults," Justine murmured.

"Some of you are the wrong figure type," Ian continued. "If we call your number, you may leave." He joined the bunched judges.

"Number three," Edith called. "Numbers nine and twenty-eight." All had bulges of fat.

"Number ten, number thirty, number forty-nine." Justine clipped off the numbers. "Forty-two is impossible with those bow legs."

Yvonne cringed at the open criticism. Ian whispered in her ear, "You didn't think Justine had mended the terror of her ways, surely."

Too fat, too short, too tall, too knock-kneed, swaybacked, bad posture, ungainly figure: all were reasons for instant dismissal. Either slowly with embarrassment or quickly with tears the girls left the room until less than twenty remained. The second large group was decimated at the same speed. Then the male candidates entered in a group.

Ian shrugged. "Will we keep them all for the class?"

"Of course," Edith murmured. She looked at Yvonne, an

eyebrow upraised. "What else? There are never enough boys for the school."

Again three groups formed, but this time smaller ones. Noel lined them around the room. "Let's begin."

Yvonne watched carefully. The *petits battements tendus* showed the arch and point of the feet. Back bends displayed flexibility. How good was the turnout of that girl in black? How straight that back? Hip movement, strength—the girls became isolated parts.

One by one the judges pointed, dissected, ruthlessly cut. With only a limited number of places, it couldn't be helped. This was business. To the tears that dribbled down despairing cheeks, Yvonne had to turn a blind eye. To a sudden sob a slender girl of no more than fourteen emitted in response to Justine's accusing finger, she had to turn a deaf ear.

"We can't take any more than fifteen," Edith whispered. "Girls, that is."

Yvonne huddled next to Ian, scanning résumés over his shoulder. How old? How much training and where? Anything to help decide who might have potential and who might not. More curt dismissals. Fatigue lined Edith's face, tightened Ian's smile. Justine coolly surveyed the room. Edith murmured something to Justine, and Yvonne overheard the name "Eleanor Alexander."

Ian also caught the words and leaned close. "Just a visit," he soothed. "She and Roland are just coming for a visit. Just a visit."

"Girls in the middle for *adagio*," Noel barked.

"Look at seventy," Edith pointed. "Not enough training yet. She's only thirteen. She can come back next year."

"And number ninety." Justine's eyes gleamed. "Too . . . I don't know. Too *something*."

Something. Yvonne closed her eyes. Competition screamed through the audition; in the company, it only murmured. But it whispered her name. Soon she might be found too "something." Or lacking something. Eleanor—young, healthy Eleanor—was coming.

Auditioning—being inspected, judged, evaluated, accepted, rejected, placed on hold, eliminated, rediscovered—never ended for a dancer. Not even for a ballerina who was—who had been, Yvonne corrected—at the very top.

Maxine treated her to dinner that night. Yvonne, still in shock, sat wringing her napkin. "It isn't fair," she repeated over and over.

"Little is."

"But to change someone's entire life after watching her for a few moments?"

"It will be good for them. Builds character." Maxine picked at her salad. Fleming had been busy lately, an important case. She was half-thankful. No awkward questions from Yvonne about her evenings. But she missed him. Soon she would introduce them. Soon. But not yet.

"What if we missed someone wonderful?"

"That's possible. Why should I offer false hope?"

"That's dreadful. I can't stand the responsibility."

"Now, Yvonne." Maxine took her friend's hand. "If they are wonderful, they will come back to another audition and be accepted. Or another company will take them. Or they'll get discouraged, give up, marry, and have five children."

"You are a fountain of encouragement."

"Yvonne. Part of talent is staying in there—not giving up. If they don't have that, they won't make it."

But Yvonne wasn't convinced. Would *she* have come back after such an impersonal rejection? Would *she* have kept trying after such a public humiliation?

In the next days, she tried other things. A soloist with the company taught the beginning ballet class and invited Yvonne to watch.

The children looked so young, only partially formed, yet at the same time breathtakingly complete and beautiful. They reminded Yvonne of young deer or small colts who might suddenly wobble away on their thin legs.

"Children, look this way. Try to pay close attention. All the ballet steps are based on five basic positions. This is the first position. Watch me. Legs are straight, heels together, and the toes of each foot are turned outward, pointing straight to the sides."

With awkward movements the children anxiously adjusted their feet, sneaking frantic glances at their teacher, at other children, never at themselves in the mirror.

"The round wooden rail that runs around the room is

called the barre. You'll hold on to it when you do exercises. So you don't fall over.''

They giggled nervously.

"Every day, every class we start with the same exercises: *pliés*. First we'll do a *demi-plié*, which means you bend your knees just a little, then we'll do a *grand plié*, which means bending your knees and going down as far as you can. Place your hand on the barre, place your feet in first position, and watch me. Down we go.''

Yvonne remembered her first dance class. She recalled excitement mingled with fear, a feeling of cotton candy in her stomach and ice cubes in her hands. Vividly she could see the image of her first teacher, slim, graceful, beautiful as an orchid.

But one class followed another. Hundreds, thousands, years of classes that would continue for the rest of her dancing life. A lump rose in Yvonne's throat. If she were lucky, that was. *Pliés, relevés, battements tendus, ronds de jambes à terre, développés, grands battements*—deep knee bends, small beats, floor circles, extensions, high kicks—the steps progressed one after another, one thousand after the next, marking each minute of a dancer's life. For now, Yvonne's count had gone awry, leaving her floating without rhythm.

"I haven't the patience," she confessed. Not to tell the blond girl in the blue leotard to face the front for the fifth time, without raising her voice. Not to explain a *plié*, class after class, correcting and guiding. No, no, Yvonne felt sure she wasn't meant to teach beginning students.

She tried an advanced class. Here correction was a matter of inches, emphasis, interpretation. Here impatience didn't perturb Yvonne. But watching strong, whole bodies leap and whirl, she choked with envy. And feeling her muscles ache with desire to stretch and pull, she tingled with fear.

They were dancing, she was not. They were seen in triumph, she in defeat. Their careers progressed, hers had stalled. A career not moving forward was slipping backward.

She hid her complaints from Maxine. The redhead was busy with her collection and new plans, making lists, decisions, excitement wherever her interest landed.

To Yvonne, Maxine seemed preoccupied, a condition she assumed involved work. Sitting in Maxine's office one day, Yvonne desultorily flicked through a book of material samples.

"How's the class going?"

"All right." Yvonne threw down the samples and sank into the chair.

Maxine pushed back a strand of unruly hair. "I can see that. You're so happy and excited. What have you decided about the apartment?"

Yvonne still camped out, as Maxine called it, in the guest bedroom of the apartment she and Gregory had shared. She had to find a smaller place, but was mired in indecision. Questions crowded around her, stifled her, oppressed her. What career? What way of life? What future? What? What? What? All questions, no answers.

"You've stalled out," Maxine told Yvonne.

"I know."

Kili hovered in the background. "Here is the material you were looking for, and also a list of calls you have to make."

"I understand you're helping Ian with the preliminary sketches," Yvonne said to Kili.

"Yes. I love it."

"I think you have a crush on him," Maxine grumbled. "You're always more excited about working with him."

"His temper is so much better." Kili smiled sweetly.

"Maybe he's getting soft in his old age," Maxine snarled. Fleming, now in Paris on that case, wouldn't be home for a week.

With the usual neurotic and hysterical passion of an injured dancer, Yvonne made the rounds of doctors, massage therapists, and acupuncturists. Frantically she rubbed in menthol and camphor, submitted herself to massage, wrapped her foot in special solutions, and slept with heat pads.

Before, she would never have given in to her fear. Before, she had been sensible, calm, even scientific. Now panic would win, if she didn't do something soon.

But finally the morning came when Yvonne decided she would at least try to best her panic. The time had come to explore possibilities for her future career. Yvonne carefully brushed her hair and painstakingly applied makeup. She dressed in leotard and tights, slipped on a pair of light tweed slacks, and topped them with a silk shirt.

Ever since she and Maxine had packed and cleared upstairs, Yvonne had not wanted to enter her studio. The rooms upstairs shouted Gregory. By seven-thirty she had slipped into the company building, then down a dark hallway to a small practice room, sure that she would be alone at that hour.

The room was empty, haunted only by memories. Here Karina, already lapsing into semiretirement, had coached her in *Swan Lake*. Here Ian had fashioned Eve on her, working late into the night to find the steps to define and expose the character.

Slipping off slacks and top, Yvonne stared at herself in the long wall of mirrors, noticing no outward signs that marked her from the last weeks. With the cast now removed, her figure was trim and sculptured, her cheekbones heavily accented, her eyes large and dramatic. She looked like a prima ballerina. That wasn't enough. Could she dance?

The room was empty, haunted only by her hopes. The doctor had been coolly noncommittal. She was lucky, very lucky. After all, she could walk. The word caught in her throat. Years of ballet training were spent learning how not to walk, but to glide, to swoop, to fly.

Gingerly she approached the barre, fear and nausea rising. One shaking hand extended out to the barre. She gripped the smooth wooden circle, her fingertips seeking to draw strength and energy from the same place years of ballet hands had touched. With graceful practice her other hand moved out from her side, until her whole arm formed a smooth line from shoulder to hand, perpendicular to her body.

Slowly she turned her feet outward into first position. Her muscles, long inactive, pulled slightly, resented the demand. Gradually she moved into a *demi-plié*, beginning a knee bend that ended with her knees only partially bent. Pain radiated along her thighs, but seemed equally bad in each leg.

With hesitant, sometimes awkward movements, she continued. Second position, like first, but her feet spread, an inverted Y, her body the upturned tail. Third: she placed one foot in front of the other, each heel touching the middle of the opposite foot. Fourth: cautiously she extended her front foot out, parallel to the other. Fifth: she placed one foot in front of the other, the heel of each foot pressed into the toe of the other.

First one side, then the other, all the while testing, feeling, evaluating each movement, each change of her muscle position. When she turned and began the *grand pliés*, deep bends, the pain increased. Although the effort left her gasping and exhausted, down she bent, inch by inch, her muscles shimmering from the concentrated control.

So far so good. Before she continued, Ian appeared in the doorway. "I was wondering when I would find you here."

Yvonne looked over, sweat forming all over her. "Do you know everything?" she asked.

"At my age, I won't be learning much new. I always come early now. Sleep is getting too close—permanent sleep, that is. I don't like becoming an old man." Ian moved slowly into the room, relaxing against the barre.

"You aren't." Yvonne reached out, touching him lightly on the cheek.

Ian shrugged. "I won't argue. Let's see you do something."

"What did you have in mind, big boy?" Yvonne batted her eyelashes wildly.

"Some nice *développés?*"

Gradually Yvonne raised her right leg, skimming lightly her left, then extending it fully into the air, one side, then the other. A series of *échappés*, small jumps opening the position of the feet. More slow extension work followed. *Pas de bourrées* in combination—transferring the body weight from one foot to another.

Her breath caught in her throat and sweat glistened over her body. Although not a difficult lesson, she was conscious of every muscle, every stretch. "What do you think?" she asked with forced casualness.

"I know you will be fine. I can't believe anything else. You will be my Colette." Ian looked away. "This will be my last major ballet, I think. . . . Who am I kidding? At my age, I *know* this will be my last. I need you, Yvonne. I can't do it without you."

Yvonne smiled wanly. "I'm not fighting the idea."

"How is teaching?"

"Not for me."

"You didn't give it enough of a try."

Yvonne didn't answer immediately. "Maybe not."

"Remember I asked you about teaching Eve to someone for the Irish performance?"

"Yes."

"I haven't forgotten. I'm thinking about Aisling. It would give her a chance to test the role before premiering here."

"That might be better than teaching a class."

That night, Yvonne dreamed, for the first time since the accident, of ballet.

She danced. Skimming along the floor, soaring and gliding into the air, floating down to earth. She starred in the best of all performances, of all possibilities, of all dreams.

She glanced at her tiny form, and noticed her Swan Queen costume. Music swelled. The glorious feeling died, replaced by panic and confusion. Had the ballet started? Had she lost her place?

Gradually she positioned her feet and posed in an *arabesque*, then softly bent her cheek against her shoulder in a gesture reminiscent of a swan smoothing its feathers. She was the innocent Odette, dancing by the lake formed from her mother's tears, fated to inhabit the body of a swan.

A male figure entered. Enchanted, he watched her. But when Yvonne spied him, her body trembled with terror, her *pointes* beating a frantic tattoo against the floor as she retreated.

It was Siegfried, her own love who looked like Gregory, was Gregory. Joyously she opened her arms, preparing to leap toward her husband, but instead she retreated, caution marring each of her steps. All wasn't as it seemed at first.

Gregory's costume was not that of Siegfried, but of Albrecht, her love from *Giselle*. The gray pond was the cold lake of *Giselle*, surrounded by the *Wilis*, spirits hovering near, waiting to possess Yvonne as one of their own.

In frenzied passion, Yvonne whirled toward Gregory, seeking to protect him. Myrtha, the *Wilis'* Queen, lurked in the shadows, eager to condemn Gregory to death.

Frantically Yvonne moved across the ground in *pas de bourrées*, pleading with the *Wilis* for help, but they refused. Gregory's attempt to leap across to her failed, and he fell to the ground, stricken. He weakened before her eyes.

Gently she approached his side, encouraging him to rise,

coaxing him to dance on. All to no avail. Gregory took her hand, drew it to his lips for a final kiss, then plunged to the ground, dying. Before she could sink to his side, the *Wilis* gathered around her, tearing her away from her love.

Her feet slowed, became clumsy. Looking down, Yvonne couldn't see her shoes. Below her knees lay nothing, nothing but space.

She awoke with a gasp, as if she had held her breath for the entire dream. Gregory was gone. Yvonne gazed wildly into the dark. A chapter of her life had ended, finally closed. The knowledge struck her heart as if a chamber within her very chest had slammed.

16

The future belongs to the determined, Yvonne decided, starting company classes again. An hour into a lesson, pale and sweating, she amended that thought: the determined and the masochistic.

She would not give up, would not acknowledge any difficulties. She was Yvonne St. Cyr, prima ballerina. Her presence in the class made the others whisper as she slid into position at the barre wherever an opening presented itself, concentrating with hushed anonymity. But her presence shouted with a blare of trumpets, her glare clearing a space among the frivolous gigglers and silencing her chattering lessers.

Ballet grew grimly serious to her, a task of survival and competition. Each young figure reflected in the mirror before her, each casual swing of hip and arm, cut into her confidence. Practicing a series of supported turns with a partner, she threw her leg too hard, pushing herself off balance. Down she flew, a tangled pink lump at his feet.

Silence fell, as other couples froze in place like illustrations in a ballet manual entitled *fouetté rond de jambe en tournant* finishing in *arabesque:* one couple with the girl *en pointe* in fifth position, her feet both on the floor; another her right leg extended before turning; yet another fell off her *arabesque,* her extended leg terrified into awkward descent.

As her partner stuttered an apology, Yvonne rose to her feet, her eyes black with fury. "How dare you! Can't you do anything right? Do I have to have my life threatened by such incompetence?" Snatching her towel from the barre, she stormed from the room, choking back tears and screams.

Alone in the bathroom, she studied her face through the falling tears. What was happening to her? Once she would have sprung to her feet and laughed an apology for her clumsiness.

The incident caused no comment, only a sorrowful glance from Ian, an appraising stare from Justine, darts of fear from the other dancers. Yvonne ignored them all, willing her body into more difficult positions, commanding her feet to move, move faster, move more exactly, move, move, move.

Inch by hard-won inch, she progressed, a wave moving along the beach, only to be suddenly sucked back, leaving Yvonne floundering on the shore of the practice room. But the tide slowly gained. She waved away Ian's tentative suggestions that she might be pushing too fast.

Justine pranced on the sidelines, evaluating, pausing to see if Yvonne would ever return. Yvonne dismissed with lip-curling scorn the doctor's warning about the healing process. Hadn't he told her she might never dance again? What did he know about ballerinas? What could he guess about the desperation in her soul?

Then, one day while at the barre mentally preparing for class, testing her foot, stretching her leg, Yvonne felt a stir in the room as if a wind had swept through. Turning, she saw Justine, silkily elegant for such an early-morning hour, enter, then turn to beckon someone forward. With a jolt of emotion comprising fear, remembrance, excitement, and envy, Yvonne recognized Roland Martin and Eleanor Alexander. Insecurity pinned Yvonne against the wall, forced her to stare limply at her hands.

"And of course, Roland, you know Yvonne. However, I don't think you two have met, Eleanor."

"No." The young woman's voice was light and high. Did Eleanor know that Roland had once briefly been her lover? Yvonne wondered. Of course, considering the sheer number of women sharing that distinction, Eleanor might not think about it, or might not care.

"Yvonne." Roland beamed, nothing but delight at seeing her again apparent from his tone. "It's been too long, much too long." With uninhibited pleasure he drew her into his arms. "You look wonderful! Just wonderful."

"Roland. And you also." It was true. Although forty,

Roland was still handsome in his exotically Slavic style, with white frosting his black curling hair, adding a note of distinction. Sexy and distinguished, Yvonne thought with displeasure, seeing his sharply planed face and strong muscular body. Roland showed little sign of his age.

"Very nice, I'm sure, to meet you," Eleanor chirped. Yvonne had seen Eleanor only in ballet photographs: a vivid Firebird, a soulful Giselle, a romantic Aurora. Eleanor's colorless blond hair hung thinly around her bony shoulders. Without makeup, her face lost definition—no high cheekbones, no eyebrows, no lashes. Her smile revealed slightly bucked teeth. Like a rabbit, Yvonne thought, but her eyes should be red, not pale green. How could Roland the ladykiller marry *her?* How could Eleanor the ballerina replace Yvonne St. Cyr?

"Is this your first time in America?" Yvonne asked Eleanor, determined not to show any displeasure. She felt Justine's probing eyes; the director, she knew, waited for a sign.

"Yes. It's so exciting. New York is so big."

Roland cut in, ignoring his wife. "I heard about . . . It was horrible, Yvonne, just horrible." His tone caressed her name.

"Yes." She looked up with a wan smile. "How long do you intend to be in town?"

. Justine acted swiftly, allowing no time for a reply. "Not too short a visit, surely. It's been so long, too long." She drew the dancers away, waving the class to continue.

Roland glanced over his shoulder. "Later, Yvonne. Lunch. I insist. 21?"

While stretching and pulling, turning and leaping, Yvonne wondered if Roland meant to bring his wan little wife.

He didn't. "How have you been, really been?" Dark smoldering eyes burned into hers.

"Tired." She attempted a bright smile to take the edge off her words. They sat in the barroom of "21," ignoring curious stares.

"Aren't we all?"

"Really, Roland, I'm not surprised. With such a young wife." Her smile teased with a flirtatiousness she had almost forgotten. Roland was charming. His charm didn't seduce her now, but left her cold, like she was examining a beautiful painting she didn't own or even covet. Still, an almost forgotten tingle bubbled like champagne around her.

"Youth isn't everything," he murmured softly. "Tell me, tell me it all." Roland had always been a wonderful listener.

Around the company, rumors flew faster than feet. Eleanor *would* be signed for next season. Eleanor would be signed, but *only if* Yvonne couldn't perform.

That was just the business gossip. The corners whispered with talk of Roland and Yvonne, speculation fueled with innuendo.

Roland and Yvonne alone knew the truth, and maybe Eleanor. Each kept silent.

Not Maxine. "You aren't . . .?" She almost couldn't find the words. "He isn't . . .?"

"No. I'm not and he isn't." Yvonne changed the subject.

They weren't, but Yvonne hoped Eleanor would find the British Isles more congenial.

Eleanor liked competition, and she turned the hours of lesson into a battleground between the women. Who could leap higher, turn longer?

Justine's intentions hid behind the fortress of her bland smile.

After a lengthy siege of intimate, expensive lunches, afternoon drinks, and late dinners, Roland launched his attack. "We once meant so much to each other," he whispered, clutching her hand.

"You're married."

"Not for long. She doesn't understand me."

"Then you'll probably be married even longer."

"Don't tease me, darling. Paris would be lovely now."

"Fall is turning into winter, Roland."

"Is it my age?"

"Don't be silly, Roland. You are devastatingly handsome. I would like to, really I would. It's just too soon. I can't."

Roland accepted her decision with good grace, charming compliments, and, Yvonne thought, relief. He was getting older after all.

The lunches, dinners, intimate moments ended.

Eleanor, as if confused by Roland's sudden reappearance

in her life and his renewed husbandly concern, flared into jealous tantrums. In the dressing room she was discovered crying. During lessons she alternated between brief moments of defiance when she glared at Yvonne and missing steps with regularity.

Justine Stelle sat in her office wearing bright glorious red but feeling damp frightening gray. A ballet magazine lay before her, her own face featured on its cover. It displayed her well, she thought. No one would look at her face and realize that she and Ian Thorn were contemporaries. Of course, he didn't look his age either.

No, she didn't look sixty, and certainly not seventy. Her figure was petite, her face almost unlined, her chin firm. But as far as Justine was concerned, the headline had erased the impression of youth. "OLD AGE HITS BALLET AMERICAN COMPANY?" Question mark, indeed. Who would notice that it was a question? At least the magazine had gallantly not mentioned her age. Not that Justine Stelle had ever been so careless as to tell anyone exactly how old she was.

The subheading which floated over the featured article struck again: "The Ballet American has been one of our most exciting young companies. The latest season is dull, dragging, and drab. What happened to the famous Stelle sparkle and glow? Has the hour arrived for new influences?"

Sparkle and glow, Justine fumed; she would like to show them sparkle and glow by burning their building to the ground. Where was a new Thorn production? the article continued. Where was Yvonne St. Cyr? Where were exciting new dancers?

As if that weren't enough, *Ballet News* led with her picture in the Footnotes section. Footnotes! Justine beat on her desk with a small fist. "Gossip" was more like it! "Asked to comment on rumors sweeping the New York ballet world that she would soon be retiring from her position as artistic director of the Ballet American Company, Justine Stelle replied: 'Absolutely not. It is ridiculous and untrue, and I have nothing else to say about the matter.' It has been reported, however, that the board of directors is discussing possible successors."

They wouldn't dare.

But they would. Some board members had been waiting for years to revenge one slight or another.

Yvonne had to come back, come back and dance. This ridiculous emotional tantrum had to stop. Oh, Justine knew Yvonne had been hurt. Dancers were always being hurt. A pulled muscle, broken bone, twisted back: the list reeled endlessly. If it wasn't one excuse, it was another.

Now Ian's ballet had stalled. Changes had to be made, a new performance readied, a prima ballerina whipped into line, the company revitalized.

Justine neatly stacked the magazines in the bottom drawer of her desk, checked her makeup and hair in the concealed full-length mirror leading to her private washroom, and settled her shoulders. If the company needed revitalizing, Justine was the one to do it. Terror. She had always found terror revitalizing. The sword was, after all, mightier than any pen.

Yvonne had just finished her second class of the day, a private session with Ian, when the door to the small practice room crashed open. "There you are!" Justine accused.

"You were looking for me?" Ian asked with surprise and alarm.

"No, of course not. I can always find *you*. Yvonne, it's Yvonne I need."

"What is it, Justine?" Yvonne asked.

"It's terrible. Marilyn has broken her foot."

"That is terrible. How is she?"

"Not dancing, of course. How did you think she would be? *Giselle*. Gala. You must fill in, you just must."

Ian snapped to attention. "Yvonne isn't ready to dance. The doctor hasn't given her permission."

"Ready to dance?" Justine was distraught with excitement, her hair fluttered slightly. "Her foot isn't broken, her leg is whole, her—"

"Not ready"—Ian beat on the barre for emphasis—"to dance through a performance."

They glared at each other. "Now I know how the child feels in a custody fight," Yvonne interjected.

Justine smiled weakly. "Of course. If you can't. We will have to carry on. I don't know what came over me." She straightened her creaseless skirt. "Yes. Eleanor."

"What?" Yvonne's hands clawed into fists.

"Eleanor hasn't left town yet. Not that I'm looking forward to asking her. I have to admit she hasn't been herself these past few weeks. But she is a name, a definite name, and this group will expect . . . insist upon a real name. Yours would have been so much better and bigger," she added artlessly.

"I'll do it," Yvonne agreed suddenly.

"But—" Ian began an objection.

"I really am ready, Ian. There is no point in putting this off forever."

He didn't object further, and Justine left with a satisfied smile.

That night, Yvonne dressed with special care. She had refused a company dresser. Everything was different. No Nellie, who knew her routine; no flowers from Gregory, no little present: it was difficult to prepare herself when everything cried no, no, no.

Healthy young peasant, she thought, adding more color to her cheeks. Happy, dancing, stupid young girl. No, that wasn't the right thought. She slowly, carefully added long, thick lashes to her own and tried to think long, thick thoughts of love and innocence. Young, sweet Giselle, waiting for Albrecht, her own love, she thought. Waiting to dance, to enjoy life. Waiting—Yvonne stared at her shadow-smudged eyes—for disaster, reality, for the results of true love.

Or, she decided, I'm a dancer fighting for my career. Tonight that seemed both safer and more truthful. Now that she was without Gregory, now that she hadn't danced a performance in weeks, Justine would enjoy the revenge of replacing her.

From offstage Yvonne watched the curtain rise on a small wooden village on the Rhine. Peasant couples crossed the stage, talking, waiting to celebrate. *Giselle*, Yvonne thought, trying to recapture her past. Just the *Giselle* she had danced a hundred times before. Nothing new, nothing innovative.

Trumpets blared across the empty stage. Hilarion, the game-keeper who secretly loved Giselle, entered, followed by the Duke disguised as Albrecht and accompanied by his squire Wilfrid. Yvonne felt her feet must be encased in cement as she attempted to wiggle her toes and she pounded her slippers on the floor.

Beyond the curtain and the orchestra pit lay reality. The audience sat waiting, watching.

Moving into position, Giselle stood behind her cottage door. Albrecht knocked, the music wailed her theme. She couldn't remember entering, the audience's applause, or Albrecht's firm hands.

Now, *ballotté*, her mind ordered. Stand on your left foot, right foot behind lightly on the floor. Spring and join both feet under your body, and then land lightly on your right foot with your left leg extended. *Now*. Yvonne stood; she leaped, she joined feet, but she landed with a sickening crack.

17

"How are things at the company?" Maxine had invited Yvonne to lunch, taking Kili along. It was the first time she had dared to mention ballet since Yvonne's stage accident.

"The same, I suppose." Yvonne still heard the crack of her ankle, still saw Eleanor's triumphant smile as she sailed onstage to replace Yvonne, still heard the thunderous applause as the English dancer was recalled for encore after encore. Yvonne had watched the future float away as lightly as Eleanor, her eyes now large and luminous with shadow and liner, her figure lithe and ethereal, had flown across the stage *en pointe*. As if to demonstrate her total victory, Eleanor had immediately packed and returned to Europe with Roland. Once again, Yvonne had begun the slow process of healing.

"I understand there is a new soloist."

"Yes. She's only fifteen." When Yvonne thought of the child's slim figure and innocent good looks, she poured another glass of wine. "Can you imagine?"

"Only with difficulty—and distaste." Maxine built a tower of sourdough rolls, then swept it away, scattering bread around the table.

"You are looking well, Yvonne." Kili picked up the pieces and neatly replaced them in the basket.

"Thank you."

"Maxine is looking plump." Kili smiled guilelessly.

"Just what I need in my old age"—Maxine defiantly chose a poppy-seed roll and piled it with butter—"an uppity assistant." She took a big bite.

128

"You don't get enough exercise," Yvonne soothed.

"I do. Just last week I walked from Tiffany's to Van Cleef's."

Yvonne and Kili laughed. Maxine glared. "Anyway, about ballet. Things are no better."

"Was that a question or an answer?" Yvonne picked through her salad, rejecting the radishes, ignoring the olives, casting aside the tomato. She had lost her appetite again.

"Either." Maxine looked unusually serious.

"Maxine enjoys handling both sides of the conversation," Kili noted.

"Behave yourself."

"Justine brought me a contract to sign. Considering I don't know if I'll be able to dance next season, it was good of her."

"You mean she has you by the short ribbons," Maxine said.

Yvonne shrugged. "I'm in no position to complain."

"On to business," Maxine abruptly changed the subject. "That's why I wanted to talk with you. Business."

"That's what you told me," Yvonne interrupted. "What kind of business? Why are you being so mysterious? I called you last night, and your housekeeper said you were out. I thought you had given up on both Jack and Leon."

"I did. New conquests, my dear." Maxine leered.

"I should think that would be tiring."

"I don't want to get out of practice." Maxine pushed away her plate. "It is business—my company. I've definitely decided to expand. Men's and women's scents for a start. We're also going ahead with the popular-priced line, the Andies."

"How about towels?" Yvonne asked. "Wrap yourself in Maxine. Nothing between you and your Maxine." She tilted the wine bottle. "Empty." She motioned for another.

"Almost as good." Maxine smiled. "I'm going to do a luxurious line of underwear. Very sexy."

"Licensing arrangements?"

"For everything but the clothes."

"You won't just front, will you?"

"No, I'll design everything. Or rather, we will. I want real control, down to the lettering on the cologne bottle. You can be thinking bottles, as a matter of fact.''

"Doesn't it take a while to devise a new scent?" Yvonne interjected.

"I started work on it the same time I had Yvonne devised."

"What will the perfume be like?" Yvonne asked.

"I've decided to name the men's line Patina."

Kili raised an eyebrow. "Isn't that the sheen age produces on an antique surface?"

Yvonne giggled. "Will this line be for men over eighty?"

Maxine remained unamused. "Patina evokes expensive articles, famous paintings. Respectable wealth."

"And for the women?" Yvonne chirped.

"Panache."

"That's good." Kili nodded.

"Panache—dash, swagger, verve. Lively style. The modern woman. The Andrus woman.

Kili smiled as Maxine continued. "The scents will be exquisite by themselves, but will also blend together. Couples wearing Panache and Patina won't clash, but compliment."

"The answer to the divorce problem," Yvonne teased. "How did you manage that?"

"Each fragrance is made of separate scents that have to 'accord,' as they say. Every fragrance divides into three separate scents, each built around a distinctive 'note.' You wouldn't believe how this works. People who devise scents are called 'noses.' They decide when a fragrance is 'balanced' and 'round.' I wanted Panache to be the more noticeable and memorable of the two, of course. But the note from each scent of Panache blends and enhances those of Patina. They will be perfect."

"To perfection," Kili toasted.

"It sounds perfect," Yvonne said wistfully.

"Not completely." Maxine stared closely at her friend. "The products need a unifying symbol."

Kili and Yvonne considered, as well as they could. "Doesn't Gloria Vanderbilt have a swan?" Kili asked.

"I know!" Yvonne leaned forward. "I've got it! A platypus. I'm sure it hasn't been used."

"I'm not sure it would be tactful." Maxine wrinkled her forehead in thought.

"Why not?"

"Sounds too close in appearance to many of our customers."

They giggled. Kili poured another glass of wine each.

Maxine gathered herself. "Maxine Andrus Inc. needs a Maxine Andrus symbol."

"I see." Yvonne stared at her friend, perplexed.

"She will symbolize the line, travel around the country on promotionals, meet the women who buy the Andrus line, and project glamour and excitement. Do you see why I need you?"

"No."

"I need a glamorous, beautiful woman who will become synonymous in the public's mind with Maxine Andrus clothes. I want . . . I need you to be the spokesperson for me."

"*Me?*" Yvonne squeaked.

"Who better? A ballerina. Incredibly beautiful and a real career woman. Much better than a model. A personality."

"Why not yourself?"

"I don't have time. Someone has to turn out designs." Maxine's eyes fluttered nervously in Kili's direction, but her assistant appeared to examine the wine bottle.

"I couldn't." Yvonne, intrigued by the thought, was frightened also. She would meet and talk with people, crowds of people. "I think I'm too shy."

"You perform every night."

"It isn't at all the same. Now, if I could dance through the crowd, explaining your clothes with steps, a little pantomime, it might be possible."

"That gives me an idea." Maxine smiled smugly. "I'll talk to you about it later. I don't intend to take no for an answer. And . . ." She paused dramatically. "It will pay very well."

"I have a dreadful headache," Maxine groaned.

"No wonder, considering all the wine you drank for lunch." Yvonne avoided mention of her own discomfort.

"*With* lunch."

"Not the way you drank it."

"You will do it, won't you, Yvonne? You will be the look for my company?"

"Absolutely not. I can't." Yvonne had decided not to give in to Maxine.

"I need you."

A flip reply died on Yvonne's lips on hearing the plea in Maxine's voice. "If you really need me, I'll try." Yvonne suddenly changed her mind, trying to ignore how capricious she had become.

"You can do anything." Maxine's voice smiled. They slouched in two large chairs at Yvonne's apartment. "Let me tell you a story. Once there were two little orphans . . ."

"They were going to be famous and rich." Yvonne's voice was hushed.

"One would be a world-famous fashion designer."

Yvonne remained silent.

"Yvonne?"

"I don't think I'm going to be able to dance again, Maxine. I won't be a ballerina."

"Once a ballerina . . ." The designer fought to keep her voice steady. "The doctor told you something new?"

"No, it's just a feeling I have."

"Then we'll change the Tale." Maxine couldn't keep a note of despair from her voice.

"But if we change it, there wouldn't be any Tale. There might not be any Yvonne St. Cyr."

18

"How are you?" Maxine looked anxiously at Yvonne.

"Terrified." She was white, drained with fear and excitement.

"How have you managed to perform all these years?"

"It wasn't this hard. I never had to be myself."

"I would think that easier." Maxine carefully inspected the models. "Try a little more adobe shadow," she told one slim young woman. "I want vivid eyes."

"Maybe I need more makeup." Yvonne ran to a mirror and studied her appearance with discontent. "Or less. I put on too much."

"You look perfect." Kili ran past with an armful of shoes. "Don't touch anything."

"Yes, ma'am." Yvonne resumed pacing, worrying.

"Nothing will go wrong." Maxine patted her friend on the arm. "You'll see. It will be perfect."

"Ha!"

Why hadn't she refused Maxine? Why was she here? Yvonne didn't feel confident about the show, and saw disaster hiding in corners.

Ballet was different—not easier, but the advantage lay with dance. Once the curtain rose and the music swelled, the body could usually be relied on. Feet formed positions with a degree of automation, arms swung into position. A dancer didn't fly through the Swan Queen role thinking to herself: ten *bourrées*, three turns. If she did, there would be no time or energy left for art.

Here, waiting for the show to begin, Yvonne had too much

free time. Maxine, Kili, models rushed back and forth
preparing. She was ready; she only had to wait.

Kili, snowed under by lists, plowed back and forth, issuing
orders as if she were Maxine's clone. "What do you mean
one hundred chairs? We need one hundred and fifty. Within
twenty minutes." Kili's bangs flew as she yelled at the
department-store representative.

Yvonne laughed. "I think you've been around Maxine too
long."

"Did I hear my name?" Maxine absentmindedly held up a
jacket to the light, smoothing the velvet.

"It was nothing good." Yvonne smiled, her mind drifting
back to Kili's words. "One hundred and fifty?" she asked
weakly.

"That was just the advance audience. We didn't announce
the showing until yesterday, since this is supposed to be a
trial run. I'm sure there will be more." She hurried off
pleased at having reassured Yvonne.

So much had happened in a month. Once Maxine had
obtained Yvonne's consent, however tenuous, she worked
twenty-four hours a day.

"Luxury." Maxine had paced the office and hugged herself with excitement while Yvonne and Kili watched. "Investment dressing. Big money."

"Everyone doesn't have big money," Yvonne remarked.

"Exactly." Maxine sat on the edge of her desk. "That's
where the Andies come in—the moderate-priced line. First
we promote the new Andrus look and the perfume. Then, in
the select department stores allowed to carry the more expensive line, we open boutiques. They will carry the clothes, and
a line of shoes, accessories, perfume—everything working
together, coordinated. Custom control. Good quality. With
the prestige and éclat of the custom haute-couture collection.
It will be thrilling."

"How soon?" Kili asked.

"Summer."

Less than a month later, Yvonne's role began. Today was
the first test show. For five dollars, the customer received: a
seat on a rickety chair, a glass of champagne, a sample each
of Patina and Panache, a shopping bag with "Maxine Andrus"
in distinctive pink lettering, a fashion show of the new Max-

ne Andrus line, and a chance to meet Yvonne St. Cyr, the
dazzling ballerina. Neither perfumes nor clothes would be
available until the spring.

The perfume packaging had proved difficult. Maxine ordered Kili out on a buying spree, collecting perfumes. She
had lined them on the floor like soldiers on display. "Mary
McFadden. The pleated surface is evocative of her pleated
evening clothes."

Yvonne ran a finger along the fluted surface. "Elaborate
bottle. Very nice."

"At the other extreme: Chanel's classic square bottle."

"I've always like that," Yvonne commented.

"I can see you're going to be very helpful." Kili giggled.

"I'm a ballerina. What do I know?"

An impressive variety of flacons dotted the floor. Pavlova,
a floral fragrance, used flower-painted bottles to proclaim the
ambiance. Estée Lauder capped Cinnabar with cinnabar-colored
tops. Even more elaborate were the figure of a kneeling
woman gracing the top of Isadora and a carved frieze of
art-deco-designed women embellishing Molinard de Molinard.
In contrast, Silences was enclosed in a black half-circle, and
Halston Night displayed a pointed, multifaceted container.

"What can we use for Patina and Panache?" Maxine
mused, repeating herself over and over. "What look do I
want? Elegant?"

"That's understood," Yvonne agreed.

"Decorative? Stark? Simple? Complicated?"

The decision remained unmade. For this show, samples
would be distributed in plain vials with shocking-pink letters
spelling out "Maxine Andrus" on one side of the outside
cover, and "Panache" (or "Patina") on the other.

"Why are you giving out the Patina samples at a women's
fashion show?" Yvonne asked, fingering a sample.

"Sixty percent of all men's scents are bought by women.
Given as gifts, I suppose. I don't care if they use it
themselves."

A quarrel broke out between two models over a beaded
suit.

"I'm supposed to wear it," Jennifer snapped.

"I am." Olive appealed to Maxine. "Aren't I?"

"You would both fit into it." Maxine stared at the suit,

then at each woman. "Fit into it well." She closed her eyes
in consideration, then snapped them open and grabbed the
shoulder of a passing model. "Bambi will wear it. Both your
complexions are too sallow."

Kili laughed and whispered to Yvonne, "That's called
pouring oil on troubled waters, then setting fire to it."

"How many minutes?" Yvonne asked, desperation reas-
serting itself.

"Ten."

Yvonne fought an impulse to slide into the back room and
sneak away. She didn't want to be there. Not that she had
much to do, just a few words of introduction before the
fashion show, and a question-and-answer session following.
What could go wrong? Everything, Yvonne worried.

"Five minutes."

Just like curtain call, Yvonne thought. She walked to the
mirror, inspected herself, and wished she had worn something entirely different. This was her first choice: a black silk
suit with a shocking-pink blouse, black pearls with a diamond
clasp, an elegant feathered hat. Maxine hoped to encourage
hats. Of course, there had been five other choices in between,
but both Kili and Maxine liked the softly fashioned suit best.
Yvonne looked romantically elegant, her hair wrapped in a
soft knot at the nape of her neck.

Yvonne stood in the back room. A doorway and short hall
separated her from the stage, with the audience gathered in a
half-circle around the platform which V-ed out into the crowd.

Kili's voice floated backstage. "Thank you all for coming."
Yvonne walked down the hall, standing just out of sight of
the audience. To the left side of the stage stood a beautiful
black-and-gold oriental screen hiding the doorway, to the
right a small glass table with two dainty iron chairs. "Welcome
to a preview of the Maxine Andrus collection for spring. We
are pleased to invite you to dance in elegance from dawn till
dawn with Yvonne St. Cyr and Maxine Andrus." Kili, dressed
in a softly romantic silk dress of persimmon, basked in the
admiration of the crowd. Yvonne cringed from the rising
murmur. "We hope you like what you see and will be
looking for the new Andies boutique, coming soon to this
store. Now, Miss Yvonne St. Cyr, prima ballerina."

Only ten short steps separated Yvonne from a high-legged

chair next to the oriental screen. But to Yvonne those ten
steps took an eternity, walking infinitely more difficult than
dancing ever was. Gracefully she floated over, as the audience buzzed with ahs and murmured comments. "So beautiful," Yvonne heard. "Elegant."

"Elegance." Yvonne felt her throat catch with nerves, but
continued. "Not quiet, boring elegance. Not little white gloves,
gray lace, nice polite hats. Elegance with panache—with
excitement, distinction, glamour, and élan. From dawn till
dawn with Maxine Andrus, you can live in elegance, dance in
elegance, love in elegance.

"These clothes from the Andrus haute-couture group repre-
sent investment buying. Clothes with style that transcend
time. Clothes with stamina. Clothes with éclat—their brilliance will be yours. Let's start, then, as we see 'Elegance
from Dawn Till Dawn.' "

Romantic vignettes, Maxine had called them. "I don't
want an ordinary show. No commentary. No dancing down
the runway. We haven't two hundred models to get through,
after all. I want the women to see the clothes in action."

Following Yvonne's introduction, the lights dimmed. Soft
music drifted through the room, strings and light woodwinds
speaking of romance and love. One spotlight bathed Yvonne
in soft pink light, another moved along the left stage area,
awaiting the first model.

From behind the oriental screen a model sauntered toward
the front of the stage, yawning and stretching. She was
appropriately dressed in a slip of a satin nightgown the color
of tea-rose petals, appliquéd and embroidered with butterflies;
her hair was in romantic disarray. She walked around the
stage as if she were entirely alone, in her own apartment,
perhaps. With a final pirouette she turned and left the stage.

Maxine had evaluated each model for her grace and
movement, not just for her appearance. Their stage presence
was to suggest dance, choreographed movements of grace
and charm.

No sooner had the first model disappeared behind the
screen than the second sashayed forth. A faint gasp rose from
the seated women. The model wore black bra, panties, and
slip—all of silk lace—with no more than three small ribbons
tying it all together.

When Yvonne had first seen the model in rehearsal, she'd been shocked. "Are you sure they won't object?"

"They'll love it," Maxine predicted. "They have always wondered what a model looked like without her clothes on."

Maxine's prediction proved true. Members of the audience leaned forward, gasped, then leaned even closer.

The model centered herself on the V-shaped extension and tilted slightly forward, peering straight ahead. With efficient gestures she primped her hair and pretended to apply her makeup. The audience understood that an invisible mirror stood before her. Both the nightgown and underwear models wore black wigs, creating the illusion that they were the same woman. Finished with decorating her face, she turned, and a tiny patter of applause followed her from the stage.

A red dress, full-skirted, a twisted white-and-red belt around the waist, swirled out. Carrying a Maxine Andrus shopping bag, the model shopped with enthusiasm.

Next came an elegant suit, the skirt Persian rose color, the long, fitted jacket dusty pink. Wearing glasses, and carrying files, the model cocked a finger toward backstage. Out raced a handsome man, steno pad in hand. She proceeded to give dictation to her secretary, stopping only to send him off for her cup of coffee. Less than thirty seconds had elapsed, yet the women understood and appreciated the scene.

Now the clothes, a large assortment, began to follow more quickly. Pants for every taste and body—jodhpur, Zouave, Bermuda, kilt—juxtaposed with suits and dresses for both business and pleasure. But no blazers—Maxine was bored with them and used only kimono or three-fourth-length coats. All were in soft materials, cloth that shimmered, bounced, leaped, danced.

For Maxine, elegance that danced was more than a theme involving Yvonne; the entire collection moved and glided.

As evening gown followed evening dress, jewels sparkled from wrists and necks and ears: squared art-deco settings for sapphires, diamonds, and rubies, delicate clusters of pearls, large pieces of hewed jade, cascading diamonds casting drops of light around the stage.

The last gown, Maxine called her quintessential ball gown: purple-iris silk, small straps holding a fitted bodice from which sprouted an enormous ruffle. The waist was fitted down to the hips, where the dress bloomed outward. A dress for Ginger Rogers, Yvonne thought wistfully. Yvonne would have loved one, but had no need of it. She never again would need a ball gown.

A handsome tuxedoed partner strode onto the stage, a bottle of Fleur de Champagne by Perrier-Jouët in one hand, two tulip crystal glasses in the other. The model in the flowing dress twirled to his side, fingered the flower design on the bottle, then kissed him. He opened the bottle; they drank a toast.

The music died, the man left. The model, elegant and beautiful, again seemed to be looking at herself in the mirror. She admired, preened, danced in admiration. In the silence an arm reached out from the backstage wall, a man's arm, pajama-clad. The index finger motioned, calling the model back. Back to bed? With one last admiring look, she turned and ran backstage.

After a delighted burst of applause, a question-and-autograph session followed. Yvonne wrote her name on shopping bags, napkins, programs. She answered numerous questions about her career. No, she could only dance *en pointe* in special toe shoes; she didn't know when she would be dancing again; thank you for watching in the past; thank you for the prayers; yes, every role was her favorite role. Eventually it ended.

A success. A triumph. The beginning of a successful partnership, Maxine raved.

19

Kili briskly entered Maxine's office, clutching an armful of dresses, then stopped abruptly. Maxine stood in the middle of the room, wearing a new sample—wide-legged pink silk pants which pooled around her ankles and a vivid purple halter top, beaded and appliquéd. It wasn't the outfit that had caught Kili's attention, however. It was Maxine.

The designer wore a paper bag over her head, two round holes cut out for eyes, and appeared to be watching herself in the mirror. Kili couldn't tell exactly where Maxine was looking.

Kili smiled sweetly. "May I assume this is a symbolic gesture?"

Maxine gazed into the mirror, preoccupied.

"Yvonne will be here shortly?"

Maxine turned her back to the mirror and peered over her shoulder. "Yvonne? Yes, anytime now."

"You haven't told her about Fleming?"

"No, and a little oriental nightingale better keep her beak shut if she knows what's good for her."

"Yes, ma'am"

"I *am* going to tell Yvonne."

"Why bother? Sooner or later she'll find out. When the children call him Daddy. Sometime like that."

"Kili." Maxine spoke in her prepare-to-die tone.

"If I may offer a small word of advice?"

"Have I ever been able to restrain you?"

"It's hard to be impressive with a paper bag over your head."

"I can be impressive anytime or anyplace, sweetie, and don't you forget it."

140

"Your words are carved on my heart. By the way, I saw that the *American Questioner* has picked up Silvia Rosen's column."

Even under the bag, Maxine hissed. "If I ever see that woman again, *she'll* have to be picked up."

"You two aren't fighting, are you?" Yvonne's voice drifted in from the doorway. "Maxine, what in the world?"

The designer snatched off the bag, flushed deep pink from the heat. "I was just seeing how I looked."

"Under the bag?" Yvonne smiled.

"No, I meant the rest of me. It's a trick I learned from Edith Head. She told me that if you really want to see how you look and not be prejudiced by the fact it's you, put a bag over your head."

"And how did you look?" Kili asked.

"Not so good."

"You didn't need a bag to find that out." Kili snickered. "What do you think an assistant is for?" She left the room, sidestepping Maxine's counterattack.

"You look wonderful," Yvonne said.

"I think a paper bag is more reliable than a best friend."

"Maybe, but it's true. There's a new sparkle in your eye, a light bounce to your step."

Kili's head poked back in. "Maybe someone's given her a hotfoot."

"Hotfoot it out of here!" Maxine pointed to the door. "And don't come back until I call you." She glanced once more at the mirror. "I really think I'm looking fat."

Yvonne laughed, knowing consolation was impossible.

Laughter more and more surrounded Yvonne. She hadn't heard from Jerry Brandner. No allusion to the business deal, no hints of scandal, no insinuations of illegality, so perhaps the deal had worked out even in Gregory's absence.

Of course, she had not forgotten Gregory, or their happiness together. The pain still visited regularly, but at first she had a moment here and there of reprieve, then followed a scattered hour, and now, she realized with guilt-edged shock, a day or even two passed without her thinking of either Gregory or the past.

Slowly she was rebuilding her life. The apartment where they had loved, lived, and languished disappeared. Out of sight, she had hoped. Now moved, she awoke to a modern, functional bedroom, swept of memories, washed of the past. Gone were the samurai guards, the dramatic ram-headed table, even the serpent-circled mirror. The ballerina setting upstairs was disbanded, the wealthy-socialite ambiance downstairs dispersed. Even Gregory's things were packed away in storage.

Now she had a small bedroom, a moderate dining room, and a sufficient living room. The kitchen she managed by herself, the housekeeping also, with the help of a once-weekly visit from the maid.

Maxine, who had helped select the apartment, made no comment when Yvonne spent a thousand dollars on burglar alarms. Yvonne could not name the fear that woke her at night, nor could she describe her periods of frantic anxiety. She could only hope they would fade with time.

Only ballet remained in abeyance, her career undecided and unfathomable. Every day she completed a partial barre—not pushing too fast, not straining too hard. Still her muscles remained weakened, her leg undependable.

When Ian spoke of *Ballet of Desire*, she didn't listen closely. Maybe her future lay in a different area. The fashion show had been an unqualified success. Maxine's advisers were excited and pleased. Plans included a perfume bottle with a ballet theme for Panache, and an advertising campaign capitalizing on Yvonne's presence. She would be a world-famous ballerina, Yvonne noted with wry humor, whether or not she ever danced again. Perhaps, as Maxine once had suggested, once a ballerina . . .

The next showing was scheduled for Chicago. Yvonne, fresh from the success of the trial run, happily anticipated her visit. Kili accompanied her on the flight. "I haven't been in Chicago for a long time," Yvonne commented.

"We won't be there long, I'm afraid. You'll soon get used to seeing nothing but airports and the insides of department stores. It won't be as glamorous as everyone thinks."

"I'm not surprised. Ballet wasn't either."

The setting was more elegant and opulent at the department store in Chicago than it had been in New York. Backstage, Yvonne prepared herself, still nervous but slightly more relaxed than the first time.

This audience was larger, and as starting time approached, Yvonne heard a buzz from the front of the curtain. She saw Kili peering out, and joined her. "There's less to this than meets the eye," Kili murmured.

"What?"

"Nothing. There seems to be a lot of press."

"That's good, isn't it?"

"Of course." Kili erased her worried frown before she turned to face Yvonne. "You're even more magnetic than we thought."

"I hope so."

The show worked its magic once again. From the audience's reaction at seeing Yvonne, to the swirl of fabric and the sparkle of magical glamour surrounding the performance, all was perfection. The question-and-answer session followed, and as in New York, most questioners displayed a superficial knowledge of ballet life. But their questions were friendly and warm, and Yvonne enjoyed answering.

As the session drew to a close, a woman at the back of the room rose. A television reporter, Yvonne realized, as camera lights blazed on, blinding her.

"Miss St. Cyr. You haven't danced since the accident. Is this the end of your ballet career?"

"No. I don't know when I'll be able to dance, but I work out every day." Yvonne and Maxine had already discussed the possibility of that question being raised. Yvonne waited for another audience question, hoping for a change of subject.

But the reporter hadn't finished. "Do you have any comment on your late husband's corporate activities?"

"I'm here to discuss Maxine Andrus' beautiful line of clothes. I never was active in my husband's affairs." Yvonne instantly hoped "husband's affairs" wasn't an unfortunate choice of words.

"What about reports that hundreds of people are losing their life savings? That Gregory Reed's business activities are under investigation for fraud? That he allegedly swindled his investors from the Reed-Mellow group out of millions of dollars!"

"That isn't true!" Yvonne gasped. "Gregory would never do anything illegal—have done anything illegal."

"If not illegal, were his activities the months before his

death, at the least, ill-advised?'' The ambiance of the presentation was destroyed, cast to ugly scandal.

Kili appeared at Yvonne's shoulder. "That will be all." She smiled with clenched teeth. "The fashion presentation is now over. Thank you all for coming."

She dragged Yvonne backstage, ignoring shouted questions from the reporters. "Come on, you're going back to the hotel to pack. We have to get back to New York."

Issuing a series of sharp instructions to the models and assistants, Kili smuggled Yvonne out a back door. Of course, Yvonne had read the latest gossip about Gregory. A scandal was being uncovered. "He left a wealthy widow," the headlines screamed. "But Reed left hundreds in ruins." Details of Gregory's business dealings had been slanted into the worst possible light and supported by lurid details, all lies. His business ventures were distorted to appear as irresponsible gambles, with Gregory shielded from disaster. Yvonne was sick with pain and rage. None of this could be true.

Kili worked efficiently, arranged a flight to New York under assumed names, and planned a strategic retreat from the hotel. All went as planned until Silvia Rosen spied them at the airport. Kili gasped with shock as the heavyset woman ran over, waving a notebook and shrieking Yvonne's name.

"Beating a hasty retreat?" she asked with false pity. "Why not tell our hundreds of thousands of readers *your* side of the story?"

"I have nothing to say." Yvonne hurried along, doing her best to ignore Silvia.

"Did you realize what he was up to?"

"Gregory was up to nothing he shouldn't have been," Yvonne turned and yelled.

"People ruined—"

"No one will be ruined. I will use my personal estate to cover any moneys lost!" Yvonne didn't realize tears were tumbling down her face. "Now, leave me alone!"

For a week Yvonne hid, refusing to speak to the press, refusing to discuss the situation even with Jerry. She merely ordered him to sell everything except the ranch and report to her how much more money he needed to compensate the investors. When Maxine called, Yvonne pleaded exhaustion, a cover for the deep humiliation she felt. Gregory had protected her; now she found herself powerless, unable even to defend his memory.

Ian and Maxine arrived on the doorstep, in no mood to accept her rebuff. Yvonne wasn't dressed, but pulled a dressing gown around her shoulders and sat in a chair, pale and thin. "I just don't quite feel up to seeing anyone," she reiterated, her voice cracking in spite of her efforts at control. "Maybe next week. I can't yet."

"That's tough." Maxine's brisk exterior hid her concern.

"We've decided it's time you stopped sulking." On the last word, Ian's voice quivered slightly. The lecture was for Yvonne's own good, he reasoned, but her pain was so obvious, her vulnerability screamed around the room.

"I'm not sulking." She stared at her hands, then looked up with a trembling smile. "I just don't feel well."

"You're not bouncing back," Maxine admonished.

"Back to what?" Yvonne's eyes filled with tears. "To ballet? I can't, not yet. To Maxine Andrus Inc.?" Her laugh shimmered with pain. "That's all the new promotion needs. A symbol of corporate mismanagement, of sharp dealings, of failure."

Maxine winced, Yvonne's words all too close to those of her own backers. Gone was the ballet theme for Panache, gone the advertising campaign using Yvonne.

"I don't have anything left."

"All right. So now isn't the time for you to travel with the collection. Not," Maxine hastily added, "because of the Andrus image. A little scandal never hurts, I always say. But to protect you. Those vultures won't give up for a while, and I won't have them hounding you across the country."

"There are other aspects," Ian cut in. "Both for the collection and ballet."

"Teaching?" Yvonne cringed. "Advising on color selection?"

"And what about Gregory?" Maxine pressed.

"What about him? I can't help him. People are determined to sully his memory. Little people who couldn't touch Gregory when he was alive."

"You have to realize, Yvonne, that they do have to investigate. All that money. And you need to carry on as he would have wished you to. Show them you won't be frightened into retreating to your apartment. Gregory would expect more of you.''

"I don't know what he would expect of me,'' Yvonne lied.

"You are determined to be an impossible little fox, aren't you?'' Maxine sighed.

"I am not. The situation is determined to be impossible. My life has determined to be impossible. I haven't determined anything for myself for some time.''

"Then it is time you started,'' Ian said. He stared at her, a dreamy look crossing his face. "I remember the first time I saw you.''

"A million years ago.'' Yvonne closed her eyes as if to shut out the thought.

"You were doing an *arabesque* in class. Badly. Your balance wasn't secure. You had no presence, no projection.''

"Then why did you choose me?''

"A scent of passion. A soupçon of brilliance. It's still there. It's survived all the blows and ill luck. Great passion has never been my fate, thank God, so perhaps I don't fully understand, but I do know you have to continue.''

Yvonne looked up. "Continue what?''

"I want you to go to Ireland for me. For *me*. Surely, no matter how little you like teaching, you owe me something. Only a few months of a life you don't value that highly right now. I need for you to accompany Aisling to Dublin, to teach her Eve for her Irish performance, to watch and coach the rest of the group. I'll come, but not until close to the performance. I have to be here, with the company. When I come, I'll bring the beginning of *Ballet of Desire*.''

"I'll never be able to dance it. I'll never dance professionally again.'' Fear marked her face.

"We'll see. I intend to mount it on you, but we'll see. Aisling will be there, after all. Will you go?''

"No. No, no, no!'' Yvonne felt disoriented, unable to think. When she tried, the room swirled and shook. Oh, what did it matter where she was? The taste of ashes in her mouth, the glistening pain of tears in her eyes, all could be enjoyed just as well in Ireland as in New York. Perhaps Maxine was right. Gregory was no longer able to defend himself or safeguard his reputation. So she would have to act. Ireland would at least be a beginning, a way to show her that life continued. She had to build a new life for herself somewhere, somehow. "When do you want me to leave?"

Her friends exchanged glances at Yvonne's sudden shift of mind. "The end of the week." Then Ian drew a packet from his coat. "I already have the ticket."

"All right."

After a few more encouraging words, he left. Maxine sat quietly for a few minutes. "I'm sorry."

"*I'm* sorry. It could be a deadly blow to the company."

"The company will survive. So will you."

"Despite everything?"

"Yes."

"Maybe so. I don't really care at the moment."

"I'd like you to do something for me in Ireland."

"What?"

"A company over there manufactures handmade shoes. I'm thinking of having them develop a line for me, and I would like you to make contact, see what the plant looks like, see if they can handle specialty work."

"I don't know much about shoes, but I'll do what I can."

Maxine smiled. "Ireland is beautiful, and you've never seen it. There will be lots for you to do."

"I'm not in the mood for sightseeing."

"Maybe your mood will change when you get there." Maxine hesitated. She had planned to mention Fleming, but tripped over the words. Mention him how or as what? Maxine felt oddly shy. "You never know what might happen. Things change, people and situations."

Yvonne thought the conversation had taken an odd turn. "You don't."

"But I do." Maxine searched. Her mood was bittersweet: sad for Yvonne, yet happy about Fleming. They had suffered through their first fight the night before. The throws of passion, Maxine thought, enjoying her own pun. Fleming was a good fighter—spirited, fair, and enthusiastic when it was time to make up. Especially when it was time to make up. "I don't always want to go on as I have. I'm getting older and tireder. Sometimes I don't want to be alone forever."

"You won't be. You'll meet the right man. Someone with everything you want and need. Then it will be perfect."

Maxine looked flustered. "Maybe. You wouldn't mind?"

"Of course not." Yvonne tried not to make it a lie. "Is there someone?"

"Not really. You know how it is." Maxine could not bring herself to admit what was happening.

Later, Yvonne wondered if Maxine had someone special in mind, but by then she was on a plane heading for Ireland.

Her flight over the Atlantic was uneventful. If on schedule, the jet would arrive in Dublin at eight in the morning, Irish time. "A terrible hour," Yvonne had joked with Maxine. "Not the time to meet either a new man or a country."

Yvonne herself felt frozen. She was coming to Ireland, not for adventure or a new beginning, but to train a young, new dancer—in a role she had once danced. To see a role that would have been hers made on some young thing. It left a bitter taste.

In the early morning as she peeped through dark clouds, glimpses of green countryside became apparent. Although visiting Ireland for the first time, she was unmoved.

When Dublin came into view, she apathetically gathered her flight bag and departed in a light rain. The airport was small for a capital city.

She passed immigration, collected her luggage, and cleared customs. Maxine had arranged for her to be met in Dublin.

Near the ticket counter a driver waited, scanning the arriving passengers. "Miss Andrus?" His voice was uncertain, but distinctively Irish.

"No, I'm Miss St. Cyr, I work with Maxine Andrus." The company and designer names must have become confused.

"Good, good. Let me take your things."

Docilely, Yvonne followed.

The driver opened the back door of a blue Mercedes, then placed her luggage in the trunk. Yvonne slid gracefully in. In the dark interior, a figure sat back, smoking a cigarette that sent small circles of smoke swirling through the air.

Yvonne turned, froze, and finally gasped, "Seán Fitz-Gerald!"

The dark-haired man showed an ill-concealed dismay. "I expected Maxine Andrus."

"She asked me to come." Wild thoughts raced through her

mind. Was this the love Maxine had hinted at? Had she sent Yvonne ahead to smooth the way and not told Seán? Staring at Seán, she read his expression as disappointment at seeing her instead of Maxine.

"Of course, I'm delighted to see you, Yvonne."

Yvonne managed a brief smile in response, but fear soon stiffened her expression. She never should have allowed Maxine and Ian to bully her into taking the trip. She was not ready to resume her life. Her losses were too severe, too recent. She had no defense against Seán, no shield of dance, no Gregory for protection. With all her security stripped away, she felt exposed and naked.

How could she cope with Seán FitzGerald, a suave man, who would amuse himself at her expense?

"Been to any good parties lately?" Seán asked. It seemed to Yvonne his smile pulled into a leer.

20

The graceful nineteenth-century furniture of the luxuriou
Shelbourne Hotel—inlaid writing tables overhung with gold
wreathed mirrors and lit with glittering chandeliers—provide
an evocative and romantic decor. That first morning, Yvonn
realized, was something of a lie, a commitment she had n
intention of keeping, a promise to the past she didn't believ
in, to the future she didn't trust, to others, even to herself.

Why had she agreed to come to Ireland?

Her suite overlooked St. Stephen's Green, a park stil
green and lush under an autumn sun. By the window, Yvonn
sat in a padded chair, reviewing the cars passing the bus
sidewalk. Sat as the morning rains cleared. Sat as the lunc
crowd grew, then thinned.

What would she do?

Seán FitzGerald's face came to mind—a face from a Euro
pean men's fashion magazine. Arrogant turquoise eyes, eye
that seemed to mirror perverse pleasures. He was arrogan
and obnoxious, just as she had remembered him from Maxine'
party. Maxine was the reason she had agreed to see th
impossible Seán. Of late, her friend had been acting strangely
busy almost every night, preoccupied with a dizzy confusio
that didn't spell work.

Had Maxine been seeing Seán? Yvonne didn't know. She'
been preoccupied herself, building her new career. But as sh
remembered the fashion show, her smile grew cynical.

At the airport, the car had begun with the discreet hum o
money. As Seán continued smoking, Yvonne sat bolt upright
Still, she was pleased she had refreshed her makeup on th

lane, an automatic gesture left over from the past. And
Maxine had almost dressed her for the flight, a casually chic
gray suit of medium-weight wool with a pink silk blouse,
light pink stockings, and delicate gray lizard heels. She only
cared about her appearance because of her own self-respect;
Seán FitzGerald's opinion of her meant nothing. She had no
interest in conceited men, no matter how handsome.

When the car swung around a corner, Yvonne's tense body
was thrown across the seat toward Seán. Making a deft catch,
he intercepted Yvonne only inches before they collided, and
held her momentarily a kiss away before releasing her. To
Yvonne, his half-smile implied that she had slid across on
purpose. After all, he seemed to proclaim silently, I am
irresistible.

She jerked herself free, pressing herself against the door of
the car. "Textiles," she nervously blurted out. The car sped
through darkened streets, a sudden shower choking the windows with fat drops. "You're in textiles—tweeds, isn't that
right?"

"I am." He smiled a practiced, charming smile and extended an arm, well-suited in gray tweed. He was impossibly
self-assured.

"A shoe representative was supposed to meet me. Or do
you make tweed shoes?"

"What an original idea!" He beamed. "Actually, though,
father waxed active and industrious. The clothes factory
expanded into shoe manufacturing, then galloped into horses,
plowed into farms, and finally bloomed into a French winery.
So to speak." His smile was fleeting.

"How fascinating." Seán was a playboy; one look at him
confirmed it. *Father was active and industrious,* a voice in
her head mimicked. And lucky Seán had inherited all the
family businesses. Unlike Gregory, she thought with bitter
loyalty; Gregory had started with nothing, had worked for
everything.

"Sour."

"What?"

"You said fascinating. Actually, the wine never worked
out. Sour grapes. Literally." He laughed at his own joke. Her
sour expression discouraged further levity. "Beautiful piece

of land, though. I could never bear to give it up. Littl
cottage there. I take friends sometimes.''

In his voice Yvonne could hear the discreet slither of silke
underclothes, the dissolute popping of champagne corks. ''Ho
fortunate for them.''

''You must come sometime.''

''Yes,'' she said; never, she meant. If Maxine had falle
hopelessly in love with this affected, impossible man, then a
the worse for poor Maxine.

Seán looked quizzically at Yvonne. ''By the way . . .''

''Yes?''

''I didn't know you worked with Maxine. Her last lette
didn't say exactly who was coming, but did imply it wa
herself.''

''Kili must have written it—she usually handles th
correspondence.''

''I assume, then, that isn't your job.''

''Answering letters? No. Maxine asked that I look at th
shoe factory and see what I think.''

''Then I'd better be nice to you.'' Seán's voice deepenec
''My future partnership with Maxine Andrus might depend o
it. Well, let's see, you can have the personal tour of Dubli
first, with drinks and dinner to follow.''

''I couldn't put you to all that trouble.'' Continuing conta
with the man was an agonizing thought.

''Not at all. I do it for all the visiting businessmen, l
alone women. Your husband didn't come with you?''

Yvonne froze in momentary shock. ''My husband?''

Seán's eyes narrowed, as if sensing he had said somethin
wrong, yet unable to imagine what. ''Gregory Reed.''

''Gregory is . . . Gregory was in a car crash in Texas. H
didn't survive. Several months ago.'' She stared rigidly ahead
refusing to cry in Seán FitzGerald's presence.

A burst of contrite apology followed before Seán smoothl
changed the subject, outlining the sights of Ireland she woul
have to see. ''Dublin is, of course, the capital of Ireland. Th
name Dublin comes from the Gaelic *dubh*, meaning 'dark,
and *linn*, meaning 'pool,' referring to the dark waters of th
River Liffey, which flow through the city, and perhaps th
color of Guinness stout.''

Out the window, Yvonne saw a broad roadway lined with stores. "Where are we now?"

"This is O'Connell Street, one of the widest in all of Europe. It measures twenty-five men or twenty-seven and one-third women."

"What?"

"One hundred and fifty feet, actually."

"I'll have to remember you drive on the left here."

"Sure you can use my car while you're here. Liam will drive for you."

"That isn't necessary. I can rent something, and you need your car."

"I have another little one," Seán reassured her. "It won't be a bit of trouble. That's the General Post Office." He pointed across the wide street to a large building of gray stone with a high pillared front entrance. "It was the focal point of the Insurrection of 1916, when the building, except for the facade, was destroyed by fire. Riot with an eye to the tourist trade."

The streets, filled with morning rush-hour traffic, reminded Yvonne that whatever the country, some things were unchanged. The rain cleared as they reached the Shelbourne Hotel, graceful yet solid, its facade red brick trimmed in white.

Seán insisted on accompanying her inside, on ensuring that her suite was waiting, even ordering breakfast to be sent to her room. Though she insisted she wasn't hungry, he wouldn't listen. "It was a long flight. Until four, then. We'll take you on a short jaunt around the city. Nothing too strenuous."

Overcome by exhaustion and inertia, she didn't object. She had too many decisions, too little time to make them. A whole new future to plan. Would she ever dance again? The doctor wouldn't say or guess. If not, what else could she do? For now, teaching Aisling and helping Maxine would suffice, but that didn't constitute a career. Twenty-five seemed old, but decades faced her, years to be faced, years to be planned for.

At three o'clock she got up to bathe and redo her makeup before Seán arrived. Approaching her suitcases, she wondered if she had something suitable to wear for dinner. Maxine had packed for her.

The day before the flight, Maxine had visited Yvonne's apartment to find her sitting abjectly on a sofa, clothes scattered in an untidy pile, total indecision marring her face. Muttering a cryptic remark about orange panty hose, Maxine exiled her to the living room and called Kili, who arrived with enough merchandise to open a boutique. Three hours later Maxine emerged, a limp Kili dragging behind. "All finished," Maxine announced.

"Me too," Kili panted.

Unpacking, Yvonne found something suitable for every possible occasion, a full array of costumes ranging from evening wear to clothes for a formal morning wedding. Much to her surprise, a pair of jeans was included, but eyeing the elegant Shelbourne, she couldn't imagine wearing them.

She chose a lavender wool dress, tucked at the waist and full-skirted, that opened down the front with a multitude of tiny buttons. She had never seen it before, and assumed it was part of Maxine's new collection. Antique cream-colored lace ruffled the neck, touched the wrists. Gregory would have liked it.

There wasn't much else he would have liked about her in these last few days. Letting those mad dogs—she refused to dignify the mob of reporters snapping and snarling around her apartment that last week with a more grandiose phrase—drive her away like a wounded doe. No wonder the predators howled around her: they smelled blood in her wilting posture and terrified face.

Well, after all Maxine had done for her, the least she could do was to charm Seán, to let him see the graceful, successful side of Maxine's best friend.

She dressed, then made up, matching her eye shadow to the hue of the dress. Next she parted her hair in the middle, secured each front section at the side with a gold hairpin, and allowed the back to flow freely.

At exactly four o'clock Seán found her waiting in the lobby. He was clearly impressed, Yvonne noticed with pleasure, though only for Maxine's sake, she reminded herself. Besides, her hours with Roland had left her with a recent distaste for any kind of flirtation.

Seán greeted her with an assured smile. "How elegant.

Not just elegant, but exotic. Calm and of perfect bearing. A real ballerina.''

"Not very real at the moment." Yvonne smiled sadly and abruptly changed the subject. She wouldn't display to Seán how unarmed she was without her career. "Anyway, I think the word might better describe you.''

"Me? Not me, my dear. I'm a simple Irishman, after all. Nothing exotic about yours truly. Nor about my work." He smiled modestly.

Yvonne was not fooled. "Shall we go?''

"Of course. About this afternoon. I'm very sorry about your husband. The Irish papers must have covered his . . . passing, but more than likely, I was away in Japan.''

Yvonne only smiled. A simple Irishman who made regular visits to Japan.

"Anyway, this will be a perfect evening. I'll take care of everything. How lovely you look." He reached out to help her to her feet.

She managed to ignore his proffered hand. "Thank you. This is one of Maxine's new dresses. She has such exquisite taste.''

Liam waited out front by the car. "I've arranged a little driving tour of the city for now. You might like to walk around early tomorrow. Don't want you getting lost. Later we'll go back to the famous sites for closer inspection.''

"How nice of you." Yvonne tried to sound gracious and knew she failed. Days with Seán stretched before her.

At dinner that night, Seán asked Yvonne how she had happened to come to Ireland for Maxine.

"Don't you think I can do the job?" Her tone was ominous.

"I'm sure you can. I just meant, isn't the ballet season starting? Don't they need you back at the company?''

Yvonne took a breath. "I was injured in the accident, then reinjured during a performance. I don't know if I'll ever be dancing again.''

Seán sighed. "Do you think it's because you're so beautiful?''

"Excuse me?''

"I mean, could something subconscious cause me to forever put my foot in my mouth when around you? I am sorry.

There was the slightest suggestion of a limp, but I didn't realize. Sorry.''

''Thanks.'' Sorrow didn't change anything, but what could people say?

21

For the three days following the dinner, Yvonne eluded Seán, offering exhaustion, mild illness, plans. She explored Dublin, walking at first to avoid Seán's calls and questions. She was gradually entranced by its charm. Every corner revealed the past, gracefully intermingled with the present. In the Georgian areas, she examined houses and castles, parks and corners where time had held its breath. The muted light calmed her, the soft sounds soothed.

O'Connell Bridge bulged with smartly dressed career women, affluent cars, and an accordion player surrounded by children. She hurried on, sorrow clouding her eyes at the sight of their small faces. Remembering, always remembering.

One block from the row of glittering department stores displaying a plethora of twentieth-century goods sat Moore Street. The open-air market bustled with apple-cheeked women of another time, crying their goods in a cockneylike chant.

The sights distracted Yvonne, the sights reminded her. A hundred times she thought she must remember to tell Gregory, only to catch her breath, realizing she never could.

A haze of rain slickened the steps to the hotel as Yvonne returned on the fourth day. "Hello."

She whirled to find Seán standing just inside the lobby. "Hello." Feeling guilty, she took the offensive. "Checking up on me?"

"No. Not at all, I was just concerned. You might be lonely or . . ."

Despite herself, Yvonne laughed at the look of panic crossing his usually suave face. Perhaps it was the magical atmosphere of the city which surrounded her, or the cozy knowledge that a warm fire waited in her room, with tea only a request away, but Yvonne felt herself thawing.

Seán wore a golden tweed suit, nipped at the waist in European style, its color emphasizing his clear blue-green eyes. His lightly tanned skin made him look younger than she remembered. "It's nice to see you."

"Really? I mean, I hope you've been well."

"Yes, it must have been jet lag that left me feeling so washed out. Thank you for the flowers."

"Nothing. Just a few petals to cheer your room."

A few blush-red petals delicately attached to three dozen long rose stems.

"Would you like to see the factory today?"

"Actually, I have a bit of work. I have to meet Aisling Nolan, a ballerina, at the airport. I'm going to teach her one of Ian Thorn's roles. Eve from *Honoré et Eve*. But I forgot— you aren't a ballet enthusiast."

Seán shrugged elegantly. "I can always learn. But tell me this. How can you teach the role if you can't dance?"

"Words." Her voice grew cold.

Seán hurriedly changed the subject. "Actually, I know Eve."

"Do you?"

"After meeting you, I was curious and went to see you dance. You were Eve. Nice work."

Yvonne studied him briefly, for insincerity or sarcasm, but saw only concern and admiration.

"Why don't we have lunch, and afterward I'll drive you out to the airport?" he asked.

"All right."

"Where would you like to go?"

"Go?" Yvonne looked vaguely around the lobby. Decisions, more decisions that Gregory always handled. "Is there a restaurant here?"

"Three days and you don't know?"

"I've been out a lot." She wasn't about to admit she'd eaten most of her meals in her room. She had never liked eating alone in a restaurant.

"There is the Horseshoe Bar. We could start with a drink there. You never know who you might see in Dublin."

"No, thank you. I really don't want a drink."

"The main restaurant has good French food, but I think you might like the Saddle Room."

"Fine."

"Intimate."

She cringed at the word, but followed him meekly to the entrance, stopping to admire the hand-tooled saddle.

"I usually come here for business meetings. I don't go out that often on pleasure. Not that this isn't." He took her elbow and pointed toward an empty table. "Let me see. What about over there?"

"Okay." For an instant she heard a rustle as his coat brushed against the jacket of her suit. That sound, his masculine presence, his scent and touch, brought a catch to Yvonne's throat. So strange to be this close to a man who wasn't Gregory. Roland had never affected her this way. He was more silk and cologne than tweed and tobacco. Realizing they were being examined by other diners, she followed the maître d'. They must make an attractive couple, she noted with some embarrassment, and some pleasure.

Idly Yvonne studied her menu, decorated with the copy of a brown-tinted antique print of horse and rider. "What would you like?" Sean asked.

"I don't know. What do you suggest?"

Seán eyed her warily. "The beef is especially good, but there is fish and also chicken."

Gregory had been decisive. Into her chair he swept her, out of her hand he swept the menu. Suggestions, orders, pleadings to try one delicacy or another always followed, for when entertaining her, Gregory knew not only his own mind but also hers. Seán wouldn't even guess. "Roast beef, thank you. Potatoes."

"Potatoes are a safe choice in Ireland." Seán gave their orders to the black-and-yellow-vested waiter, then turned to face Yvonne. "This is very popular with the horse set."

"Really? I wouldn't think horses could fit in such delicate chairs."

"Your sense of humor is back. Tell me, what have you seen of the city?" He looked up and saw the waiter approaching. "Here we are."

"Yes, here we are."

The waiter set a basketed bottle of wine on the table. "The roast beef for your wife, I believe, sir?"

Yvonne bristled on hearing the word. "Not wife."

"Ah," the man misunderstood, "I see." He beamed approvingly at the lucky young couple. Yvonne snatched up a fork but stabbed her salad instead of the man.

Seán studied his meat without comment, and when the waiter left, he continued as if nothing had occurred. "Did you visit Trinity?"

Yvonne carefully cut a small portion of meat, then slowly chewed before answering. "Yes." Two could play his game of great good friends. "I saw the Book of Kells. It was stunning. I've only seen pictures of an illuminated manuscript before."

A national treasure, the book was a copy of the four gospels handwritten in Latin by monks in the Kells monastery during the ninth century. "You know that a different page is turned every day?"

"Why is that?"

"So the pages won't be exposed to the light too often. The designs are so complex and minute. Seeing it is a good beginning for anyone visiting Ireland."

"I'm so pleased you approve." She smiled. "I saw the National Gallery."

"What pictures did you like best?"

Yvonne inspected her meal, confident that her first feelings about Seán had been correct. He would never let up. After all, this conversation had overtones of a quiz, an evaluation of her culture and education. "The Dutch school, I think. There is a distance, a coolness I like." Her wide eyes looked pointedly into his.

"I like the warmth of the French school." He changed the subject to ballet, Ian's other ballets, what roles she liked best. The conversation followed the impersonal lines of an interview. "I'm impressed with the dedication and work ballet demands," he finally admitted. "And the years of study. As a child, I would never have stuck with anything so completely, not for years and years."

"Tanaquil LeClercq once said that dancing was similar to training a racehorse and being a racehorse at the same time."

"And who would she be, might I ask?"

"Tanaquil was married to Balanchine."

"Balanchine. Even I know that name."

"In 1954 she contracted polio and became crippled." Yvonne's voice tightened as a chill ran through her. Although less dramatically crippled than Tanaquil, she too might never dance again.

"What did she do then? Isn't a career in ballet like burning your bridges before you?"

"Too true. She teaches at the Dance Theatre of Harlem. I think she's very brave. Seeing those healthy new students, involving herself so much with ballet, but all the while knowing she'll never dance again. Perhaps like me. . . ."

Then Seán said softly, "I'm sorry about everything—your career, your husband, your life. I know words seem trite, and personal experience has taught me that pity isn't necessarily a desired reaction to tragedy." His tone darkened. "Anyway, it's time to leave for the airport."

On the drive out, Yvonne saw the distant mountains. "The countryside here must be beautiful."

"Of course it is. But I have been so inconsiderate. You must come out to the farm tomorrow."

"Farm?"

"Mine. It's out in the country. Birds. Trees. All that sort of thing. Very restful. You've only seen Dublin, and the most beautiful parts of Ireland are out in the country."

"I don't know if I'll have the time. I have to meet the ballet company, see the theater, and start coaching Aisling."

"Surely you could take the afternoon off?"

"Well, yes . . . I suppose I could."

"Good, it's settled. Tomorrow after lunch, Liam will pick you up. You can stay for dinner. We'll go horseback riding."

"Dancers aren't supposed to ride horseback!" Yvonne snapped indignantly.

"But you aren't a dancer now, are you?"

22

As they stepped from the car at the Shelbourne, Aisling shivered. "I hadn't expected it to be so cold."

"Ireland is perpetually air-conditioned," Seán responded. "You will be warm enough inside. I'll see you tomorrow," he addressed Yvonne, then faced Aisling. "We're going horseback riding. Would you like to join us?"

"Horseback riding?" Aisling looked aghast, as if he had suggested a nude stroll down O'Connell Street. "No way! Justine would kill me."

"She wouldn't know," Seán replied good-naturedly.

"Justine is into information," Aisling whispered. "She'd know."

Seán laughed and bade farewell.

Yvonne helped Aisling register and then invited her for tea and cakes. "It will help you warm up." And perhaps warm their relationship as well, she thought. On the ride from the airport, each had realized they were virtually strangers, marooned in a foreign land. To Yvonne, Aisling suddenly appeared young and unserious. To Aisling, Yvonne must seem old and now out of it. A dancer who was finished. The thought was discomforting.

"Thanks." Aisling looked as if she would rather not, but didn't know how to refuse.

"Good flight?"

"Very nice. I saw a little of London. Not much, though." Aisling's smile flickered mechanically.

"Is this your first time out of the country?" Yvonne asked

when they were in her room, drinking tea. There should be some way to break through Aisling's nervous reserve.

"Yes." Aisling picked up her cup, spilling a few drops of tea as her hands quivered.

"Day after tomorrow, we'll meet with the Irish dance-company management. Sometime in the morning."

"Terrif."

"You must be very excited to have been chosen for this role by Ian."

"Yeah." Aisling's tone wasn't enthusiastic.

Yvonne raised an eyebrow.

"I know he does super ballets," Aisling admitted. "A little old-fashioned sometimes. I've heard the company's going to have a new choreographer."

"Of course. The company has never used only Ian."

"But at his age, he can't be at the top forever. A new choreographer . . ." Aisling broke off in thought. "I was not sure this was the place to be. But of course, I told Ian I would come," she quickly added.

Yvonne felt herself bristling in response to Aisling. This wasn't going at all well. How could she reach her? Ian wanted Yvonne to teach her the role of Eve, to pass on the essence of emotion and character that brought the role into reality.

But emotion and character must come from Aisling; she must fuse with the role. To help Aisling discover these feelings, she would have to know the young woman, to establish some degree of trust and communication, superficial though it might be. "When did you first decide to become a ballet dancer?"

Aisling shrugged nervously. "Well, you know how it is. Real early. Sometimes I wonder if it was such a great idea."

"I see." Yvonne's tone primly disapproved.

Aisling nervously shook back her long hair. "Mother took me to see *The Nutcracker* when I was young. I thought it was so beautiful, so romantic. The costumes, shoes, floating like a cloud, a handsome prince . . . you must know the feeling."

"Those illusions wouldn't have lasted long."

"You know it! But my mother was so enthusiastic. When I showed some talent, she developed great ambitions."

"I see." In an instant, Yvonne remembered the auditions

and the agitated scene as she left the hall. The mere handful
of winners stood apart, either elated with private joy or still
pale and trembling with nerves. At the time, Yvonne had
seen their different reactions as individuals recovering from
tension. Now she wondered if some winners would be forced
to continue in ballet, a career they didn't want.

"Not that her ambitions weren't for my own good," Aisling's
voice broke into her thoughts. Ambition was a desirable
quality for a young ballerina. Justine would cremate a lacka-
daisical dancer right where she stood.

Yvonne wavered a moment, considering Aisling. She appeared shy and placid, but surely there must be more. After
all, Ian had chosen her to dance the passionate Eve.

The blond sat, her head bent awkwardly forward, as if
inspecting her feet with fascination. Her body slumped in the
chair like a gawky letter K. "Maybe you would like to walk
through the park before dinner. Work out some of the kinks
from the airplane ride."

As Aisling tumbled out the door, Yvonne wondered if she
had expected too much. After all, they were competitors, not
friends. So she would teach Aisling the steps of Eve's role
and let the young ballerina find the rest for herself.

But by morning, Yvonne had reconsidered. She would not
fail Ian. "What do you think about while dancing?" Yvonne
asked while they were eating breakfast in Yvonne's suite.

"Think about?"

"Yes. Do you try to remember just the character and her
emotional reactions, or something out of your past?" She
watched Aisling twirl a long strand of hair around her finger.
"When Ian makes a new ballet, I try to read about the
characters or at least about the historical period. Some dancers don't do that, but try to find the role within the steps.
How do you develop the character? What do you think about
when you dance?"

Aisling wouldn't meet her eyes. "Well, usually when I
dance, you know, I think about the first step. Then, when it's
over, I think about the second step. I mean, I think constantly
about the steps and what is coming up and about my partner
and how good or bad he is." Her glance darted briefly at
Yvonne's face, then drifted to her own plate.

Yvonne had known this would not be a good day when she woke to find it bright and shining outside. She awoke early, cozy in her warm bed until she remembered Seán and his plans. She didn't want to see him, didn't want him to see her. She didn't want to be at his farm, nor to go riding, but could think of no plausible excuse. So the night before, she had hoped for rain. And she had to succeed with Aisling.

Ian had chosen Aisling and must feel her capable of dancing Eve in the Thorn manner. This pale, uninterested girl must have a core. "Maybe we should talk about this later," Yvonne hedged. "After you have gone over the steps a few times."

"Terrif!"

"What are you planning to do today?"

"Sightsee, I thought. You are going to Mr. FitzGerald's farm?"

"Unfortunately."

Aisling looked at her with curiosity. "He's a real hunk."

"I suppose so. However, he doesn't interest me. I'm taking care of some business for Maxine Andrus with Seán. There is nothing personal between us."

"Oh!" Aisling pushed away her plate. "Thank you, but I think I will go now."

"You've eaten so little."

"Can't gain any weight." She slid toward the door.

"Will we meet for dinner?"

"Let's see what gives." On that tentative note, Aisling disappeared into the hall.

How could a girl whose voice rose at the completion of every sentence become determined enough to play Eve?

How could a dancer who couldn't dance play Colette? Maybe Ian was losing his touch or his mind.

That morning when she had woken, it was too early for breakfast. Glancing around, she spied a large parcel, a gift from Ian for her trip. Knowing its contents, she had resisted opening it.

In some ways the package was a Pandora's box. Inside were promises for the future, promises for her which might prove to be taunting, elusive dreams.

Still in her nightgown, Yvonne had brought the box to her bed and slipped off the cord. Her eyes skimmed an array of books: biographies such as *Colette*, by Yvonne Mitchell, and Margaret Crosland's *A Provincial in Paris;* an annotated picture book, *Belles Saisons*, by Robert Phelps; a collection of Colette's own works, *The Vagabond, Sido, The Pure and the Impure, Gigi, Earthly Paradise*.

She felt unhappy, unsettled by the unanswered questions released from the box. Despite agreeing to come to Ireland, she wanted to remain aloof from her own work in ballet, frightened that only disappointment lay in aspiring to the role of Colette. Secretly Yvonne was convinced she would never dance again. Since arriving, she had performed a barre each day—a perfunctory, undemanding barre. Her foot had not healed.

But the feel of the books in her hands, the pictures of the writer, the clothes and settings of a bygone era, combined to stimulate her. A familiar hunger to create, not just to dance.

If she couldn't dance, other worlds might open for her. But the thought of a life without dancing horrified her, and she fought her rising terror. She would manage, would conquer her problems. She would pretend to be brave and in control.

For the present, she would teach Aisling, and try to uncover what Ian saw in the young dancer. He had entrusted her with this task, the only thing he had asked of her all these years. She would put aside her panic and would work with Aisling to prepare for Ian's visit.

And she would charm Seán FitzGerald for Maxine. Why didn't she like him? After all, he radiated charm and handsome self-confidence comparable to Gregory's.

Liam would arrive shortly after lunch. What to wear? She briefly examined the jeans before throwing them back in the suitcase. Self-respect—that was her problem. During the last painful months she had lost all her self-respect. All her self-esteem had been built on her talent in ballet and her pride in Gregory's choice of her as his wife. She was still Yvonne St. Cyr, still an accomplished and exciting woman. Eyeing herself critically in the large mirror, she saw a woman neither exciting nor glamorous. What would Gregory say? What would Maxine?

First, she painstakingly brushed her hair into a thick bun at the top of her head. She didn't want a scarecrow's tresses flowing awkwardly while she rode.

Setting out her makeup, she chose violet and gold shadows, lightly but skillfully applied, so her eyes would shimmer and dance with life and excitement. Her complexion glowed peaches and cream, thriving on the moist Irish weather. How strange to seem so well when she felt hollow inside.

Today Seán FitzGerald would meet Yvonne St. Cyr, *ballerina assoluta* and he would find nothing less. No matter how frightened she might be, she could still pretend and project the product of her imagination.

Horse riding at the farm. Another typical understatement, no doubt, like the flowers. Nothing like the casual riding in Texas with Gregory. Probably his friends wore riding outfits. Picking up a bedside copy of *Ireland of the Welcomes*, a guide magazine, she turned to a picture of the hunt. All those stiff costumes with little black hats and red jackets.

It was almost time for Liam to come, much too late to rent an outfit. She would have to make do. First, she needed jodhpurs. Luckily, pants were in style, and Maxine had included several pair in assorted styles, plus a pair of black jodhpurs. Of course, at five hundred dollars, they were never meant to be worn while clasping anything so vulgar as a horse between her knees. No, Maxine had envisioned the gabardine elegantly crossed while sitting on a velvet sofa or gracing a restaurant stool, and closer to no animal larger than a Persian cat. But they would do.

The blouse she chose, a white silk with trim long sleeves and a tiny collar, tucked nicely under a red blazer. The jacket fit neatly at the waist, flaring around her hips.

Soft leather boots added the final touch. Almost two thousand dollars on the hoof, she thought, staring at herself in the mirror, counting the white silk scarf she had added at her throat. She probably cost more than the horse, and still she trembled inside.

Car, complete with driver, appeared punctually, and Yvonne found herself almost looking forward to the afternoon. The promise of the early morning had been fulfilled in the bright, warm day. Knowing she looked well, Yvonne tried to anticipate an enjoyable afternoon. For a beginning, Seán would not get the better of her this time. Something about his handsome face stimulated her competitive spirit.

The car was warm and comfortable. Soon they moved

through the environs of the city, passed the suburbs, and entered the countryside. Although barely released from winter, the land hung a patchwork quilt of greens.

Yvonne began to relax. Animals—sheep, cattle—dotted fields barren of crops. Isolated cottages hugged the road, edged with the daffodils of spring. Ireland was a peaceful, beautiful country, far from the bustle and crowd of New York.

Eventually Liam veered off the narrow thoroughfare, following a byway for almost a mile before branching off onto a lane. Thick trees draped the path, occasionally scratching the roof of the car as they drove under the low canopy.

Suddenly the trees fell away to reveal a farm and a two-story cottage-type house bathed in soft sunlight.

The walls gleamed with fresh white plaster; the roof shone golden with thatch work. It was the perfect setting for a pastoral film, with white fencing separating narrow paths and carefully laid beds of flowers. This was more a comfortable second home of a wealthy man than a farm. Happily, Yvonne smoothed her pants and tugged her jacket into place.

Liam drove the car to the rear of the house. "Himself will be with the horses," he explained in his thick brogue.

When Yvonne climbed out of the car, Liam drove off. She looked around the yard, searching for Seán. A wedge-shaped Maserati Merak nestled against the house. Seán's other little car. A nice little forty-five-thousand-dollar sports coupé. A long white building stood before her, so she crossed the yard and entered the stable, recognizable by its pungent odor.

"There you are." Seán was grooming a large black stallion rippling with muscles and spirit. "I thought Liam had kidnapped you." Turning, he halted in awed silence, his gaze fixed on her.

"Here I am," Yvonne agreed. As she stared at him, a sinking feeling grew inside. In contrast to Seán's well-bleached pair of jeans topped with a red wool shirt, her sartorial splendor clamored for attention.

"You look . . . very nice." He shut the stall door and walked toward Yvonne, still staring. "Wouldn't the weather be beautiful?"

"Beautiful." Yvonne stood up very straight but tugged self-consciously at her jacket.

Seán seemed unable to take his eyes off her. "You liked the drive, then? You hadn't been out here in the country before, I suppose?"

"No. We never even visited Dublin in the past." A conspicuous green stain on the jeans—paint, she guessed—matched the color of a building she saw in the distance. "The countryside is so picturesque, I never thought it would look so vivid." She lowered her eyes to avoid his, and her shining boots seemed to wink mockingly at her.

Seán wore battered and unpolished work shoes. "Yes." Finally he forced his eyes away from her. "You need a cup of tea before we go riding. It's chilly today."

"And getting colder." She followed him into the back of the house, discovering a luxurious kitchen complete with a neatly dressed young woman.

"This is Jane O'Malley. She's the housekeeper."

"Nice to meet you." The brown-haired woman smiled warmly. Her eyes were wide and thickly lashed, her figure lush.

So much for the old gray-haired faithful family retainer, Yvonne thought. "And you. What a beautiful kitchen!" She looked around the well-stocked room, suitably equipped for a gourmet restaurant of intimate size.

"Isn't it?" Jane replied with evident pride.

"Do you think all this gleaming marvel could produce a simple cup of tea?" Seán asked.

"Well, then, go on with you." She hustled them out toward the large sitting room.

The room had luxurious furnishings and a captivating ambiance. Large windows built into the walls allowed the warm glow of sunshine to enter; lighted ceiling panels brightened with artificial illumination during Ireland's more usually cloudy days. There was an imposing stone fireplace centered in one wall, with a thickly cushioned sofa before it.

A secluded reading corner along one wall provided a more traditional look, with two wing chairs in a most untraditional Chinese red. Three different oriental rugs covered the wood-tiled floor, their rectangular settings defining the various conversational areas.

Nothing appeared undersized, quiet, demure. Without being restricted to tweed and brown, the room seemed masculine.

And Seán looked quite comfortable in the room, as much as the room befit him.

"This is beautiful," Yvonne approved. "The view through those windows is exquisite. Is that your land?"

"All the way to that line of trees in the distance."

"Been in the family for years?"

"No, my family doesn't come from Dublin. Galway."

"Across the country?"

"Right. The sun goes down on Galway Bay and all that. Very pretty place."

A soft tinkling rattle announced the tea tray. "How lovely." Yvonne's head started to hurt. Why was she sitting in a costume from an old English movie doing old English things?

The white china tea service had tiny blue hand-painted flowers. Next to a steaming pot of tea sat hot water, cookies, soda bread thick with raisins, raspberry jam, white bread, tiny cakes, and a covered silver tray. "Just a bite to keep you going." Jane smiled at Yvonne. "Don't let him eat too much. He's getting fat."

Jane clearly adored Seán, Yvonne thought, and with a twinge of irritation wondered about their relationship.

"Will you pour," Seán asked when Jane left, "or shall we be modern and have me do it?"

"I will. I wouldn't like to start a trend around here. How do you take your tea?"

"Milk and sugar, please."

"I can't get used to that. Milk and sugar, I mean. Makes it seem like coffee."

"In most parts of Ireland, tea is served black enough to look like coffee. I became used to a weaker blend while in Japan. Could I have a cake?"

"Certain you are allowed?"

"Jane is just the housekeeper."

"I see. Is that the latest Irish saying?"

Seán looked up in surprise, then laughed heartily. "I assure you that is all. We're cousins, actually. She's a French-trained chef, to be precise. Works normally in London for a very posh restaurant, but was in poor health this past winter, and is spending a few months here recuperating. There is little enough housekeeping to be done."

"Oh. It's not really any of my business, of course." Yvonne flushed the color of her jacket.

"I wish you would eat something. She'll be terribly hurt."

"What's on the tray?" Yvonne asked.

"My treat." He lifted the cover to reveal darkened toast. "Just the way I like it. How is Aisling?"

"It's very hard to tell."

"Don't you two get along? Same company and all."

Yvonne hesitated. "We get along, of course. She is so much younger." How tempting it felt to explain her apprehensions to Seán, as she would have to Gregory.

Seán laughed at her reply, spilling his tea. "Oh, yes, I can see that. You are such an old lady and she's just a sweet young thing."

Yvonne withdrew all intentions of confiding. He would not understand. "In terms of dancing, that sums it up well."

"I had been wondering. If you can't dance, how can you teach Aisling a role?"

Yvonne flushed. "Well, Eve isn't totally unfamiliar to her. She has seen the ballet a number of times, and has a general idea of her part. Then I tell her, show her without really dancing, just marking the steps." Her tone was wistful.

"As long as I'm being my usual tactful self . . ."

Yvonne acknowledged his comment with a faint smile.

"Are you certain you want to wear those beautiful clothes on a horse? They are dirty creatures, in truth, with rude manners."

"I thought this was the proper attire. The hunt and all."

Seán slid down in his chair, making an unpleasant face. "I don't hunt. Nasty idea, I always thought. Chasing a little creature around. Very unkind."

"You're very kind." She half-teased, half-mocked.

"Not necessarily. I like to fish." He sat up. "However, I think the scarlet coat is usually reserved for gentlemen."

"Oh, I see." Once again Yvonne felt foolish, embarrassed at her mistake.

"Do you know Oscar Wilde's description of a fox hunt?"

"No." His conversation darted faster than she could follow.

"The unspeakable in full pursuit of the uneatable."

Yvonne laughed. "I don't know what to do about my clothes. I look like the unspeakable *and* the uneatable."

"Jane and you are about the same size, I believe, and I'm certain she could lend you a pair of jeans and a sweater. Of course, I suspect you'll fill them out a bit better." With a wicked grin he left the room before she could reply. "Jane, your presence is required!"

Jane took Yvonne to an upstairs bedroom, all pink roses and sheer white drapes, then brought her jeans and two tops. "The black would be striking on you"—Jane held out one—"but also the white. I couldn't decide."

"This is very nice of you. The black, I think. These aren't good clothes, are they? I'd hate to ruin them."

"Not at all, at all." She closed the door. The jeans slipped easily over her hips with at least an inch to spare. The sweater fit, but clung so that Yvonne suspected where the difference in their measurements lay. Seán had an exacting eye.

When she met Seán in the backyard, he wordlessly admired the change, then led her toward the stable. "My horse is Othello."

"The black stallion." Yvonne acknowledged the literary allusion.

"*Very* clever."

"Ian considered doing a ballet based on *Othello*."

"At least he develops only the best themes."

"Ian is wonderful." And far away.

"And you're his most prominent ballerina. Forever and ever."

"There is no forever." Yvonne quickly changed the subject. "Someone once said that every artist should have a strong temper and a stronger temperament. When it comes to ballet, I have both."

"Sounds like Noble."

"Who is Noble?"

"The horse you're about to ride." As they passed several horses on their way to a back stall, they heard a deep snorting, followed by a whinnying cry coming from the darkened corner.

Barely concealing her dismay, Yvonne watched a large white horse prance out. "Noble?"

"Really he's quite gentle."

She stared at the large eye coolly regarding her. "Does that mean he hasn't eaten anyone lately?"

"Not for weeks."

Noble raised a hoof.

"Maybe he's hungry again."

"No, just spirited. I'll saddle him for you."

"Don't go to any trouble." She should refuse to ride, but pride would not let her. Seán was testing, she felt, waiting to see her fail again.

"None at all. Just take a minute."

In the open air of the courtyard, Noble looked smaller, at least an inch. After all, Yvonne thought, he was just a horse. Anyone who faced Justine Stelle regularly should be able to face a horse.

With Noble saddled, Seán brought out Othello, already fitted. To Yvonne, both horses appeared to breathe fire and flames when annoyed. Worse, Noble was fitted with an English saddle, both small and frail when compared to her accustomed heavy western one with its reassuring saddle horn to clutch.

"He's a good-sized horse."

"You are certain you can manage him?" Seán asked, a challenge lighting his eyes.

"Of course." Pride burnished her cheeks, and reaching for his bridle, Yvonne mounted. The fresh air apparently invigorated Noble, who tossed his head.

"Let's just explore the land."

"Lead on."

"I don't really farm here."

"I'm surprised." Yvonne clutched at the reins. "I can just picture you out on the fields, sowing and reaping."

As Seán directed his horse beside hers, Yvonne couldn't help but notice the attractive way his hair ruffled in the wind. Out of a suit, his shoulders revealed broader lines, less delicate good looks. Embarrassed by her heightened attraction to him, Yvonne abruptly turned her horse. Noble either disliked the maneuver or misunderstood, and with a leap he reared into the air, then bolted across the fields. With a scream, Yvonne tightened her knees, trying to stay on. If they hadn't approached the stile, she might have.

23

When Maxine saw Fleming, she still floated from her latest fashion showing.

Fleming's arms encircled her. "I like this dress." They stood on a balcony overlooking the park.

"The color?" Maxine preened.

"That is beautiful." The gown's hue called to mind the ocean along the Florida coast being ruffled by the March winds—blues and greens kissed with white. Fleming drew her close and kissed her neck.

"The shape?" Part of her new collection, the dress swept from a low neck, skimming her waist, and flared into waves around her feet. Constantly shimmering and moving.

"Since it fits yours, the shape is entrancing."

"The design?"

"I'm certain your collection will sweep the country." Fleming's low laugh sent a familiar thrill through her stomach.

"I haven't found what you like best?"

"No."

Maxine swirled in his arms, turning so she faced him. "If not the color, shape, or design, then what is it?"

"The touch, the feel." He fingered the light, gossamer material. "Soft as a woman's thigh."

Maxine flushed with pleasure. "Not just any woman's, I hope?"

"Only the most special." He gestured back to the party. "Want to join them?"

"Not really."

"Want to join me for a bite to eat, then home?"

174

"Whose home?" Maxine fought the mushy feeling that spread through her at the sight of his half-smile, the sound of his gravelly voice, the touch of his firm hand. Next she would be blushing and swooning at the sight of him.

"I've wanted to talk to you about that. Wouldn't it be easier to let one of them go?"

"Go where?" she joked, as expected.

Unexpectedly he pressed the point. "You know what I mean."

Maxine wasn't certain she did. She had never lived with a man. Her career overflowed from her two offices, spread through her personal life, dribbled through her apartment. Models, Kili, Yvonne, manufacturers, Melvin—all were free to roam at will. "You wouldn't want to compromise me, would you?"

"Actually"—Fleming kissed her hand—"I was proposing."

Maxine stared. "Proposing what?"

"Marriage. What else?"

Maxine raised an eyebrow. "I've known other things to be proposed."

"Maxine." Fleming moved slightly away and looked over the balcony, until his eyes rested on the passing cars far below. "Have I mistaken your feelings? I know we haven't known each other long. And I don't go around proposing to women in droves. It isn't one of my vices."

"That's a good thing. Could lead to bigamy."

"I love you."

Maxine clasped her hands, unclasped her hands, moved to the rail, then away, took a deep breath, then slowly released it. There it was. A suitable, serious man—no tennis pro or half-baked playboy—loved her. Maxine Andrus. The woman who had long ago decided to settle for a brilliant career and satisfactory sex life. Now she was loved and wanted. Dizziness swept her; a ringing filled her ears.

Love. Maxine had never taken it seriously. Not for herself. Love at first sight, regret at second—another of Maxine's Maxims. Wasn't this almost first sight?

The silence grew. Finding the right words to express her fear and apprehension proved difficult. "Fleming." Her voice sounded strained and hoarse. "Fleming . . ." Must collect myself, she thought. "I would love to marry you." Surprise choked her, but as she swung across the abyss, Maxine instantly knew it was true.

"Then you will marry me?" Fleming was laughing, hugging and kissing her, all at once. "I wasn't sure you would. All I could think of was the Duke of Westminster proposing to Chanel. She refused, saying that there were any number of Duchesses of Westminster, but only one Mademoiselle Chanel. There is only one Maxine, but I was hoping you could share part of her with me."

"There's one thing."

"Anything." He was incandescent with pleasure.

"I don't want it announced yet."

Fleming moved a step away. "Why not?"

"Please understand. It's Yvonne. She's unsettled and lost right now. Once she's certain of the fashion career, she will understand, but not now."

He looked over the city. "A month. I'll give you a month. But I can't do without you any longer than that." Drawing her close again, he kissed her.

Maxine settled happily in his arms. She had found a new maxim: Romance is a fool's name for fate.

The transatlantic line cracked and snapped. "How are you?" Maxine sounded like she was underwater.

"All right."

"What?"

"All right," Yvonne yelled. "I hit my head."

"You fit what?"

"Hit, hit. Hit my head."

"How? What happened?"

"I fell off a horse."

"This line is impossible, Yvonne. I thought you said horse. Who hit you?"

"Seán's horse."

"Seán hit you?" Her shriek carried nicely through.

"No, the horse."

"You did say horse."

"I fell off."

"I see. Yvonne, have you been working too hard?"

"No, I was just riding with Seán and I fell off the horse and I'm fine. More or less."

"You don't sound fine. You sound very strange."

"It's the phone."

"Maybe."

"What's happening in New York?"

"Madame's on . . ." The line crackled, Maxine's voice grew faint.

Madame's on the stage? Yvonne pictured the wizened form in leotard and tights twirling onstage. "Madame's in a rage," Yvonne guessed. That sounded very possible. "What about? What is she mad about?"

"No, onstage. With Tor N. Curtain. I'll send the pictures. You'll never believe it without them." Maxine's voice grew fainter.

"We might as well give up. The connection is terrible. Is there anything else you want to tell me?"

"I just wanted you . . . love . . ." Maxine said.

"What?"

"Later . . . Seán . . ." Static ended the call.

Yvonne stared with dismay at the phone as she replaced the receiver. Maxine was much more serious about Seán than she had dreamed. Why did that leave her feeling so upset?

She remembered opening her eyes, seeing the sky, and gradually noticing its surrealistic location was due to her own strange position flat on the ground. Seán had dismounted and run to her side, his worried face joined almost immediately by Noble's large white head. "Are you all right?"

"All right is a relative position. I don't know if this qualifies."

Seán waved the horse back. "Maybe I should get a doctor."

Noble pawed the ground and whinnied with what Yvonne knew signified jubilant success. "Don't gloat!" she yelled at the horse.

Seán looked worried. "You shouldn't move until I get help."

"The horse," she said.

"Noble is yards away. He's all right." He might have been soothing a child. "He won't hurt you."

Yvonne started giggling at Seán's tone. "Stop looking at me like that. I'm fine."

"You're sure?" Seán remained unconvinced.

"I'll sit up and relax for a minute, then we can continue."

"I'm so sorry." He sat beside her on the grass. "Noble is frisky, but he hasn't done that before. Leaped right over the stile. Too bad it was without you."

"Yes, and I don't believe it was an accident." Yvonne finally sat up, then tried to rise. Seán put a supportive arm around her. She felt the power of his strength. "Thank you, I'm okay." She moved uneasily away, strangely affected by his touch.

"Certain?"

"Perfectly. Shall we continue?" Her arm was sore, her back bruised, but she refused to let him or the horse know about either.

Seán looked at her admiringly. "You have lots of spunk," he admitted.

Carefully placing her foot in the stirrup and swinging gracefully over the animal, Yvonne remounted her horse and guided him toward the drive. "Do you have beautiful sunsets here?"

"Only in the evening."

She smiled. "Do you know we've talked only a little about shoes." Yvonne wondered if the fall had disarranged her hair.

"I didn't want to interrupt your ballet business too much."

"What exactly did Maxine have in mind?"

"Glamorous shoes to match a line of evening wear. Also decorated beaded evening shoes. Would you like to see samples?"

"Of course, whenever it's convenient for you and I can get away from the ballet."

"Where would you like to go for dinner?"

"I didn't know we were dining," Yvonne pointed out.

"It's the least I can do after my horse attacked you."

There was no reason to go out with him, and it would be easy enough to plead a previous engagement. "All right," Yvonne found herself saying. How could yes and no change so rapidly in her mind?

"I'll take you by the hotel so you can change."

"Not a jeans-and-sweater place we're going to?"

"Not even hunting scarlet."

Seán looked admiringly at Yvonne as she came downstairs. "Hunting scarlet of another kind?"

"Oh, yes. Most definitely." Her hair loosened in black waves around her shoulders, Yvonne had chosen a long red dress, cashmere of bias cut so it swirled out from her waist. From high neck to hem, the front fastened with tiny pearl buttons. It was not a haphazard choice. She had wanted to impress him.

"While that dress might not capture a fox, the male hunters would gather in a pack."

"Maxine is so talented."

"Not exactly what I meant. How did you two meet? Well-known women-around-town?" He ushered her out to the car.

"No, we were in boarding school together."

"You two were exceptions, then. School friendships often disintegrate."

"We were both orphans, more or less, and we clung together. To our mutual benefit, I admit."

"Perhaps not the happiest of memories for you. I'll try to be tactful and change the subject."

"Where are we dining?"

"Just down the street to the Royal Hibernian Hotel—their Lafayette Restaurant. Superb French food."

They drove the short distance through a light rain. "Changeable climate."

"One of the kindest things to be said of Irish weather, I'm afraid."

When they arrived, he helped her out, and through the blue-gray facade of the Hibernian. The lobby, topped with a domed skylight, spread white and spacious. "This was once the Dublin terminal for stagecoaches."

At the door to the Lafayette Yvonne stopped in admiration. "Beautiful. I assume they didn't park the horses here."

Decorated in Georgian style, the room displayed regal elegance. Scarlet plush flooded the floors; crystal chandeliers flowed from the ceiling; gold-crusted mirrors splashed the walls with the shimmering motion of reflected light. Muted lights kissed gleaming silver, shining china, shimmering crystal.

Silent and impeccable service completed the atmosphere of continental elegance. Yvonne chose *brochette de fruits de mer*, while Seán asked for *noisettes* of lamb, and ordered a delicious wine. Yvonne pointed out an elegant passing gown; Seán indicated a famous actor entering with a party. They looked at each other and wondered what to say, the easy chiding of the afternoon suddenly buried deep under something else.

Dinner arrived. "I know!" Seán said. "Champagne. We will celebrate your safe escape with champagne." The first wine disappeared, replaced with a chilled silver bucket and an inviting green bottle.

"Very nice." Yvonne quickly drank a glass, thankful for the warm glow from the tickling drink.

Seán spoke of the farm, then asked Yvonne about the season in New York. "Do you miss dancing?"

"Yes."

"I suppose it is an adjustment."

How cool he sounded. "I don't know what to do with myself, really."

"There are the shoes. Working for Maxine."

"I hardly think my inspecting your shoes is of earth-shaking importance to Maxine. I'm afraid it was charity on her part. Your shoes are probably already firmly established in her line." She smiled wanly. "See, you don't have to take me out to dinner."

"This isn't entirely business. You need to find something to make you happy."

"Coco Chanel said that happiness consists of bringing one's thoughts to realization."

"Not bad advice."

"Not very useful. I no longer know my own thoughts."

Seán refilled her crystal tulip. "Only the shallow really know themselves."

Yvonne laughed. "You're quite cynical, aren't you?"

"Always glad to entertain," Seán covered. "By the way, would you like me to send your meal back?"

"Why would you do that?"

"You aren't eating it."

"I am." Yvonne felt defensive. Not since the death of her baby had she been able to eat with any enjoyment.

"You never eat! You transfer a small portion of food to another place on the plate, spread it around so it looks larger. Occasionally you take the fork touched with food to your lips, and fake chewing. You don't eat. I don't think you appreciate good food."

"You eat burned toast!" She changed the subject quickly.

"Not burnt, just well done. Besides, the carbon is good for you."

"I eat plenty. I don't want to get fat."

"Not much chance."

The atmosphere was charged. "No dessert, thank you," she said.

They finished their meal in near-silence. Outside, Seán suddenly smiled and nodded. From around the corner the clip-clop of horse's hooves approached. A black turn-of-the-century hansom cab drove into view and halted at the curb near Yvonne. Perched high above the street, the driver had a thick rug wrapped around his legs, and a long thin whip in his right hand. "I thought it would be a historical way to see the city," he said.

The rain had ceased as they drove through the nearly deserted streets. "Anyplace special you would like to go?"

Yvonne peered out from the window of the high cab and shook her head. "No, this is wonderful." She smiled. "You have my thanks. All is forgiven. Almost."

As the night cleared, a full moon glowed purple through a cloud, then broke out into clear white light. Pools of water glistened in the street, cracking into drops of liquid moonlight as the cab passed. Muffled figures moved along the paths; soft voices flowed out from pubs, blending with Gaelic music; the past claimed victory over the present.

In other circumstances, in other times, and with another man, it would be a romantic setting, Yvonne thought. The anniversary of Gregory's death drew near. An entire year without him, but a year not without its longings for a special person in her life.

"I expect to see Oscar Wilde popping along, or maybe William Butler Yeats. What atmosphere!"

"Dublin seems lost in time?"

"Yes, I like that. But what about you, though? How did a scholar and passionate reader of Wilde end up peddling shoes and tweed? Handed down in the family?"

"Yoked around my neck would be more accurate."

Yvonne was surprised. "I thought your father waxed active and industrious."

"He did. But like a new moon, all was dark. The family had a cloth business—grandfather's, in truth."

"Did you know him?"

"No, by the time I came, the business was almost sunk. Father had become bored and had moved into shoes. Shoes didn't work either. But he developed an interest in horses, breeding."

"How did they do?"

"They didn't. Breed, I mean. I learned to ride well, though."

"What next?" Yvonne found herself fascinated.

"The farm. Not the one we visited, another one that failed. Then the winery."

"With sour grapes."

"Right. You can see the unbroken line of family success. I don't want you to misunderstand. He was charming. Everyone liked Father, he just wasn't very practical."

"You are certainly doing well."

"Thank you. But live long enough, and disaster is bound to strike."

What did Seán know of disaster? "Why didn't you go into teaching?" Yvonne asked.

"Money, or rather, lack of it. Father had muddled along for years. Grandfather, a good businessman, had left enough money so it took Father some time to lose it all. But he did, then died without knowing we were broke."

"How old were you then?"

"In Trinity, my second year."

"You were fortunate to finish."

"I didn't, really. Had plans for postgraduate work. But I had Mother to care for and couldn't stay for my graduate degree."

"That must have been hard for you." Admiration rose in Yvonne.

"It was." He settled an inch closer. "Maybe for the best. I

discovered this disgustingly normal ability to succeed in business. I had always pictured myself as the misunderstood thinker and scholar, of course, as does three-quarters of everyone under the age of twenty-one, I suppose. Anyway, work is the refuge of people who have nothing better to do, so perhaps it was just as well.''

Yvonne was touched by Seán's serious tone and unexpected disclosures. Neither as privileged nor as superficial as she had first thought, he had a charm and attraction that were growing with every meeting. Not that she had time for an attractive man. Deliberately she changed the subject.

''Why is that bridge called the Halfpenny?'' Yvonne pointed across Seán to a wide footbridge she'd crossed earlier in the day.

''They once charged a toll. A halfpenny.'' Seán's eyes looked deeply into hers.

She noticed his high cheekbones and firm chin, how light flickered across his face as the carriage moved past streetlights and back into the darkness.

Yvonne realized how very close they were, her fingers touching his arm, which rested on the window. A vaguely masculine scent of cigarette smoke, after-shave, and champagne curled around her. He wore a plain but obviously expensive black suit and white oxford shirt. He continued to hold her gaze, then dropped his eyes to her lips.

For shared seconds Yvonne wanted to forget the past and pretend that only the present existed. She yearned for a man's scent, a man's embrace, and only inches away Seán hovered, waiting for . . . her? For long, lingering moments she thought he meant to kiss her; then panic swept her. No, she couldn't allow herself to feel passion, nor did she wish to inspire any.

With a shudder, she pulled back. ''It's getting late.'' Her tone was brisk.

Seán reached into his jacket and took out a gold cigarette case. Moistening his lips, he took out a cigarette, put it in his mouth, lit it. A small red-orange glow dotted the cab, followed by clouds of smoke.

''Well, have you been practicing for Colette?'' Seán finally asked.

''Not really.''

''Then you won't know if you can dance or not!''

"My foot and leg still hurt."

"That could be a problem." How cool he sounded.

Dammit, she wanted some sympathy. Deserved some. "It is." She tried to sound brave, unwilling to plead for his attention or concern.

"Have you seen a doctor here?"

"No."

"Why not?"

"I'm tired of doctors."

"They are boring, I admit, as is illness, but you should see one, then you can make a decision about your future." How simple and rational he made it sound. "From what you've said, you were doing very well until the second injury. The first doctor had thought you would never dance again."

"Maybe he was right, after all."

"Maybe Ian was right and you overdid it."

"Thank you. It's nice to know you have my life all figured out." She glanced at him. Why was it she always noticed how handsome he was? It made her angry and discomfited.

"I don't have anything figured out. I'm only trying to help. Listen, how about an invigorating walk along the strand—the beach?"

The beach shone with magic if not enough moonlight. Only tiny atoms of silver light touched the waves and disappeared in the white foam dancing along the water. A breeze billowed Yvonne's dress as Seán assisted her from the taxi he had hailed.

"You won't be cold?" he asked.

"No."

"Your shoes will be all right in the sand?"

"Fine. They're flat-heeled."

"Good! As a boy I often visited the seashore. We lived in Galway then. My mother still does. I would walk along the shore, listening to the waves. My mother is Síle Burns."

"She remarried after your father died?"

"I don't think so."

"What do you mean, you don't think so?"

"Mother is so independent, I'd probably be one of the last to know. Our names aren't the same because Mother is the well-known poet. She uses her miaden name." He spelled

"Síle." "The name is Gaelic and is pronounced like 'Sheila.' "

"I see." She had vaguely recognized the name.

Along the shore they walked, Yvonne's beauty taking on a new, softer quality in the hazy moonlight. Seán reached out as if to help her through the sand, then continued to hold her hand. They talked about Aisling's reluctant ambition and Yvonne's problems reaching her.

"You don't fully appreciate Aisling's youth, innocence, and inexperience," Seán said after listening to Yvonne. "Your own brilliance dictated a different path, a sparkling road to success, but Aisling's passage has twisted and turned with uncertainty. No wonder she finds you intimidating and the choices suddenly presented to her bewildering."

"She isn't all that young, Seán. She should know her mind!" Yvonne knew she was being hard, but the unfairness of his pity for Aisling overcame her. The young dancer had everything before her—dancing, success, romance. For herself, all was finished.

"But think of yourself, Yvonne. You said over dinner you didn't know *your* own mind."

"You're so calm, so cool, so passionless, Seán FitzGerald!" But she smiled. He was right. She was too busy feeling sorry for herself to understand Aisling.

"Calm, cool, passionless, am I? No one has ever called me cold. I don't like to brag, but by reputation I am charming, warm, and friendly."

"Modest. You forgot modest." Then she halted at the water's edge, gazing dramatically over the windblown expanse, ignoring him. He came up beside her and quietly asked, "What do you want, anyway?"

"I don't know what you mean." Yvonne started at his serious tone.

"For a start, do you want to be treated like a woman or a business associate?"

Yvonne turned toward him. "I didn't know they were exclusive."

"They aren't, necessarily. But on the ride in the hansom . . ."

Yvonne started walking along the beach. Suddenly Seán strode to her side, a bemused expression on his face and heat in his voice. "Cool?" Swinging her around to face him, he pulled her close, kissing her ardently. Her lips were momentarily soft beneath his, her body yielding and warm, taken by surprise. But then she pulled away.

"I don't make a point of forcing myself on women."

"Well . . . I . . ." Yvonne could think of nothing indignant enough to say. Her hair, windblown and sea-beaded, haloed her head. Tears of sea sprayed her cheeks. The impression of his lips still lingered pleasantly on hers.

"I'm very sorry," he said, but he didn't sound sorry at all. "I'll just take a walk into the sea to atone." He whirled and started blindly away, walking directly into the water. "Damn!" He lifted one Italian-leather-clad foot, then another. Water dribbled out, and an ambitious wave reached his knees. "Damn, damn, damn!"

Yvonne soon couldn't stop herself from giggling. "Your shoes will be ruined. Your trousers are all wet. Come out. Come out. I don't really think a kiss is worth dying for."

"That depends, doesn't it, on who the kiss is from? Shall we continue the walk, then?"

"In your . . . condition?"

"Sophisticated people overlook little annoyances."

"I see. Let's walk, then."

"Now . . ." Seán gestured toward the water. "Isn't this nice?"

"Yes, it is. I'm sorry about what I said." Yvonne knew she had not been rational about Seán. He aroused emotions in her, feelings that made her cheeks burn and her pulse race. She attempted to ignore them.

"Perfectly all right. Let's not discuss it now. This evening has been exhausting enough. I have a favor to ask."

"I certainly owe you one." She laughed.

"It's my mother. She is quite a balletomane and would love to meet you, if possible. Perhaps if you had time, we could drive to Galway and spend the night. She doesn't come to Dublin much. You should see other places besides the capital."

"I don't know."

"Mother is very interesting. She would never forgive me if I knew you and didn't bring you over."

"I would hate to come between a man and his mother." The visit seemed quite appealing.

Seán captured both her hands. "You are a lovely woman."

They stood facing each other, close enough to see each other clearly through the darkness. "I don't understand about Aisling and this evening. I was only trying to help you. I thought if you understood how she felt about ballet, you might find a way for her to understand Eve."

"I know. I can be very difficult. This has not been a good year, and I've become accustomed to feeling sorry for myself." A small tremor of hurt crept into her voice.

"I have a wonderful idea."

"Really?" She reclaimed one hand.

"Yes, we're going to pretend this evening didn't happen." He firmly took her hand back.

"If none of this happened, what is that squish-squish noise when you walk?"

"My heart beating loudly for you. You look sensually delicious in that dress. Especially with your alabaster skin."

"Thank you." Yvonne smiled slightly. "I don't think of myself as sensual-looking, though. I'm more romantic, if anything."

"You are both." Gradually he drew her close. "You look like a ballerina right now, only not so haughty."

"Ballerinas look haughty?"

"Yes. It is something in the way they hold their noses." Gently he kissed her on the end of her nose.

Yvonne knew she should move away, but she was mesmerized by Seán's eyes, enormous and deep blue in the dim light. He radiated a masculine warmth and security as the sea pounded coldly behind her and the wind swirled around them—protection amid her crumbling world.

Slowly he drew her lips toward his, trembling slightly with self-control, fighting his desire to crush her in sudden passion. A long kiss later, he released her a few inches and gazed into her eyes. "I've never seen violet eyes before. They're the color of thunderclouds moving over the bay during a storm. Or the first flowers of spring." He drew her close again and kissed her with more hunger.

Tightly they pressed together, and Yvonne could feel his strength and his desire bearing into her. For a moment she fought with herself, remembering her loyalty to Gregory, her feelings for Maxine, but the magic of the moment won.

He whispered her name, exploring her face and neck with his lips. Beneath her fingers she felt the warmth of his body, the pull of his muscles. Seán was so strong, so masculine, it swept her breath away.

Minutes lengthened into eternity. The world transformed into manly essence, naked desire. Yvonne refused to remember any other time, any other life, any other loyalties than to herself and to the moment.

Around them the sea murmured of love and creation, the wind whispered the secrets of life. The entire universe conspired to protect and shelter them.

Gradually the first rush of passion halted. Yvonne and Seán looked at each other in suspended silence. Now either they continued forward in headlong flight or drew back from the cliff's edge.

"Let's go back to the hotel," Seán said.

Passion mixed with guilt, moonlight with fear, all in a confusing but stirring mixture. As the taxi sped toward the hotel, she painfully felt his body only inches from hers, sensual and strong. It had been so long since she had felt anything for any man.

Suddenly Yvonne found herself in a sea of pleasure and remorse, the murmur of ecstasy washed away in waves of guilt and disgust. How could she have allowed Seán to kiss her? Worse, how could she have kissed him as she did? Passion and desire had swept over her, just like waves lapping on the shore.

Her desire she could accept. Even through her depression and pain of the last months there lurked a trace of sexual desire, the need for closeness. Yvonne understood her emotions were nothing to be ashamed of. At twenty-six, she couldn't expect to give up her sensual self or pretend her nature was virginal. It all had been a physical reaction, a temporary betrayal of her body. How could any man compare with Gregory? The idea cried treason.

Nor was it merely a matter of loyalty to Gregory. Yvonne had every reason to believe that Maxine was interested in Seán.

She refused to be maudlin. She knew Maxine well. Curiosity about Seán might evaporate overnight; or, more likely, over a drink with a handsome new man. Maxine showed little desire to settle down, and should Yvonne display attention to Seán, Maxine would disappear from the scene with a happy smile. No man could ever come between them.

But there was a chance. A chance that this might be a man who could capture Maxine's heart, the man with whom she would settle down, the man, in romantic truth, Maxine had always been waiting for. With his sense of humor, his charm, his masculine attractiveness, Seán might be the man. Yvonne tried not to linger on his attributes.

She would not stand in Maxine's way.

To Seán's surprise, Yvonne bid him good night at the door.

24

In New York, Justine Stelle and Ian Thorn were deep in conversation about the progress of *Ballet of Desire*.

"Ian, time is passing," Justine said with an edge to her voice. "Questions are being asked."

"Questions?"

"In the magazines. In other . . . high places. Really, Ian, don't you keep up with things?"

"I do try, but I've been busy here. Whatever it is, the storm will pass, Justine. You're old enough to know that."

"I'm also old enough not to be taken in by your charm, Ian. What is happening?"

"Well, I was working with the corps yesterday. It's falling into place."

"A ballet doesn't feature its corps, not this company, at least. We need excitement, glamour, an event. We need a brilliant ballerina. What about her?"

"We have the preeminent dancer of this century. I will use Yvonne for the soloist."

"Yvonne is a memory. *Yvonne isn't dancing.*"

Ian carefully kept his annoyance from his voice. "Yvonne isn't dancing *yet*. She will be."

"Maybe. It can't be someday, however, it must be soon. I want you to visit Ireland next week. See how Aisling is doing. Make certain dear Yvonne is recovering. Work on Colette. I would like to show a few of the Friends a solo from Colette, a hint of what's to come. I have your flight booked, your tickets are ready. Tuesday you leave."

"Tuesday?" Ian uncomfortably heard the clank of one metal finger. "Isn't that rather hurried?"

"If Yvonne can't dance, she can't. We might as well know now."

"And if not?"

"If not, we have Aisling."

"She isn't the star Yvonne is."

"No, she isn't. Not yet. Maybe, in the long run, she never will be. But for one season she can be. For one performance with enough advance publicity, she will be. But of course, if the dance isn't going well, if you won't have a scene . . ." Crash, the iron fist hit the table.

"There is nothing wrong with the ballet," Ian flared.

"Of course not, Ian. I would so hate to have to use a new ballet by Tor N. Curtain. I understand he and Madame are up to something."

"Curtain is not a ballet choreographer. Just a mere flash in the night over the show-business sky."

"Of course, Ian. Of course. Where is your sense of humor?"

"All right, Justine. You win. I'll see Yvonne."

Pleased, Justine smoothed her skirt and left the room.

"Today we'll start by blocking out your role without a partner," Yvonne said to Aisling. They had arrived early at the studio, Yvonne wishing to avoid Seán.

"Fine." Dressed in a well-mended purple leotard and tights, Aisling positioned herself at the barre for a warm-up. Yvonne had chosen to play a tape instead of using a pianist. "At least there won't be a witness," Aisling murmured to herself.

A half-hour later and the warm-up completed, they were ready to begin Eve. "What now?" Aisling asked.

"Let's start at the beginning."

"An original idea."

Yvonne glanced sharply at her but said nothing. "You know the first scene, of course. Center stage, Honoré de Balzac is in Paris, carrying on. Try to imagine the setting." In her imagination, Yvonne saw Ian's staging.

She remembered the group scene blazed with harsh color as women in low-cut dresses lavishly entertained the writer and his friends, harsh yellow and red lights glittering on the stage. "To the side is Evelina Hanski. You."

"Me?" Aisling's voice whispered.

"Here." Yvonne pointed. "You are lying on a white bear-skin hearth rug before a log fire when the curtains open. The fire burns brightly with yellow and gold flames."

"That is a good effect, isn't it?" Aisling sat up.

"Lie back in place. Don't think of it as an effect. There is a fire. Despite the flames, your side of the stage glows with cool blue-white lights, a moonlike illumination."

"I've never clearly understood." Aisling closed her eyes, as if picturing the scene. "Is this setting showing action in both Paris and Russia, or is the Paris scene Eve's imagination?"

"That is up to you." Yvonne smiled. "Ian never would say." For once it was pleasant not to be the one struggling with interpretation.

"He wouldn't!" Aisling muttered. "What did you think?"

Yvonne tucked back a strand of hair. "It's probably better," she eventually replied, "if I don't tell you. At least not right away. You have to decide for yourself. The first solo, for instance, do you see Paris, or do you not? Are you thinking of the famous . . . infamous Balzac yet, or dreaming other dreams?"

Aisling twirled her hair and wrinkled her forehead. "What does it matter?" Her hand tapped nervously. "I mean, a turn follows a leap which precedes a *brisé*. Ian's ballets are always a series of difficult if not impossible steps. That's enough to think about."

"Most superficial. Emotional expression, psychological understanding, and personal projection are the cement and mortar holding a performance together. The steps are just the building blocks of a role."

Aisling assumed a brooding air, as if darkly considering her approach to the role, while Yvonne turned on the tape recorder. "I'll think about it."

"Good. Now, let's see you walk through the first solo. Just to make sure you have all the steps."

"Fine." When the music began, so did she. Some sections she marked, showing she knew the steps, other parts she danced full out.

When the sound died, she looked at her feet, unable to

neet Yvonne's eyes, as if unwilling to read an immediate evaluation.

"Not bad." Yvonne joined her. "On the second turn, I think you'll find it will work better if you delay a beat longer."

"I won't come in late?"

"No. Almost, but no. It's a trick in Ian's style. Often there are tiny periods of rest, of preparation that you don't hear at first in the music. I think it's part of the sensual feel."

"A beat longer." Aisling hummed the music, turning and then repeating the turn till she had a feel for the timing.

"Now, this section"—Yvonne hummed—"is a series of *brisés*, not *entrechats*."

Aisling copied her. "Like that?"

"Fine."

"And my hands in this part?" The corrections continued, as remembered steps became choreographed ones.

"Now." Yvonne again moved next to Aisling, sinking gracefully to the floor. She motioned for Aisling to join her. "Who are you?"

Aisling finally sensed that this inquiry referred not to Aisling, ballet dancer, but to Eve. "I'm Eve Hanski, an exiled Polish countess living in Russia."

"Happily?"

"No. I'm bored. I fall in love with a famous novelist through reading his works, write to him, and eventually marry him."

"True." All this amounted to little more than program notes. Instead of voicing her thoughts, Yvonne hazily recalled her original talks with Ian. In repeated performances over the years, she had modified the role of Eve, molding and expanding it to accommodate new insights, adding her love for Gregory, her friendship with Maxine. But Yvonne's insights could not be Aisling's. Together Yvonne and Aisling must rediscover the original character Ian had devised, and Aisling must breathe her own visions into her. "Who are you when the curtain comes up?"

"I've never worked through a role in this way. Let's see. The synopsis said I'm living on an estate."

Pulling up her large carry-all, Yvonne searched and found faded notes. "When I work with Ian, I go home and write down everything he said that I can remember.'' She referred to the pages. ''You are living—in Ian's words—in oriental splendor on a fifty-two-thousand-acre estate. More than three thousand servants wait on you.'' Yvonne laughed. ''How does that all make you feel?''

''Strange, I guess.''

''Try 'important.' 'Royal.' ''

''I'll try.''

''Your home, standing in an ornamental park, is exquisitely designed by an imported French architect. A setting for a princess. A lonely princess. The oriental opulence is isolated splendor.''

Aisling wiggled nervously. ''It seems to me she could have been happy.''

''*You* aren't,'' Yvonne reproached. Aisling couldn't just dance Eve, she had to become the young woman. ''You were married at seventeen to a man twenty-seven years your senior. He's morose and silent, has nothing in common with you. The nearest large town is Kiev, more than one hundred snowbound miles away. You try motherhood, bearing five children, but lose all but the last.''

Aisling closed her eyes to concentrate. ''At seventeen, Eve had married. God, that's just two years younger than me.'' She looked stricken. ''I'm married to a man of forty-four, and have four dead children.'' Aisling giggled nervously. ''Impossible! I can't do it, Yvonne. I'll just do the steps, please, learn the foot and hand positions, and do what I'm told. All this thinking is wasteful.''

Yvonne sighed. ''You aren't trying!''

''Maybe if I think about it.''

''Why don't you try the solo again. I'll start the music.''

This time Aisling danced full out, projecting with her talent and body that which she couldn't produce through her emotions. Yvonne watched closely.

Fast and high in her technique, Aisling leaped effortlessly through the air, barely touching down before soaring again. Aisling's movements could be leaner, her landings more exactly in place, her positioning more precise, but the general effect, Yvonne decided, was of exquisite grace.

Yvonne felt torn by envy and fear. She had never been

jealous of another dancer, never had reason to be. Now the feeling caught at her throat.

The music ended; Aisling stood still and waited. Yvonne acknowledged her technical expertise, but also the lack of emotional involvement. To Aisling dance was a series of physical actions strung together like shining silver beads, but to please Ian, her dancing needed the mysterious depth of opals.

"Very nice. It's getting late." Yvonne rose from her vantage point on the floor. "Why don't you go back to the hotel now and get some rest. Stay warm! Have something to eat!"

"Yes. You aren't coming?"

"Not now. I have to work out."

Aisling looked quizzically at Yvonne but said nothing. Yvonne had not practiced alone in the studio since arriving.

Work out. Once Aisling left, the room seemed suddenly chilly. Yvonne pulled on a heavy pair of leg warmers. Another loose sweater added warmth, but drafts still crept under the door. The cold, or nerves?

Yvonne looked around the room. Mirrored walls, as usual, wooden floor, as usual, barre along the wall, as usual. She could have been in New York, London, Tokyo, or Peking. This was the constant in her trade—wood, mirror, rosin. Maybe it would bring her luck.

Demi-plié, plié in the first position as her muscles complained, *demi-plié, plié* in second position. She had to find out sometime. She had to know if she would dance again. Through the barre she worked, finally warming as her body responded to the exercise.

In a burst of ambitious hope, she moved to the center of the room and tried a cautious *pirouette*. With a gasp, she froze as pain shot through her leg.

Failure caught in her throat, a conviction that she would never build up the stamina needed for a performance. The memory of her last humiliating attempt rose before her. Unless she could dance for at least two hours, she would never be strong enough to survive a performance. Dancers had to dance.

Aisling had danced—soared, floated, wafted as if on a cushion of air. Yvonne, on the other hand, had no beginning. No beginning, no future, no hope, no dreams, all negatives piling around her, dragging her legs, pulling her to the floor till she collapsed in anguished tears. The sweet unconcern with which Aisling did the undoable, that oblivious ease Yvonne had once possessed, proclaimed the present reality— her career was in ruins, her life along with it.

What would she do? A burst of rain hit the window of the room. Ireland seemed gray and cold and unfriendly—a prison for the next weeks. And she its prisoner, caught because there was nowhere she could flee.

A week passed, a witch's blend of tears and laughter, early-morning lessons and late-night parties, austere studios and luxurious homes. From her isolation, Yvonne had again started seeing the entertaining Seán. He seemed more and more infatuated with her. The days flew by, though Yvonne did not know if she felt bewitched or cursed.

Seán never mentioned the beach or her kisses, an omission for which Yvonne was thankful. She had been silly to think a moonlit night would mean anything to such an experienced man.

Aisling's progress remained all in her feet and legs, never progressing to her heart or mind. Full of ambiguous emotions, Yvonne acknowledged the young dancer's technical delight and stylistic expertise. But Aisling would not—or could not— delve beneath the surface of her role.

"Have you tried to talk with her?" Seán asked when Yvonne complained.

"Talk's all I do, but she just won't see. Or doesn't want to."

"Why not?"

Yvonne bristled at his tone of quiet reason. "I don't know. Aisling is a professional dancer. She should be able to adapt herself to Ian's needs, even if channeled through a third party."

"If you knew, you might find it easier to get her to change. Good management, you know."

If her mornings were tedious, broken only by Aisling's tears, her afternoons and evenings were kissed by sunlight and moonlight and stars. Quickly she learned of Seán's prominence in the financial and social life of Dublin. He was a leader in his own quiet way. His position was never publicized;

however, those who knew mattered, those who mattered knew.

They visited the shoe factory, where women worked by hand and machine on a narrow range of styles. Yvonne took an interest in each detail.

"What would you like to see now?" Seán asked. "I have sketches to send Maxine. Why don't you look at them and give me your opinion."

Two dozen drawings of shoes littered the desk: half to be executed in leather and half to be jeweled and gilded. "I like this especially." Yvonne fingered a simple leather shoe in an art-nouveau design.

"What about these?" Seán asked about a group with leather frills and cutouts.

"They remind me of something Maxine once said, 'The next time you are tempted to add just one more necklace, remember: excess should never be mistaken for style.' "

"Oh."

"Yes. But we'll send all these sketches to Maxine and see what she thinks."

"Actually, I rather liked those. I thought they looked sprightly."

"Fussy."

"As Oscar Wilde would say, I don't like arguments of any kind. They are always vulgar and often convincing."

Yvonne tapped the pictures. "These are always vulgar but never convincing."

Far from taking offense, Seán regarded her with apparent admiration.

Much to her chagrin, Yvonne came to enjoy herself when with Seán. Except when working with Aisling, she stopped thinking of her hazy future or of ballet. Life flew and dipped, and she with it.

How much of her pleasure was due to Seán?

Yvonne didn't want to think about that.

25

___

Yvonne fingered Ian's telegram, feeling lost in space, darkness all around her.

"COMING SOON. HOW IS AISLING? HOW IS YOUR DANCING? LOVE, IAN."

A chill swept her. The terse telegraphic style didn't sound like the nervous paraphrasing and piled-on enthusiasm of her friend and mentor. Nothing in her life felt as it had before.

She stood alone in Ireland, abandoned by her friends, bereaved by her losses, forsaken by her career.

This could not last, this separation from the real world. But the aloneness drew her along through life, allowing her to survive a difficult transition, to ignore her confusion about what her future would be.

Justine must be pressing him. Yvonne knew how insidiously the artistic director could fight for her whims and desires. Ian felt her knife thrusts; his telegram appealed for help.

She couldn't, Yvonne thought desperately.

Torn by her fears, she left early for the ballet studio and her lesson with Aisling.

When Aisling wasn't in the rehearsal room, Yvonne walked to the stage area.

"She isn't dancing, is she?"

Still hidden in the shadows, Yvonne froze on hearing a young man's voice. The "she" had to be Yvonne. Moving closer, she saw Aisling onstage, a dark-haired young dancer from the Irish company by her side.

"Not that I can see." Aisling lightly turned while he supported her.

"And the company thinks she's finished, don't they?"

Effortlessly Aisling extended her right leg while balancing *en pointe*. "You know it. With Yvonne at the top, I thought any ambition on my part might mean I lose everything and gain little." Aisling thoughtfully inspected her hand, trying different positions. "But now I don't know."

"Don't know what?"

"Everything has changed now, hasn't it? I mean, Yvonne is injured and not dancing. Ian has chosen me for this performance."

"I'm glad about that." He gazed adoringly at her.

Aisling didn't appear to notice him. "Now, maybe everything is changing. It's like a magic wand, you know, but I can't tell if the fairy is good or bad. Before, my head was safe, if not crowned. Now, before I left, the vibrations around the company were different. Like everyone was looking at me, seeing if I would take over Yvonne's place, seeing if they could gain some advantage."

With a chill, Yvonne imagined the scene. Yvonne is finished, they would have hissed. Never will the Swan Queen dance again, they would have predicted with malicious glee.

"So why don't you make a bid for the crown?" He nibbled on her ear.

"Thing is, I don't know if I want to." Aisling seemed to continue an argument of long standing with herself. "I think Justine might favor me. For her own reasons, of course."

"Well, then?"

"It isn't that simple, believe me. Justine called."

Surprised, Yvonne almost stepped from hiding.

"When?"

"Last night. After I came back from dinner."

"And?"

"Justine's voice just crackled over the line. 'Aisling! Where have you been?' " Aisling mimicked with frightening reality. "Scared the hell out of me, I can tell you."

"Yeah. She's not the pussycat type, from what I've heard." He smiled.

"A tiger is more like it." Aisling snickered.

"What did she want?"

Yvonne desperately wanted to know that too.

"My first thought was a long-distance bed check, but that

seemed extreme even for Miss Stelle. I pulled myself together and told her I was out with Yvonne at dinner.''

"Sounds harmless enough.''

"With Justine, who knows? She just said, 'I see,' in her drop-dead tone. I tried to be polite, asked her how she was. Was that a mistake! She informed me she hadn't called at that hour to chat.''

He whistled. "Friendly.''

"She wanted to know what was happening here. Well, believe me, I knew she wasn't asking about the weather or foreign affairs. Ballet is all to Justine. Even more so than to Yvonne. She asked how Eve was coming. I wasn't about to tell her anything discouraging. I said well. Why should I die young?''

"Was that all?''

"No. She wanted to know how Yvonne was.''

"What did you say to that?''

"I said she was fine, working well with me. Listen, in our company you don't complain to Justine, not about anyone or anything.''

"All sounds safe enough.''

"Then she asked if Yvonne was dancing. The only reason for the call, of course. Everything depends on Yvonne.''

From her niche, Yvonne held her breath, waiting for Aisling to continue. But the young dancer's attention had shifted.

"And I'm not so sure Yvonne's finished.'' Aisling shivered. "When I've seen great dancers—Baryshnikov, Nureyev, Makarova—they seem to dance in a light of white talent, you know.''

Momentarily distracted, he nodded. "I do. Like they're in a trance.''

"I'm not like that,'' Aisling admitted. "But Yvonne has it. And so maybe she isn't finished. I can just see her rising like a phoenix, the flames licking around her as she rises up.'' Aisling's voice glowed.

"She's helping you with Eve, isn't she?''

"Yeah.'' Aisling sounded glum.

"Isn't it working out?''

"You wouldn't believe it. Emotional expression, psychological understanding, personal projection . . .'' Aisling mimicked Yvonne's tones. "I have enough trouble learning the

teps, dammit. I don't know about this other stuff. It seems
o old-fashioned to me. I don't know if I can do it. I really
ry,'' Aisling whined. ''But Yvonne just stands there and stares
t me with her regal bearing and imperial expression.''

So that was how she appeared to Aisling. Yvonne cringed.

''Maybe she's just trying to prepare you for what Ian
vants.''

''Yes, I know. But it seems like a lot of trouble for a role,
nd so heavy. It's out-of-date to do it that way.''

Yvonne fled the scorn in Aisling's voice. Out-of-date,
ld-fashioned. So that was how they saw her. Probably twenty-
ix seemed ancient to them as they stood with their lives
tretched out before them.

But Yvonne had a more immediate concern. What had
Aisling told Justine?

''You look wonderful,'' Seán said when he saw her.

''Thank you.'' Yvonne was despondent.

''What's the matter?'' He looked into her eyes.

''Nothing.'' She smiled widely.

''Didn't you want to go out to dinner?'' He thought for a
noment. ''There is a new restaurant opening in the mountains,
f you don't mind a ride, or—''

''Yes. No, it doesn't matter. I'm just a little depressed.''
he couldn't explain to Seán. Aisling's scorn, Ian's pressure,
ustine's conniving: her problems reached across the water,
rying to engulf her.

''We could go to Galway,'' Seán teasingly suggested.

''Yes.''

''What?'' Seán looked startled.

''Yes.''

''You've always said no before.''

Yvonne tried to look casual. She knew her sudden changes
f mood and mind both confused and bemused Seán, yet she
ouldn't stop herself. And in this case, the trip seemed heaven-
ent. A few days to escape the reality she knew had to come,
ut that she still hoped to outrun. She needed time away; then
he could face the music. ''Changed my mind.''

''Well, of course. Now?''

Yvonne realized how impossible that would be. ''We could

hardly just drop in on your mother without warning.'' Her fac
fell. ''It was a silly idea.''

''Not at all,'' Seán heartily cried. ''It's a wonderful idea.
was surprised, but I'm also pleased. We'll go to Galway a
soon as you pack a few things. Then, tonight we'll stay at
hotel.''

''That would be wonderful.'' Yvonne appreciated hi
spontaneity.

''We could drop in on Mother, but she keeps early hour
and I don't like to disturb her.'' Seán gave her hair a playfu
tug. ''However, first thing tomorrow, we'll visit her. It wil
be just fine,'' he soothed. He glanced at his watch, the
chucked her under the chin. ''I'll give you ten minutes t
pack.''

''I only need five.'' Yvonne grinned.

Yvonne awoke in her Galway hotel determined not to thin
about ballet, Ian, or Aisling for four days. A beautiful da
promised, so she would take advantage of the weather an
her visit to the west of Ireland to have a few days of relax
ation and enjoyment.

Seán looked up when Yvonne came into the restaurant fo
breakfast. '' 'Morning,'' he cheerfully greeted her.

''Good morning, Seán. I'm very hungry. What's good her
for breakfast?'' How handsome he appeared, framed by a lov
window overlooking a main thoroughfare, Eglinton Street.

''Omelets.'' He handed her a menu. ''Ham and cheese o
mushroom?''

''Mushroom sounds delicious.'' She looked at the listing
''And some rashers and sausage.''

''You *are* hungry.''

''I am.''

''Does this indicate something?''

''I want to enjoy Galway.''

Seán stared. ''Good.''

''Where shall we begin?'' Yvonne smiled brightly.

''How about a walk through the city?''

''Perfect.''

''I think this afternoon will be soon enough to see Mother
That should give us enough time to look around the city.''

"I would like to pick up some flowers and chocolates for
ıer."

"That's easy enough, and very nice of you."

Time passed quickly. Galway was smaller and quainter
han Dublin. The same sense of history that lurked in the
apital's corners flourished in Galway as well.

"The town retains traces of the ancient plan, but the town
valls with fourteen towers and gates have disappeared. Do
ou feel like a tourist?" Seán asked.

"Like a time traveler."

A church in the center of the old city lay behind metal
ailings. "This is the Church of St. Nicholas, founded by the
Jormans in 1320." They walked down the first of three wide
isles. "This was the largest medieval church in Ireland.
Columbus is said to have prayed here before setting out for
America."

Soft light flooded through a narrow window, and for a
noment Yvonne caught her breath. The aura of mystical
ilence reminded her of Gregory and her child. With determi-
ation she pushed the thought away.

Along the streets by the church, an open-air farmers' mar-
et sprawled, thick-accented merchants displaying fresh vege-
ıbles and eggs. "This is still farming area," Seán pointed
ut.

The Corrib River branched through the city on its way to
Galway Bay, and during the day, when Seán and Yvonne
rossed over the many bridges dotting the river, they leaned
ver the railings to luxuriate in the sound of the swirling
vater below.

Back on Shop Street, the main street, Yvonne looked
appily around. "This city is perfect. It has good shops and
estaurants."

"A strand."

"History."

"A library."

"A university."

Yvonne smiled. "I think I would like to live here forever."
.mbarrassed by the implications, she turned away, pretend-
ıg to inspect a jewelry-shop window.

"I accept, I accept. Come on." Seán pulled her into th
shop.

"Accept what?"

Ignoring her confusion, he turned to the jeweler. "Coul
we see your Claddagh rings?"

"Surely." The man pulled out a tray.

"You accept what? And what are Claddagh rings?"

"Claddagh rings are traditional wedding rings from Galway
See, two hands clasping a heart. Isn't that romantic?" Seá
studied the tray with an appraising eye and chose one decor
ated with a diamond. "Do you like this?"

"Seán, I . . ."

Seán kissed her. "I want to accept your proposal and sta
here forever."

The jeweler looked amused if surprised.

"I did not propose!"

"Fickle." He turned to the jeweler. "We'll be back."

"No, we won't." Yvonne glared with discomposure a
Seán. "But thank you anyway." Why did Seán impulsivel
tease her so? "Isn't it time we went to your mother's?"

"Good idea. Maybe she can talk some sense into you, an
tell you what a wonderful man I am."

Back at the hotel, they separated to gather their luggage
"Seán"—Yvonne turned—"I meant to ask you. What shoul
I wear?"

"Wear?"

"Yes, clothes. Something suitable for your mother."

"You always look lovely," he assured her. "And it won
matter."

Though irritated, Yvonne decided that arguing with Seá
was useless, he would never lend her the direction Gregor
had. In her room she chose, after much consideration,
shirtwaisted wool dress in wine-and-black plaid. She wrappe
her hair in a French twist.

During the short ride to the house, they did not speak, bot
involved in their own thoughts. Yvonne wondered about th
poetess she was about to meet.

Turning off the main road, they drove down a tree-line
lane, then turned into a circle drive that fronted the house.

A country house in miniature, Síle Burns's home had th

open lines of a villa. Rectangular, the plastered gray-stone facade was broken by a collection of equally spaced high windows.

"This is very old, isn't it?" Yvonne asked.

"Yes, but I'll let Mother tell you about it. She does a tour that rivals mine."

A woman with gray hair came to the door. "Mary," he called. "How are you?"

"Fine, Mr. FitzGerald. My husband will get your bags."

"Mary is Mother's housekeeper," Seán explained as he introduced Yvonne. "Where is Mother?"

"Resting in her room."

Seán took Yvonne into the house and escorted her into a large room. "This is the main drawing room. I'll leave you here for a minute and get Mother."

"Take the flowers and chocolates to her for me, will you? What a lovely room!"

"It's Mother's decorating, all the way. She helped me plan my farmhouse."

"It's beautiful!"

"Mother has exquisite taste," he said proudly. "She'll love you."

The drawing room had white-painted walls with ornate stucco flowers and ribbons decorating the ceiling and dropping to the top of the walls. It reminded Yvonne of a wedding cake of perfect beauty. A horizontal band along the upper part of the wall, the frieze, was painted blue and gold.

Like most Irish rooms, a center fireplace added its own form of cheer. Around it Síle had arranged a couch with two chairs decorated in pink and needlepointed in an ornate flowered design. Another wall displayed a white sofa highlighted with pink and purple pillows. The furniture was traditional, but the unusual choice of pink and purple gave a contemporary air, erasing Yvonne's expectations of a little old lady. The same deep purple echoed in the cushions of two chairs settled by the windows.

The wood floor was light parquet, contrasting colors of wood worked into an elaborate mosaic pattern. A carpet, a muted oriental of pinks and purple, covered the center of the room. On the mantelpiece perched a series of framed pictures. One ornate gold-and-white frame held a picture of a dark-haired woman of great beauty and a boy, much like her in appearance, obviously Seán, aged about six.

"My dear." A tall white-haired woman walked into the room. "How nice to meet you. Welcome to Ebbtide."

"What a pretty name."

"It's from an eighth-century poem: 'Ebbtide has come to me as to the sea; old age makes me yellow.' " She wore a simple but beautifully cut expensive black suit with a bright red blouse.

"I think the name is inappropriate if you are supposed to be in old age." Síle looked young and vigorous.

"Thank you for the chocolates and flowers." Pulled back into a tight bun, Síle's hair showed in clear detail the lightly lined but beautiful face with high cheekbones and a firm chin. Her eyes were clear blue. "Shall we sit by the fireplace," she suggested.

Seán and his mother sat on the sofa, Yvonne across a low table on a chair. Mary brought in a tray with tea and quietly served them. "I was just telling Mother you admired the house."

"It's wonderful. How old is it?"

Síle smiled. "I'm afraid loving this house as I do, I may become boring, so feel free to interrupt. The architect was John Smyth, who took the general idea from an illustration in Colen Campbell's *Vitruvius Britannicus*, which was published in 1727." Her voice was low and melodious. "The design was adapted from a house by Palladio, the Italian architect. Smyth also designed the Provost's House at Trinity College."

"So this is a famous house."

"Well," Síle demurred, "of some historic interest. Seán says you have already had a quick tour of Galway." Síle rarely looked directly at Yvonne, and the dancer wondered if she were shy.

"Yes, we did. I really like it."

"I know. Its charm has always struck me. The Normans seized the river crossing in the thirteenth century and established a castle and settlement there. By 1278 there was a walled town." Her hands, with long tapering fingers, spoke a graceful language of their own.

"Mother is an expert in the city's history."

"It's very hard for me to appreciate how much history has taken place in this area," Yvonne told them.

"Maybe Yvonne would like to see the rest of the house," Seán suggested.

"Yes, very much."

Síle led the way, indicating interesting architectural features as they walked. Everywhere, little touches attested to Síle's taste and the intrinsic beauty of the house. Yvonne noticed Síle lightly touched everything they passed, as if caressing the walls and furniture. The dining room had a painted ceiling of clouds and cupids. The study had Chinese-red walls thick with books, not decorative showpieces, but well used and loved volumes.

Of all the rooms, Yvonne liked best the small sitting room with French doors opening onto a tiny walled garden. The room seemed to smile, painted yellow and white with red accents and a flowered carpet. "Like sitting in a garden," she exclaimed.

"Yes," Síle said. "I love it." She touched the small love seat covered in yellow velvet. "The textures, the colors, everything is just as I wanted."

A series of small hints suddenly wove themselves together, shocking Yvonne into embarrassment. Síle was blind.

26

"You didn't tell me," Yvonne wailed.

"I thought you knew. Síle Burns is an internationally famous poet. She's known as the blind poetess, a title she doesn't care for. Mother doesn't wish to be known as the blind anything."

"She is excellent at not appearing blind."

"It's her house. All the furniture is kept exactly positioned. She knew and loved every inch before she lost her sight. But it is still amazing, I agree," Seán said.

"She's overwhelming."

"What do you mean?" He laughed.

"The house is beautifully decorated, she's a famous poet in Gaelic and English, she's beautiful, and she raised a very nice son."

"Thank you."

They sat in Yvonne's cozy bedroom on the second floor. A large room decorated in flowered prints combining blue, pink, and yellow, it also had a fireplace. The large windows overlooking the distant sea had padded window seats. Gaily painted ribbons and flowers festooned the small mantel.

Planned without clutter or distraction, the entire house had an airy, comfortable atmosphere, with just the right blend of paintings, beautiful things, and interesting collections to delight the senses. A house Colette would have loved, Yvonne thought.

Seán still kept a room in the house. He had shown her his boyhood telescope, a set of dully colored antique maps framed on the walls, his old coin collection.

The days slipped by like light through her fingers. The mornings, she and Seán spent walking the streets of Galway, a source of unending charm for them both. She grew accustomed to his broad shoulders beside her own slim ones, his wide step outdistancing her own petite stride. With a start, she realized hours passed without sadness.

The afternoons were spent with Síle, listening to her stories of Ireland, her discussions of architecture, art, music, and ballet.

"I saw you dance once," Síle told her. "At the very beginning of your career. You were so lovely. I thought you could fly. I was so jealous."

Life stretched with pleasure, expanded with leisure; a picture of eternal bliss shimmered before Yvonne.

Nights, Seán and Yvonne walked along the beach, reached through a path between the house and the sea. He told her of his childhood in Galway as the wind ruffled his hair; she began speaking of her marriage to Gregory. They never mentioned Maxine, and suddenly she seemed unimportant. Desire tempted her, but something held Yvonne back. She knew he loved her now, but could she love him?

Despite her blindness, Síle missed very little. Yvonne noticed that when the older woman sensed the unsaid, she turned her head slightly as if catching high-frequency waves, unavailable to ordinary mortals. The last afternoon, Síle and Yvonne sat together in the private garden while Seán went into town on business.

"Here is the tea," Yvonne said, and wheeled the cart out onto the lawn.

"Isn't the weather beautiful?" Síle cried. Long, graceful fingers reached for the light and heat. "You mustn't get the wrong impression. This is especially nice weather. In your honor, I suppose. And rightly so. Aren't the flowers pretty?"

"Beautiful, but how . . . ?" She broke off in embarrassment.

"Did I know? I feel them. And I arranged the flowers to be planted before I went blind. Would you like me to pour?"

"I will," Yvonne offered.

"I wanted to show off, but I will be modest for now. You pour. I take tea black."

"When I first saw you, I didn't realize you couldn't see."

"I must not be as well adjusted as I thought." Síle stirred the tea.

"Why?"

"I felt so good when you said that."

"But you have adjusted so well! I don't see how you did it. I couldn't have." Empathy surged from her to the older woman.

"Yes, you could. There isn't any choice."

Yvonne fell silent momentarily. "Maybe. I don't think I could stand it. I'd not be as wonderful as you."

Síle laughed. "I wasn't wonderful, you know. I had an enormous adjustment to make, and I didn't want to make it."

"Sounds reasonable."

"Of course, that wasn't what I told myself. I told myself that I *couldn't* make the adjustment. There is a difference. I took to my room for days, crying, depressed. I planned to withdraw from life. Stay in my room. Not be a burden. Not have anyone feel sorry for me. Oh, I was very proud of that."

"But you aren't a burden."

"Not now, but I was."

"I'm sure that having Seán helped." Yvonne thought of his cool appraisal of her own difficulties, at first angering her, then helping her.

"Dear Seán."

"He must have been a consolation."

"He certainly tried. He felt terribly guilty."

"Why guilty?"

"For no reason. Because I was his mother who was going blind and he couldn't prevent it. Not good logic but excellent emotion."

"How old was he when it happened?" A youthful image of Seán, the way he looked when his hair blew in the wind, came to mind.

"He had been out of Trinity for two years. That was part of the problem, of course. With his father gone, Seán saw me as his responsiblity. We had almost no money. Dear Edward left a beautiful house, debts, and little else."

"Seán told me."

"He thought that having more money would have made a difference." She tucked back a wisp of white hair.

"Would it?"

"A bit. But I already had excellent care, the best possible. Seán felt so sorry for me."

"Well," Yvonne objected, "he should have."

"No. My poems, you see, were known for their sensual exploration of Ireland, nature, and life itself. Without my sight, how could I know the world of the senses? So, I was lucky."

"Lucky!"

"Lucky!" Síle stated firmly. "At the time, I didn't think so. I went on a maudlin trip around Ireland, visiting the sights I would never see again. I took the Ring of Kerry tour, stopping at each noted view. I visited the purple Cliffs of Moher. And I cried and cried."

Yvonne's voice choked. "I am so sorry."

"Think of all that wasted time. What a fool I was! But I suppose it couldn't be helped. I romantically decorated this house, refining the colors, the furniture, the ornaments that I would mentally live with for the rest of my life. That wasn't a bad idea."

"What did Seán do?"

"He coddled me. Anyplace I wanted to go, he took me. He even brought me to live with him."

Yvonne liked Seán more and more.

Silence fell between them, broken only by the call of birds in the trees. " 'A wall of forest looms above, and sweetly the blackbird sings; all the birds make melody over me and my books and things,' " Síle recited quietly.

Sympathy welled in Yvonne. How bravely Síle had faced her situation; how badly she had stood up to her own. Yet Síle was an exceptional woman, talented in many areas, and mature before she faced her trial.

Yvonne had alternated between feeling very old and very young. But never mature enough to take hold of her life and bring it under control. But why had Síle considered going blind lucky?

From the house, they heard Seán coming.

"When I could see"—Síle's voice was low—"I sometimes wondered if my poetry had a reality outside my life, and my life a reality outside my poetry. I write better than before. Being blind allows me to *see* better. My life has its own reality. I am happier that way.''

Their last night in Galway, Seán and Yvonne walked along the beach, watching the moon dip into the bay.

"Can I assume it's safe for me, this close to the water?'' Seán teased.

"Safe?'' Yvonne asked innocently. "You know the area better than I.''

"Familiar areas lose their bearings when I'm with you.'' Seán smiled. "You have a most unsettling effect on my surroundings.''

"You mean you might fall into the water again.''

"I never precisely fell into the water, but I'll let that pass. How do you like Galway now?''

"I love it. I'm surprised you left.''

"I come back a lot. I wouldn't want Mother to think I'm keeping track of her. She wouldn't like that.''

"I know. She is amazing.''

Seán laughed. "A friend of hers once said that while her world is limited, her limits aren't worldly. It always is a shock to find out from the little I tell her how much she knows. She likes you very much.''

"More than the rest of your girlfriends?'' Yvonne teased. "Or doesn't she know you keep a harem?''

"She has never met any of them. You are special.''

"Thank you.'' She glowed with pleasure.

"Careful in the sand.'' Seán caught her hand, helping her along.

His touch caused her heart to race. If she were a poet like Síle, she could find the words to tell him of her feelings; now she could not even dance her meaning. They walked on in mute affection.

Seán slowed, then stopped and turned to face Yvonne. His lips lowered to hers. Gently at first, then with more demanding pressure, he kissed her. His hands moved down her back, caressing her naked shoulders, following her spine in soft, fluttering motions that brought Yvonne's breath in sharp gasps. "Yvonne, I've been wanting to talk to you. About us.''

Yvonne looked down to avoid his eyes. "There isn't really any *us*, Seán.''

"But I think there is." His hand reached under her chin, tilting her face toward his and forcing her to look into his eyes. "Haven't you enjoyed being with me?"

"Very much."

"Well?"

"Thank you. It had been a long time since I had enjoyed anything, and I certainly appreciated your taking the time to show me Dublin and Galway and everything," she ended lamely. Her heart pounded. Under her fingers Seán's suit of tweed teased her skin. Masculine sensations, long absent from her senses, tantalized her.

"Is that all?" his voice lazily teased.

"What else did you want, Seán?"

"You."

Tightly they pressed together, his body strong and commanding, hers soft and yielding. It had been so long, so long since she had felt the complete desire to surrender. It left her trembling and faint. Logical decisions could no longer determine her feelings for Seán. She had thrown her heart over, her misgivings, to find herself in his arms.

"Would you like to go in?" he whispered. "You must be freezing."

"In where?"

"To your room."

Yvonne hesitated, tottering on the edge of a deep valley, wondering if she should turn and run. Did she want to commit herself? Did she want to love again?

But as Seán kissed her once more, moving in a slight swaying motion against her, she didn't believe she had any choice.

"Your mother . . ."

"She won't know, and would be delighted if she did."

"Seán!"

"Listen, Yvonne"—he searched deeply for new patterns in her eyes—"at my age and still unmarried, Mother must wonder if something is wrong with me."

Feeling his masculine hardness, Yvonne laughed softly. "I'll be glad to give her a testimonial."

Gently he drew her back along the path, half-holding her as they walked. At the door to the house he stopped, kissing her again, murmuring her name.

She must have mounted the stairs and entered her room, but she couldn't remember.

"Are you sure?" he asked once.

Yvonne tried to draw back, to scrutinize the situation like one of Seán's antique maps, to fathom the depths of his affection in his gaze, the latitude of his love in his touch.

"Yes."

He lowered her onto the bed, then lay beside her, both fully dressed. "I've wanted you so long."

"You haven't known me that long."

"I've known you forever; I just found you recently," he corrected while playing with her long flowing hair.

She cradled one of his hands in hers, kissing it tenderly. Slowly he moved his free hand to the buttons of her blouse, unbuttoning them one by one till the silky fabric slipped open and off her breasts. Only the sheer, lacy fabric of her bra remained, her nipples thrusting boldly into the cloth.

His lips sought her neck, nibbling at her gently, then moving down farther and farther till they closed over her nipples, teasing them through the fabric.

"Seán" she moaned, and turned to her side, facing his body. With quick gestures she opened his shirt, felt the bare smoothness of his chest and the warm muscles of his arms.

With one deft move he unsnapped the last restraint from between them, pressing his bare chest against her breasts. For an instant they clung together, his face buried in her hair, her hands clasped behind his back, holding him close.

Still Seán did not allow himself to hurry, but kissed and licked till all her skin burned and tingled with passionate desire.

"Seán . . ." She couldn't wait, couldn't do without having him more intimately.

With maddeningly lingering movements he unclasped her skirt, taking it off, then removed her slip. Only a touch of black lace remained, held on her hips with slim satin ribbons.

Standing, Seán removed the rest of his clothes and nestled close to her. Yvonne felt him thrusting against her. She moved a hesitant hand along his chest, down past his waist, leaving it there while they kissed.

Reaching out, Seán untied first one ribbon, then the other. He bent down, and with his lips moved away the lacy covering, revealing all of Yvonne. The moon flooded the room with soft light, gleaming off Yvonne's breasts, highlighting her nipples, leaving only the triangle between her thighs in shadow.

Propping himself on one elbow, Seán leaned slghtly back and looked at her. Yvonne thought even in the gentle light her blushes must show, but she didn't move or attempt to cover herself. His eyes gleamed blue in the light.

Slowly he lowered himself toward her, and with his lips brushed hers, then her nipples, then to her stomach, and continued down, down, and kissed her center. With first gentle, but then firm and more demanding movements, he explored her more intimately.

She moved her hand then, encouraging him, feeling him grow larger and stronger beneath her touch. With more frantic gestures she urged his progress, touching his hair as his lips explored the inside of her thighs, pulling him up and encouraging him over her body, holding him tightly as he slowly entered her.

Together they moved in a *pas de deux* of love, new and yet familiar. Desire exploded within her as she boldly responded to his thrusting power. Beneath her hands his muscles rippled, and suddenly ecstasy tore through her. "Oh, Seán . . ." She cried his name over and over, completely lost in her pleasure and release.

Before she could recover, Seán's own hunger was satisfied. Tightly she clung to him, moving with his rhythm, until they both slowly sank to the bed, exhausted.

Gradually the pounding of her heart stilled and his breathing became normal. Together they lay, entwined in each other's arms.

Seán rolled to his back, drawing her alongside him, tucking one arm around her. "That was perfect, Yvonne."

"Yes." A dreamy haze surrounded her, shimmered the moonlight peeping through the curtain.

"Forever," he murmured, even as sleep crept over him. "I'll love you forever."

27

Early next morning, Yvonne arose and crept from the house. Seán had returned to his room during the early hours of morning. The house lay quiet behind her.

She needed time alone before they left for Dublin, before those hours of togetherness. Betrayal, her mind accused her, treachery.

Last night had been perfect, romantic and sensual. She should be happy, fulfilled, and at peace.

Instead, the murmuring waves with their soothing rhythm spoke in ironic counterpoint to her tempestuous thoughts. In Galway she had sought a peaceful interlude from pressing problems. Now she perceived the storm of her life had traveled with her. As it always would.

She had been betrayed by her body, by her need for love and protection. Her body had betrayed her, as she had betrayed Maxine.

She had loved Gregory completely. So quickly she had allowed herself to grow dependent, trusting him completely, wanting him to make every decision. He had promised that she could count on him, rely on him for everything. Forever. Needing him to make up for the loss of her parents and the insecurities of her teenage years, she had asked for promises no one could make.

In one careless moment she had been cast into a treacherous world, left vulnerable and without resources. Naked, exposed, she had to face her problems.

It could happen again. There was no forever.

The thought terrified her.

Then she remembered Síle's conversation about her blindness and her adaption to it. Her own situation was not that dissimilar. Why wasn't Seán sympathetic to her?

Had the poet been hinting at something? Trying to tell Yvonne about her son? In every way possible, Seán had tried to help his mother, had tried to make a life for one disabled person. Wasn't that enough? Why should he spend a lifetime caring for another?

A handsome, desirable man, Seán could choose from any number of women. Why should he marry a mixed-up, nondancing ballerina? Before long, her reputation would disappear like smoke on a windy day. The public was not sentimental about the recently departed. She would be unrecognized and unacknowledged. Seán should not marry her, Síle seemed to say.

Despite her passion for Seán, their love could not grow. Every hour, every minute spent at Seán's side increased her misgivings. She lured him on, teasing him with a relationship that could only end in pain.

That was unfair to Seán, unfair to herself.

Seán, she felt sure, would not accept her hesitations, her unreadiness to love again. Perseverance and adoration could change her heart, he would believe. She would weaken in the face of his conviction, he would hope. Her staying in Ireland would only add lingering pain to their lives.

Somehow, she had to convince him their love affair could not be.

"Thank you for everything." Yvonne hugged Síle Burns. "You have a very special life here."

"You must come again, very soon."

"We'll see," Yvonne hedged. "My plans are uncertain. But I'll never forget this house, or you."

As they drove away, a tearful Yvonne turned back to see Síle's slim figure waving in the doorway. "You should visit your mother more," she scolded.

"I know. It's your fault."

"Mine?"

"Yes. Wives handle family relations. They set up the family visits. When you marry me, you will see that I visit Mother more."

"I'm not going to marry you."

"Of course you are." Gently he touched her leg. "After last night, we belong together forever."

"I told you once, there is no forever."

"Then for as long as possible."

Yvonne burst into tears. "I can't talk about it, Seán. You'll just have to believe me."

"Yvonne . . ." He drove to the side of the road, stopped, and reached for her. "Don't cry."

"I can't help it."

"Did I do something wrong?"

"Nothing. I've made a mistake." She couldn't talk with Seán about her fears. She had never told him about the baby she'd lost, about the grave in Houston. Her life, her reality, didn't lie in the green fields of Galway. She had been pretending.

Not just fleeing the immediate problems in Dublin—the ballet, Aisling, and Ian—but her permanent trials, Gregory's loss, the baby, and her permanent inability to dance.

If only Seán would sweep her up, *force* her to marry him, she thought with a surge of pain. Make up her mind for her as Gregory would have.

But that wasn't Seán. "I think we should go on to Dublin," she said, half-wishing he would not.

Seán looked hesitant, then turned back to the wheel. "You are tired and perhaps upset about Dublin. It will be better when Thorn is there to share the responsiblity."

Worse. That would make everything worse, she thought.

Yvonne rose decisively, and without pausing to order breakfast, sat at the desk to compose a short note. All night she had agonized, trying to find the words to tell Seán they could not have a relationship. "Dear Seán." That was the easy part. Honesty, discreet honesty, appeared the best course.

She would not think of the night in Galway, that night of wild passion. Only by keeping her mind firmly on the task at hand could she force herself to continue.

"I do not feel that I can see you again. In no way do I hold you responsible for what happened, or pretend I didn't enjoy it myself, but I feel it would be best to discontinue our relationship before anything else happens we might both egret.'' Short but clear, she decided. ''Best wishes always, Yvonne.''

A soft tap on the door interrupted her as she addressed the envelope. ''A delivery, Miss St. Cyr.'' The man left a flower box on the table and withdrew.

With trembling hands Yvonne lifted the lid of the long narrow box. A single white rose lay swathed in green paper, a small enveloped card at the stem. She ripped it open, and read: ''For a beginning, may it not end.'' Gently she touched the single perfect blossom. She had always liked roses.

End it must, Yvonne resolved, refusing to soften. Although not a dancer anymore, she still had a dancer's control and self-discipline, characteristics which she could transfer to her personal life.

Solutions had to be found to her other immediate problems: Ian and Aisling.

Although she could not have fully explained it to Seán or anyone else, the night of romantic passion had awakened her emotions. It was as if in the year since Gregory's death, she had been only partly alive. Unwilling to face unpleasant realities, she had bumped blindly through life, pushing too quickly back into ballet, then bouncing into Maxine's company. She had to stop.

She would eliminate Seán from her life. She would explain to Ian that for her to dance Colette remained impossible, that her career was finished. To have been decisive, to have made decisions, pleased her, no matter how distasteful the consequences.

As the formally gray-uniformed doorman hailed her a taxi, Seán appeared at the hotel entrance. ''Yvonne.''

''Oh, Seán. You surprised me.'' His warm, familiar voice had shaken her.

''Sorry. I know you are busy with Aisling this morning, but I couldn't wait to see you. Just see you for a minute. You slept well?''

''Yes. Thank you for the rose. It is perfect.''

''You're welcome. I planned on bringing it myself, but decided that wouldn't be proper.'' His eyes seemed bluer than ever.

''No.''

''Maybe improperly proper.''

"Seán, I have to . . ." She struggled to continue.

"I know, I know, you have to go. I'll meet you fo lunch?"

"No, I can't have lunch with you." She realized she ha to tell him in person; the note was cowardly and unkind. " have something difficult to say to you."

"Then we have to meet for lunch. Difficult things alway need food to get them down."

"I . . ."

"Of course you can't. I should realize how busy you are I've been taking you away from work. Very inconsiderate o me." He reached out and took her hand. "I couldn't resist but I'll be better now."

"No, don't be silly." His touch sent her heart racing.

"Dinner! I'll take you to dinner." He drew her closer. " wish I could take you in my arms. Right here on the street."

"No, please." Gently she wriggled from his grasp.

"Sorry. Dinner at eight?"

"I can't anymore, Seán." How impossibly hard it was Her body longed for him, but she had to resist. "I'm no going to see you anymore."

"Not see me?" Seán looked stunned.

"No."

He pulled back a little. "But why?"

"I have so much to do." She looked over his shoulder commanding herself not to cry.

"I see." His jaw set in a strong line.

"And then I'll return to New York."

"I see." Seán's eyes turned almost blue-green.

"Do you?"

"No. Is it like biscuits and burnt toast?" His smile didn' reach his eyes.

"Maybe. It's too difficult to explain, but it won't work I'm not ready for a serious relationship."

"I'll force myself to accept a tawdry affair," he tried t joke, "for now."

"Seán, I have to leave now."

"So we're not to see each other at all?"

"I think that would be easiest." For a long moment the stared into each other's eyes.

"It wasn't my horse?"

"No, silly." She smiled, a smile bright if brittle. "It hasn't anything to do with you, Seán. This is my problem."

"I don't understand, but I suppose you know what is best for you. If you change your mind, call?"

"I will."

He looked at the tiny white hand he held in his. "I think this is yours."

28

"Ian!" In the mirror Yvonne caught sight of his trim, erect figure in the doorway to the studio. "You weren't due yet."

"Darlings! How well you both look, truly well. You mean I'm not a pleasant surprise?"

"Of course you are."

"Of course," Aisling echoed.

"We just want everything to be perfect for you."

"Perfect," Aisling echoed through clenched teeth.

"Pay no attention to me, not a scrap. Just continue. Let me see what you have been up to. What little treats. Surprises." The words were Ian's, but the enthusiasm sounded forced.

"Shall we start from the beginning, Aisling?" Yvonne walked to the tape recorder and switched on the now-too-familiar music.

Aisling drew a deep breath, hoping to still her quivering body. "I hope you won't be disappointed. Yvonne has really been working with me. I always feel like a wayward child, just one skip away from a scolding." She smiled to indicate it was a joke.

A mere seven years separated Yvonne and Aisling. Seven years, hundreds of performances, brilliant reviews, personal attention from choreographers like Ian Thorn—a lifetime of difference, a river of molten gold. Fall in, and Aisling would evaporate in a whiff of smoke, burned by Yvonne's position and power.

Turning and flexing, Aisling glanced quickly at the two figures watching and evaluating from across the room. With obvious concentration, she moved through the dance, missing a beat here, a step there, but all in all not doing badly, Yvonne thought. But still mechanically.

Yvonne switched off the recording. "That's as far as we've gotten."

For minutes Ian seemed lost in thought, wandering around the studio, touching the barre, the mirrors.

"You've worked with the young man who is partnering you?" Ian asked Aisling.

"Yes. He is working out very well." She turned scarlet and hung her head. "Just the right height."

"I do think it will be a good performance," Yvonne added with somewhat chauvinistic pride in their own company.

"I'm delighted, truly touched, that anyone would want to put on this old man's ballet."

Both women looked surprised at youthful Ian calling himself old, but neither commented.

"And are you enjoying yourselves? All work and no play, you know . . ." Ian looked around the room as if at a loss to know what to do next.

"What did you think of Aisling's work?" Yvonne asked.

"Very nice." Ian still had not reached a decision.

"She is having some trouble understanding the background for the ballet. The emotional grounding isn't a part I teach very well."

Both women waited. Ian stared into space, then recalled himself from beguiling daydreams. "It will work out. Sometimes it takes a while, you know, a matter of time. Do you think we could go and have a bite to eat? I wasn't hungry when I checked into my hotel, but now . . ." He shrugged.

"Of course." Yvonne gathered her clothes. "Let's all go back to my rooms," she suggested. "We can order lunch. The food is very good, and the fireplace makes everything cozy. Isn't that right, Aisling?"

"Real cozy. We could order tea and cakes. They serve a large tray of different kinds of cakes, you know, Ian, and let you take what you want." Behind his back the women exchanged bewildered glances. Though physically in Dublin, mentally Ian remained in New York.

"How is New York?" Yvonne asked. "We haven't heard much news. Maxine called, but I could barely understand what she said. Terrible lines." Tea had been served in her room and Ian sat absentmindedly stirring a cup.

"Fine. The company is preparing for the season. Everyone misses you both, of course, and sends their love. Regards from Justine, and so forth and so on."

"We weren't looking to see you yet," Aisling pointed out.

"Actually, I had tickets for last week, but postponed my trip. Justine's getting nervous, a little edgy, that is. You know how she likes to know exactly what is happening."

Maxine sketched with quick, hard strokes. "Do you think the American woman is ready for a one-piece bathing suit?"

"I think it has been tried." Kili rescued a fluttering paper before it disappeared under the sofa.

"Not where I'm planning to put that one piece."

Kili glanced at the sketch and gasped. "Really, Maxine, you won't get away with that."

"Maybe not. Maybe it's time to go in the other direction. What about a suit with long sleeves and little pants attached? A rediscovery of modesty."

"It is good to see you working so hard." Kili's cactus temper pricked.

"How are your drawings coming for Ian?"

Kili looked pleased. "I'll bring them over for you tonight. The design is good, but I'm not certain they can be danced in."

"That can be a problem at first. You'll have to show Ian, also."

"He's in Ireland."

"Ireland?" Maxine looked vaguely at Kili, still thinking of her designs.

"Justine sent him over early."

"Why?"

"He didn't say. Knowing Justine even secondhand, I doubt for any happy reason."

"I wonder what Yvonne is up to?" Maxine laid aside the drawings and paced the room.

Dressed in clinging bottle-green pajamas, her red hair newly cut to fan around her head, Maxine looked almost beautiful, Kili thought. "Up to? Probably nothing."

"That's what I was afraid of." Maxine slouched dramatically beside Kili on the sofa.

"Why? What did you want her up to? Teaching Aisling a dance and looking after your business interests is enough." As she spoke, it dawned on Kili that Yvonne's presence in Ireland for Maxine had little to do with business.

"It was more what I wanted her down to, really. A man."

"Really, Maxine, Gregory—"

"Is dead." Maxine firmly closed the sentence.

"Oh, Maxine."

"Oh, Maxine, nothing. I'm sorry, but that's how it is, Kili. And Yvonne is alive and very young."

"True, but I think she's also the pining type."

"The pining type, the pining type," Maxine repeated, raising her tone. "What an interesting vocabulary you have. Next we'll swoon with vexation. However, I must admit you are right. I send her off to romantic Ireland with a handsome young man, and she probably is up to nothing."

Kili had begun an objection, but stopped, easing back onto the sofa, looking mildly devious. Thoughts of Ian inspired her, but outdoing Maxine at her own game required fine judgment. "I wonder . . ." she said.

"Wonder what?"

"I wonder what Yvonne *is* up to. I would hate to think about her sinking into a depression way over there."

"You don't think she is, do you?"

Kili looked thoughtful. "It's too bad you can't go and see."

"I wouldn't dare. Yvonne would know why I was there. She'd be furious." Maxine felt it unnecessary to add that Fleming would insist upon accompanying her, leading to painful questions, even more painful answers.

"Maybe . . . No, that wouldn't work."

"What wouldn't work?"

"I wondered if I could go. I have an excuse—planning the designs and costumes. Then I could see what's going on. But I don't suppose you could spare me."

"Kili, I can still run my own business. That isn't a bad idea. Go pack. Make plane reservations. Since this is official business, I'll buy your ticket."

Kili feigned nonchalance, carefully stacked the drawings on Maxine's table, and walked toward the door. "I'll call you when I have details."

"Besides"—Maxine's voice lazily floated after her—"who am I to stand in the path of true love?"

Kili's heels clicked down the hall, tapping out her embarrassment.

"I think of Willy as a man of common friends and uncommon enemies." Ian held a large mug of tea and looked at the two young women.

"I think of him as a skunk," Yvonne objected.

"Now, Yvonne, a man is more than the sum of his nervous ticks. I admit Willy left something to be desired." Ian gestured with his cup toward Aisling. "What do you think, little one?"

Aisling looked white and ill. "I think I might agree with Yvonne. The way he locked Colette into a room, making her write, and then had the gall to take credit for her work."

Ian closed his eyes. "Remember what Colette said. 'My life as a young woman began with this freebooter . . . before that, it had been roses, roses all the way. But what would I have done with everlasting roses?' "

"I don't know that everlasting roses sounds bad to me," Yvonne objected. Once her own life had been roses; now it was all thorns. She longed to see Seán but refused to surrender to her desires.

"But perhaps Colette wouldn't have written without an end to the roses," Aisling said. "Maybe she needed that push."

"Very possibly, Aisling. I know this seems slow and tedious, but we must have some idea of our course before we begin."

"Have you thought about the scenes?" Yvonne asked.

"Not completely. This is mostly the dream stage. I'm thinking of 'Roses, Roses, Roses' as a title for Act I and beginning with her married to Willy. Her happy years with her parents in rural France will be in a dream sequence. I think we'll show Justine and the Friends a solo expressing Colette's frustrations in Paris, that is, her bewilderment at marrying a so-much-older man who has numerous mistresses and whose life turns out to be a lie. A famous writer, Willy had in truth paid others a pittance to write for him by the time he married Colette.''

"The first book producer," Aisling suggested. Despite her agitation, talk of Colette interested her.

"One interesting thing about Colette," Yvonne volunteered, "was her interest in acrobatics. I remember how young and athletic she was while in her thirties."

"Good idea. Maybe an acrobatic theme would work into Roses." Ian thought. "Listen, you two get into practice clothes. I'll start working on the floor."

"But I—" Yvonne mildly objected.

"Hurry up, I don't have time to talk when I'm thinking."

"Yes, Ian."

Minutes later, Aisling arrived on the floor. A black leotard hung loosely around her ever-slimming frame. Her tights were mended in long runs. She took her place at the barre and began a warm-up.

Yvonne followed more slowly. Her violet leotard and tights were immaculate. A sheer scarf tied around her waist formed a flattering skirt. From thin lines of liner to generous shadow matching her outfit, her makeup was impeccable. Her thick hair coiled at her neck.

Aisling stared at herself in the mirror as if painfully noticing her own hair, which needed a washing, and her un-made-up face. She looked resentfully at Yvonne's perfect image.

"Let me look at you both." Ian scrutinized them.

"Ian, I can't—"

"Hush!" An impatient hand covered Yvonne's lips into silence. "Roses, athletic, youth, disillusioned." He motioned to Aisling. "What about a *grand rond de jambe en dehors*?"

Aisling moved to the center of the room. Balancing on one foot, she moved her other up the balancing leg before extending it out in front and then to her right and continuing on behind her into fourth position *derrière*. "This?"

"I don't like it. Try it *en dedans*."

Aisling reversed the step, starting in back and working toward the front. Why would that make any difference? she wondered. "What about this?"

"Who knows?" Ian wandered around the room deep in thought.

Aisling stiffened, unsure if Ian expected her to know. Yvonne shook her head at Aisling's bewildered expression. "He's always like this," she whispered.

"Think of something," he turned and ordered.

"Colette's lovely thick hair, which she wore down her back in a braid," Aisling suggested.

"Her mother's ire when she cut it off," Yvonne added.

"Her catlike eyes." Aisling looked surprised at what she recalled from the few books Ian had given her.

"Eyes. I must remember eyes."

"What about costumes and setting?" Yvonne asked.

"That darling girl Kili is handling them." Ian smiled. "I haven't seen them yet."

"I'm sure they will be beautiful," Yvonne said.

"I would like some *cabriole devants*," Ian continued. The combination spring and beat in the air were impressive, ending with a *grand battement*, a large beat extending the leg high in the air. "Maybe a double." Two beats in the air. "They are brilliant."

"They are hard," Aisling murmured.

"You haven't seen anything yet," Yvonne whooped.

"Now, Yvonne. Here in the middle of the floor."

Yvonne took a deep breath. "Ian, I've been trying to tell you. I can't dance."

"Still having trouble?" Ian might have been inquiring about a strained muscle. "Doesn't matter. We'll just walk it through."

Yvonne stifled a protest, deciding to wait until she was alone with Ian. "Here I am."

"Good, good." Ian's eyes swept around the room. "My bag, where's my bag? Ah, here it is. Tape. This is the music, at least for your part, Yvonne. Not all the music has been composed, but it should be soon. Tape recorder."

"What would you like to see?" Yvonne's smile presented a brave front. No step of hers could satisfy Ian's sharp eyes. Her body felt heavy and misshapen, but the mirrors were kinder, revealing only her normal trim appearance. Perhaps she should start some mild practicing, just to stay in shape.

"Both of you pay attention," he ordered. "For now, Yvonne will walk through the positions, Aisling will dance. You might as well both learn the role, and Aisling can understudy you for performances."

Two hours passed. Both young women dripped with sweat, Aisling from dancing, Yvonne from walking through, bending and gesturing. Ian must have noticed, Yvonne thought. Surely he could see she was in no condition to dance, and wouldn't be for months, if ever. Pain tightened her throat. Before, she had delved into ballet, losing her disappointments. Now she felt ballet had betrayed her.

"We have made a good start," Ian concluded after much thought. "The same time tomorrow."

"Thank you, Ian." Aisling prepared to leave.

"Good, good. We want to be ready for Justine's little party."

"Party?" Yvonne narrowed her eyes. What was this about a party?

"Justine?" Aisling gasped.

"Such enthusiasm," Ian teased. "At the end of this season, Justine wants a few minutes of Colette to show to the Friends of the Ballet."

Party. The women eyed each other in dismay, their thoughts remarkably similar. What did Ian really mean? How would it affect them?

"Ian," Yvonne asked, "could I see you after this for a few minutes?"

"Of course. Lunch?"

"That would be fine."

"You don't mind, Aisling?" Yvonne asked.

"No, I'm meeting a friend." Ian walked to rewind the tape, and Aisling turned to Yvonne. "Are you still seeing Seán? He is such a nice older man."

"Older?" Yvonne gasped.

Aisling smiled innocently. "You know, Colette wrote about young girls being attracted to middle-aged men. I think she called it becoming the plaything. She said it was like an ugly dream, punished by fulfillment. She called it morbid, like eating chalk, reading dirty books, sticking pins into the palm of your hand. Isn't she funny sometimes?"

"Yes." Yvonne laughed, wondering how Seán would like being compared to dirty books and pins in the palm, then remembered she and Seán wouldn't be laughing together anymore.

"I have such an appetite here. Must be the cooler weather. Excitement of a foreign country. Have another cake?" Ian and Yvonne had lunched and were now having coffee and cakes.

Both had avoided topics of serious discussion while eating. Now Yvonne felt compelled to mention her bad news. "Ian, we have to talk."

"But of course, dear, we are."

"No, I mean seriously and unpleasantly." It took such determination to continue.

Ian frowned comically. "How horrible!"

"I can't dance." So simple, yet so complicated.

"I know." He patted her hand. "It must be frustrating."

"It's more than frustrating, Ian, it's permanent." Tears stung her eyes.

"You mustn't get exicted." He patted her hand.

"I'm just being realistic," Yvonne insisted, hysteria threatening to take over.

"I am a little worried, just a tiny bit concerned."

"I'm very worried," Yvonne insisted. He was beginning to understand. This was not a dancer's whim, not capricious fear on her part, but the end of her dance life.

"Justine is up to something," he continued his thought.

"That sounds normal." Ian wasn't beginning to understand. He was worried about the artistic director, not her dancing.

"Something big. She is under pressure lately."

"Aren't we all?" Yvonne half-listened, searching for words commanding enough to grab Ian's attention.

"But with Justine, there are always reactions. Like an out-of-control pressure cooker."

"I see." Despair swept her.

"The explosion might be gigantic."

"Yes."

"You don't have to dance long, just a solo. I know it will be difficult, but you must start dancing again sometime. You can do it, Yvonne, and this is so very important to me. And it will be for you.''

''Ian, I would do anything for you, but . . .''

But what? Ian wouldn't hear. Well, he would see for himself soon enough. Her most expressive dancing would prove to be awkward hesitations and inept mistakes, a clear message to all. She would never dance again.

29

"Maybe I'll take the afternoon off," Yvonne said to Ian as they finished lunch. "Do some shopping. See some sights." She smiled listlessly.

"Fine, fine. I'm seeing some old acquaintances for dinner, but I'll work on Eve with the Irish company first. No need for you to hang around. I feel sure you have more entertaining things to do."

Yvonne smiled sadly. "Not really, but I would like a change. I'm a little tired, so first I think I'll go back to the hotel for a nap."

Ian tarried over another coffee. Yvonne left the restaurant, heading for the hotel. Suddenly she remembered leaving her sweater at the studio and decided to make a short detour to the practice hall before returning to her rooms to think. Her problems were intractable; she was not that eager to tackle them.

The company had scattered for lunch and Yvonne entered the deserted studios. Quietly, engrossed in her thoughts, she ambled down the hall, hearing the strains of faint music emanating from the practice room. Someone was working out, she concluded. But that didn't matter, she would just take her sweater and leave.

She opened the door softly, being careful not to break some dancer's concentration. Across the room she saw Aisling, turning slowly *en pointe*, a dark-haired young man supporting her. Absorbed by their dance, neither heard Yvonne.

Gazing intently into each other's eyes, the young dancers moved slowly back and forth across the room, step following step. When they stopped, Aisling balanced on one foot, extended the other, and snaked it around the boy's waist. Slowly their bodies neared, gradually their lips met. "She says they'll highlight me, interviews, pictures, the works," Aisling finally said.

"Excuse me." Yvonne's voice sounded harsh and strained.

With a cry, Aisling topped off *pointe*. "I didn't . . . I didn't hear you."

"Obviously."

Yvonne nodded a greeting. "I forgot my sweater."

"This is Pat. He's a dancer with the Irish company."

Awkwardly the dancers moved apart. Pat turned toward the barre, wiping his face with a towel. Aisling balanced from one toe to the other, hands picking at her tights. "Do you plan to work out this afternoon?" she finally asked.

"I just came for my sweater. I'll leave now. Don't let me disturb your . . . practice." Across the room she saw her figure reflected in the mirror. She looked white and taut, older than her years. With stiff movements she walked awkwardly from the room.

Ian needed a ballet. Yvonne lay fully dressed on her bed, fighting her sentimentality and mawkish self-pity. Justine had insisted he produce a part of *Ballet of Desire*, although Ian had avoided the word "insisted." He had no need to; Yvonne knew the artistic director.

Ian needed a dancer. It couldn't be Yvonne, not in her crippled condition.

Nor could it be anyone in America. Time and circumstances were against him finding another dancer. Aisling was his only hope. Aisling had to dance Colette, had to be the new Thorn dancer, had to become a prima ballerina.

Tears threatened, but Yvonne dashed them impatiently away. Painful situations dictated painful solutions.

For the first time, Yvonne had understood how lost and confused Aisling felt. As despairing perhaps as Yvonne herself, if for different reasons.

Ballet had not been the easy path, the simple glittering road for her that others thought. Never easy, ballet was a constant struggle, which her exceptional talent made somewhat easier, but not easy.

Over the years Yvonne had made many sacrifices. Her time with Gregory had been slivered by her career, her choices about life and time firmly determined by the demands of her art.

Unlike Aisling's, these had not been conscious decisions. Years before, she had decided to be a dancer, and when her talent shone forth, a path both straight and clear spread before her. Each piece slotted in position, an elaborate gilded mosaic.

Aisling, on the other hand, always faced conscious decisions. Her talent not as readily evident as Yvonne's, Aisling worked her way up, always discomforted by the knowledge that she didn't have to dance. Another life, a life of normal girls, of ordinary controllable activities existed outside ballet. The thought that she should flee to that life always tortured Aisling. Her mosaic still lay in pieces—hard, sharp shards of stone and glass without a pattern.

Maxine and Yvonne knew from the beginning that normality was not their affliction.

Yvonne's personal life too had a preordained quality. She had not really chosen Gregory, nor had she found him. He had been a lucky happening she had done nothing to deserve. Her chance for ballet and romance had passed. She must step aside to make way for others. Aisling. Maxine. It was their time now.

Aisling had no glamorous career, no handsome man. She had work. Work and fear. Constant fear, which Yvonne had increased, not diminished.

In the year since the car accident, Yvonne had known fear, knew how it gnawed at your self-confidence, tripping you when you least expected it.

Surely their mutual fear was the basis for a relationship between them. And the basis for an understanding of Eve, a beginning for Aisling, a way for her to find new depths to her career. Colette might never have been afraid of anything. Yvonne knew that couldn't be true, but fear certainly wasn't the leitmotif in the writer's life that it was in theirs.

What was the point in sharing her decision with Ian? He could not accept she would not dance, at least for now. She and Aisling would work out their differences, perfect the role, and present Ian with a *fait accompli*.

Yvonne would not dance again.

It had taken time for her to accept that. Time and failure and tears, but it was true.

No dance, no Séan. It seemed the season for harsh decisions.

"Telegram, Miss St. Cyr."

"Thank you." Yvonne took the green hand-written envelope and continued to her room. What could this be? Hardly any kind of solution to her problems. Telegrams usually complicated matters, rarely offered solutions.

Anger about Aisling and Pat still bubbled inside. Now, what was she up to? Having little knowledge of Ian's needs, Aisling would have to work night and day to master Colette. That left no time for young men with clumps of brown hair and large brown eyes. Yvonne had not reached her peak allowing careless distractions.

That girl needed to be set straight. Preoccupied, Ian probably took no notice. Poor Ian. He was upset and powerless, and needed their help. Whatever her intentions, that girl would give it. Yvonne would see to that.

Down she sat, nervously tearing open the envelope. The signature indicated Maxine. "YVONNE, NEED SHEER TWEED EVENING STOP WEAR AND WEDDING STOP SOONEST STOP IMPORTANT STOP." That made absolutely no sense. More with hope than confidence, she reread the message.

Still no sense. Was New York ahead of or behind Irish time? she quizzed herself. Behind, so it was still afternoon on the East Coast. Reaching for the phone, she buzzed the front desk. "I need to call New York."

"Ah, now, that wouldn't be possible, I'm afraid."

"Why not?"

"Lines aren't working. I'll ring for you later."

"Please do. It's important."

Two hours later she still could not complete the long-distance call.

"NEED SHEER TWEED EVENING." *This* evening? "SOONEST." What was the soonest? It sounded urgent, though. What could she do?

"TWEED" had to involve Séan. If she called him, he might be able to help.

But she couldn't call him, not after telling him they could

never see each other. He would think she meant to resume their love affair.

She searched for another solution, but failed. Once again she fingered the telegram, then moved decisively to the phone. Yvonne dialed Seán's number, memories flowing back.

They were adults. They were mature. Their relationship would resume right where it should have remained—business acquaintances. Allowing her passion to spill out had been a mistake.

Seán stayed at the farm only on weekends, so she rang his town number. After a number of rings, a low, melodious voice answered—emphatically not Seán's. "Seán FitzGerald's residence."

At the point of hanging up, Yvonne scolded herself. Business, purely business. "Could I speak to Mr. FitzGerald?"

"Of course," a husky voice answered, sensual overtones overflowing. "Seán, it's for you."

"Hello?"

"Seán, it's me. I hope I'm not disturbing you."

"Of course not, I was just—"

"It doesn't matter. I have a strange telegram from Maxine. Something about tweed, which must mean you." How flustered she was! "We are supposed to be taking care of business for Maxine, we should meet about this."

"That's a wonderful idea!" His voice was excited. "When?"

"Only business, Seán."

"Of course. I understand that. Business, business, business."

She did not ask who had answered the phone. She didn't care, not one bit, and would hate for him to get the wrong idea. But he certainly hadn't wasted any time.

"You must understand that this doesn't change anything." Yvonne's voice was firm, and she ignored her racing pulse.

"Of course not. Perish the thought." Seán looked serious, except for a small gleam in his eyes. "Nothing at all."

"It would be better if we didn't see each other, but that can't be helped."

"Then we'll have to suffer on." Seán smiled slightly. "Together."

"Yes." Yvonne bit her lip. "Together." She showed him the telegram. "What do you think?"

"Maxine has not mastered the art of short, lucid messages?"

"Obviously something became garbled in transmission." Yvonne tapped the paper. "But what?"

"I agree it must mean me. I am definitely the tweed person."

"Could she really have needed it last night?"

"I did send Maxine some very sheer tweed samples. Tweed effect, anyway."

"The 'stop' could be in the wrong place. Maybe Maxine is thinking of making sheer evening wear. That leaves 'wedding.' "

"Strange for a wedding dress," Seán commented.

"Maybe for an interesting effect." They stared at each other over the paper. Yvonne wished she hadn't noticed what a finely chiseled mouth he had.

" 'Soonest'?" he asked.

"That part is simple. Whatever Maxine wants, she wants soonest."

"I see." He didn't sound enthusiastic.

"What's wrong?"

"I wasn't thinking 'soonest' when I sent the samples. That was careless. I'll have to see how much I can get hold of now, then call Maxine."

"The phones are still out."

"Just as well for now." Seán rose. "I'm off to see a man about some tweed." At the door, he turned. "Just to keep me from getting careless again, would you like to come too?"

"I suppose so." She had to safeguard Maxine's business interests. Nothing to do with Seán.

"It's a small drive. The man we need is on vacation out in the country."

"We could call."

"He doesn't have a phone. Helps keep him from being disturbed."

"By the less persistent," Yvonne suggested.

"Right."

Soon they were speeding through Dublin's traffic and out into the countryside. The bucket seats forced them closely together, much too close for Yvonne, supersensitive as she still was to his touch, his warmth, his body.

"I'm glad you were home last night," Yvonne said. She wouldn't dream of mentioning the sultry voice. "I'd hate for Maxine to be disappointed."

"Glad I was too. I'd hate for Maxine to be mad."

They whipped along the narrow roads. "Do you always drive so quickly?"

"I'm sorry, I didn't mean to frighten you."

"You didn't frighten me at all. But you might get a ticket."

"Not much chance. The Gárdaí don't patrol out here very much."

"How nice." Her hands gripped the edges of her seat. A few miles later she again turned to him. "Do you always drive so fast straight down the middle of the road?"

"Well, everyone does on these narrow roads. There isn't all that much room, you see, and . . ." He quickly glanced at her. "I'm sorry." He slowed down the car. "I forgot about the accident. I've done it again." He slowed down even further. "I don't know why. I really don't have this problem with other people. I know any number of people who would describe me as tactful."

They drove on slowly, slowly, slowly. "Seán?"

"Yes."

"You really don't need to creep along. It is nice of you, but I can stand a normal speed."

"Sure?"

"Yes." She smiled at him. "But it was nice of you to remember. I'm afraid there is a lot to remember about me." She blushed and looked ahead. In certain ways Seán knew her so intimately.

Gradually Yvonne noticed the sky clouding over. "I think it's going to rain."

"It ususally does," Seán agreed. "At any time in Ireland, any day, you are safe looking at the sky and saying it looks like rain."

"I hope this man can help."

"So do I."

"What's that noise?" Yvonne asked suddenly. Trying to ignore Seán's nearness, she paid close attention to any passing detail.

"What noise?"

"The engine is making a pinging sound." She cocked her head to listen. "There it is again."

"Seán glanced at her out of the corner of his eye. "I am going too fast."

"You are not! I heard a noise."

"I didn't." He slowed the car.

Yvonne indignantly looked at the scenery. "Have it your own way." Carefully she cultivated annoyance, preferring it to other emotions. Around a corner they came upon a flock of sheep blocking their way. Three dogs and two men whistled and clicked them along the road. "Why are we stopping?"

"To let the men get the sheep past us. If we drive straight through, they will panic and scatter."

The large furry animals still had their coats and looked to Yvonne like large cotton balls. Dirty cotton balls, she decided, noticing bits of twig and leaf caught in their coats, as if they were nature's dust mops. One black-muzzled animal peeked into the low car window, examining Yvonne with an enormous golden eye before moving away.

"I think I'll retire to Ireland and raise animals." Yvonne smiled. "It's so peaceful here."

"That's a wonderful idea." Seán looked adoringly at her. "I know a wonderful farm in need of a woman to look after it."

"Your farm has a woman looking after it. I'm sure Jane does a good job." To say nothing of his helpful friend from the town house.

"It isn't the same." Seán reached over, searching for her hand.

"Seán, we agreed. Just friendship." Confusion came over her at his touch.

"I believe in warm friendships."

"I don't. Besides, you need both hands to drive."

"All right, for now. I just want—"

"Seán?" She hurried to stop any talk of passion.

"I want to be sure not to miss our turn." Seán smiled innocently. "But I haven't given up hope," he added quickly.

"You should," she said firmly. As she looked at his strong profile, a flicker of happiness burned, conflicting with her intentions.

"I think we turn this way."

"Don't you know?"

"I've only been here once before." Seán frowned with thought. "I remember that clump of trees."

"Isn't there an address?"

"Yes. Willow Grove."

Yvonne looked suspicious. "That's an address?"

"It is in the country. Roads aren't exactly named and numbered out here." Seán gestured toward the tree-lined fields. "But this is beautiful, isn't it? Not a bad place to get lost in."

"We aren't supposed to be getting lost, we are supposed to be here on business." The pastoral scene contrasted vividly with the tumble of feelings he set off within her. She should never have called him, Yvonne realized.

"We are." His mouth tilted into a half-smile that touched her heart.

"Remember that." When Yvonne again heard the sound from the engine, she said nothing.

The noise grew louder; Seán cleared his throat. "I think I hear something."

"Indeed."

"Sorry." He grimaced.

"Thank you."

The pinging stopped suddenly; so did the engine. "Oh-oh."

"Oh-oh?" Yvonne echoed.

The car glided to a halt. "I think we have a little problem."

"Are you sure?" Yvonne regarded Seán with suspicion. "Isn't this a bit of a cliché? Car trouble out in the middle of nowhere." She glanced anxiously down the deserted road.

"You don't know your clichés. Running out of petrol is the cliché."

Yvonne stared severely. "Maybe you were being creative."

"Honestly, no," Seán insisted indignantly.

"I'm sorry. That was silly of me." Yvonne blushed.

"Of course, now that we are here . . ." Seán reached over and pulled her close, familiar hands brushing her body.

"Seán!" Yvonne struggled free from Seán and her desires.

"Sorry, I forgot. Just friends."

"Where are we?"

"Not far from where we are headed."

"We'll walk."

"I hate to walk," Seán grumbled, but left the car.

Together they sauntered down the road, little more than a hard dirt path. Not the most suitable substance for her heels, however. They soon reached a division in the road. "Which way?" Yvonne asked.

"This way, I think. Yes, I'm sure. I have an infallible sense of direction."

"I see."

The sky darkened further, the wind picked up, and a splash of rain hit the back of Yvonne's head. "Just around this bend."

They rounded the bend to find road and scenery, nothing else. "Infallible?" Yvonne murmured.

The rain fell in blowing sheets, and they sheltered ineffectively under the trees. Seán dripped. "I get wet a lot when I'm with you."

"Are you sure you don't have an infallible sense of misdirection?"

Seán laughed. "It's you."

"Me?"

"Yes, I'm hopelessly in love with you and I've been left confused. Bewildered."

"Let's change the subject."

"To the weather?"

"To where we are going and how we'll get there." Indignantly she charged down the road with pounding steps, only to sink into the mud, heels first. "And when I die in this quicksand, that too will be your fault."

Seán laughed heartily. "Let me help you out to firmer ground." He reached out with both arms, pulling her forward, then paused, gazing down into Yvonne's eyes. Slowly he pulled her close, gently kissing her lips, touching her hair, damp though it was.

"Seán . . ." her voice warned.

"I know. Friends." He released her.

Just then she saw a lone figure coming in their direction. "Rescued." She nodded.

Dressed in what looked to Yvonne like a tweed suit, a flat tweed cap on his head, and a pipe in his mouth, a man shuffled toward them. "A farmer," Seán identified. "A real sower and reaper."

"Why is he wearing a suit?" Yvonne asked.

"Because that is how they dress. Wouldn't be caught dead in jeans, you know." He hailed the man. "Good day to you."

"'Day." The man, dripping as they were, looked at the sky. "Damp."

Yvonne laughed at the understatement. "Yes."

Seán smiled. "If we were in a gale and freezing, it would be 'brisk.' Farmers are stoic."

Yvonne turned to the man. "We're looking for Willow Grove."

"Long walk." The man wheezed with laughter.

30

―――――

"Plot!" Yvonne pretended to grumble.

"Pardon?" Seán asked as they drove up to the front of his farm.

"I think this was a plot."

"You are becoming unbecomingly suspicious," he scolded, a gleam in his eye. "I didn't invent that mysterious noise, nor did I conspire with the gods to arrange the shower that soaked us."

"You did suggest we get back in the car, stop and dry off here instead of going back to Dublin." She tried, with little success, to look severe.

"I was only thinking of you, my dear. I wouldn't be wanting you to catch your death of cold."

Although she could not regret the extra hours with Seán, Yvonne intended to firmly control the situation. Nothing would happen while she was at the farm, she firmly decided. "Well, at least Jane will act as chaperon."

"Ah, yes, Jane." Seán stuck his hands in his pockets and looked toward the sky.

"Jane. Cousin. Housekeeper. Remember?" Yvonne walked toward the kitchen.

"How could I forget Jane?" His accent deepened. "But she's in Paris."

"In Paris?"

"Lovely city." Seán opened the door, and taking her elbow, firmly steered her inside.

She would be alone with Seán.

"Only a brief trip," he pleaded.

"Brief enough so she'll be back within the next few minutes?" Yvonne moved toward the door. "I think we'd better leave for Dublin. Now."

Gracefully he moved to block her way. "Now, Yvonne. Don't be silly."

"Seán, I told you this had to be business." Agitation grew as she stood before him, unwilling to touch his body, which stood infuriatingly between her and the door.

"It is. What would Maxine say?"

"What?" Yvonne stepped back with guilty shock. "Say about what?"

"You catching pneumonia, of course. Out in the country on tweed business—isn't it lucky he can help us, after all—out in the country, caught in a sudden shower, and then . . ." —he moved dramatically toward her as she hastily retreated across the room—"Yvonne is mortally stricken. Oh, woe is me."

Yvonne started to giggle.

"Easy for you to laugh. Do you know what Maxine would do to me?" Seán looked around the kitchen. "I'm hungry."

"I thought we were going to dry off and leave."

"I'll have to set the fire, and you can put our clothes in the dryer, and we might as well have a bite to eat."

Yvonne wondered if she looked like a drowning river rat, and patted nervously at her hair. "Well . . . I still think you might have planned this."

"Did not. Did not." A dark comma of hair had fallen across his forehead. "I can prove it."

"Yes?" Yvonne distrustfully drawled out the word.

Seán opened cupboards, peered into the refrigerator. "Yes. There is almost nothing left to eat that isn't frozen. I planned to stay in the city while Jane was gone. I can assure you, if I were planning seduction, I would have prepared a more delicious meal. All I have is cheese." He pulled out a round of the golden dairy product. "A few crackers in the tin there. And"—he smiled—"a chilled bottle of champagne."

"Just happened to be there, huh?"

"In my house, chilled champagne is a staple." He turned toward the living room. "Now, take off your clothes."

"Seán!"

"I meant so you could change. Upstairs, you know."

"I bet," she murmured. Business, business, she chanted mentally, determined to remember even if Seán was determined to forget. Still, she looked anxiously into the mirror of the bathroom. A wilted wildflower, pale yellow against her black hair, clung behind one ear, where Seán had placed it before getting back into the car.

Drawing it out, she carefully placed the fragile blossom in her wallet. That morning she had pinned her hair severely back, as if to proclaim her attitude toward Seán, but now it clung unbecomingly to her head. Taking out her brush, she fluffed her hair around her shoulders in soft curls.

Downstairs she heard Seán moving around. "What shall I change into?" she called.

"On the bed," he answered. "Bring down your clothes when you come."

One of Seán's white shirts hung from the bedpost. "Seán, this isn't what I had in mind."

"Sorry. Jane didn't leave anything, and besides"—he appeared at the foot of the stairs—"it will cover everything vital."

Yvonne hesitated, but the clinging of her damp, clammy clothes changed her mind.

Her clothes in a pile on the floor, she toweled off and slipped on Seán's shirt. Its arms dangled off her hands, so she rolled them up to her elbows. The tails of the shirt at least covered her thighs, she thought with relief as she carefully buttoned the shirt to her chin.

She walked downstairs, holding the dripping clothes in her hand, feeling the carpet under her bare toes, and trying to pretend the situation was totally within her control.

"There you are." Seán appeared not to notice her physical appearance, the soft curve of her breasts thrusting through the thin cloth. "Hand those over and I'll slip them into the dryer, if that's all right?"

"Fine." She handed over her jeans and shirt.

"You go into the sitting room by the fire. I found some pâté and bread to go with the cheese, and the champagne is cold." He smiled with apparent charm and not passion. "I'll change and be right back."

Yvonne settled on the couch, feeling a ribbon of disappointment. A tray held their dinner. Seán hadn't mentioned assorted relishes, two other cheeses, an apple tart, and thick cream. A silver cooler held the champagne.

"There. Won't take long." Seán entered the room looking pleased. "Is the fire high enough?"

"Fine, thank you." Only one lamp was lit in the room. Soft light came in through the large windows, muted by a gentle rain. The setting was cozy and familiar, Yvonne thought.

Seán helped her prepare a plate of food; then, as she settled back, he opened the champagne with a cheerful pop. "I think we can gather a line of tweeds and send Maxine samples by tomorrow night. And maybe phone her by then."

"Good. I know she'll be pleased at your efforts, Seán."

"And yours."

The idea made Yvonne edgy. Her efforts had included becoming romantically involved with a man Maxine cared for. "Yes." She briskly turned away and stared into the fire.

Seán handed her a tulip glass of bubbling wine and sat on the other side of the couch. Even without looking at him, Yvonne was painfully aware of his presence. A subtle scent . . . his weight on the cushions. . . . Memories flooded her.

His gentleness combined with strength, the curve where his thigh swept into his body, the startling blue of his eyes—impatiently she pushed memories away. This was the present. It couldn't work, no matter what she might feel. Maxine, Síle's advice, her own confusion, all prevented their relationship from progressing.

How could she trust her reactions? During the last year her moods had swung wildly, propelling her first toward one decision, then abruptly in the opposite direction. How did she know her love for Seán wouldn't follow the same path?

"Yvonne?"

His voice made her start as if from guilty thoughts. "Yes."

"I don't want to pry, but what are you doing about your career?"

"Which one?" she tried to smilingly evade the question. "The shoe-and-tweed concern is looking up, thanks to you."

"I meant ballet."

"Oh." It seemed so tiring to talk about. Yvonne sipped her champagne. "Nothing."

"Then you are certain it's over."

"I don't know. In New York . . ." She glanced to see if he

looked uninterested, and saw his eyes fixed on her. "In New York, I was determined after Gregory died to resume my career." How many details that left out, she thought. She swallowed, "There were monetary problems."

"What kind?" Seán clearly hadn't suspected.

"It doesn't really matter. You must not read the scandal sheets." She explained Gregory's business problems. "I don't know what is happening now. Jerry wasn't going to bother me unless an emergency arose." She tried to smile. "A further emergency, I mean."

"Then you aren't . . . wealthy?" Seán searched her face.

"I'm having trouble staying afloat," Yvonne admitted. "I suspect Maxine invented this job so she wouldn't be in the embarrassing position of giving me money."

"I'm so glad." He moved closer to her.

"Seán, what a terrible thing to say."

"Well, it was bothering me. It suddenly occurred to me that as the widow of an enormously wealthy man you might be terribly rich. I didn't want people saying I was a fortune hunter." Seán looked dignified. "I think you should realize I'm not rich, just comfortably well off."

"I'll keep that in mind."

"Now we can get married."

"No, we cannot," she objected. "Will you pour me some more champagne?" She moved to the corner of the couch, safely out of reach.

"Why not?"

"I don't want to. That's all."

"Then we'll talk about ballet again. After the accident, you intended to dance?"

"Yes." Yvonne closed her eyes, thinking of those days in New York. It seemed years before. "Just when I thought I was ready, there was the accident onstage. My Achilles tendon. It wasn't broken but badly strained. A side effect of everything else that had happened, the doctor thought. Minute changes in the way I dance added extra strain to the area. He didn't know if I could build it up enough to dance professionally."

"Then he didn't say you absolutely couldn't dance again?"

"No. But I had worked so hard before, trying all the

half-crazy remedies that dancers find. It just didn't seem worth the effort. When Maxine's job offer came, it seemed perfect. I was tired of dancing and the emotional effort it took. I'm getting older. My career couldn't last forever. I thought working as her representative would be the solution.''

"But it wasn't."

"No." She vaguely realized Seán was sitting very close.

"So now?"

"I don't know. Ian believes I will dance Colette."

"He still has confidence in your ability."

Yvonne considered. "No, he's desperate, he sees what he wants to."

"You aren't limping as you were when you first came."

"No, but I really don't think I'll dance again." She waited for the mandatory pep talk. Of course you can dance, give it all you have, Gregory would have enthused. You have to, I won't accept less, Gregory would have ordered. But Gregory wasn't here.

"Well, if you don't dance, what will you do? Teach?"

His cold nonchalance slapped her momentarily into silence. "No. It isn't working out well with Aisling." To cover her hurt reaction, she poured herself another glass of wine.

"Have you considered you aren't dancing because you don't want to? You've been dancing a long time. Maybe you need a rest." Seán put an arm around her shoulders.

Yvonne's head began to swim, either from Seán's nearness or the champagne or the nervous reaction to the discussion. "Well, I'm getting one." She nodded in the direction of the windows. "Look. It's really pouring outside."

"Isn't it nice to be inside on a day like this?" Seán pulled her closer so her head rested on his shoulder.

"Especially when you've been out on a day like this." It was so safe and comfortable in the shelter of his arm. Deceptively safe and comfortable, she tried to remind herself.

"True. You think Maxine will like the tweed?"

"It's very hard to tell. Maxine's mind can change like the wind." Yvonne laughed. "But then, who am I to talk anymore? It seems I do the same constantly."

"I should think that a rather understandable reaction

to the year you've been through." One hand moved around her shoulder and to the base of her throat. Gently he played with the top button, which seemed to slip open.

"Maybe, but it doesn't help me feel stable." At his touch, a growing warmth spread through her body. She should move away and insist they start back to Dublin, but she hesitated, enjoying the flames of excitement that licked through her.

"Perhaps I could help there. I am very stable." He drew her face toward his, kissing her with butterfly touches around her lips, down her throat, then darting toward her breasts.

She grasped his hair, pulling his head up to a less dangerous position, only to find his lips pressed demandingly against hers. She was captured in a trap of love, she thought, imprisoned by ecstasy—hers as much as Seán's.

Pulling her onto his lap facing him, he opened the rest of the shirt's buttons, revealing her white body, and crushed her to him. "Yvonne, just give in to this," he told her. "I love you. Want you. Need you."

Yvonne tried to fight her deep need, but as his lips found the burning points of her breasts, as she felt his passion thrusting through his clothes, she knew all was lost. Later she might regret her weakness, but for now Seán was everything she needed.

31

"You don't know what this means to me." Fleming carefully slid the key into the lock. "Thank you for delaying your trip to Ireland." He touched her hand. "Thanks for everything. I'll never forget this."

"I don't mind." Kili nervously peeked over her shoulder. "Couldn't we get out of the hall, though?"

"Sure. It will be all right. Really." He was an entire head taller than she.

"Not if Maxine finds out, it won't be."

Together they slipped into the front hall of Maxine's apartment. "You are certain that Maxine will be busy all day?" Kili heard a nervous flutter in Fleming's voice.

"Until three."

"Did you warn the manufacturer to keep her busy?"

Kili looked aghast. "If you don't know her any better than that, you should call off the whole thing. Just a hint, a whisper, and Maxine would know something was up. She's always there until three."

"How did you get away?"

"I told her I had to pack. Either way, that's true. If she finds out, it will be permanent."

They walked to the living room together. Kili tiptoed behind Fleming. "Why do I expect her to leap out at me?"

"Experience." Fleming laughed, feigning a confident air.

Kili looked around the familiar apartment. "Are you sure you want to do this, Fleming?"

"Positive." He smiled slightly, reaching out to hold her hand. "You won't desert me now, will you?"

"Of course not."

Kili checked her lists for the hundredth time and glanced nervously at Fleming. "What if I forgot something?"

"It wouldn't matter. Maxine will be too nervous to notice."

"Ha!"

"Now, Kili, everything will work out."

"Easy for you to say."

"I'll protect you." Fleming smiled boyishly.

"You aren't big enough."

"Where do these go?" The butler who had been waiting for Kili and Fleming, appeared carrying Maxine's wedding bouquet.

"In the bedroom," Fleming directed.

"How did you get her agreement on obtaining a marriage license?" Kili nervously adjusted a bouquet of flowers spilling off a low table, spreading lacy baby's breath onto the floor.

"It wasn't that hard." Fleming's eyes were glazed. "She said that the road from license to wedding was littered with wilted white roses, limp grooms, and yellowed marriage licenses."

"She always was a romantic."

A few hours later, Kili wore a shocking-pink dress with a panel of lace decorating the bodice, and a river of tiny pleats flowing from the body of the waistless dress. The room had been transformed into a bower of flowers, white and yellow, most exotic. No roses, Kili had screamed repeatedly to the florists, who kept baby rosebuds dancing in their heads.

The guests had been carefully chosen, and they had all arrived promptly. She directed the caterers toward the kitchen, where Maxine's French chef could be heard swearing in frustration at the invasion. "If he quits . . ." Kili whispered. "Are you sure we'll survive this?"

"No."

"Oh. That's nice."

Fleming shrugged. "The only way to get her to marry me is to catch her by surprise."

Kili pondered. "Weddings aren't exactly a birthday. I wonder if she will fire me for this."

"I'm sure not."

"I'm *not* sure."

"We'll blame it entirely on me."

"Don't think I'll forget that offer." Kili's eyes darted around the decorated apartment. "This setting is stunning. Maybe we can plead artistic insanity before the ax falls."

"I don't understand what she's afraid of." Fleming sighed.

"Being left?"

"I would never."

Kili shrugged. "Maybe not. Afraid of leaving?"

"You are heartening. On the eve of my wedding, telling me I might become a deserted husband."

"If you want security, Fleming, buy stocks, invest in gold, do anything before you marry Maxine."

"I never could take good advice."

When the hall phone rang, Kili answered. "Yes. Thank you." She turned to Fleming. "Maxine is on her way up. Do you want to meet her, or shall I?"

"No, you go in to the . . . party. And pray it doesn't turn into a wake." He set his shoulders and waited by the door.

"Fleming!" Maxine looked surprised but pleased. "I didn't know you would be here. What's that noise? It sounds like—"

"A wedding."

"A wedding?" Maxine stepped back and looked up at Fleming. "A wedding?"

"Yes, it's a quaint little custom. People stand before a minister and tell all their friends they intend to live together. Some of the best people have them."

"A *wedding*?"

"I knew you would be pleased."

"Whose?"

"Whose?" Fleming took a deep breath. "Ours."

"You are kidding!"

Fleming expected the flowers in the room to wilt. "I hope not. Now, once and for all, you will marry me!"

Maxine gazed at him, burst into tears, and ran for her bedroom. Fleming resisted an impulse to run in the opposite direction, and followed instead. "Can I come in?" he called through her door.

"Yes," she sniffed.

"Oh, Maxine, I am sorry."

"What is this?" She pointed to a dress lying on the bed by her bouquet of orchids.

Simply cut, of a vaguely oriental design, the dress accented the green of her eyes and flowed to the ground from quilted shoulders.

"Your wedding gown. Kili designed it."

"Damn! That woman is getting good. She won't be with me long."

"What about me?"

"I don't think you could learn to design dresses."

"Maxine, do you hate the idea of marrying me so much?" Fleming walked to her side, put his arms around her.

"No, it's just . . ." Her lower lip quivered.

"What is it?"

"I won't make you happy."

"Don't you think I would be the best judge of that?"

"But, Fleming. Don't you want a wife who will follow you around, gazing adoringly at you, saying, 'Yes, dear,' all the time?"

Fleming looked adoringly at her. "No, dear. I want you. Forever. Now, let's make it that way."

"Now, Aisling, we have a problem here." Yvonne had invited Aisling to lunch on neutral ground—the Shelbourne Grill. She was determined not to think of the night before. Not the hours with Seán at the farm or the later dinner he took her to at the Grey Door. Seating only thirty-five diners, it was a romantic setting glowing with Georgian antiques, candles, flowers, and a bright fire. Over fresh salmon cutlets cooked in a sauce of fresh cream, dill, onion, and mushrooms, they held hands, laughing for no reason and every reason.

"Yes. Bundles of problems." Aisling cringed, as if wondering which Yvonne meant: Ian, her dancing, Pat?

"I have been . . . difficult with you, Aisling."

"Difficult?" Aisling said softly.

"Yes, this has been an unpleasant year for me. I have not been patient. I have not been generous. We still have time to work on Eve. You have improved a great deal, and I will find a way for you to reach new heights."

"Eve?" Aisling had clearly expected an upbraiding, and Yvonne's friendly attitude stunned her.

"That leaves *Ballet of Desire*. You will have the privilege of dancing Colette."

"Colette? But I can't. Ian is making it on you." A gleam suddenly woke in her eyes, seeming to evaluate Yvonne's words.

"He is. But I obviously won't be dancing it. Let's avoid pretense. Once you are settled in Colette, I will retire and leave the company."

"No, you can't mean it. You are at the top."

"Now, you mustn't worry about that. You must concentrate on Colette."

"What will Ian say?"

"We won't tell him."

"Won't tell him! You must be kidding. We won't tell him you won't be dancing in his ballet?" Aisling's eyes widened and she paled.

"Ian is so quiet, preoccupied. Of course, he's getting older. I guess that's the problem," she murmured. "However, whatever it is, he doesn't understand the seriousness of my injury. He is planning to make the ballet on you, with me watching, so I can then take over the role. I'll start practicing again, working out as I can. Ian will presume I'll be able to take on the role, that I'm learning the more difficult sections in private."

Distraught, Aisling fell back in her chair. "I can't, Yvonne, I really can't. What would Ian do to me? Dancers don't make these decisions. And Colette will be worse than Eve. I've seen you dance Eve; Colette is all new. I can't do it."

"Of course you can. Ian knows you have talent. That's why he chose you."

Aisling was unconvinced. "Maybe he was wrong. Anyway, Justine would never let me." Her eyes dipped nervously to her hands, then opened wide and innocently as she looked at Yvonne.

"Justine won't know until it's too late. You'll do a wonderful job, and she won't care, I assure you. Justine allows anything that works."

"I'll try." Aisling tottered to her feet. "I think I'll rest until class."

"Of course, dear, but you haven't eaten."

"I can't. Not right now. I'll order some tea and toast up in my room while I relax."

"All right, but be sure to take care of yourself."

Aisling smiled in timorous reply and left the room. Yvonne thoughtfully watched her leave. Aisling trembled with nerves, looked thin and harried. Was it just the pressure of working on Eve? Or perhaps Aisling's doubts about her own ability? Was Justine pressuring her in some way? Yvonne wondered if Aisling would make it.

To her embarrassment, Kili found her heart pounded as she walked toward the studio. Perhaps coming to Ireland was a mistake. Perhaps he wouldn't be pleased.

The door opened, and Kili saw that Aisling and Yvonne leaned toward Ian at the end of the room. Ian turned, but the light glowed behind Kili, blurring her outline for a moment. "Yes?" Ian's voice was brisk.

"Hi. It's me."

"Kili?" Yvonne ran toward her. "What are you doing here? Is Maxine here?"

"No. Just me and my designs." In minute detail Maxine had explained what would happen if Kili told Yvonne about her wedding. "How are you?"

"Wonderful."

"And you, Aisling?" Kili edged along the room.

"Fine, Kili. I think I'll take a break," Aisling announced, and disappeared into the hall.

"Hello, Ian."

"I didn't expect to see you so soon." Ian inspected her gracefully but thoroughly. "You are looking well—very well."

"Thank you." She lightly touched her expensive Chinese-ed silk dress for reassurance. "I have the sketches. I thought you might like to see them."

"I would. And you." They looked at each other.

Yvonne stared in disbelief.

Ian gestured toward the hall. "I have to make some arrangements so I'll have the afternoon free. If you don't mind waiting here."

"Of course not." They looked longer, then Ian tore himself away.

"Well, Kili. How are things in New York?" Yvonne tried to look normal.

"Fine." Kili avoided her eyes. Just one little thing. The surprise wedding of your best friend. "Nothing special happening."

"Maxine's busy?"

"Oh, you wouldn't believe how busy."

"Kili, tell me."

"What?"

"I've gotten the impression that Maxine has a new romantic interest. Do you know anything about that?"

Kili gulped. Just as she had always thought. Those two didn't need telephones, they communicated telepathically. "Well, I guess you could say that."

"I see." Yvonne looked away from Kili, hiding her disappointment.

"Here we are." Ian bounced in with energy Yvonne hadn't seen since his arrival in Ireland. "I have a car out front, Kili. Why don't you get in?"

"Thank you. I'll see you later, Yvonne."

"Of course." Yvonne stared as the slim young figure retreated out the door.

"Oh, Yvonne. This is a first for me," Ian bubbled.

"At your age, Ian, it wouldn't seem possible there would be any firsts left." Yvonne raised a graceful eyebrow.

"I'm in love."

"That isn't a first for you, Ian. Not even a second or third."

"But with someone fifty years younger."

"There may be a good reason you've never tried it before, Ian. Are you certain you know what you're doing?"

"Yes."

"Well, you're too old to lecture. But"—she turned with a smile—"don't call in the middle of the night claiming you are trapped in some bizarre position. You're not that young anymore."

"No . . ." Ian smiled. "Younger. Much younger."

After an intimate lunch, they went back to Ian's hotel. "You aren't sorry I came?" Kili asked.

"Very pleased. The sketches are truly perfect. Just like you."

"I'm glad both are suitable."

"How long can you stay?"

"At least a couple of weeks."

"How is Maxine?"

"On her honeymoon."

"Honeymoon?" Ian stiffened with surprise. "As in trip fter marriage?"

"You've got it."

"Yvonne doesn't know?"

"No, and we aren't to tell."

"No, that isn't an honor I would dream of taking from laxine."

Kili smiled. "There will be several days before the storm reaks." With a shake of her head, she tossed thick black air over her shoulder.

Ian leaned back and looked at her. "Oh, Kili, if only I ere ten years younger."

Kili giggled. "I'm so glad you had the honesty not to ask r twenty."

"I don't need twenty."

"You don't need ten."

"Kili, I do love you." He looked at her.

"Really?"

Ian walked across the room and stared out the windows. Well, no, but almost."

"Thank heavens." Kili laughed and joined him.

32

Yvonne awoke each morning in an ocean of despair and indecision, resolving not to see Seán, only to find herself unable to keep her resolve. No sex, Yvonne had insisted, and Seán agreed to abide by the terms of their relationship. He did. Just barely. Yvonne was determined to remain strong—at least until she could speak with Maxine.

Now Yvonne sat pensively looking over the stage of the Gaiety from their seats in the lush red auditorium. Seán had asked to see a rehearsal of Eve.

"I heard something that might interest you," he said. "About a doctor."

"A doctor?"

"Yes, a specialist. Works with leg injuries in some new way. Would you be interested in seeing him?"

Yvonne remained silent and moved her hand slightly away from his. "The company asked Aisling to give a small preview tonight."

"Did she agree?"

"Of course. It will do her good to perform."

"Does she think so?"

"I don't know. I didn't ask her." Yvonne took a deep breath. "She is working much better into Eve. I suggested that Eve too was frightened, frightened that life would pass her by. Aisling had been thinking about using her fear onstage."

"That sounds very revealing."

"That sounds like a great dancer."

"That brings us back to the doctor."

"Really. Is he a dancer, too?"

"No, he is an expert on soccer injuries."

Yvonne patted his hand. "You've found a new career for e!"

"Oh, you would look so cute in those little shorts." Seán oved as if to kiss her.

"Thank you. What do you think?" She leaned back in her air and regarded him fondly.

"About little shorts?"

"About the doctor." She didn't look at him. Did she want m to insist? Yvonne thought she knew what she wanted, yet e hung on his words.

"I think he is probably very good and he might tell you mething definite about your leg."

"I meant, do you think I should go? I don't think I'll ever nce again."

"So you've said."

Her hand moved onto her lap and curled into a tight fist. What does that mean?"

"I just mean, I can't believe that after all those years, all at suffering and struggling, you are ready to give up with-t a fight."

Yvonne raised her head proudly high. "I did fight."

"Not as hard as you can." He kept his eyes pointed toward e stage.

"Then you think I should go to the doctor?"

"I won't say that."

"Why not?" She turned to face him. "Why won't you tell e?" If he loved her, he would.

Seán gestured with impatience. "Because I don't believe in ving advice, certainly not about something so important. ou may be right, and this would only be one more sappointment. So this has to be your decision. I can't make for you."

Gregory would have made it for her, he would have known actly what she should do. If Seán were strong enough, if he red enough, he would too. "There's Aisling. She's going rehearse her solo for tonight."

The music began. Aisling stood in the middle of an almost pty stage, settling into position, flexing her *pointe* shoes.

Coming to rest, she froze for a moment before beginning
dance.

"That looks good."

"She is a good dancer," Yvonne said with some prid
She and Aisling were not best friends, but their relationsh
had improved immeasurably. At least, most of the time.
periodic attack of nerves would occasionally overwhelm th
young girl, leaving her shy and ineffective when with Yvonn
At least twice when Aisling had begun to speak, she quivere
slightly as if frightened by the significance of her words. C
both occasions she halted, an anguished look on her fac
Nerves, Yvonne assumed. At nineteen the featured role in
world-famous choreographer's new ballet was enough to pe
rify the most seasoned of dancers. But, Yvonne thoug
confidently, Aisling could do it.

"I think Aisling has lost weight since coming to Ireland,
Seán commented.

Yvonne stirred with guilt. Working with Aisling and seeir
Seán meant she'd been neglectful of Aisling's diet. "Th
excitement of the trip. A new place."

"Hasn't affected you like that. You've gained a few pounds.

"Do you think so?" Yvonne was alarmed.

"Relax, you needed it. When you first came, you weren
looking so good."

"Thank you very much, Mr. FitzGerald. I'm so sorry
didn't meet with your approval."

"Oh, you always met with my approval." He leaned clo
and kissed her on the cheek.

"Seán."

"You did."

"Let's watch Aisling."

The blond girl swirled and dipped, covering the stage
dramatic gestures. Then gradually she slowed.

"Am I wrong, or is something amiss?"

"I don't know. She's off beat." When the dancing su
denly ceased, Yvonne stood up, straining forward. Emitting
slight cry, Aisling tumbled to the floor.

"Please leave me," Aisling asked. She gestured everyor
out of her dressing room. "Please, Ian, I'll be all righ
Yvonne can stay." Aisling curled up in a humiliated ball.

Silence fell. "I know it's embarrassing to faint onstage, but it isn't the end of the world."

"You would never do such a thing, never. This was my punishment for not eating breakfast, or dinner the night before, or much lunch before that."

"You should have."

"I couldn't. The thought made me ill."

How astute of Seán to notice Aisling had lost so much weight. "Aisling, I think you need a doctor."

"No. That isn't necessary, Yvonne. I just fainted."

"But look at you. You're wasting away."

"I'm not ill."

"Of course, you are. I should have noticed earlier. I am responsible for you, after all."

"I just haven't been eating very well. Nerves."

"Aisling, you weren't this upset in New York."

"I wasn't working as a soloist in a Thorn ballet in New York."

"Yvonne. Seán. Look who's here." Ian's voice rang out from the stage.

Yvonne walked, head down, her mind still ruminating on Aisling. Something else bothered her, but what?

Ian met them, and asked quietly, "Aisling?"

"I think she's all right," Yvonne replied with a tight smile. "She'll eat first, then resume. But you were saying . . . ?"

"It's our English friends." Ian gestured. "Roland and Eleanor are here."

Yvonne's dismay could scarcely be hidden. Justine would have been a more welcome sight.

"Yvonne." Roland sprang across the stage toward her, enveloping her in a bountiful hug. "You look wonderful. Gorgeous."

Seán stared.

"Oh, Roland, this is Seán FitzGerald."

"Nice to meet you." Roland nodded, his eyes fixed on Yvonne. "Lunch?"

"Yvonne and I have a date," Seán quickly interjected.

"But you are welcome to join us," Yvonne mischievously added.

"Hello." A faint voice came from behind Roland. "How are you, Yvonne?" Pale Eleanor appeared.

"Fine, Eleanor. You must come to lunch too." Yvonne tried to smile warmly. The animosity in New York had been her own fault, after all.

"I wouldn't miss it," Eleanor assured her.

"Ian?" Yvonne asked.

"Thank you. Very nice, but Kili and I have to mull over some important details. Designs." He smiled at Kili. "Scenery. All those boring details." He looked back at the group of dancers. "Later, children. Later."

As a native, Seán chose the restaurant. Roland, ignoring Seán and Eleanor, escorted Yvonne. Effusively he tucked her in her chair, hovered over her choice of dinner, almost, Seán thought, fed her bite by bite.

"What do you think of Ireland?" Seán asked Roland.

"That it is more beautiful now that Yvonne is here." He gazed intently into her eyes.

"I bet you haven't had time to see the sights. You and your wife."

"Roland doesn't like to sightsee," Eleanor volunteered.

"We have lovely scenery."

"I know." Roland leered at Yvonne. "Wonderful."

"Of course, there is too much rain." Seán glared.

Roland didn't notice. "When will you be back in New York?" His tone implied civilization.

Yvonne gazed at Roland in wonder. She had never before realized how tacky he was. Roland's bedroom eyes, his passionate leer, his constant touch, all could pass for a romantic hero from a silent movie. But now his lack of subtlety made it all seem humorous. His manner was as intimate as the rustle of sheets. Too intimate. What had she ever seen in him?

"What are you two doing here?" Yvonne finally interrupted his compliments to ask.

"Stopover," Roland murmured, making it sound like an invitation to bed.

"Stopover?"

"To the gala in New York. Everyone will be there,"

Eleanor cooed, for the first time sparkling with satisfaction. "Roland and I have a *pas de deux*. It is very romantic."

The rest of the conversation passed in a blur, Yvonne hardly noticing what was said, what was eaten. "Gala" rang in her ears, a gala replete with a full act of Ian's *Ballet of Desire*.

33

"I have decided to visit the doctor." Yvonne had agonized over her decision all night, unwilling once again to raise false hopes, yet determined to do what she must.

"Have you?" Seán's voice was cautious.

"I thought you might be pleased." His nonchalance stung.

"I want you to do whatever you think best, Yvonne." Seán's voice was gentle, and he gave her a hug. "Soon?"

"Today."

"Would you like me to take you?"

"No, I'll go alone." Yvonne did not wish to sound like a martyr, but she felt frightened and exposed, unsure if she were truly doing what she wanted. "Whatever she thought best," Seán had said, but Yvonne had not known what she thought best for the past year.

"Good for you."

She smiled tightly. "I try." With little encouragement from him.

"Let's meet afterward. I'll want to know what he says. Unless you would rather be alone for a while."

"No. I would love to meet you. Where?"

"Just in case I'm delayed, I'd rather you didn't wait on the street. Let's meet on the first floor at the National Museum."

"Fine. It's close to the hotel."

"Yes." He stared at her without speaking, took a deep breath, and carefully chose his words. "I hope . . ."

"Yes?"

"I hope . . . I hope Roland is enjoying his visit." He didn't sound as if he meant it.

"I'm sure he is." What had he been about to say?

"Really?"

"Wherever Roland is, he's always in his favorite company because Roland *is* his own favorite company."

"Thank goodness."

"What?"

"I thought maybe you two were dear, close friends."

"No." His undertone of jealousy brought a pleased flush to her cheeks. She glanced at her watch. "I have to leave."

"Right." They stood. "Yvonne . . ."

"Yes?" She hoped for some commitment on his part, some direction.

"Good luck."

"Thanks."

Yvonne walked the short distance to FitzWilliam Square, home to Dublin's elite medical specialists. She sauntered through the small public park enclosed by green railings at the square's center. Dr. Murray's office was located in one of the large Georgian houses, and elegantly furnished like a private home. A pert nurse settled Yvonne in a comfortable chair with a list. "Just fill this out, dear, and the doctor will be with you in a jiffy."

Too soon, Yvonne thought, listing her bits and pieces of body on the paper, noting her ailments. When finished, she sat back with a sigh, stifling an urge to flee. If she didn't know for sure about her injury, she wouldn't be forced into a choice.

"Miss St. Cyr? Dr. Murray will see you."

A large, bluff man with an absentminded air and sharp, shrewd eyes welcomed her with kind words about her career, careful questions about her body.

He poked and probed, watched her walk, flex her foot, bend, and stretch. "Hmmm."

Yvonne watched with large, frightened eyes.

"Let's see you run in place."

Under his eagle eye she ran, surprised at not feeling ridiculous. She jumped, walked once again, then sat, waiting.

"Are you in pain during other activities?"

"No, just dancing."

He sent her with the nurse for X rays. When back in his comfortable office, Yvonne braced herself for the bad news.

"You are hoping to resume dancing professionally?"

"I don't hope anything any longer."

"I have something that might help." He spoke of bone chips, of calcium buildup, and of a series of shots that might dissolve both. "What do you think?"

"Can I call you in the morning?"

"Of course."

She would ask Seán. Now that she had definite information, he would advise her.

She took a taxi to the museum. The first floor. Seán had said he would wait for her there.

But much to her disappointment, Seán was not to be seen. A few visitors passed, as did the guards, but no sign of Seán. He must be in the main area, she thought. Without wandering through the exhibits, she scanned the room, eager to see him, expecting his broad shoulders to come into view. He was nowhere in sight.

She would be patient. Something had detained him; he would arrive any moment. She paced by the door, searching the face of each male figure who entered.

Fifteen minutes passed, then thirty. Yvonne felt deserted and disappointed; she hated to wait. When about to leave, her eyes drifted up the staircase to the second floor.

There stood Seán, his arm around an attractive woman, his head close to hers. The woman with the husky voice, Yvonne was convinced. With a gasp, she stepped behind a display box and watched in despair as the woman kissed Seán goodbye, then walked down the stairs. She passed so closely to Yvonne that her perfume swirled around and Yvonne could admire her beautiful brunette appearance, examine her lush retreating figure.

"Yvonne!" She heard her name called from above. "Wait right there." Quickly Seán descended. "Where have you been?"

"Me? Right here, on the first floor."

"Oh, I forgot."

"Forgot?"

"This isn't the first floor."

"What do you mean? Of course it is." Angrily she blinked back tears.

"Not in Ireland. This is the ground floor. How silly!"

"How silly!" She laughed faintly.

"Were you waiting long?"

"No, I just came in."

"Good. Let's go somewhere more private and you can tell me what the doctor said."

Once installed in Seán's house in town, Yvonne told her story and waited for his advice, concealing her devastation. She was the one who insisted they must have no claims on each other. She had insisted they had no future together.

"What will you do?" Seán asked.

"I thought you might advise me." When he didn't answer, she bit her lip with annoyance. "No, that's not right. I should do what I think best."

"Now, Yvonne."

"Never mind. I would like to go back to the hotel, please."

Seán insisted upon accompanying her into the Shelbourne. He had been unusually quiet during the ride. "Yvonne . . ."

"Never mind."

"Yvonne, I think you should take the treatment."

"Really?"

"I really think certain things are better worked out by yourself, but yes."

She took his hand, then remembered the brunette and quickly released it.

"Miss St. Cyr, message."

Seán reached over and took it, handing the paper to Yvonne.

"It's from Kili. She says we are to come to her hotel room. Right away."

"Why?"

"Doesn't say, but it sounds important. Can you come?"

"Wouldn't miss it."

They crossed to the Royal Hibernian, where Ian and Kili had their suites. Yvonne and Seán went right up to the room and knocked. "Come in." The voice was muffled.

Seán held the door open for her and Yvonne walked in.

"Yvonne!"

"Maxine! What are you doing here? Where have you been?"

"Good to see you," Seán said. "Yvonne wanted to send over the Marines to look for you."

"What a good idea! All those handsome men." Maxine laughed, sounding, Yvonne thought, nervous.

Ian and Kili stood by the windows, talking quietly. Yvonne noticed a tall man standing behind Maxine's chair. "Have you heard? Roland and Eleanor are here."

"Wonderful."

"We have your tweed."

"Great."

"It caused some confusion when we received your telegram."

"I see."

Yvonne looked at the man. "I don't believe . . ."

"Oh, yes." Maxine turned toward Fleming. "This is Fleming James. You've met."

"I am afraid I don't . . . Oh, yes, the restaurant. Nice to see you again." She tried to remember if Maxine had ever explained who Fleming was. Handsome man, she noticed. "I was worried when you disappeared. What are you doing here?" She turned back to Maxine.

"I'm on a little vacation . . . a trip." Maxine looked very white.

"Midyear?"

"Yes. I think it's called a honeymoon. Fleming and I are married."

34

"Married?" Yvonne squeaked.

"Married." They sat in Yvonne's suite, each with a drink in hand.

"I don't know what to say, Maxine. I'm so happy for you." The sudden change sent Yvonne reeling. Mixed thoughts of what changes this meant overcame her. What would happen to her relationship with Maxine? And if Maxine were married, she didn't love Seán. Love Seán—the words repeated over and over in her mind.

"Yes."

"You don't need to sound so mournful." Yvonne smiled.

"No."

Yvonne laughed. "He seems very nice."

"You haven't been around him long."

"You mean he isn't?" Yvonne quickly asked.

"Yes, he is." Maxine blushed.

"Maxine. I am really, really happy for you. It is a surprise. You didn't tell me." Yvonne was happy. Deliriously happy, when she thought of Seán.

"I couldn't, Yvonne. I tried, but I was afraid you would think I had deserted you."

"I suppose so." Yvonne bounced around the room in sudden excitement. "You're married and I am so happy for you."

"Thank you."

"Fleming is very lucky. I'll tell him so when I see him at dinner."

"I'm lucky too. Although, I admit, it's a trick."

"Trick?"

"Show James Blond a pound of Godiva chocolates and he'll follow you anywhere." Maxine smiled faintly in self-mocking humor.

"He is very handsome." Soft sunlight flooded the room. Maxine sat in a chair, wearing a white wool dress that caressed her figure; Yvonne curled up on the small sofa by the fire. "And you are looking wonderful. Marriage agrees with you."

"I've only been married a week. I've plenty of time for lines to gather in my face. What's been happening here?"

Yvonne mentioned the ballet, the shoes, the tweed, Aisling, Ian, and Kili, concluding with the doctor. "I suppose I will make one more effort to see if I can dance."

"Of course you should." Maxine touched her arm.

"That's all."

"Really?" An eyebrow arched.

"What else?" Yvonne swirled her drink.

"When I saw Seán with you at the door . . ."

"Business," Yvonne primly stated. There was, after all, nothing really to tell Maxine.

"I see."

"No, you don't."

"I had hoped for more, I admit. Look what the Irish air did for Kili." Maxine laughed.

"I don't think it's fair to blame the air. Ian is looking wonderful, isn't he?"

"Yes, disgustingly so."

Yvonne looked at her friend. "You don't mind if I ask you something personal?"

"Of course I do. After all our years together, I am not about to let you get personal." Maxine smiled. "What is it, silly?"

"What made you decide to marry?"

Maxine laughed. "The shock of being asked."

"You've turned down enough men to fill this room. What was it that finally made you take the chance?"

"You know what they say."

"What?"

"It's better to have loved and lost than to eat only hard-boiled eggs for a month."

"Will you be serious?"

"I hope not. What about you and Seán?"

"I told you, business." Yvonne still felt evasively shy about Seán.

"You lie. I saw a look in his eye that had nothing to do with business."

"Those were his eyes, not mine."

"I see. You are coming out to dinner with Fleming and me tonight. A celebration. Tomorrow we'll have a larger gathering. Include Ian and all. I understand Aisling is to dance a solo."

"Yes. I hope she's all right. She fainted today onstage."

"Oh, Yvonne. What have you been doing to her?"

"Nothing!" Yvonne was indignant.

"I have a wedding present for you," Maxine quickly changed the subject."

"But you're the one who got married."

"I know that. I don't remember the occasion, but Fleming assures me we did." Maxine walked over to a box she'd brought into the room earlier, without explanation. "Here."

Inside Yvonne found a dress. Sheer blue, it dipped revealingly in back, breathtakingly in front. "It's beautiful, but isn't that a little brief?"

"Brevity is the soul of fit."

"I'll catch a cold."

"Or something." Maxine looked into the fire.

"Now, Maxine."

"Now, Yvonne. I can't stand to see that nice man here, and him floating away from you."

"Seán FitzGerald is held in place by any number of women." Yvonne tried to sound disinterested.

"None can compare with you."

"I'm not in the contest," Yvonne insisted. She couldn't admit even to Maxine how complicated it all was.

"You should be."

"Love, Maxine Andrus, is for the young and foolish. And you."

"Cynicism, Yvonne St. Cyr, is a gift to be kept under control."

"You are a fine one to talk."

"Yvonne, you've done your bit. It's time for the mourning to end."

"Right. That's easy to say, Maxine, I don't know if I have the ability. Gregory and I were so happy."

Maxine moved beside Yvonne on the sofa and again stared into the fire. "I know. I thought of that, you know. I thought about loving Fleming and then having something happen—death, or just divorce, lack of interest, a change of heart. I wanted to run when he first mentioned marriage."

"You know what they say." Yvonne faked a smile. "Better safe than sorry."

"Ha! I only know what I say. Better sorry than safe."

"A Maxine Maxim?"

"You bet! When did we ever go for safety in our lives? Why should our love life be any different?"

"But it hurts."

"I know. That's how you know you're alive."

Yvonne laughed. "Your usual encouraging self, aren't you? Did you think this all out when you agreed to marry Fleming?"

"Yes. I was very logical."

"Thinking made you decide?" Yvonne looked deeply into Maxine's eyes as if to find the magic that had captured her determinedly unmarried friend.

"No. I thought it all out, then discovered it wasn't a matter of logic. I had already thrown my heart over, over the fear, the uncertainties, the possible broken dreams. I didn't really have any choice."

"Aisling." Maxine hurried down the hall in her direction. "How have you been?"

"Fine, thank you."

"Yes, I heard about your fainting onstage. You must feel wonderful."

"It will be over soon. Excitement and all that." She had always liked the designer, but did not know her well.

"If you get any more excited, it might prove fatal."

"Best wishes on your marriage."

"Thank you, Aisling. It was a surprise, but an enjoyable one, as it turns out."

A surprise? Aisling liked but didn't always understand her.

"You know I'm having a dinner after your performance tomorrow night. You are coming?"

"Yes, Miss Andrus, I mean . . . Mrs. James."

"I'm remaining Andrus. It took too many years to perfect Maxine Andrus to give her up now. But call me Maxine."

"Thank you. Maxine."

"And bring your young man."

Aisling gasped. "Young man? What young man?"

"I don't know, but at your age, you must have at least one. Seems normal to me."

"I don't think I'd better."

"Why on earth not?"

"I don't think Yvonne approves."

"Really?" Maxine leaned close. "Does he do something very naughty?"

Aisling laughed. "No, he's a dancer."

"That sounds legal and moral. Don't worry about Yvonne. I'll take care of her."

That did not sound good, Maxine thought. If Yvonne weren't careful, she would become like Madame—a lovely woman, but not Maxine's choice for a best friend, not a vestal virgin of dance. She was determined that Seán and Yvonne get together, no matter how much work she had to invent for them. Her deliberately cryptic telegram had helped. Sheer tweed evening wear wasn't a bad idea, and Seán and Yvonne were still seeing each other. That wasn't enough. Yvonne's entire trip seemed to have been wasted. The dancer wasn't even engaged to Seán. Yet.

"Isn't this nice?" Maxine looked around the Lord Edward Restaurant. "I'm so pleased you suggested this for our first night, Seán."

"Very glad you approve, but I should be taking you two out."

"No." Maxine smiled sweetly. "This is my party." They were seated in the bar by the open fireplace, where chunks of turf blazed. The beamed ceiling added a note of romance to the white stucco walls.

"The martinis are delicious," Seán volunteered.

"Martinis don't seem very Irish," Maxine protested, "but they are good."

"We can look over the menus while we drink."

"What a choice," Fleming said. "What is a prawn?"

"Shrimp," Yvonne answered.

"I love shrimp," Fleming enthused.

"I didn't know that." Maxine stared at her husband.

"The subject never came up. You don't have to know everything about me."

"You would get bored too soon," Seán put in.

"Maybe." She looked suspiciously at Fleming. "On the other hand, should a person who doesn't know another person's taste in seafood marry that person?"

"Too late now," Fleming said. "Seán, what about another drink? Or," he added in an undertone, "maybe two?"

"Maxine." Yvonne trilled a warning.

"Maybe so," Maxine replied obediently, as if temporarily preparing to continue the evening in a sweeter tone. She stretched her toes toward the fire, and as she glanced at the door, smiled with enjoyment. "Oh, good!" Maxine purred.

Yvonne looked suspiciously at her friend. "Good?"

"The rest of the party." Maxine smiled.

Yvonne turned to greet Ian and Kili, but instead Roland bounded toward them, Eleanor following like a late tug outdistanced by the ocean liner. "Yvonne."

"Oh, no," Seán exclaimed. "I mean, how nice to see Roland again."

"Maxine, Fleming, Seán . . ." Roland stared at Yvonne. "My dear Yvonne . . ." He drew out her name. "How nice to be here."

Yvonne smiled weakly at Roland. "What a surprise." In desperation she looked at Maxine. "Maxine hadn't told us."

Fleming looked like he was getting a headache. "Let's go upstairs for dinner." Firmly he put an arm around Maxine, drawing her close. "What are you up to?" he whispered.

"Why, dear, whatever do you mean?"

The dining chamber, one floor above, was softly lit with Victorian shaded lamps, graced with bay windows. "How tiny!" Maxine admired the chamber, which had no more than thirty seats.

"How romantic." Roland rolled the R.

"Yes," Seán hissed. "If I had known the party would be so large, I would have chosen something more brightly lit."

"This is perfect." Roland smiled, and arranged to sit between Yvonne and Eleanor. "Just perfect." He moved his chair closer to Yvonne.

"Perfect," Seán snarled.

"Nice view," Eleanor said.

"Smashing," Seán said.

"Lord, I hope not," Fleming muttered.

"Does anyone have a cigarette?" Maxine asked.

"Allow me," Seán volunteered.

"I thought you'd given them up, Maxine." Yvonne passed is case across the table.

"Now, Yvonne," Maxine chided. "I am responsible for ny own bad habits."

"All of them." Fleming peeked over his menu at Roland aressing Yvonne's hand and shuddered.

Maxine passed the cigarettes back to Yvonne, who turned ne gold case in her hand and silently read the inscription: "To Seán for his help that important night. Jennifer."

"A match?" Maxine asked.

"She could light it off this inscription," Yvonne muttered.

"Now, now," Seán cautioned.

Yvonne remembered the lush brunette. Although she should emove her hand from Roland's attention, the temptation to nnoy Seán proved irresistible. "Tell me, Roland . . ." She aned toward him. "What will you do in New York besides ance?"

Dinner didn't linger; it merely seemed so to Fleming and eán. Maxine, Yvonne, and Roland all seemed to enjoy nemselves. It was so difficult to tell what Eleanor thought.

Maxine whispered to Yvonne as they parted. "How exciting! ve never been with the belle of the ball before. Such xcitement to have two bees buzzing around you."

When Roland insisted upon escorting Yvonne to her room, ne didn't argue, leaving Seán in the lobby with a cheery ood-bye.

Yvonne opened the door. "Thank you, Roland." Her tone as suddenly crisp.

"A nightcap?" Roland leaned toward her.

"I don't think so." She quickly entered, half-closing the oor. "Roland . . ." She peeked out.

"Yes," he breathed hopefully.

"When you were a little boy, what did your mother read to ou at night? *The Memoirs of Casanova?*"

* * *

The next day, Yvonne commenced a course of treatmen
with Dr. Murray. "How long . . . how long before we'll
know if it's doing any good?"

"There could be some reaction within a couple of weeks
Have you been practicing?"

"Not very much."

"It won't hurt. There is no danger of greater injury to the
area. We must know if your foot will strengthen enough for
you to dance, if the pain will lessen. You do your best, and
I'll do mine." He smiled paternally.

"I don't remember my best anymore."

"You athletes have reserves."

"I don't usually think of myself like that."

"As an athlete? Maybe you should, less pressure that way
It's hard to think of yourself as a failed artist."

Failed artist. The phrase rang in her ears as she left the
doctor's office. Failed artist. At least now she had a title.

Luckily she had a full schedule for the day to distract her
First, at the studio, she planned an hour of practice. Nothing
heavy or demanding, just enough to stretch her thighs, exer
cise her calf muscles.

Afterward she would go to the hotel and change for Aisling
performance and the dinner after. At Maxine's insistence, she
was wearing the new blue dress.

She had promised to accompany Aisling to the theater, a
the young dancer had asked that Yvonne keep her company i
the hours before the performance.

Yvonne had resolved to remain busy, leaving herself n
time to think. She was so happy for Maxine, delighted he
friend had finally found the man to make her happy; a ma
who didn't earn a living with tennis balls or surfboards;
man who was handsome and smart and nice.

She truly was. But she was also lonely. Never again woul
she and Maxine be as close. This last year she had nearl
lived at Maxine's apartment, feeling free to drop in wheneve
she wanted, or needed to. That would end.

In addition, she saw the irony of her relationship wit
Seán. At the very time she realized Maxine had no interest i
him, Seán had another female interest.

She should have told him that she knew, that she'd see
him at the museum, but her pride prevented it. She ha

insisted they would remain only friends. At least she had found out in time. From the casual intimacy of the kiss, Yvonne knew the woman was not a new interest of Seán's, but a long-standing relationship.

"Are you ready?" Yvonne coached Aisling with her makeup. "A little more blush."

"Yes. I could dance this in my sleep."

"I don't want to plant evil suggestions, but if you need to hold back, do. This isn't the important performance. Just a preview."

"I will. Really." Aisling smiled crookedly. "I just keep remembering that terrible moment. Falling to the floor. Opening my eyes, you know, with everyone crowded around staring at me."

"Don't think about it," Yvonne ordered. "Just dance. You must not let this get out of hand. And when the ballet is over, we will have a party with Maxine. It will be very nice. Maxine's parties are always very nice."

"Yes."

"How are your shoes?"

"Fine. I'm wearing a new pair, I want them stiff for this role."

"Good." Yvonne thought frantically. How could she soothe Aisling, ease her worry about the coming performance?

"I . . ." Aisling hesitated a moment. "I saw you go into the practice room earlier. How did it go?"

Yvonne groaned. "As if I had a ninety-year-old body."

"Maybe you should ask Ian for whatever tonic he's taking."

Yvonne darted a glance at her, but realized the girl had no idea what brought a smile to the older man's lips, the spring to his step. Then she remembered Aisling quoting Colette. To the young dancer, Kili and Ian as a couple must be unthinkable. "I don't know if I could stand to feel that good."

Aisling giggled.

"Maxine told me that you are bringing Pat to the dinner."

"Oh. I don't have to."

"There is no reason why you shouldn't. I can be a little difficult, I know."

"That is all right." Aisling closed her eyes. "I would like to be alone now."

"All right, but if you want anything, just send for me."

Aisling's steps dragged through backstage corridors until she stood at the edge of the stage. Around her buzzed the stagehands, the corps from the last act, the other dancers. She seemed to neither hear nor see them.

She stood alone, completely alone. Music played, and for a frightening moment she hesitated as if struggling to remember the first step.

With a magnificent leap, she floated onstage. As one note followed another her body automatically positioned itself, her feet curled onto *pointe*.

The audience caught its breath at her slim, graceful form. She whirled and flew, turned and leaped.

In a flash she was backstage, dancers crowded around her, offering congratulations, whispering her name. Hands propelled her back onstage, presented her with flowers. The lights blinded, leaving the audience noise and glare.

Once back in her dressing room and wearing a robe, Aisling greeted Yvonne and her friends. "Thank you," she murmured.

"Oh, Aisling." Yvonne's eyes glowed with tears. "That was wonderful."

"Really? If you say so, it has to be true."

"The best, the very best I've ever seen you do. Truly. I am so excited."

Aisling knew Yvonne referred to Colette. "I'm glad I didn't let you down."

"You change. Come back to the hotel and I'll help you get dressed for dinner. I have a surprise for you."

"I won't be long," Aisling promised.

Aisling hesitated at the edge of the room. Yvonne came over to greet her. "Hello, Pat." She smiled pleasantly at the young dancer. "And, Aisling, you look wonderful."

"Thank you very much for the dress." As a present, Yvonne had given the young woman a white lace dress. Deeply ruffled at the neckline and wrists, the gown floated romantically around Aisling's slim figure. "I've never owned an Andrus before." Maxine had given the dress to Yvonne, but she had never worn it, finding it too youthful. "It looks stunning on you," Yvonne assured her.

"Your dress is beautiful," Aisling returned the compliment.

Yvonne's hair floated around her shoulders. From Maxine's dress, her figure flowed with an unusually lush display, her breasts white and swelling, her exquisite back fully highlighted.

When Seán met her backstage at the theater, she obviously took his breath away. Yvonne greeted him coolly, although with a small kiss, chatting about Aisling's performance. "She is doing so well. So very well. I know she'll be splendid, and this is just the beginning. Her career will blossom."

"I hope so. If that's what she wants."

"Of course it is."

Maxine had found a restaurant with a band, inviting not only her immediate friends but also the entire Irish company. "How are you?" She floated to Yvonne and Aisling's side. "You were perfect, Aisling."

"Thanks. It was very nice to ask everyone to your party."

"I'm just sorry I won't be here to see Eve." Maxine smiled.

"You can't stay?" Yvonne asked wistfully.

"Not a chance. Maxine Andrus Inc. will find out they don't need me, and my days of designing will be finished." Maxine dramatically closed her eyes.

"Maxine, you could never be done without." Aisling laughed.

The dance floor filled up. Seán approached Yvonne. "Do you dance?"

Yvonne gave him a long, querulous look. "That isn't funny."

"No, I meant real dancing." He gestured toward the floor.

"Don't let Ian hear that." Yvonne giggled.

"Well?"

"Of course."

"A friendly dance, of course," Seán said. He led her to the dance floor, holding her at arm's length as the slow music played. "This all right?"

"Perfect."

"I like your dress. Actually, this isn't a bad position. If I held you closer, I couldn't see so much." Seán leered at her décolletage.

"You are impossible." She nestled closely to Seán. "This might be the safer position."

"Oh, well, I can't have everything." Seán pretended to sigh.

The touch of his body felt familiar and yet newly exciting. Had she not known about Seán's other female interests, she would have been unable to keep her head. The music floated through her body, leaving her lighter than air. As she turned her head slightly and her lips touched his face, for a moment Yvonne thought she would kiss him, but showing enormous self-control, she turned away.

"Yvonne!" Roland moved onto the dance floor.

"Oh-oh," Seán sighed.

"I've been looking for you everywhere," Roland cried.

"Here I am!" She generously presented herself. Seán wasn't the only one who could have admirers.

"Good heavens!" Roland pretended to fall back in shock. "That dress, your . . ."

"Hello, Roland." Seán stepped forward.

"Ah, yes. So nice. But this must be my dance." Before either could comment, Roland swept Yvonne into his arms, pulling her close. "To dance again with you, my dear, is so exciting."

"I am going to bed," Fleming announced.

"But I want to see the city by night," Maxine protested. "Seán is taking us for a drive."

"You go, dear . . . unless Yvonne and Seán would like to be alone," his voice hinted.

"No," Yvonne insisted frantically.

"No," Seán interjected before Yvonne had finished.

"I won't stay out long," Maxine promised. "I just want to see what's up."

"I know, dear." Fleming smiled.

As they settled into the Mercedes, Maxine insisted on sitting in the back. Seán drove; Yvonne sat beside him.

"You must have Fleming take you in a hansom cab," Yvonne told her.

"Oh, did you?"

"Yes, Seán took me." Yvonne blushed.

"What a romantic idea!" Maxine smiled.

"Historically interesting," Yvonne stiffly corrected.

"I can see that."

Seán drove slowly down the almost deserted streets. "Anything in particular you would like to see, Maxine?"

"No, I just felt like a little drive."

"It was a lovely dinner, Maxine," Yvonne enthused, trying to keep her attention away from Seán's thigh so close to hers.

"Yes," Seán added, "thank you very much."

"I did think Ian and Kili were in good form." Maxine looked out the window. "And Roland. I don't think there is anyone quite like Roland."

"Not if we are lucky," Seán muttered.

"What's wrong with Roland?" Yvonne objected. "I thought he was charming." She deliberately provoked him. Seán's jealousy soothed her.

"Charming?" Seán gasped.

In the backseat, a noise suspiciously like a snicker was muffled. Seán and Yvonne didn't notice.

"Flattering," Yvonne suggested innocently.

"Cheap charm and foolish flattery?" Seán countered.

"Just because he appreciates my unique charms."

"The fact that you aren't a man? Those are unique qualifications you share with lots of other women, you know."

Yvonne glared.

Maxine giggled softly.

"You are no one to talk." Talking of love and all the while seeing other women. She felt her heart might break.

"What do you mean?"

"After what you did!"

"I did not have the car break down in the country on purpose, Yvonne. You heard the mechanic yourself. And as for the farm . . . Well . . . You were there too!"

"Busy, busy. How busy you two have been," Maxine said innocently.

"It was supposed to be all business," Yvonne insisted.

"All business," Seán echoed.

"It wouldn't have been necessary for me to see Seán, otherwise."

"You do have some interesting ways of drumming up business," Seán sweetly commented. "Beach, moonlight . . ."

"You must enjoy living here, Seán," Maxine said. "I understand you have a lovely farm in the country."

"And a vicious horse."

"Yes, Maxine, you and Fleming must come and see it. The countryside is gorgeous."

"When it isn't raining." Yvonne couldn't stop picturing the woman in the museum.

"Some people like rain," Seán said.

"Some people have cars that don't break down."

"Now, children. This is so kind of you, Seán."

"If you are lucky, you won't have to walk home," Yvonne added.

The front seat sizzled with silence.

"Two-timer," Yvonne half-sobbed.

"What?" Seán squeaked. "What are you talking about?"

"Nothing, absolutely nothing."

"In the morning, I could take you and Fleming on a sightseeing tour of the city," Seán addressed Maxine. "I have a regular talk."

"Seán is good at talking. Words are so cheap." Yvonne smiled bravely.

"What words?" Seán indignantly asked.

"If you don't watch where you are driving, we will end up in the water—wet as usual."

"I can drive, thank you. What cheap words?"

"You use so many, no wonder you find it hard to remember."

"Yvonne . . ." Seán's voice held grim warning.

"I saw her. You didn't fool me." No longer could she hold back her pain.

"Who? Saw who?" Seán begged.

"Those times you said you adored me. Or have you forgotten?"

"I have not forgotten, and I do adore you," he yelled.

"It certainly sounds like it," she sniffed.

"Who did you see?"

"I saw you with that brunette at the museum. She kissed you!"

"Tsk, tsk. How did you two do so much in so short a time?" Maxine's voice swelled with satisfaction.

They ignored her. "Brunette?"

"Don't you dare deny it! And she was at your house that night, wasn't she?"

"That brunette?" Seán's voice was strangely pitched.

"And the cigarette case. Jennifer. Is that her? Or do you have a harem?"

"Oh," Maxine sighed. "Young love is wonderful. I am so happy for you both."

"Really, Yvonne, if you wanted to meet my sister, you just had to ask." How pleased he sounded.

"Sister? Sister? How dumb do you think I am?"

"Never give a man an opening like that, Yvonne," Maxine advised.

"Jennifer is my sister. She gave me the cigarette case in memory of the night I helped her elope. It's a long story, of some interest and amusement, but one I don't think I'll go into right now."

"Sister?" Yvonne's voice grew faint.

"Yes, my sister."

"Oh." She should be embarrassed, but happiness rippled through her.

"Yes."

"I'm so sorry." His sister!

"Don't be. She is a most satisfactory sister."

"I don't know what to say."

"I could make some suggestions," Maxine murmured to no one.

"That's all right." Seán cleared his throat. "All of us make mistakes. All sinners have a future, all saints a past."

"Which am I?" Yvonne asked. There was no one else. And Maxine was married.

"I hope you have a future, but I don't think I'll carry that thought to a logical conclusion. I'm sure you aren't a sinner."

"I've been horrible," Yvonne squeaked.

"Just difficult. Roland is horrible." Seán took her hand firmly in his.

Yvonne moved as close as she could.

Maxine yawned loudly. "Let's go back to the hotel. I don't think there is anything left to see."

*   *   *

Maxine tiptoed across the bedroom.

"Did you have a good time?" Fleming's sleepy voice asked.

"Yes."

"Oh, God!"

35

What irony, Justine thought, that in a life so organized, planned, controlled—her own life—turmoil would often prove so useful.

Through the halls she sailed, a quiet, dangerous figure. In the business office she dived, waves of agitation spreading through the company in her path.

"Here are the ads." The business manager ran forward. "And the posters."

In the style of a Degas painting, the posters announced a commemorative gala starring Yvonne St. Cyr in an act from the new Ian Thorn production, *Ballet of Desire*.

"Yes . . ." Justine approved after careful scrutiny. "That's right. The guest list?"

"Once they found out the President and Mrs. Reagan were attending, the tickets sold out immediately, both for the gala and the party afterward. It's so exciting."

"You can't begin to know," Justine absentmindedly murmured. "The hand-delivered invitations?"

"All out. The board of directors had theirs yesterday. Acceptances are already in from Liza Minnelli, Halston, the Chows, Diana Vreeland, Walter Cronkite, Al Pacino, the Kissingers, the mayor—"

"Stop." Justine closed her eyes in ecstasy. "Send the list up at the end of the day. It's too much to take in at one time."

Not undeserved, she thought, returning to her office. What a combination of pleading, free tickets, promises, threats, and called-in favors it had taken! But everyone, anyone who counted, would come.

Come to see the former stars, the current crop, the new Thorn ballet, and Yvonne St. Cyr. Unfortunately, poor Yvonne wouldn't be dancing, would in truth never be dancing again. The top dancer of the company would, most unexpectedly, most tragically, be retiring.

What an announcement that would make on the night of the gala!

But . . . Justine closed her eyes, picturing the newspaper accounts. In the brave tradition of the theater, a new young soloist would debut.

Aisling Nolan would triumph. Or she wouldn't.

It didn't matter, really. That was the beauty of the plan. If Aisling was brilliant, the company had a new star. The directors would hail Justine's clever development of the girl. And if she failed, the company would have no star. When the ship was sinking would be no time for the board to change artistic directors.

It was truly a good plan.

"I'm sorry about last night." Seán and Yvonne walked along O'Connell Street. He reached out and held her hand.

"I'm sorry about my suspicions. It wasn't my business about your sister."

"I hope you think it is. Not my sister, I mean, but if I were seeing someone else. Jennifer lives in Paris with her husband, but should be visiting soon. You'll like her."

"I'm sure I will."

Seán looked happily around. "Isn't this a beautiful day?"

"Yes, it is."

"What do you want to buy Maxine?"

"I don't really know. She doesn't need anything. Later, when I'm feeling more creative, I'll get something unique. For now, I would like to find something, and an Irish something seems perfect."

Two hours passed as they visited the department stores, lingering in Clery's, then walking past Trinity to Grafton Street and browsing in Brown Thomas and Switzer's. "What do you think?" Seán asked as she looked at some tablecloths.

"Very nice, but not what I want."

"I have an idea." He led her back up Grafton Street toward Trinity and turned right into Nassau Street. "We'll go to the Kilkenny Design Shop. Upstairs they have a tearoom and downstairs an assortment of textiles, furniture, jewelry, ceramics, glasswear, representing some of the best of Irish crafts.''

Delighted, Yvonne chose a set of Waterford crystal in a shimmering design and a hand-woven bedspread in shades of white and blue. "There are so many beautiful things here. I'd like to decorate my house with . . .'' She suddenly fell silent.

"What is it?''

"I just remembered, I don't really have a home any longer. I sublet my last apartment. Anyway, that never seemed like home, just a place to live.''

Seán directed her upstairs. "You are in luck.''

"Really?''

"I have several homes, and the need of someone to live in them.''

"Maybe if you advertised.'' She smiled. "What would you like?''

"You.''

"I meant for tea.'' Yvonne pointed to the buffet of cakes, sandwiches, quiche, and salad.

"You are so difficult.''

"Better than horrible.'' She looked at him with pleasure.

"I was so sorry to hear Roland and Eleanor had to leave this morning.''

"You lie.''

"That's true.''

"I'll be sorry to see Maxine leave.''

"I know. I'll console you.''

"For now.''

"Forever,'' Seán assured her.

"There is no forever.'' Yvonne smiled.

"We could pretend.''

"I can't think about anything except Colette for Ian. We have a lot to do.''

"Let's go to the Zoo,'' Seán suggested as they finished tea and cakes.

"All right. I have the day off. Aisling is resting.''

A short drive later they arrived at the verdant park, cloaked in greens embroidered with flowers, one of the beauties of Dublin.

"This is very nice. Very peaceful. I'll have to bring Aisling."

"Why not let Pat bring her? More romantic that way."

"Aisling will be too busy for romance."

"Let's sit here." Seán gestured to a bench by the lake. "I have a friend I meet here sometimes."

"Oh?" Yvonne raised an eyebrow.

"Yes. I'll tell you when I see her. You remind me of her, as a matter of fact."

"How nice. I think."

"Yvonne, are you sure that your plans for Aisling are the right ones?"

"What do you mean?"

"Does Aisling want to dance Colette?"

"Of course."

"How do you know?"

"Because it's a wonderful role, a chance to star in a Thorn production, her chance to break into starring roles."

Seán remained silent for a few moments. Across a fenced moat, lions paced. The monkeys hooted. "Are you certain those aren't reasons *you* would want the role?"

"I would if I were in Aisling's place. This is her big chance."

"But maybe Aisling doesn't see it as a chance."

"Of course she does."

"Have you ever asked?"

"I don't need to." Confused, Yvonne stared at Seán. "It's an opportunity any dancer would want."

"All dancers aren't the same."

"They are about roles."

Seán said no more. Perhaps Yvonne did know best. But he noticed how Aisling grew thinner and tenser every day, while neither Ian nor Yvonne seemed to recognize the obvious.

"There you are." He pointed excitedly.

"What?"

"The black one," Seán indicated.

"The swan!"

"Sure, what else would you be?"

"It is exquisite." The swan, less than half the size of the white, had a red beak and the haughtiness of a true ballerina.

"Yes. When I first saw you dance, it was as Odette-Odile. When you came on as the Black Swan, I knew I would love you."

Days passed; *Honoré et Eve* approached. Every morning and evening without fail, Yvonne took a short lesson. Calling on the discipline she'd developed over the years, she ignored the aching muscles and continued the painful stretching. Quickly her thighs and calves strengthened, her waist and arms firmed.

But dancing with her body and legs did not make her a ballerina. It wasn't fair, she thought. If she were a man, she would have no problem. Male dancers wore soft shoes on- and offstage, never rising above half-*pointe* position.

In class, women wore those same soft shoes practicing at the barre in half-*pointe*. But when in the center of the room for the rest of the class, and while onstage, women were seldom off *pointe*. In their specially stiffened slippers, they turned and supported themselves, their entire weight resting on a tiny point. Except in preparation for steps, in some contemporary ballets, and in special effects, women always balanced *en pointe*.

Yvonne could not dance *en pointe*—not for long. She practiced using soft shoes, raising only onto the ball of her foot. But *en pointe* she could support herself for only a short while, not regaining her former elegance or style.

Mornings Yvonne and Aisling worked on Eve, afternoons on Colette. "Sometimes," Aisling grimly said, "I can't remember whether fear or sensual delight motivates me, whether I'm Eve or Colette."

The role of Colette grew and developed with Aisling herself. Occasionally an unexpected jealousy would sweep over Yvonne as she watched the young dancer prepare. The ballerina dancing Colette would be revered, remembered forever. And Aisling, not Yvonne, would be that ballerina.

At times like this, she missed Maxine.

Not that Seán wouldn't volunteer himself to be everything and anything to her. "Friend and lover," he offered. But this was no time to be making decisions. Later, after the performances, she would tell him their future was uncertain. No matter what agony it cost her, she would return to New

York. The love affair would have to end for now. Yvonne was just too unsure of herself, of what she wanted, of her ability to give herself fully to another man.

"What do the latest X rays show?" Although certain she knew the answer, Yvonne felt she had to ask Dr. Murray. Her pain had not lessened, her strength had not returned.

The doctor shuffled through the pictures, examined Yvonne's leg, and reexamined the X rays. "Tell, me, Miss St. Cyr. Do you want to dance again?"

Yvonne stiffened with shock. "Of course I do. Why would you ask something like that?"

"Ballet is a very demanding career, filled with pressure and anxiety. Like athletics, it generates a limited life. You have only so many years."

"What are you getting at?"

"Your leg and foot have healed."

"That's not possible. There is terrible pain. I can't possibly dance in a performance. I can't stay *en pointe*."

He leaned earnestly forward. "I'm certain there is pain. You haven't danced for a long time and the area may never adjust completely. Surely *pointe* work brought discomfort before your injury."

"Yes, but not like this. Not this intensity."

"Maybe it isn't all in your foot. Maybe you should consider getting another specialist to help."

"What kind?"

"A therapist perhaps could help with . . ."—he shrugged—"certain ambivalent feelings you have about ballet."

"It isn't true." With dignity Yvonne rose, picked up her purse, preparing to leave the room. "It is not true. I cannot dance. Dr. Murray, I'll never dance again."

Later, in her room, Yvonne fingered a letter from Maxine and considered that it perhaps worked out for the best.

Maxine sent word that Aisling Nolan had been featured in *People* magazine as the rising young dancer in the company. She glimmered in gossip columns, was pictured in the papers. "I don't, to be fair, know that Aisling has anything to do with this," Maxine continued. "The photographs look old to me. I think that Justine is up to something.''

Well, perhaps so. Yvonne closed the letter, placing it in the bottom of her purse. Perhaps she and Justine had come to the same realization. Aisling would dance Colette.

36

Aisling roamed the dressing room like a tortured animal, white and shaking.

"How about some honey and water?" Yvonne suggested, hoping to draw the young dancer's attention away from her fear.

"No. I want to die," Aisling wailed.

"Aisling, calm yourself!" Already dressed in an evening gown for the night's performance, Yvonne would join Seán in the audience just before curtain time. He had promised her a surprise.

"It's the end!" Aisling threw herself on a cot and sobbed. "I can't go on, I can't."

"Of course you can. You need to start your routine."

"Routine? I don't really have one, you know."

"Of course you do," Yvonne comforted, then added in an undertone, "or you should. What do you do first?"

"Oh. I . . . ah, I don't know."

"You should have something to eat."

"I've been sick twice already."

Yvonne chose to be firm. "Now, Aisling. You must gain control of yourself. Most dancers suffer from stage fright. I do, heaven knows. You have to learn to deal with it."

"Worse," Aisling cried. "This is much worse. I can't go on."

"Don't be silly, of course you can. Now, think. Just two weeks ago, you did wonderfully at the preview. This is just the beginning. You have a whole future ahead of you, a future of famous roles that will be linked with your name."

292

Aisling lay on her back, her eyes closed. "Yeah. Linked like a prison chain, you mean." She shuddered.

"And you were very good at that time," Yvonne continued, ignoring Aisling's comment.

"You don't know how it was. I stood backstage waiting, and everything was a blank. Zero. I just remember finally coming off, you know, and hearing the corps whispering around me, and I could smell the bouquets of roses—but I couldn't remember anything of the performance. Anyone might have danced that role."

"Oh, Aisling." Yvonne felt at a loss to confront such passionate and earnest fear.

"I couldn't remember one turn, one *arabesque*, one extension, one preparation, one *sissonne*, one *jeté*, or one *bourrée*!" Aisling yelled.

"But you got through it perfectly."

"That time it was swell. It worked. I mean, it was a solo. I was alone on stage. My positioning didn't have to be right on the mark. I wasn't going to bump into someone if I got a little out of line, you know. The space was mine. But what will happen in a full ballet? What will happen when I have a partner and a stage full of dancers? Disaster, I know it. It's only a matter of time!" Aisling burst into tears.

"You are allowing yourself to become too upset about this." Yvonne's tone was less patient. "You've danced often enough, Aisling. What is it? I know Ian's ballets are demanding, but you're a Thorn dancer now. Thorn dancers take risks—a step from a strange angle, a virtually impossible turn."

"It was bad enough before, when I was just one of the soloists." Aisling stared at the ceiling now, eyes fixed and tragic. "Every time I stepped onstage it was like . . . like . . . a pit to hell opened under my feet. You know, I danced Princess Aurora in *The Sleeping Beauty* last year for the first time? I didn't think about character or motivation like you would have. I just wondered when disaster would strike. During the Rose Adagio, I had to balance while the four men make up to me? Stay *en pointe*, you know, balance with my hands above my head. Balance while one man releases me and another replaces him? No wobble, no clutching, no pawing the air, smile, smile, smile?"

Aisling's constant questioning tone gave her nervous speech a singsong quality. "It can be dreadful, I know, but then it's over."

"And when it is," Aisling whispered, "more and more I just feel relief. But relief doesn't seem enough, Yvonne."

Seán met Yvonne in the lobby. "You look beautiful," he whispered when he saw her. "Beautiful," he said with pride and admiration.

"You too." She smiled, still shaken by the intensity of Aisling's reaction.

"How is Aisling?"

Yvonne hesitated, searching for the right word. "Nervous," she finally managed. Once she reached the stage, Aisling would be fine. A dancer's tension always eased once the music started.

Seán studied her eyes a moment, as if sensing Yvonne hadn't disclosed all, but didn't comment. "I have a surprise for you." He guided her toward their seats.

"So you told me. What is it?"

They walked down the aisle, and as Yvonne slipped into her seat, she noticed the woman sitting next to her. "Síle!"

"Hello, Yvonne. How are you?"

"Fine, thank you. What a nice surprise!"

"Yes, I don't come to Dublin anymore. My life in Galway is so peaceful, but when Seán told me about the ballet, I thought I would make an effort. I can still hear the music and enjoy the performance in my own way."

"I'm very glad you did," Yvonne enthused. It was good to see the poet again.

"Síle's fingers touched the air like graceful antennae. "Yes, it should be a beautiful evening. And afterward, you and I have a date with Seán." Síle smiled happily. "If you don't mind my tagging along, that is."

"That will be wonderful," Yvonne agreed. With Síle, she felt content, as if the poet's inner peace reached out to touch and console her.

The music swelled; the light faded. "It's starting." Síle took Yvonne's hand and squeezed it in excitement.

The performance was not as elegantly set as it would have

been in New York, Yvonne thought. But the Irish dancers displayed enthusiasm, verve, and excellent technique.

Waiting for Aisling's entrance, Yvonne grew rigid. As she heard the theme for Eve, she held her breath with nervous anticipation.

Aisling had seemed calmer when Yvonne left her—clamer or frozen with fear. She still muttered about not coming onstage, but Yvonne felt certain she didn't mean it.

When the performance ended and was pronounced an elegant success, Aisling would be praised and feted; then she would feel better. After all, this was a temporary excitement, the cumulative effect of a trip to Ireland, Ian's sudden interest in her career, and perhaps the pressure of knowing Yvonne wasn't dancing.

A flash of white and fur announced Aisling's presence onstage, and Yvonne relaxed. She looked perfect—vivid and exciting. Aisling's personality lacked tension, the cutting edge necessary for the role of Eve, but nerves helped her to project the wild, passionate nature of a woman who left her family to find love in Paris.

Act I concluded.

During the intermission, Síle and Yvonne discussed Galway and made plans to visit parts of Dublin the next day.

Act II finished. Aisling had again performed marvelously.

Yvonne wondered if she had underestimated the joy of coaching. Perhaps she could learn to find satisfaction in teaching.

Act III began, and Yvonne felt her body easing into complete relaxation. Almost finished, she thought, her first task for Ian almost complete.

She still had Colette to develop, but that should now work out as satisfactorily as Eve had.

Onstage, Aisling began a turn, then hesitated. She paused no longer than a beat, but as the rhythm of Eve pounded in Yvonne's pulse, she instantly felt it. A leap, and again Aisling stammered with her feet. Yvonne caught her breath; Aisling slowed. A murmur broke out in the audience, then grew as Aisling lost the beat and finally stopped.

Even from their seats Yvonne could see Aisling's large and

frightened eyes. With an awkward toss of her head, Aisling fixed those large frightened eyes on the audience.

Yvonne knew that from the stage the audience was only a blur of lights, yet she felt as if Aisling gazed directly at her with an accusing stare. Then, with a moan, Aisling ran from the stage.

37

Yvonne's breath came in gasps as she tore from Aisling's dressing room. Seán followed more slowly and calmly but with a red flush of anger flooding his cheeks.

Silently he helped her into the car. Síle was in the corner, waiting.

As they drove toward Seán's house, Yvonne felt tension growing.

"That poor girl," Síle finally ventured.

"There was no excuse," Yvonne cried. "None. She was doing so well."

"I'm sure she didn't run offstage on purpose. She said she was going to faint." Seán's tone was neutral.

"You can't run off by mistake," Yvonne snapped. "It would have been better to faint. There was no excuse. A dancer doesn't leave the stage. Not unless she's injured or overwhelmed by sickness."

"Now, Yvonne," Seán insisted. "Stage fright might be considered an injury or an illness. I'm sure she did the best she could. You might have been a little . . . kinder."

"Kinder!" Yvonne sputtered. "Aisling doesn't deserve *kindness*. She ruined the ballet. Ruined Ian's performance! Take me to my hotel room, Seán. I don't feel well."

Next morning Yvonne woke up, not numb, not sad, not confused, not bitter. She was furious. Anger straightened her back, sparked her eye, tightened her muscles—intense emotion she had not experienced since before Gregory's death. She was furious—with herself.

She had felt annoyance, irritation, and other watered-down forms of distress, but the blazing emotion that swept her was new.

Nothing had been totally satisfying since that horrible day in Houston. She had discovered herself a small vessel caught in the storm of life, crashed by hostile waves, blown here and there by the whim of the winds of misfortune. It made her mad as hell, and it had to stop.

She slipped down to the ballet studio early and warmed up. Alone in the room, she prepared to battle her fears and weaknesses.

Aisling might not dance Colette.

Yvonne still didn't want to believe it. The young dancer had the potential to develop into a great ballerina if only she conquered this temporary though crippling fear.

She stared at herself in the floor-to-ceiling mirrors, dark eyes sunken into white face, body tense. Aisling had allowed undefined fears to cripple her. But it wasn't the same for Yvonne. She had been injured, then reinjured. From the beginning her prognosis was clear—she might never dance again. But Aisling remained perfectly capable of dancing, only psychologically hobbled.

Yvonne began her warm-up, ignoring the pain in her body by concentrating on another kind of discomfort. What would she say to Seán?

Before Maxine's marriage, Yvonne had told herself she couldn't love Seán because her friend might desire him. That, she now knew, had been self-evasion. She had been afraid to love Seán, afraid to risk her heart again.

Maxine had married, despite her fears. What had she said to Yvonne? It hadn't been a matter of logic. Maxine had thrown her heart over, over the uncertainties, the possible broken dreams.

It sounded so simple. Yet, if she threw her heart over, who would be there to catch it? Seán loved her, but not enough to take care of her.

She practiced stretching and leaping. Somehow she must find out what her future career held. If Aisling couldn't dance Colette, Yvonne might have to. If she could.

Sweat poured from her tortured muscles; pain shot through

her body. With work, she *would* be able to dance. But not dance as she once had.

The pain still stabbed. She had tried, had done her best. Expecting to land with shooting pains, anticipating the sharp thrusts, Yvonne knew her dancing lacked grace and precision. Her former brilliance was absent.

Amid every soaring leap and turn, she heard that jarring crack, remembered her last fall onstage. There was no hope those memories would fade before Justine's gala.

Back at the hotel, Yvonne heard her name, and saw Síle.

"What are you doing here?" Yvonne asked, peering over Síle's shoulder, expecting to find Seán glowering at her.

A delicate cane in one hand, Síle crossed the room toward her. "It smells more modern," she told Yvonne. "And sounds noisier. I haven't been in the Shelbourne for years. Since before. I thought we might walk across the street to the park in St. Stephen's Green. All this city noise and bustle is strange to me." Her smile was gentle as always.

"Of course." Yvonne reached her side and extended her right arm. "Why don't I help you." She guided Síle down the front steps and across the street. Through the railed entrance they walked silently down a path, and finally Yvonne stopped at a bench. "Would you like to sit?"

"That would be nice. What a sunny day!"

"Yes, it's beautiful." Until that moment, Yvonne hadn't noticed the weather.

"I'd like you to come to dinner tonight with Seán and me."

Yvonne's body was too tired for anguish, but mention of Seán's name constricted her throat. "I don't know that Seán wants to dine with me. He was very annoyed with me last night about Aisling. He didn't think I was understanding enough."

"Perhaps it wasn't the time to be understanding." Síle was tranquil. "Just remember, we always get angriest at those we love."

Yvonne chose not to comment on Seán's love. "I'm afraid I wasn't thinking of Aisling at the time. I was embarrassed that she was letting me down. And Ian, of course."

"How did Mr. Thorn take it?"

"I don't know. I haven't seen him. I've been busy trying to figure out my own life."

"Often hard to do."

Yvonne smiled a secret bitter smile. "Yes."

"Especially in a time of change," Síle continued.

Yvonne's laughter tolled hollowly. "You have a message for me there?"

"Not completely. Maybe reminding myself. And trying to help you understand Seán."

"I'll be leaving for New York soon. I don't suppose Seán and I will be seeing each other very much." Yvonne carefully shielded her tone from Síle's sensitivity, not wanting Seán's mother to feel her pain at the thought of leaving him.

"I'm sorry."

"Sorry?" Yvonne recalled her talk with Síle in Galway and the message for her.

"I know you've been under a great deal of pressure lately. Not that Seán and I have been gossiping about you. He tells me little." Síle's laughter tinkled like a silver bell. "But like most children, more than he knows, of course. He did say that you were injured and aren't dancing. I know that must be very upsetting for you. When I watched dancers, I thought that in some ways they saw with their feet, with their dancing. You must feel as blind as I do." Her head cocked to one side.

"You think I should find another world for myself?"

"Oh, dear no. I could not, would not, dare to presume to know your life so well. I think you should decide that there is a world.

"I learned that I couldn't escape blindness by running from it, or by hiding. I had to embrace it, know my blindness as my secret lover, to accept it that thoroughly. Maybe that is what pain must mean for you."

Yvonne concentrated on Síle's words. She admired the woman enormously. Síle had a stable and solid quality which equally balanced her artistic sensitivity.

Strangely, a memory of Madame flashed through Yvonne's mind. She had told Yvonne that pain wasn't always bad: "Pain can be growth, and understanding, and new beginnings. The trick is to live through the pain, to dance through the pain."

Síle had learned to live through her pain, to reach beyond her blindness and find happiness and satisfaction. Well, Síle was a better woman than she, a stronger woman. And Seán had helped his mother. He said he loved Yvonne, said he wanted to marry her, but he couldn't mean it. He wouldn't direct her in her decision about ballet. He didn't offer her sympathy, or guidance, or help.

"Seán was very good for you," Yvonne answered Síle indirectly. "I remember what you told me. How he took care of you."

"Indeed. He almost destroyed me." Síle's tone was light, but her expression serious.

Yvonne gasped in shock. "What? But you told me . . ."

"Oh, he didn't mean to, of course. He meant to help."

"What happened?"

"He coddled me. By taking such care of me, he drew me out of my room only to enlarge the prison. Anyplace I wanted to go, he took me. He even brought me to live with him at the farm. Eventually I couldn't find anything in the room for myself. I could scarcely move. I was frightened, unhappy, and Seán was always there. If not Seán, the housekeeper he hired for me. I became an invalid."

"But he only tried to take care of you." Yvonne spoke in a hushed voice, imagining Síle held captive by her handicap.

"I know he meant well, but you cannot take care of adults, not unless they are to become children."

"What changed all that?"

"I decided to kill myself." Her voice was still emotionless.

"Oh, no!" Yvonne cried out despite herself.

"It made sense to me, at the time. I had nothing to live for, my life composed only of darkness and muted images. My husband dead. Me a burden to my child." Síle seemed lost in old memories.

Yvonne didn't mean to pry, but she had to know. "But you didn't?"

"No. I got lost." A twinkle shone in Síle's eye.

"Lost?" Sometimes conversation with Síle proved as confusing as talking with Seán.

"One day, after deciding my days were numbered"—Síle's voice was even-toned—"I was alone in the house. I went for a walk here in the city. Perhaps half-thinking about throwing myself under a car in traffic. I don't know." Síle took a deep breath. "Well. Off I set. The first time I'd been alone on the street. I was frightened. The traffic seemed so close to the path. Everywhere people pushed and jostled me. My fear helped me, it helped me forget I was blind and notice life. I discovered something very important: the world still existed! There was light—not the light I had known, but light. There were smells. And images were all around me, as sharp as glass. The feel of pavement under my feet. The smell of life in a flower. The world was full and vivid. Suddenly I had something to live for."

Yvonne daydreamed on her bed, considering her life.

Never had it occurred to her how determined her future had been from the moment she had arrived as a young, frightened girl at the boarding school. Her overwhelming sense of loss and rejection had left her with a need for love and acceptance—both of which found fulfillment in her dreams with Maxine, then in the dreamlike reality of ballet, and finally in the dreamy-eyed marriage to Gregory.

The time to wake up had arrived.

The time to grow up and retake charge of her own life had come.

That afternoon she saw Síle back into a taxi taking her to Seán's, then visited with Ian.

As he had packed in his room, the choreographer's eyes glazed with images of New York and Colette. "Unfortunate, my dear. It was, oh yes, I hadn't expected that. Aisling is still a young dancer, little more than a girl, you know. Didn't really matter. Sense of drama. Half the audience probably thought it part of the ballet . . . yes, I'm sure that is how it was interpreted. The future, always toward the future, and Colette is so wonderful. And you will be too."

Her good-bye crinkled with sadness, an atmosphere of loss and a breaking of ties. He would still love her if she never danced again, but their intimacy would never be the same.

Yvonne waved to him, never explaining her attempts and failures of that morning. He couldn't see clearly now. In fact, now that he didn't consider Aisling a possibility for Colette, he could see less clearly.

Yvonne was not prepared to give up on the girl. This was

an unfortunate episode, an emotional sunspot that had briefly flared but would now subside. Aisling was a ballerina, Yvonne believed, and ballerinas danced.

Yvonne had two weeks, just fourteen days before she and Aisling would follow Ian to New York, then another week before the performance. She would give herself a present of these days and hours, and try to define the limits of her own abilities while helping Aisling regain her poise onstage.

Dinner with Seán and Síle was light and graceful. Síle spoke of the poets she'd known in New York and Europe. Yvonne offered ballet tales. Seán proudly displayed Síle's qualities, and showed in a thousand and one small ways that he regretted scolding Yvonne the night before.

Síle excused herself early. Seán and Yvonne sat before the fireplace, suddenly aware of being alone. "Would you like some coffee, a liqueur?" Seán perched on the edge of the couch.

"No, thank you. That was a very good meal. And Síle's wonderful."

"True. I feel with such a mother I should have done better with my life." He smiled in affection.

"You have done so well." Yvonne examined his sensitive hands.

"Do you think so?" Seán appeared to search for an answer in her eyes.

"Of course I do." Yvonne felt oddly shy around Seán.

"What are you planning now?"

"Aisling and I will stay for another two weeks, then go on to New York."

"Are you looking forward to that?" He reached out and took her hand. "Have you missed it?"

"Missed it?" Yvonne mused. "I don't know. Everything in New York is a mess for me. My life, I mean. I haven't a real job. My house is only an apartment I'm unaccustomed to. Maxine is newly married."

"You don't mind?"

"I'm very glad," Yvonne assured him. "I've wanted her settled and happy. But she has always been busy with work. Now her spare time will be taken up with Fleming. I have to start building my life from scratch. The time had to come, though, and it might as well be now as later.''

Seán nervously stirred. ''Actually, I had an idea about that.''

''My life?'' Yvonne teased, trying to avoid a more serious discussion.

''Yes. Do you like Ireland?''

Yvonne raised an eyebrow at the sudden change of subject. ''Very much.''

''The rain and wild horses, too?'' Even his smile seemed half-serious.

''I wouldn't have missed Noble for the world.'' Yvonne thought Seán had never looked more handsome. ''I wouldn't ride him again for the world, mind you, but that's another story.''

''If I kept him carefully penned up, I don't suppose you would consider marrying me?'' Seán didn't look at her, but squeezed her hand tightly.

''Is that a proposal?'' Was he teasing?

''Yes. Not an elegant one. Maybe I should try again. I haven't had much practice. Will you marry me, Yvonne?''

''I don't know what to say.'' She hadn't expected a serious proposal.

''A simple yes would be nice. You know I love you.'' Gently he pulled her to him, kissing her with love, not passion. ''I believe that you love me.''

Yvonne rested her head on his chest, listening to their hearts beat. Did she love Seán? She believed she did, and had loved him for some time. It still shocked her. Not that long ago, she had loved Gregory so intensely she couldn't imagine ever loving any other man. How could his image and her feelings for him fade so quickly? It seemed more disloyal to love Seán than to have become his lover.

Maybe this was one more of her whims, a temporary attraction lasting only a few months before being replaced by another and then another.

''I don't know.'' Yvonne turned to face him, staring into his deep blue eyes. ''I need time and space, Seán. I have a lot to think about.''

''Ballet and all?'' He looked sad.

''So much all.'' He knew her problems, but wouldn't give

her the answers. Why didn't he command her to stay, insist she needed him? Why didn't he sweep her up, order her to love him? Why didn't he truly love her? A cry started from her heart which would never reach his lips. He would never acknowledge her anguish in words.

Perhaps because of his efforts on Síle's behalf, he couldn't reach out to help her. It might well be asking too much of him. If it were, if he cared that little, she wasn't certain enough to risk her heart.

"Well, if you are sure for now."

"Yes." She wanted to leave. He wouldn't insist she marry him, and before long, tears would rush forward uncontrolled. She didn't want him to see her pain.

"I was picturing little Yvonnes and Seáns," he murmured. "Playing with Noble, I suppose."

A small Texas site rose before her closed eyes. Once more, no forever.

Yvonne was determinedly cheerful with Aisling. "It's time we go all-out with Colette. Only two weeks, you know."

"Yes." Aisling hung listlessly on the barre.

"I'm sorry I was so rude to you last night." She had to spark life into the girl. Quickly.

"I shouldn't have run off the stage. I couldn't help it."

"I know."

"What did Ian say?"

"Took it very well. He didn't seem upset at all."

"Really?" Aisling clearly wondered if Yvonne lied.

"Of course. I suppose by Ian's age, one gains perspective. He must have seen a goodly number of dancers flee the stage."

"How dreadful." Aisling hung her head.

"There's nothing to worry about. One performance isn't worth dying over."

"Yes! That's what I finally decided."

"Ian left me with a set of scribbled notes for Colette." Work. Aisling needed work and direction. Yvonne would allow nothing else to interfere, and had told Seán she would not see him during her last days in Ireland. Although he looked stricken, she remembered sadly that he hadn't tried to change her mind.

"I have something to tell you." Aisling's voice quivered.
"Yes?"

"Justine called several times while we were here."

"I see." Hadn't she expected that? Still, Justine's deviousness always came as something of a shock. "What did she want?" Yvonne carefully controlled her voice.

"To know if you were dancing. To see what Ian was doing. I tried not to tell."

Yvonne grimaced, knowing Aisling was no match for Justine. "That's all right."

"She told me I could have Colette." Aisling couldn't meet her eyes.

"And you will." Yvonne allowed no hint of bitterness to permeate her tone. "I certainly won't." The decision was not Justine's, but Ian's, but it had become academic.

"I'm not going."

Aisling's voice was so low, Yvonne didn't hear what she had said. "What?"

"I'm not going." Determination shone in Aisling's eyes.

"Not going where?"

"Back to New York. Back to the company."

"I know this has been a terrible experience, Aisling, but you can dance Colette. It will be an important step in your career. *Ballet of Desire* will be your success, your triumph."

"I'm not going."

"But you have to."

"No, I don't have to. You know, it just isn't worth the pain. Not even for Colette."

"Later, you'll regret this. You'll feel you were too hasty. Don't decide yet. Work with me. You can't turn your back on the excitement, the glamour. You can be a prima ballerina, a world-class artist. This stage fright is temporary."

"No. I don't expect it to get better. It isn't the same at all for you. You *know* you are a great dancer. I just know I don't do badly and that my mother thought it would be nice. I'm getting too old to make Mother happy. I wanted a nice solo career. There is too much glare now. And the politics," Aisling burst out. "I never wanted to be caught in that mess. Justine against Ian. You in the middle. I just don't care about ballet that much."

"But everyone is giving you a chance," Yvonne protested.

"No. Everyone is using me." Aisling's eyes filled with tears. "Ian wants to lure you back to dancing. Justine is trying to work against the two of you, and I'm convenient. I'm not as smart as you, Yvonne, but I finally figured it all out. And you."

"Me?"

"You just want me to dance Colette so Ian will have a dancer. You want to believe ballet was worth all *your* sacrifices. That *your* life meant something. Otherwise, you gave up everything for a meaningless nothing.

"Well, I don't want to end up like you. Alone. No husband. No career. All washed up before you're thirty. You have no life outside ballet, and no life inside. I won't give up everything. I want a life of my own. A real life."

Clouds hung low in a dreary sky as Yvonne checked her luggage at Dublin Airport. In a few hours she would be back in New York. Home once again, she thought with bitter irony.

She had only seen Seán once since his proposal, a disturbing, indecisive visit that left her in tears. Their situation was impossible she had decided, refusing his phone calls and his visits. Now, she was leaving Ireland without telling him. She couldn't face the pain of saying good-bye.

When Yvonne discovered her flight had been delayed she wandered aimlessly through the airport, finally heading toward the newsagent. A magazine would distract her, she decided.

Through the plate glass windows, she noticed the rain falling in sheets. It seemed appropriately sad.

"Yvonne." Seán's soft call startled her.

"How did you know I was leaving?" The uncontrollable leap of joy his presence brought to her heart quickly disappeared.

"I have spies everywhere." Seán attempted a faint smile. He looked tired and sad.

"It's almost time to board. I need a magazine." Yvonne wanted to touch his cheek and comfort him, but sternly held her emotions in check.

"You didn't tell me you were leaving."

"Just something to read for the flight. It gets boring sometimes." Yvonne pretended not to hear.

"Not even a last good-bye?"

"I have to be back in New York and I have been busy and there isn't any point to this, Seán," she blurted out while choking back a sob. "There's nothing for us to say."

Seán inspected her lips, reached out as if to touch her hair, but instead moved slightly away. "There isn't any point to anything." For the first time she noticed a small bouquet of roses in his hand. "Here's something to brighten your trip."

"Thank you." She took the flowers, careful to avoid his touch. As she leaned forward to smell them, a single tear fell onto a yellow petal.

"And a book. Just in case you've nothing to do on the plane." He thrust a slim volume toward her.

"I'll be able to use that." She turned her head slightly. "I think it's boarding time."

"You could still change your mind." Seán's voice pleaded as he inched closer to her. "You could stay in Ireland."

"I can't." Bravely she held back her tears.

"You really are going to leave." He sounded as if he couldn't believe his own words.

Other passengers lined up for the flight to New York. "I have to," Yvonne replied.

"You want to," he accused suddenly. "You would stay here if you really wanted to."

"I don't know what I want and there isn't anyone to tell me."

"There's your heart."

"I have to go. My ticket . . ." Nervous hands opened her handbag then dropped it, spilling its contents across the floor. "Damn! I won't be on in time."

Seán quickly collected the last rolling pence and in returning the bag, he captured her hand in his. "Yvonne."

"There isn't time." Frantically she clutched her ticket. "I have to leave." Ignoring the tears trickling down her face, she smiled brightly. "Take care of Noble. Tell Síle I'll miss her. Be sure and call if you are in New York."

"Yvonne?"

"I really can't stand this."

Seán looked down at her hand, at her fingers interlocked with his. "I always have to give it back, don't I?"

She couldn't answer, and taking tear-blinded steps she hurriedly left him. It was far over the Atlantic before she opened her blue bound book. It was a volume of poems—love poems—with the title *Forever*.

38

Yvonne looked up as her dressing-room door opened. "She's here?" she gasped.

"No." Ian looked grim. "No one has seen or heard from her."

Yvonne had finally left Ireland for New York after a week of resorting to pleas, praise, even threats—to which Aisling would only repeat, "I'm not going." Yet Yvonne had left Dublin certain Aisling would be shocked into following.

Two weeks had passed. Aisling had not arrived on her scheduled flight, nor on the next or the one after that, could not be reached and had not contacted anyone at the company. Maybe Aisling was not coming.

In New York, Yvonne found Ian had developed Act I with the corps and had blocked out Colette's role. Despite her protests, he worked with her to perfect it. When Aisling came in from Ireland, Yvonne told herself, she could teach her the steps quickly. Meanwhile, another soloist understudied. She could do it. Yvonne unsuccessfully fought terror. The understudy could dance if Aisling didn't arrive.

On the day before the performance, the understudy twisted her ankle. Aisling ahd still not arrived. No one was prepared to dance Colette.

"She will come. She has to come." Yvonne stared straight ahead, unwilling to meet Ian's eyes.

"And if she doesn't?"

"If she doesn't, there will be an announcement. Due to circumstances beyond anyone's control, the act from *Ballet of Desire* won't be shown. It won't be the first time, Ian."

"It may be my last time, Yvonne."

"Don't be ridiculous." She didn't want to feel Ian's pain.

"I'm not. Justine has been busy."

"She can't touch you." Yvonne wondered if that were true, if Ian's loyalty to her had not undercut his position.

"I think this time she has. Tor N. Curtain has a dance on the gala."

"But he'd never replace you."

"There is talk that the company needs a new look."

Yvonne shivered. "But Justine is the one on the defensive. I've caught up on past gossip in the last few days." Desperately she sought good omens. Some sign to help fight her guilt.

"There is no such thing as a defensive Justine, my dear. She's been on the offensive since we've been in Ireland. It won't take much, just a skip, to convince the board that a new choreographer is needed. Not just one, probably. Oh, no, at least I'll have the consolation of being replaced by a group, a whole herd. But I will be replaced."

"Where is Aisling?" Yvonne wailed.

"It isn't really Aisling I want for Colette. It's you. I really thought if you had no choice, you would be able to," he admitted.

"I . . . cannot . . . dance." By pausing slightly between each word, she hoped it would make Ian understand.

"You could try."

"I don't think whirling onstage like a second-year student would help you."

"I talked with Dr. Murray."

"Ian!" She sprang to her feet in rage. "How could you? How dare you!"

"I had to know." Ian looked embarrassed, and tugged at his beard.

Yvonne had never seen Ian look so woebegone, and felt her anger melt. Ian was desperate, desperate enough to intrude into her personal life. How could she blame him? A long career and life were coming to an end; why shouldn't it be on his own terms? Walking across the room, she put her arms around him. "It's all right."

"You'll try?"

"It won't do any good. No matter what the doctor says, I

can't dance well enough." Tears filled her eyes. "I would if
I could, Ian, truly." How close her words were to those of
Aisling's. Yvonne banished the unhappy thought. Aisling's
condition was different. Stage fright slashed through a dancer's
confidence, but once challenged, the hysterical fear dissolved.
Hers was a physical pain, not to be danced through.

"Madame . . ." she murmured.

"What?" Ian looked at her curiously.

"Nothing. Why don't you check and see if Aisling called
in."

With a concerned glance, Ian left.

Yvonne's thoughts traveled back in time to Madame, after
the horrors of the accident, Gregory's death, and her collapse.
Again Madame's words echoed.

She told me to forget. Pain isn't always bad. It can be
growth and understanding and new beginnings. The trick is to
live through the pain, to dance through the pain. She could
almost hear Madame's voice.

But her pain had been none of those things. Her pain had
been endings, backward moves. Dancing through the pain
was a familiar concept to dancers; they often did. But her
pain could not be danced through. It was too severe.

There was a knock. Aisling? "Come in." Yvonne turned
toward the door, hope lighting her face.

"Hello, Yvonne." A ruffled Seán stood before her.

"What are you doing here?" Since leaving Ireland, she
hadn't heard from him. Once she had weakened after a
session with Aisling. Going to his house, she had begged for
a clear decision. Stay or go. Dance or not. Sadly he had
refused to choose her life. He hadn't loved her enough.

"I want to see you." His eyes devoured her. "You're
looking well."

"I am looking like hell." Uncomfortably she remembered
she still wore jeans and a crumpled blouse. Her makeup had
faded, her hair fallen.

"I missed you."

Yvonne searched his face, hungry for the sight of him. The
weeks seemed like months. "I missed you."

Their eyes locked and Yvonne walked a step toward him
before halting.

"What's happening?"

"Aisling isn't here. She never came back from Ireland. There is no one to dance Colette. Everything is a mess." She trembled. Why wouldn't he sweep her up in his arms, tell her that he would take care of everything? She couldn't take care of her life any longer.

"How's Maxine?"

"Fine." She almost smiled. "You came all the way from Ireland to ask how Maxine is?"

"No." Seán braced himself. "I've come to take you back to Ireland."

"It would have been cheaper to send me a ticket."

"I'm serious, Yvonne. I tried to fight it, tried to tell myself that you should know what you want."

"I don't think I've known what I want for a long time." He had come. Yvonne felt dizzy with relief.

"I've come to tell you." Seán cleared his throat. "You want to marry me and return to Ireland. You don't have to dance anymore. Don't have to decide if you can dance. You don't have to decide anything you don't want to."

Yvonne walked to him, softly touched his face. "But, Seán, you don't believe in telling people what to do."

"I know."

"Why did you change your mind?"

"Because I have to have you as my wife. No matter what the terms." Drawing her nearer to him, he kissed her. "Will you? Marry me, that is?"

In his eyes she read love and patient adoration. She saw that he couldn't live happily without her, but she saw more.

Yvonne knew that Seán remembered a woman who in despair wanted to walk into death because he had thought he knew what was best for her. His willingness to take over for Síle and make her decisions had almost resulted in tragedy.

His eyes held love, but also fear and disappointment. Fear that this too might ruin a life, disappointment that she would not choose what *she* wanted. Seán would be happy for her to retire to Ireland and give up ballet.

But not as an escape from life. Not when she feared the dance, was running from life. Yvonne ran, she knew, ran from life, from ballet, from love. She had to stop.

"Yvonne, will you marry me?"

For long seconds she waited. Scenes of another life, another love, flashed through her mind. There was no forever, only a chance to throw your heart over the fear of the temporary. Only a chance for new pain, new disappointment. Only a chance to live. "Seán, could you wait for my answer? For just a few more hours?"

"I'll wait as long as I have to. Provided the answer is yes."

Maxine and Fleming found Seán backstage sitting on an unused piece of scenery in what appeared to be a riot. The designer recognized it as pre-gala confusion. "Seán!"

Maxine ran over and kissed him. "What are you doing here?"

"Trying to find a wife."

"Congratulations!" Fleming shook his hand.

"Premature."

"Where is Yvonne?" Maxine asked.

"I don't know. In the dressing room when I last saw her."

"And Aisling?"

"Not here," Seán said, "last I heard."

Maxine looked grim. "Yvonne must be beside herself."

Just then Justine flew past, Ian following. The small woman exploded with anger. "How is this possible? A company of dancers and there is no Colette. I can't believe this, Ian. It is all your fault."

"My fault!"

"Yours. Taking Aisling to Ireland."

"That was your idea, Justine."

She didn't appear to hear. "Mounting the ballet on Yvonne when she can't dance." Justine whirled to face him. "The posters, the advertising promise Yvonne!"

"That is also your fault. You didn't ask me. You didn't ask Yvonne. It was immoral to announce Yvonne if you weren't sure she'd be capable of dancing." Ian backed down not an inch.

"Morality, as someone once said, is expediency in a long white dress. And Ian, this is becoming very unexpedient."

Maxine shot after Justine like a rocket. "Listen, you . . ." Her voice trailed away as they whisked through the halls.

Seán looked alarmed for Maxine. "Aren't you going to intervene?"

Fleming sighed. "It's tempting, but anyone who picks a fight with Maxine deserves whatever they get."

"Uh—oh," Seán moaned.

Roland and Eleanor moved toward the stage. "This time, don't take that extra step," Eleanor whined. "Make sure you don't cover my face in the lift."

"Yes, Eleanor."

"And try to prepare better for your leaps."

"Yes, Eleanor."

"And be sure to wait until they've finished applauding my variations before you come back onstage."

"Yes, Eleanor."

Roland looked up and saw Seán. "Yvonne? Is Yvonne here?"

Seán exploded. "Roland, just stay away from her. I mean it!"

Fleming waved Roland away. "I think you're being too hot-shouldered," he said to the dancer.

Maxine returned. "How is Justine?" Fleming asked her.

"Poisonous!" Maxine hissed.

"She may mean well," Fleming mildly soothed.

"Fleming, in kindergarten I learned a sweet little saying." Maxine stood primly, her hands clasped before her. "There's so much good in the worst of us and so much bad in the best of us that it ill behooves any of us to trust the rest of us."

With shaking hands Yvonne changed into white leotards and tights. Over them she fastened the brief dress Kili had designed for the first act. The gown was white decorated with pastel flowers.

Ian sat watching her. "No one in the audience has ever seen this act before."

"Is that some consolation?" Her voice held no emotion.

"No one will know if you are doing the correct steps. If it gets too painful after the first variation, you can sail offstage early."

Act I contained two major solos for Yvonne, one she had learned in Ireland, the other in New York. Between the solos, Yvonne could be offstage.

"I think I'm going to be sick." Terror receded, a distant memory. She was beyond any description of fear.

"It will be all right." Ian swore softly, unexpectedly. "You don't have to do this, Yvonne. I'm old. What the hell! I have to retire sometime. I'll tell Justine." He moved toward the door.

"No, Ian, this is too important. For us both." She drew her makeup on, and affixed the long braid to her own hair. "There's no color in my face at all."

A soft knock caught their attention. Ian opened the door. "It's Kili."

"Hi. Maxine wants to know if you want her. Seán wants to know if you want him. Fleming wants to know if anyone has seen Justine alive recently."

"Hi, Kili. No. No. I don't care," she answered the questions in order. "Tell them to take their seats in the auditorium, and if I live, I'll see them later. Ian, why don't you visit the rest of the dancers?"

"You want to be alone?"

"Please." Ian and Kili left arm in arm.

She choked on fear as she walked toward backstage. Onstage, a triumphant Eleanor finished a spectacular turn and sailed offstage.

"Yvonne, how nice to see you." She smiled victoriously on her way to accept her curtain call. "You giving it another try?" she called back over her shoulder.

Yvonne closed her eyes. Later Maxine would take care of Eleanor. Dance through the pain, she told herself. Embrace the pain, don't run from it. She felt neither less sick nor less frightened.

The sets changed. The Colette dancers moved around her, murmuring frightened wishes for luck.

The music began.

The curtain opened.

Yvonne waited for her cue, uncertain if she could move onstage when she heard it. She felt frozen with fear, but knew the icy sensation would not stop her foot from hurting.

Dance through the pain, she chanted. Dance through the pain. The music called and beckoned. With a leap she landed onstage, turned, and started the demanding solo Ian had devised for Colette's introduction.

It hurt, it burned, it pulled. But Yvonne would not give up.

She would finish this solo, if not through skill or strength, then through determination.

Extend, jump, faster, she thought. You are young and beautiful. You have all of life before you. Turn, turn, turn, dance through the pain. Don't pretend it isn't there, accept it, use it. The pain that is coming to Colette.

Before she expected, the solo had ended and the audience screamed its appreciation. Yvonne leaped offstage, into Seán's arms.

"I did it," she cried. "I did it."

"Of course." He held and kissed her.

She had danced through the pain, and now she knew she could love through the pain, too. Her love for Gregory, the pain she knew at losing him, all had to be accepted, lived through.

"Yes," she told him. "Yes, yes, yes."

He smiled at her answer and reached into his pocket. "I told the jeweler I'd be back." He beamed, slipping the Claddagh ring on her finger. "That's forever."

39

"My ice is melting." Seán swirled his glass. "Do you think we could see if they are ready?"

"Not unless you want something melted besides your ice."

"They are always on time when they're separated," Seán complained.

"I know, but when they're together, they work on Max-Von time."

"Is that like Mex-Tex cooking?"

"No, much hotter if disturbed."

Yvonne lay on one side of Maxine's bed, her black hair fanned out around her head. Maxine lay on the other. Head to head, hair mingled red and black together, they relaxed. Two months had passed since the gala.

"Is it time to leave?" Yvonne asked, her eyes closed.

"Just about. I think I hear pacing from the living room. We'll wait till they whimper at the door."

"Do you feel we have a secret desire to be dominated?" Yvonne giggled.

"Only by fame and wealth."

"Your ideas for the new promotion are so wonderful, Maxine. All based on your sayings. Maxine's Maxims. What your mother never told you. It will be perfect. Having Fleming running the corporation, you'll never be apart."

"That was one of the better parts of the idea. You would have been a more beautiful symbol of Maxine Andrus Inc., though."

Yvonne waved a hand. "Beautiful in a different way. You

318

ave a contemporary, fresh look that will sell, sell, sell. I did
wonder . . .''

''Yes?''

''How did you think of those perfume bottles? Panache and
'atina in two curved shapes that nestle together?''

Maxine smiled, remembering that night with Fleming when
he inspiration hit. ''My wedding ring,'' she lied. Max-
ne held up her hand, and Yvonne saw the three interlocking
old bands of her wedding ring. Some things she didn't share
ven with Yvonne.

''How is Kili? I saw her and Ian together last week. They
ooked so happy.'' Her voice bubbled with laughter.

Maxine joined with happy gasps. ''I know, it is almost
idiculous. But when I see them together now, it doesn't
eem strange. They're just a normal couple.''

''I don't think 'normal' is quite the word I'd use. Do you
hink it will work out—her setting up her own design firm?''

''Yes. Having worked with me, she's learned to take care
f anything or anyone. No other assistant of mine ever lasted
s long as Kili.''

''What is that strange sound coming from the living room?''

''Fleming rattling his keys. He thinks of it as a subtle
int.''

''We are very naughty to be late for the party,'' Yvonne
aid.

''Madame won't mind. She is basking in the glare of
ublicity like the old turtle that she is. Besides, you don't
ally want extra chatting time with Justine, do you?''

''Oh, things are quite congenial there. She has decided I'm
he centerpiece of the company, now that I might disappear at
ny time into the wilds of Ireland.''

''Like Aisling?''

''Yes. I got a card from her last week. She's happier there.
he dance company is much lower-key, and she now has the
anache of having been with a large American company.''

''That cute Irish dancer, Pat, won't hurt.''

''No, I suppose not.''

''You won't, will you?'' Maxine asked.

''Won't what?''

''Disappear into Ireland?''

"Really, Maxine, you know where Seán's houses are," Yvonne teased. "I would hardly disappear."

"I'm waiting."

"That tone doesn't intimidate me."

"Please."

"No, not yet, at least. I will be here less, as we'll live part of the year in Ireland. But now that Seán is opening the company in the United States, we won't have to be separated when I dance with Ballet American. Besides, a contract is being drawn up, and Ian is hard at work on a new ballet."

"Really? I thought *Ballet of Desire* was his last. Isn't it amazing what a change of bed can do for an old man?"

"I'm happy for him."

"What's this one about?"

"It's to be called *The Importance of Being Oscar*, based on the life of Oscar Wilde."

"Considering Oscar's sexual preferences, doesn't that leave your role skimpy?"

"Oh, I'm going to be Oscar." Yvonne giggled.

"I should have know that Ian in his old age wouldn't be any tamer."

"Maxine, what is that noise?" A whishing came from the living room.

"That's Fleming."

"He's turned into a rocket and is taking off?"

"No. He's opening the curtains to make sure life still exists outside the apartment."

"We have to leave. Our husbands can only take so much. After all, they are still new at husbanding."

"I think it's a good idea to break them in correctly. Let me tell you a story." Her voice was dreamy. "Once there were two little orphans . . ."

"They were going to be famous and rich."

"One would be a world-famous fashion designer . . ."

"One would be a world-famous ballerina . . ."

"And"—Maxine slowly sat up—"that was just the beginning."